Hope Clark's books have been honored as winners of the:

EPIC Award (three-time winner)

Silver Falchion Award (three-time winner)

Imadjinn Award (three-time winner)

Daphne du Maurier Award (finalist)

Route 1 Reads East Coast winner for the state of South Carolina

"C. Hope Clark delivers addictive, character-driven suspense. Every. Single. Time."
—Debra Dixon, award-winning novelist and bestselling author of *GMC: Goal, Motivation, & Conflict*

"Those who haven't read any of C. Hope Clark's books are short-changing themselves. You can't begin one of her books and then put it down. Two-time Killer Nashville Silver Falchion Award winner.
—Clay Stafford, *Killer Nashville Noir*, Founder of Killer Nashville

"Author C. Hope Clark brings to life the uniqueness that is Edisto, peppering the island with endearing and strong-minded characters that linger in your mind long after the last page."
—Karen White, *NY Times* Bestselling Author

"Hope Clark has created another fascinating heroine in former Boston PD detective Callie Morgan. A fast-paced mystery set against the backdrop of a tiny South Carolina island where murder never happens—or so the locals would like to believe."
—Kathryn R. Wall, author, *The Bay Tanner Mysteries*, St. Martin's Press

The Novels of
C. Hope Clark

The Carolina Slade Mysteries

Lowcountry Bribe
Tidewater Murder
Palmetto Poison
Newberry Sin
Salkehatchie Secret
Lake Murray Money

The Edisto Island Mysteries

Murder on Edisto
Edisto Jinx
Echoes of Edisto
Edisto Stranger
Dying on Edisto
Edisto Tidings
Reunion on Edisto
Edisto Heat
Badge of Edisto
Edisto Bullet
Edge of Edisto
Edisto Storm
Hidden on Edisto
Edisto Lethal

The Craven County Mysteries

Murdered in Craven
Burned in Craven
Craven County Line

Edisto Lethal

iii

Book 14 of The Edisto Island Mysteries

By C. Hope Clark

Edisto Bridge Books

This is a work of fiction. Names, characters, places and incidents are either the products of the author's imagination or are used fictitiously. Any resemblance to actual persons (living or dead), events or locations is entirely coincidental.

EDISTO BRIDGE

Edisto Bridge Books
140A Amicks Ferry Road, PMB 4 Chapin, SC 29036
Print ISBN: 978-1-968423-44-5

Visit Hope at chopeclark.com

Cover design: Debra Dixon
Interior design: Hank Smith

Dedication

Dedicated to Chef Paulette Bilsky Phillips

Chapter 1

Allan

FAMILY REUNIONS rank just short of funerals in terms of mandatory appearances, assuming you give credence to Southern etiquette. Especially when inheritance hangs in the balance, though Heaven forbid you mention that. Regardless, it does tend to sway plans to attend. One must claim to love an elder with all of one's heart, you know. Bless their heart. Bless everyone's heart.

Allan Poe had argued with himself for the whole drive east from New Orleans. "Heaven help me." Whatever his feelings about Grandmother, he was in no position to decline her eightieth birthday bash at Edisto Beach. The occasion gave him a chance to grasp how close she'd inched to the grave while measuring where he stood when they one day doled out the estate.

He corrected himself. No, he refused to act like the other Poes. Normal people weren't that callous.

He took deep breaths to still his thoughts, failing miserably. How was he to behave? The reunion required proper deportment in an awkward, ostentatious manner that Allan despised, but surely he could manage for a week. He had to.

In some ways he felt almost . . . whoreish.

He pushed the gas pedal back up to the speed limit, something he'd been forced to do off and on for the whole trip. His mind would take off, and his foot would ease off, delaying him more. Everyone else should have arrived yesterday, Saturday. He'd excused himself to Sunday thanks to the distance and choosing to drive. Arriving any later would put him in the doghouse of doghouses.

All this preparation dredged up old emotions with few of them positive. Cold was how the Poe clan rolled. If he didn't get a grip on that fact and recall how to interact, they'd eat him alive.

Who cares what they think?

You gotta adapt, bro, or you won't see them coming.

Then don't go.

I've gotta go.

Then don't show weakness, man.

How many times in how many ways had he had this conversation with himself?

Pragmatism ran hard and deep in Poe DNA. *Survival of the fittest* was spoken in undertones, the quiet joke that wasn't all that much of a joke.

Every other member of his family jockeyed for relevance in the eyes of the grand dame, Doris Woolf Poe, because bloodline alone didn't guarantee a cash-in when the ruling family member passed. His great uncle had learned that the hard way, then drank himself to death after he drew the short straw, with most of the estate going to Grandmother Doris.

Tensing as he crossed the McKinley Washington Bridge onto the island, he stayed that way for the fifteen minutes required to reach the beach and pull up to the address. Scouting the packed collection of cars, he judged how to park in an area designed only for four. Breath held, he squeezed his ten-year-old blue Honda Civic partway into the yard at an angle, tapping the bumper of the silver Volvo. He allowed a tight grin at the pleasure. He'd arrived. Time to play this game.

Tagged POE 1, the vehicle belonged to Grandmother who no longer drove, which meant being driven by his Aunt Lacey, the youngest of that generation. There were three siblings to include the two aunts and Allan's father. Lacey lived with and took care of the old woman. Allan could not imagine being fulltime nursemaid to an aging, worn-out mother, sacrificing one's life into middle age, which made him believe Lacey had to be hedging her bets on her inheritance. The others, however, would play to their strengths doing their own thing to gain favor.

Allan's father's tag read POE 2. He was the eldest of the three. The middle child, Allan's other aunt, Kimberly, drove a Lexus, with the tag POE 3, of course. The fourth car, however, bore a Georgia tag, hopefully belonging to a particular visitor he couldn't wait to see.

His two younger cousins must have arrived with their mother. One in college and other recently graduated, they'd still be living at home, not allowed to move to another state.

With the old woman's first line progeny being in their fifties, they were old enough to be grandparents but weren't. Adding people to the clan meant diluting the inheritance or risking a new favorite. None of these people had any idea how to live without the tether of Grandmother Doris.

Allan threw his car into park, but despite the lower backache and cramps in his legs, he froze, unable to exit. Jesus, he didn't want to mingle with those people. Hands affixed to the steering wheel, he steeled himself, locking into place the persona needed to fit in.

He massaged the knot in his chest then took ten breaths, as he'd learned in therapy. His name was Poe, but he wasn't them. Not really. His therapist told him he was his own man, and regardless of how he was molded, by nurture or nature, he wasn't bound by the Poe behavior. He had options. Blood did not lock him into any destiny.

You're half Koulouris, remember.

His mother had been half Greek. Dead for ten years now, her love for Mediterranean food was what he remembered most of her. That and her humming. She was as un-Poeish as anyone could be, and for a year or so after she died, he wondered what in the world made her want to marry into this crew.

Son of a bitch. Slowly counting to ten, very slowly, he willed his pulse back down. Better. Backhanded, Allan wiped hard the corner of one eye. He couldn't afford a trigger. Not now. Not this early in the game.

When he entered, those faces would flash amazement then happiness, hopefully, pleased he came all this way after three years. He could wish. Especially from his dad.

But later, however, when the warmth of reunion had cooled, everyone's true colors would come to light. They would ask about his profession as a chef, and he had to decide whether to lie. He hadn't been employed for months.

Whispering his mantra, "You're only half Poe," he got out.

His father had called six months ago, warning Allan to carve out time from his busy restaurant schedule. *There is no excuse not to come*, he'd said. Not, *We'd love to see you.*

Not everyone reaches the age of eighty, Eddie Poe went on, like Allan was still seven. *Grandma Doris might not last another year.* Dear old dad emphasized how the whole family owed the woman their life's blood.

But Eddie's unspoken and true message was that the matriarch owned a fortune that had to go to someone, and he preferred his son to get his share, after his own, of course. Nothing like a noble first-born son spawning the eldest grandchild.

Let the jockeying begin.

Unfolding, he stretched himself out of the car, popping joints that had sat stagnant for too many miles. He retrieved his suitcase from the back seat. He'd packed a duffle first, then realizing he needed a pair of khakis and a few items that didn't look like beach clothes, he ditched the duffle and packed the suitcase. He had no idea what kind of party there'd be, or if a formal dinner was planned.

All this for Grandmother Doris. She wasn't the sweet grandma who'd told you stories, baked cookies, and let you stay up until midnight when you slept over. His mother's mother had died before Allan was born, so a real grandmother was foreign to him.

Case in hand, Allan scrunched his eyes shut, mentally returning to the mission-oriented person he'd told himself to be for almost eight hundred miles.

He opened his eyes. A dozen feet off the ground on pillars, *Maelstrom Manor* posed like other ocean-front properties rising two stories only with a small turret on the western side for sunsets. Named for the Poe story, *A Descent into the Maelstrom*, the name instilled a belief in a few of the family that naming the house after a violent whirlpool jinxed them all.

Allan's grandfather's great-grandfather came from Boston, and the Edgar Allan Poe genetics somehow came from there. Allan just told people yes when asked if he was related, tired of trying to explain how.

Sliding sunglasses back in place, he squinted up. Last he remembered, the manor sported a coral Miami-ish exterior, but here it was all softened wearing baby blue. A gray roof instead of tan. Like it no longer had anything to prove.

Allan eased his car door shut, resituated himself, and approached. *Let's do this.*

Nobody was on the front porch. They'd either be out back facing the water or scattered between the dining room and kitchen since the Poes claimed to be a culinary lot atop of being real estate moguls. His grandmother had literally published a cookbook, rife with original recipes. His aunts handled themselves adeptly around food, and his dad could taste a missing pinch of cardamon. All possessed a strong palate, and this appreciation for food along with his natural mother's genes, had given Allan training and inherent desire for the career he chose. . . and a genius idea for this vacation.

At his recommendation they hired his former co-worker, a chef who owned an upper crust, but not quite top shelf, eatery in Atlanta, to handle the meals for Grandmother's birthday week. Chef Pauline Vitalis had a reputation that allowed her the luxury of catering upscale events for well-heeled clients. She'd worked alongside Allan in New Orleans at The Red Lacey on Canal Street. She used to love Allan. She accepted the gig, so that had to mean something.

Fingers crossed, he hoped for a serious conversation with the chef. The earlier the week the better. *Best birthday present ever*, his father had said. Allan hoped so. His professional future depended on it.

The front door gaped open, April ocean breezes channeling from the back through the house. Stepping in, he caught a whiff of crab, parm, was that cayenne?

Long slender arms of surprise wrapped around him from behind. "Allan!"

Cousin Kimi had always been his favorite.

The tall brunette spun him around and pecked him on the cheek. "Drop that bag and give me a proper hug, you idiot."

He did and almost melted at the scent of whatever she wore. "You've grown."

"I'm a working woman now," she said. "But I can still race you to the Pavilion and back." Her smile widened. "Beat your lame ass then still drink you under the table."

That smile was infectious. Fit and beautiful, the dark-haired beauty could be ruthless, he recalled. Or at least she used to be.

"Which room?" he asked.

"The small one at the end of the hall . . . beside Ogden."

Ugh. Kimi's brother. Not one of his favorites.

She leaned in. "Seen your father yet?"

"Nope."

Her eyes darted to the side, toward the next room. "Grandmother's in there. She looks like shit."

"She's old as dirt," he whispered back. Even if Grandmother couldn't hear, no telling who else listened on the other side.

Kimi did a puff with her lips. "She can't hear you."

"Everyone else can, and I don't have a lot of currency with this family."

"But there's a lot of currency to spread around when the time comes," Kimi whispered back, tickling him under his chin.

He'd forgotten how emboldened she was.

"Uncle Eddie?" Kimi hollered, likewise alerting the entire household. "Your baby boy is here."

A chill skirted down Allan's back at being thrown straight into deep water. "Damn, Kimi!"

She pointed to his forearm. "Better roll down those sleeves if you don't want to be criticized for the ink," she muttered under her breath.

Shit! He hustled to unroll his sleeves. The eight-inch tat consisted of a black raven, entwined trails of ivy, and a chef's knife, the combo once upon a time defining him when he thrived in that old New Orleans kitchen. The artist was famous in the town, the quality evident in the raven's eyes.

But nobody in the family had seen the ink. No point in feeding them more reasons to judge.

Edgar "Eddie" Poe, the nickname attempting to hide the obvious, rounded the corner, acting downright pleased. Khakis creased (thank goodness Allan packed some), soft plaid button up, and Italian loafers. "Son, you got here. We're eating in about twenty minutes." He lifted his chin and sniffed. "Smell?"

The question was a challenge.

"Crab Oscar," Allan replied.

"Good man," the father said, gripping his son's shoulder and giving a shake. About the time Allan thought he'd be embraced, the man let loose. "Go get washed up. Don't be late." He turned and was gone.

Kimi looked at her cousin, her mouth downturned with sympathy. "That almost hurt to watch."

Allan stood at the crossroads of sting and disappointment, no words at the ready.

Kimi filled in the silence, though. "This family sucks, Cuz. Surely you remember that."

"I know," he said.

She touched the sleeve covering the raven. "Ogden's on the beach. Go unpack. I promise to be your wingman this week." She winked and left.

Didn't take six steps for him to feel more eyes on him. At the far end of the dining room, Grandmother Doris sat silent, alone, watching him walk toward the steps. She'd been parked at the table, her walker off in the corner too far to retrieve.

Discarded, almost. He stopped himself from feeling sorry for her, because he couldn't trust feelings like that amongst these people. Sympathy showed weakness.

With a hesitant wave, he gave her notice.

The family was known for gray eyes, but Grandmother's shined almost silver, and she had a way to pierce you with them. You could never tell if she was looking at you or through you. Some blamed cataracts, but one could never be sure.

He scurried upstairs, heart pounding. By the time he reached the room, he was back to rubbing the center of his chest.

Disappearing into the Jack and Jill bathroom that connected the two bedrooms, he locked both entrances and leaned on the sink. When his pulse refused to slow, he opened the cold-water spigot and splashed his face once, twice, then filling cupped hands he sank into the puddle.

Fuck, fuck, fuck.

Finally, he dared rise and peer into the mirror. *You won't last like this. Suck it up.*

God, was all this worth a face-to-face with the chef? Pauline didn't know yet, but she held his culinary future in her hands. He still possessed talent, despite what had happened in New Orleans. He knew she knew, too. But if his family demoralized him this easily, how would he appear to the chef? Good culinary experts had to function solidly under fire.

Snatching a towel, the towel ring bounced off the wall, and his heart leaped again as he muffled the noise. Out of frustration at his own wimpiness, he bounced the ring once off the wall on purpose.

Do this, man. Pull yourself together.

He'd come with two goals, and he would remain steadfast in his mission. He'd remind his relatives of his existence, staking his claim as to the inheritance, and he'd seek to regain his role in the culinary community. If he couldn't have one, he'd have the other, hopefully walking away with both before the week was over.

The effort he'd be forced to make was yet to be seen. The pretense depended on the others.

Chapter 2

Callie

CHIEF CALLIE Jean Morgan hadn't worked a weekend since September's hurricane, making her feel it time for her to pull one and give her officers a rest. The time of year on Edisto Beach dictated the flavor and number of its visitors, and with this being early April, tourists consisted mainly of stragglers left over from Spring Fling, most students having gone back to school two weeks earlier. These holdovers kicked up sand and drank too much on Saturday, lying around exhausted and hungover on Sunday. Minimal activity.

Non-students consisted of adults snaring a cheaper rental before prices doubled in the hotter months. Daring day trippers played the odds on the weather because even the sixties could comfortably bake you lying flat on a blanket, a soft drowsiness after winter with the sun straight down on you, unencumbered by clouds.

This was the time of year when nothing much was crime-worthy for a police chief.

Callie's son had been one of those earlier college students, having left with the herd two weeks ago. A junior, he attended College of Charleston, a university one hour away and squeezed in the middle of The Holy City. However, he had announced he would be returning for the weekend with something to discuss that merited face-to-face, not a phone call.

Any mother on the planet would mull those words over a zillion times to guess what was so wrong to merit more than the standard text.

Sure, she'd love to see him, but the hidden reason made her wary. The topic, or rather a certain topic, had been in the back of her family's minds since Jeb had turned eighteen. Three years into his collegiate life, here they stood on the cusp of adult reality . . . and his career choice.

Changing his major to political science with a communications minor last year sort of tipped his hat as to where his interests were, but the bigger issue was what he would do with that.

He and his girlfriend Sprite were on a fast track to permanent couple-hood, a yet-to-be-discussed part of the equation. Callie loved the girl, and the girl's mother Sophie, her best friend next door. The union could be fun for everyone. That was not an issue.

Callie preferred that he attend graduate school. Her mother Beverly, Jeb's grandmother, had political aspirations for the young man as soon as she could get her hands on him. After all, he was sixth generation of a family of politicians . . . having skipped Callie, a hard wedge that remained steadfast between daughter and mother.

Intentional as hell, too. Callie would rather take a bullet than enter that realm.

Jeb was expected home tonight, after dinner with his grandmother in Middleton, forty miles away. Beverly could stretch a dinner date into oblivion, and she'd retain you until she and her guest were of one mind over whatever the issue. That fact tightened Callie's chest. Her mother was relentless in slipping in her influence.

Chief of police wasn't totally political, but it was close enough to the game to know the rules, the players a cesspool of scheming egos.

All these thoughts swirled in her head while she patrolled the main thoroughfare of the quiet beach community. Up ahead, a smoke gray Dodge Ram didn't even slow enough to roll the stop sign, and she instinctively popped on a light and mashed the gas. The driver blew onto Palmetto Boulevard from Dawhoo Street, empty trash cans rolling around in his truck bed.

Seeing the lights, however, he promptly pulled over. One point in his favor. He already had at least three against him.

This man lived over on Edings Street, having closed two months ago on an older home titled *Tan Time,* repairs needed on flooring, porches, steps and dated fixtures inside. Not a total overhaul, but enough to take some time. A nice-looking gentleman in his late thirties from what Callie had learned, and he'd been carting his building scraps to other people's dumpsters.

Mrs. Chester happened to live on Edings Street and had caught him on a Ring camera just yesterday and filed the first formal complaint. She captured the tag, make, and model of the vehicle clear and legible on a cam, the picture attached to the complaint sporting a red arrow drawn on the photo toward the steering wheel side where the driver hadn't done a thing to hide who he was.

Callie never ceased to be amazed at how pure stupidity kept her and her uniforms in business.

She pulled up behind him, not bothering to run the familiar tag.

"Johnny Scott," she said, walking up on the driver's side. "How have you been?"

Well-tanned for his short time there, even with this being the off season, he had acquired a beach image. He kept his truck washed and shining, though, so she could give him that. Pride of ownership, something respected out here, was important. Trespassing and disrespect of other's property was not.

She did the whole license and registration thing, going back to her car and taking her time, a luxury afforded her, especially this time of year. She returned with three tickets, weighing in on the high side of the financial spectrum for each.

Johnny flipped through them. "What the hell?"

She waited until he finished and peered up. "That doesn't include others I overlooked," she said. "We have a formal complaint filed against you, Mr. Scott. Dumping your construction trash in other people's receptacles is neither cool nor legal. There's a beach trash facility for that, not to mention you're supposed to rent your own dumpster."

"Mine's full."

She raised her brow to acknowledge the futility of what he'd just said.

"If someone's dumpster isn't full, the bin ought to be fair game," he added.

This one was full of foolhardiness today.

Then he tried turning things around on her. "You cannot prove that's what I was just doing, so that makes this third ticket illegal."

She expected that. "A complaint was filed yesterday, photo taken with you all but smiling at the camera. Time stamp on the photo, tag number on your truck. That house is the only one with a dumpster on the street you just came from. Your trash cans in your bed are empty. Again, did I mention the Ring camera on that house?" Her mouth turned up on one side. "I know which houses are under construction around here."

He held up his hands, tickets pinched between fingers. "Uncle, chief. Uncle."

"Other officers will be watching you, too, Mr. Scott, so don't think the cover of night will make a difference. We're a small lot out here, and to be caught by one is to be known by all."

The man had no idea how spot on Callie was with that remark. She may have exaggerated knowing every address of every repair job and new build, but Scott's tag would be on every officer's mind for a while.

Movement caught her eye up ahead on the sidewalk, and in two seconds Mr. Scott noted as well. "Does she work for you?" he asked. "It's like she walks a vigil."

Councilwoman Donna Baird was two houses ahead of them, walking her Harlequin Great Dane appropriately named Horse. Scott hadn't lived there long enough to have weathered a voting season, so he wouldn't recognize her.

"That's your newest council person," Callie said.

"Maybe she'd listen to me," he said. "When my dumpster gets full, the Edisto trash is often too full for my stuff. That has to be a community issue."

Callie gave him a mild shrug. "Well, there she is. You have a good day." She returned to her cruiser, her mirror showing Scott parking his truck and approaching the lady and her beast on foot.

Callie chuckled as she put the vehicle into gear and pulled out. Donna had been in office only six months, but she'd learned fast. The good old boys that formerly dominated the council now had a woman who could keep pace, and her positive public image surpassed all of theirs. She put herself out there, walking Horse every chance she could, the result being she'd become a well-known fixture with an approachable personality, fast becoming a local favorite. Half of Edisto had no idea who the other council people were.

Her also having been a veterinarian and being the owner of such a sweet gentle giant as Horse, elevated her almost to the level of perfection.

And they'd learned to have fun passing constituents back and forth. What Callie couldn't do a thing about, she passed to Donna. What Donna couldn't fix, she passed to Callie.

Callie waved at Donna in passing and continued her perusal of the beach.

Half a block later, she noted cars at a house on Palmetto that wasn't readily occupied and not always leased, meaning they could afford it to remain empty at the owners' whim. *Maelstrom Manor* was owned by the Poes, who'd arrived en masse no less. She didn't know the people, but everyone knew *of* them. They hadn't had a family reunion since she'd been chief, and she would've thought the place was rented out except for all the POE license tags. Big money people. Nobody could say anything nice about them, but neither could they say much from personal experience, either. Tightly knit with well-defined circles of acquaintances.

The house was known for its turret, and rumors spoke of a direct lineage to the mystery author. Someone had to explain the house's name to her, taken from a short story she'd never heard of. One would expect *The Raven* or *The Gold-Bug* or something about a pendulum. One might expect a dark gray cloud hovering over its roof.

Callie continued taking Palmetto, appreciating the lack of activity. Those here were indoors at their evening meal and worn out from the sun. In no time she canvassed full circle through town, ending with a pass by her own home to see if her son had arrived. He hadn't.

Sprite's car, however, sat parked in her mother's drive next door. Callie's good friend Sophie Bianchi had the most beautiful, sweet daughter named as whimsically as the mother lived. The son was even named Zeus. Sprite had been dating Callie's son Jeb almost since they met four years ago, prompting the girl to attend the same school, The College of Charleston. For Sprite to return to the beach alone said something to Callie. The two traveled together, their young love tethering them tight.

Curious, Callie pulled over and texted her son. *You staying with your grandmother tonight?*

She waited, trying to judge whether a quick answer was good or not.

By the time the kid got to Edisto, she'd be so full of questions he wouldn't have a chance from the time he walked in the door.

Still no answer . . . no floating dots telling her he was typing. Just stillness.

Jeb knew her well and owned a maturity beyond his years, but her expectation for a response remained foolishly on overkill. She knew, and he knew. Therefore, he ought to text her right back, right? She put down the phone, scolding herself.

She remained on duty until seven that evening, and with ten minutes left, she headed to the eastern end of town, near all the commercial venues, and slowly took note, rounding Palmetto at The Pavilion. She'd meander back down to Dawhoo Street where she'd earlier pulled Mr. Scott, and if she saw nothing by then, turn around and end her day at El Marko's for dinner.

She caught Donna and Horse turning onto Atlantic Street and eased next to them.

"Saw you talking to the guy in the pickup. Grab a new supporter?" she called through the rolled down window. "He wasn't around to vote last time."

"Johnny Scott," Donna replied. "Lives on Edings. Doesn't like his ticket."

"Tickets," Callie corrected. "Three."

Donna paused. "He didn't mention that. He asked if I could get a ticket reversed, and I told him that wasn't in my job description, but if the topic of the ticket was something that the town needed to address, I'd take it under consideration."

"Glad to hear. Need a lift?"

Donna walked everywhere. Endless energy. "No thanks. Two more blocks and we're done."

Donna had moved in with Stan Waltham, Callie's old Boston boss who'd decided after his divorce if Edisto was good enough for his favorite detective to relocate to, the Southern beach was good enough for him. Back in the fall after the hurricane, in attempt to gather his belongings, Stan had slipped on his steps and broken his leg, then got stranded with Callie for the duration of the storm.

When Stan came home after his surgery a week later, the town regulars pondered how to he'd manage care due to steep stairs and him being the bachelor he was. Donna Baird, however, took caregiving to another level and moved in until he was literally back on his feet. He needed help, the storm had caved in her roof, and the arrangement seemed right.

Her repaired house was now rented to tourists. Necessity was not only the mother of invention, but also the birth of romance. Stan remained in quite good spirits these days, and Donna seemed adoringly content.

Callie couldn't be happier for them. She relied upon Stan for both professional and personal advice, and they'd protected each other for going on for twenty years. Donna had proven herself worthy of decent advice as well, making the team rather tight.

"Stan okay?" Callie asked, a question Donna had become accustomed to.

"Limp's almost gone," she replied, like Callie never saw the man. Edisto Beach was two and a third square miles. The only way Callie hadn't met anyone was if they came for a few days then left. Like the Poes.

"What are you doing for dinner?" Donna said. "I was about to park Horse back at the house and take your old boss to El Marko's. Are you off duty?"

Callie looked at her watch. Jeb had responded to her text. *Probably.*

Probably meant spending the night with dear old grandma.

Donna stepped to the rolled down window. "Something wrong?"

"Jeb," she said.

Donna sobered. "Is he okay?"

"Oh yes. He has some news to break to me, but instead of using his phone or coming home, he chose to dally with his grandmother. Now he's spending the night at her place."

"And you're racking your brain trying to dissect what he wants to tell you. Oh, honey." The council woman stroked Callie's arm hooked over the downed window opening. "You don't think he and Sprite are . . . expecting, do you?"

That option hadn't even crossed Callie's mind, and for a confusing second, she couldn't figure out why not. She'd almost welcome that situation with the grandmothers being herself and Sophie, the two kids likely living close enough to take advantage of their assistance.

"Thanks for planting that thought," she said.

Donna burst out laughing. "What the heck else would you be more worried about?"

"Long story," Callie answered, not thinking Palmetto Boulevard the place to discuss family issues. "But sure, I'll meet you at El Marko's. Let me change clothes, and I'll be right there."

Donna waved as the cruiser left, Callie pulling out to take an immediate right turn onto Dawhoo Street, which would lead her to Jungle Road. Right two and a half blocks would take her to *Chelsea Morning's* front door, the house she'd been gifted with by her parents and shared now with her significant other, Mark Dupree, owner of El Marko's. She and her tight group of friends traveled in close circles, within walking distance of each other with El Marko's not being over a mile from any of them.

Her stomach told her dinner sounded great. Her mind said she needed light, social conversation. Her sweet man would be right there. Life was good. . . except when rationalizing family affairs. She was much better at managing crime.

Chapter 3

Allan

DINNER PROVED superb. Crab Oscar wasn't difficult to make but wasn't easy to make perfect. The dish, however, turned out flawlessly. Chef Pauline had outdone herself, and from the looks of the eight seated diners, everyone agreed. The low hum of conversation spoke clearly of satisfaction.

Most of his relatives hugged Allan when he showed for dinner, nobody as warmly as Kimi, of course, who made a public display of making up for the others. Even a brief pat on the back from Ogden surprised Allan though the youngest cousin seemed to have grown darker, stiffer, and more internally focused over these three years.

There was no such thing as a functional family, but there were degrees of dysfunction. In the game show of screwed up families, Allan rated the Poes in the top ten percent.

Give me Screwed Up Families for 600, Alex.

Allan picked at a tiny remnant of crab left from the meal as small talk traveled around him like he wasn't there. The food had been too good not to consume quickly, and he had arrived hungry, having declined the endless array of fast food enroute. He'd eaten clean for far too long, and as a chef, he understood why.

He listened to Chef Pauline in the kitchen, preparing for dessert. He'd managed a quick hello to her before dinner, a snatch of a courtesy because she had her hands full plating and serving the meal. They shared a brief hug, and she'd even winked once as she carried plates to the table. A warm wink, like she felt sorry for him having to endure this event, acting as if she remembered their late nights at the restaurant after closing when he'd spoken of his kin. Like she would like to talk later. Like time had passed, and she was happy to see him. Like she understood the predicament he was in.

For God's sake, he read a lot into one wink. Just how starved was he for validation? Yet he couldn't stop hoping his future held promise in that wink. A promise of employment.

A sarcastic laugh and a nudge under the table from Kimi brought him back to the present.

He'd been seated to the right of Aunt Kimberly, Kimi's mother, the second child of the three middle-aged children. Like Allan's father, she was also a broker, but she hadn't the desire to run the firm, so Eddie assumed the reins. Loved the checks, but didn't like being confined to an office, she often said.

"Where exactly are you working, Allan?" Then she gave a quick, "Thank you, Pauline," as her dinner plate was taken away, spoken as if the professional chef were a bus boy.

Kimberly's specialty was making people uncomfortable, and if you dared take her up on a verbal challenge, chances were you'd lose so shamefully you wouldn't dare but answer succinctly in the future. You quickly learned not to waste words with her.

"I'm working nowhere at the moment," Allan replied, like that's how everyone functioned. Working one day, not the next, taking one's leisurely time to find the perfect place worthy of one's talents. He'd decided before he came down from his room that he'd just come out and speak his mind, update the family, and take any judgment head on. Somehow his nerve had taken a break and left him dangling.

She ingratiated him by turning to make direct eye contact. "Are you still a chef though? If you aren't running a kitchen, do you lose your chef's toque, your apron, or whatever tells the world who you are?"

He started to ask if she was still a broker, with her not doing anything broker-like, but he knew better. "Yes, I am still a chef. Trained and pedigreed."

Aunt Kimberly turned to her brother, acting appalled. Kimberly never allowed herself to be caught on her back foot about anything. She embraced drama in a dry, condescending manner. "Then tell me why we aren't using *him* to do all this cooking?"

Well-versed in all things Kimberly, Eddie wasn't fluffed. "Allan thought hiring his former mentor would be special. He could mingle with family while being assured the food was above and beyond. Isn't that right, Allan?"

Kudos to his father. "Spot on, Dad."

"So, you're unemployed?" Aunt Kimberly continued, not to be bested. "Seems all the more reason for you to be doing the meals. At least be a sous chef. That's what you call the secondhand person in the kitchen, right?"

This time Eddie didn't jump so fast to Allan's defense.

That paternal energy sure had wilted fast.

Grandmother watched, head still, neck stiff, only her eyes shifting from person to person as they spoke. She hadn't said a thing to him, to the point he wondered if she'd had a stroke and couldn't speak for real. While she had a nurse, Shannon had been around long before Allan left home. He hadn't really had a chance to ask about Grandmother's health, and he wasn't asking in front of the family. He liked to think of himself as the more mannerly Poe.

"We're not trying to be mean, Allan." Lacey, the other aunt, spoke this time. With no husband or kids, she justified her existence tending Grandmother. Lacey sat to Grandmother's left, Shannon to her patient's right.

Allan thought of Lacey as the gentlest soul in the group, and the most fragile, which in this horde meant the least respected, short of maybe himself.

"What are your plans?" Lacey asked.

If she hadn't asked, someone would have. *Bless her heart.*

"Resumes just went out," he said. "I'm waiting for interviews. Didn't want anything to interrupt this affair, so here I am, uninterrupted." He stopped at that.

Lacey's genteel grin told him she didn't need more, her own *bless your heart* clear but unspoken.

Cousin Kimi threw her napkin on her plate. "Damn, family, would y'all just cut the guy some slack? We haven't seen him for three years, and you greet him with this ration of shit? We'll never see him again if this is the welcome he gets." She gave him a real smile, not a Poe smile. "I'm thrilled to see him, myself, whether he's panhandling or serving the White House, he's still my adorable cousin."

Allan welcomed her warmth with a wink, not caring who saw.

"Tell me again why he hasn't been here for three years?" asked Aunt Kimberly.

"Mother," Kimi warned, and Aunt Kimberly gave a slight nod of pomposity in agreement the subject be closed.

Silence hung around the table until Ogden spoke. "I might be visiting a friend and staying the night." He hadn't said a word before now.

"You will not," Aunt Kimberly said, like that was that.

"I'm an adult now . . . *Mother.*"

"This week is centered around your grandmother, so cancel your plans."

"And pretend we want to be here? Like we cherish her and honor and adore her?" he said.

Aunt Kimberly held up her dessert spoon, dictating *enough*.

Damn. Ogden had evolved into a far bigger self-centered ass than Allan remembered. Talking back to Aunt Kimberly? He'd pay for that. And so bluntly about Grandmother right in front of her? He had no hopes of being in the will, did he?

Grandmother hadn't flinched. Forever thick-skinned she'd always given as good as she got. Yet she'd tolerated this crap with nary a response.

"I know I haven't been around for a while, and you've grown up some, Ogden," he heard himself say, "but your remark was uncalled for. Your plans were rather thoughtless as well. This week is for Grandmother."

Everyone turned to him. He mentally replayed his words, wondering if he'd erred.

Ogden laughed. "Like I'll listen to you, the man who contaminates people and can't keep a job. Who's to say you're still in the will?"

Kimi lightly gasped. The others turned to Grandmother, waiting to see if she was inclined to take sides, maybe hint at Allan's financial future one way or the other. Or now Ogden's.

Like Kimi, Allan poised for a response. They'd finally addressed the elephant in the room. He had not been the kitchen party responsible when two diners at his old employment, a New Orleans restaurant called The Red Lacey, had collapsed after dessert. One died. The other was hospitalized. He'd not been charged because nobody could confirm who did the deed, but since it was likely an item they ate, the restaurant was sued, he was fired, and word crept through the city, making him unemployable for a fifty-mile radius. How much further than that he had yet to determine. He'd been too ashamed this past year to apply for serious work for fear of being recognized for the worst moment in his life.

The nurse cleared her throat.

Aunt Kimberly looked at the noisemaker like she hadn't been invited.

Shannon shifted attention to Grandmother. Aunt Lacey did as well, like she had to oversee the nurse. Neither, however, physically aided the matriarch. Almost like Secret Service, they remained in the shadows, ever vigilant, indicating Grandmother still called the shots.

Allan knew better than to say more. His silence, interpreted as surrender, allowed his tarnished reputation to fall from discussion. All the rules were coming back to him.

They ate their lemon sorbet in silence.

Allan had a spoonful and quit. A week of this stifling intimidation would give him a damn panic attack. Maybe he would leave tomorrow night, having given the birthday thing a full twenty-four hours. He could say he heard from one of the resumes, and time was of the essence. He could hopefully squeeze in a chat with Pauline.

Chef Pauline entered the room with hot tea in two china pots wrapped in quilted cozies. At the sideboard, she set them on the tea tray that held the precise number of cups and saucers. "As thanks for making all these arrangements on her behalf, Grandmother Poe asked me to set up a tea service, and she will prepare tea for everyone."

Wait, the old woman was up to that?

Grandmother rose from the table. Allan expected the nurse to jump up and retrieve the walker, take her elbow. . . something.

But nobody did. Lacey may have looked a bit tentative but remained seated, which radioed to Allan that this part of the evening had been orchestrated.

Grandmother was more on the ball than he thought.

The matriarch wasn't speedy by any means, but she managed to shuffle to the sideboard and perform all the ministrations of tea pouring. Chef Pauline remained within reach as backup, making no move toward assistance. The nurse had pushed her chair back to be ready.

Clearly everyone had been told not to interfere.

With two cups prepared in painful slow motion, Grandmother passed them to Pauline to deliver.

Finally, Pauline returned to Grandmother for the last cup which was placed at the old woman's own place. Honorable, he guessed, Grandmother wanting to do for the family instead of always being the one being done for. Someone her age probably tired of being waited on.

The patience of the family in her doing so was admirable, too, and Allan squelched his earlier nerves.

He wasn't a tea aficionado, at least hot tea. Cold green tea more suited him, but he welcomed the pomp and circumstance. Little formal moments like this could change the tone of a room, putting everyone on the same page in being proper in honor of something or someone. Etiquette had purpose.

Nobody picked up their cup until Grandmother did. She took her time with a puff of a blow across the surface, and once she drank, the rest blew theirs then sipped.

The first sip felt odd on his lips, so Allan took a second taste. Too hot, he thought, but then a numbing sensation slowly filled his mouth, coated his lips. He sucked in air, trying to define why, but the numbness shifted to a tingling burn.

"Anyone feel that?" he asked, his tongue running over and around the inside of his lips.

Kimi looked perplexed. "Feel what? It's tea. Do they not do tea where you've been?" She took another sip to show she didn't have a problem with hers.

"Too much McDonalds." Ogden laughed, as if he were a skilled practitioner of decorum.

"He's used to Cajun tea," said Lacey with a chuckle.

Allan almost started to take another sip, to retest what this experience was, but instinct stopped him. A flutter in his chest made him go for his water. He drank the glass dry, then reached for Kimi's and did the same, a sudden awareness in his chef's mind as to what this might mean.

Pauline reached his side. "What is it?"

"Monkshood?" he whispered, afraid to be right, but equally afraid to be wrong.

Panic flashed in her eyes. She disappeared into the kitchen.

The damn nurse jumped up and followed her instead of tending to him.

Allan motioned for Ogden to pass his water glass. When the young man hesitated, Kimi snatched the glass and handed it over with a slosh. By the time Pauline returned, Allan had swallowed over a quart of water.

Pauline handed him two black capsules. "Here."

Shannon nodded beside her. "Take them, then drink some more."

Allan tossed them back with the last mouthful from his current glass. Nurse Shannon ran to her seat and brought back her glass. He drank again, stomach bloating.

His breathing ran faster than comfortable, his heart fretting a bit. His shirt mashed wet against his chest from the frantic effort to drink with a numb mouth. However, he recognized the activated charcoal often used for poisonings atop the water used to dilute the effect of whatever he'd ingested. Nurses and chefs alike understood what charcoal was for.

"It wasn't me," Pauline said under her breath, but the room remained so silenced that everyone couldn't help but hear.

"I called 911," Shannon said.

He didn't want an ambulance and started to protest, but to have these two professional women peering down on him so worried, made him afraid to say no. What if he wasn't thinking clearly?

Shannon took his pulse. "It's up."

"You think?" he said before he could catch himself.

Kimi looked stunned, even fearful. Ogden wasn't much past intrigued. Everyone else remained affixed in their seats, including his father.

Allan's temper spiked despite feeling ill. "Jesus Christ, people, none of you give a damn I was poisoned?" He looked to his father. "Dad?"

"Allergy maybe?" his father said. "But certainly not poison. Either way, best to get you checked out. You do have insurance, don't you, son?"

Lacey pointed at her brother. "Ooh, good point since he is unemployed."

Allan couldn't believe his ears. "Seriously?"

"You sure you aren't exaggerating your symptoms?" Aunt Kimberly said.

His voice came out screechy. "I'm a chef. Don't you think I would know?"

"But you aren't an active chef," Aunt Kimberly reminded. "Maybe you're rusty."

"She's right," Lacey echoed. "Maybe you have a bug, and the tea didn't agree with you. Or maybe the crab. Do you fare well with seafood? These things happen."

Ogden's grin spread, unsettling. "Yeah. These things happen, man."

The entire damn family sat, unmoving, watching to see how this spun out. Grandmother acted no differently than when they'd first sat down.

Nobody asked how he felt until Pauline knelt before him. "Charcoal working?" she asked, studying him hard. She waited for Shannon to add something. "I'm not a doctor," she said.

"I only need to lie down," he said, the page in his culinary school textbook about noxious plants so crisp in his mind's eye. Purple hooded flowers. The leaves. Especially the root. One of the toxic plants that could easily turn fatal. This didn't feel fatal, but what did that feel like?

Pauline spoke to him like he'd zoned out. "Allan? You still with us?"

He nodded, worried why she'd ask that. So, he forced himself to take measure. He was young and strong. He hadn't had but two sips of whatever this was.

He started to rise. Pauline stood to assist, but he waved her off. Honestly, he was almost giddy that he was this stable, so stable that he began to question his own doubts about what he'd ingested.

"I'll see y'all in the morning," he said.

The nausea came over him like a King tide wave.

Pauline ran to the living room and brought back a small trash can which he promptly filled with sorbet, crab, and asparagus, stained with the black charcoal. The smell brought up another wave, then another until his gut had emptied.

"Ew," said Aunt Lacey, standing to position herself behind her mother, who remained seated, taking in the commotion.

"I need . . . to lie down," he said, a weakness seeping into his limbs. He wanted to escape these cold Poe eyes.

Pauline took his arm and with little effort pushed him back into his chair. "Wait right here until the ambulance arrives."

He shook his head. "Sleep. Need sleep." But in attempting to stand he found himself too washed out to do so. He was stuck waiting for medical help.

Some left the table, but he wasn't sure who. He could hear people in the kitchen, his name filtering back.

Shannon remained, having pulled up Kimi's seat who now stood behind her brother. The nurse kept taking Allan's pulse. Time escaped him as he felt worse.

He peered down the table at the lone person who'd said nothing.

Those silver eyes watched, teacup still wrapped in her hands, as if to say her tea was fine. She lowered her cup and raised a brow. No words, but he felt a message. He just couldn't grasp the meaning.

Something told him she was far from senile.

Someone knocked at the door. Good, he thought, his eyelids clinched as he fought a fresh stirring in his gut followed by a hard, encroaching headache. He was losing touch with who was who or what time meant.

As the room spun, he heard his father's voice at the door. His greeting was followed by the sound of a woman. "Edisto Beach Police Chief Callie Morgan," came the voice. "Who called 911?"

Chapter 4

Callie

CALLIE WAS HALF out of her uniform when the call came through, a 911 from an address on Palmetto Boulevard. At hearing the house number, an even number, she made a mental tally down the row of addresses on the ocean.

The Poe house.

She redressed, texted Mark she had received a call, and left. Jeb's delay coming home might be for the best.

She took scant minutes to reach *Maelstrom Manor*. With all the cars blocking the drive, she hugged the curb and parked.

A middle-aged man answered the door. Salt and pepper hair, he was built like a tree trunk, no waist. With him not acting rushed, flustered, or fearful, she questioned whether the call was a mistake.

Callie introduced herself. "Who called 911?"

"Yes, yes, of course. Eddie Poe," he said, and let her in.

She wondered if Eddie was short for . . . hopefully his mother didn't do that to him. "What's the problem?" she asked, studying the current room, beginning to catch a scent of something sour. Nothing seemed to be amiss, nobody was down, but he acted attentive to the room to his left, so she made her way there without invitation. There was some hesitation in his actions which could be shades of shock. She preferred that to people losing their minds.

A nice-looking man in his thirties rested in a chair a few feet from the dining room table, listless and pale. A middle-aged woman held his wrist, measuring a pulse, and he was letting her. Somebody medical, she assumed. A much more senior woman remained at the head of the same table, almost like she was unaware of her surroundings.

At first blush, the man could be related to Eddie, minus the salt in his hair and a build that hadn't gone to seed yet.

People filed out of the kitchen, resembling Eddie's attitude. They assumed places behind the chair of the old lady, and Callie swore they stood in some sort of order, especially when the man joined them, easing in on one end.

Dark hair or dark mixed with age, all had gray eyes. The room held the oddest air of a creepy controlled panic.

Someone broke through the zombie crowd, trotting toward Callie and the young man, wearing a chef's coat, *Chef Pauline* embroidered above a pocket. She laid a hand on his shoulder and explained. Her effort exceeded that of all the others combined and the creepy bubble of an atmosphere popped.

"This is Allan Poe," she said, pushing herself to be firm. "These fine people are the Poe family. This week is an eightieth birthday celebration for the grandmother seated there." She pointed. "They were eating dinner. Everything was fine through dinner, but when tea was served after dessert, Allan had a reaction. He's woozy, has numbness in his mouth, and from the way he closes his eyes, he's a little loopy and probably fighting a helluva headache."

Callie noticed the trash can eight feet away and went to peer in. "And nauseous?" The black gunk took her aback. She'd never seen that before.

"Yes, yes, nauseous. But he's probably done with that."

The can had to hold a half gallon of substance. "That's a lot of vomit," Callie said. "And why is it . . . black?"

"We loaded him down with water and activated charcoal." The chef remained standing, waiting, breathing slightly above normal.

"Now," Callie said. "Who are you?"

"Pauline Vitalis." She gave a slight bow, then caught herself like now wasn't the time. "Sorry. I'm the chef they hired for the week."

A person of interest. Callie would question her later. "How long ago did he react?"

"Not quite thirty minutes."

"Who called 911?"

The woman seated next to the man rose her hand. "That would be me. I'm a nurse."

"Are you a Poe?" Callie asked.

"No, the nurse. Shannon Kirby. I'm assigned to Mrs. Poe there." She pointed to the old woman.

"So why aren't you still on the phone with 911?" Callie asked.

"You came. Thought I'd be more needed here."

Great, she had hung up on 911. "They didn't call you back?"

"Yes, but I didn't answer, because I'd be more helpful beside him," she said. "But I agree with Allan that this might be some sort of poison."

Say what? "Allan thought he was poisoned?"

The nurse looked to the chef. "What did he call it?"

"Monkshood," said the chef. "You might know it as wolfsbane."

Callie didn't know it as anything and instead studied the patient. He was watching, not participating. He looked spent. "His name is Allan, you said?"

"Yes," said the nurse and the chef in unison, frowning at each other like the other one was wrong to talk.

Callie called 911, gave her title, and confirmed the ambulance. "Poison involved," she said.

"Monkshood," said the chef.

"Also known as wolfbane," whispered the nurse.

"Here," and Callie pushed the phone at the nurse. "This time stay on the phone until they tell you otherwise."

Callie took a knee before the man. "Allan, can you understand me?"

He gave a sluggish nod.

"Allan Poe?"

Another nod.

"Do you think you ingested something toxic?"

Same nod.

"Any idea who doctored your food?" she asked. "Or how?"

The nurse bent over. "He could have poisoned himself."

Callie held back saying what Allan managed to slur. "Are you shitting me?" he said, the effort taxing. "Would I have eaten. . ." His words deteriorated to mumbling. "There are better ways. . ."

Callie got the message. He felt sabotaged.

"His tea," Pauline whispered in her right ear.

"Pardon?" Callie asked.

"He reacted to the tea, not the food," the chef corrected. "He was fine after eating. He'd even lasted through the lemon sorbet, so not in the food. No, ma'am."

Says the chef. "Who served the food?"

"Me, but monkshood wasn't in the food."

"So you keep saying."

The nurse leaned in, speaking low to her counterpart like Callie couldn't hear. "Anyone would expect you to say that, Pauline. I believe I'd be quiet about that whole school of thought."

Allan closed his eyes. He was probably as annoyed about this dialogue as Callie was. "Who then served the tea?"

Pauline pointed to Grandmother Poe. The nurse darted her eyes in the direction of her charge. The others stood motionless and silent.

"Wait." Callie came up from the floor. Allan wasn't saying much, and she needed better answers. "You're saying that older woman over there tried to off him? And she did this all by herself."

"No, no, no, that's not what happened," exclaimed the nurse.

Pauline shook her head in clipped motions that made her short dark brown ponytail shake. "We mean Grandmother poured the tea. Nothing else."

The nurse spoke up. "She handed the cups to you, and you served the people. She poured."

Callie paid hard attention to Pauline. "Kind of points back to you as the chef then, doesn't it?"

Pauline leaned in, her jaw tight, and muttered in Callie's ear. "Any one of these damn people could've pulled this. Those cups have been sitting on the tray on that buffet since well before the meal, with everyone coming and going through here." She whispered, "Damn people won't let me cook. They all consider themselves sous-chefs. Add this, stir that, don't forget she likes less of this spice, more of another."

Callie sure wouldn't want to sleep under this roof without two locks on the bedroom door. "Ever think this was an accident? Like someone grabbed the wrong ingredient?"

"Not in my kitchen. Assuming I'm the only chef."

Callie would've looked down her nose at her if she'd been taller than her five foot two. "I thought you said the others—"

"I didn't pour the tea," she murmured, again so as not to be heard by the others. Then she turned toward the living room, chewing on the inside of her mouth like she recognized the proverbial corner she was painting herself in.

Callie continued. "Who is Allan in relation to the older woman in question?"

"Grandson," Pauline said.

"Grandson," Callie confirmed.

"I know what this looks like . . ." Pauline said, nervous and eager to justify herself.

Her radio beeped and Callie held up her hand. Dispatch announced the ambulance was two miles out. Everyone stirred. "Thank goodness," said the father.

Callie headed to the front door, making sure all the outside lights were on. "I need y'all to move some of these cars out of the way." When nobody moved very fast, she raised her voice. "Move the cars, please."

Eddie and Ogden ran out, and POE 1 and 2 were promptly repositioned on the street. Before the two drivers could return to the steps, the ambulance arrived.

EMTs trotted up and inside, Callie leading them. The chef stood by Allan, and Callie suddenly got an image of church. Pauline acted the preacher, the patient the bowed individual being saved, the others lock-kneed behind the grandmother. If they'd had robes, they'd have been the choir. She'd freak if they started singing.

That's how weird this household was. Oddest behavior at a scene Callie had experienced in a long while.

The medics took information from Callie, with Pauline confirming, the nurse echoing a couple of times but clearly deferring to the chef. Then after the two medical staff took Allan's vitals and labeled him stable enough to transport, they left. Eddie followed in POE 2.

The excitement gone and noise reduced, Callie returned to face the remaining family. Then she noticed the trash can had disappeared. "Where's the vomit?"

Kimberly sniffed in disgust. "I told Eddie to toss that thing away from here on his way out."

How had Callie missed that? Just wonderful. She didn't have the means to test the contents and would have had to ship said evidence to Walterboro, if she were to do so. But they'd no doubt pump Allan's stomach at the hospital. That would have to do. Let them use their lab and formally note the medical record. She returned her focus to the others. "I will need statements from each of you."

"When?" asked the next oldest woman to the grandmother, broader in shape than Eddie.

"Now."

The woman scoffed. The young guy who appeared college-aged cursed under his breath.

"We're all traumatized," said the younger middle-aged woman. Callie had about figured the three middle-aged adults within three or four years of each other were siblings. The one talking seemed the youngest and sported shoulder length black hair with very little of the white the others had. She spoke softer with less attitude. "Can't we wait until morning?"

"Here or at the station?" Callie replied. Nobody wanted to commit, so she kept going. "Introduce yourselves, please. Discussions are a lot easier when you aren't Female 1 or Male 2."

The young guy reacted first. "I'd be Male 1, don't you think, since

I'm the only penis in the room?"

The young woman elbowed him. "Shut up, moron."

Oh, wasn't he fun? "True that, Male 1," Callie said. "Let's start with your name so we don't make these kinds of mistakes."

"Ogden."

"Poe?"

"You think?"

These manners . . . thus far she believed any one of them would poison the other.

Callie had her pad out and motioned with her pen to Ogden. "You're Ogden Poe." She motioned with her pen to the young woman.

"Kimi . . . Poe."

The list continued, with the nurse telling Callie who the grandmother was. Doris Woolf Poe. Then so on. With a few more brief queries, she learned who was related to whom. Callie had pegged the siblings correctly. The two young adults belonged to the eldest sister, Kimberly. Allan belonged to Eddie, and Lacey had no children and lived with her mother, Doris. All used the last name Poe, and nobody appeared married. Another oddity.

The only unrelated folks in the room were the two who spoke up first and came to Allan's aid. The nurse and the chef.

"Where can we do these interviews?" Callie asked. Nobody replied. "Fine, let's use the dining room table, and y'all can listen in."

"There's a small study off the living room," Kimberly said. "And you can start with me."

Ah, this one considered herself queen bee. Which meant she would not be first. Callie could see this one coming back after her interview and telling everyone else what to say and how to say it. "Let's start with. . ." She swore they leaned forward in expectation. "Ogden."

"Why me?" he protested, looking to his mother who harrumphed with bored irritation.

Callie shrugged. "I don't know. Maybe you seem the most eager to be noticed, so I'm noticing you. Come right this way, Male 1."

"Boom," said his sister to their backs as they left the room.

Alone in the study, Callie pulled out her phone on which she'd be recording conversations with these people. She could not afford them collaborating overnight. With so many of them, there would be enough of that as it was.

Edisto Beach Police Department had nine uniforms counting the borrowed deputy from Colleton County. All beat cops. No detectives.

While they could interview someone for a traffic violation, potential murder was another thing altogether. So that put the onus on her and her fifteen years of experience running cases in Boston to handle this case almost solo, her officers managing the rest of the town.

She texted Mark about where she'd be and why. Then she texted the officer on duty for the night and made him aware, in case something got out of hand.

This was quite the unique scenario. She couldn't recall a poisoning under her oversight, or on past records, for that matter. Anaphylaxis due to seafood, sure. But monkshood?

She read introductory information into the recording and set the phone before Ogden, who followed her every move with his eyes, leery, appearing every bit the spoiled brat. "Don't I need an attorney or something for you to do this? Or my mother?"

"Are you over eighteen?" she asked.

"Yes. I'm twenty-one."

"No mother. Do you have something to hide about Allan Poe's health situation?"

His brows almost touched in the middle. "Um, no."

She waited to see if he would ask for an attorney. He could have, but he didn't.

"Let's move on then. Cover your movements and conversations since Allan Poe arrived here at *Maelstrom Manor*. He's your cousin?"

"Yes."

"When did he arrive?"

"Right before dinner. Say six thirty. My sister and uncle saw him in. The rest of us weren't there." He paused. "Maybe Grandmother, I don't know. She doesn't talk much to anyone anymore, but she'd been parked at the dinner table for an hour, so she might've seen him. Don't know if he said anything to her or she to him."

Real warmth in this Poe clan, wasn't there?

"Were you around when the food was prepared?" Callie asked.

"Sure. Everyone was. Me probably less because I'm not fighting those people. They were giving the chef fits."

The term *too many chefs in the kitchen* came to mind. "Why? Is the chef not up to standards?"

"Personally, I think she's awesome, but these people. . ." He flipped his hand in a wave motion toward the direction of the dining room. "They all think they're friggin' Gordon Ramsay and Bobby Flay rolled into one because of Grandmother's influence."

"How so?" she asked. If the kid wanted to flap his mouth, let him. If he went off topic she'd bring him around, but what he thought important might be information she could run with.

Allan's symptoms were indicative of something gastrointestinal, but he could have the flu or have eaten bad seafood. Someone said they had crab. Still, she'd knock out the interviews she could and let tomorrow's medical details point out the need toward subsequent effort.

"Back to the kitchen," she said. "All of you love to cook?"

He seemed to be settling into the interview. Good. His arrogance helped keep this moving.

"You haven't heard of Grandmother's cookbook?" he asked.

"No, tell me," she said, acting intrigued.

"*Southern Silver Spoon*," he said. "Older than you are, maybe. She first published through a press in Charleston that no longer exists, so the first editions are valuable relics. Then some New York publishing house showed interest. Most of the kitchens on the peninsula have it." He nodded toward the dining room, which Callie assumed meant the kitchen. "There's a copy in there that everyone uses."

The peninsula meant Charleston proper. The city had more than its share of famous cookbooks and a history of great cooking with many top-notch chefs having left their impact there. If Grandmother Poe was that esteemed, kudos to her.

"Do you cook?" she asked, noting how readily he drove attention toward the others.

"We're made to learn how from the time we can walk. I hated that crap as a kid, but cooking is not a bad skill to have. Of course you can get accused of poisoning people easily enough." He chuckled at his own humor.

Callie tried acting like that out-of-the-blue remark wasn't off color. "Do y'all often get accused of poisoning someone?" She added a touch of naïveté at the end. "Does that really happen? Sounds awfully . . ."

"Poe-ish?" he finished for her.

She pointed at him, like he'd nailed it.

He made this laughing noise in his throat. "You aren't the first to make the comparison."

"Which makes you all culinary toxicologists, then," she said.

He hesitated. "Damn, that's about the best way to put that I've ever heard. I'm stealing that, po-po."

"Help yourself," she said. "Back to our discussion of exterminating people."

He was finding this conversation entertaining, leaning into something close to sinister. "Grandmother's the wisest about what's toxic in this world," he said. "The rest of us have maybe a third of her wisdom, but that's still more than the average chef. We threaten to poison each other, you know. My sister's been known to do some heavy research to beat others in our morbid dinner table conversations. Grandmother determines the winner, or at least she used to. Kimi does her insane best to impress her."

Then before Callie could say the thought, Ogden did. "It pays to stroke the old lady since she's loaded. One never knows what's in the will."

"You don't sound like you try too hard," Callie said.

He shrugged. "I'm the last person who'll get noticed. The underestimated underdog."

Which made Ogden a better suspect than before.

Not every person involved vied for inheritance, though. The chef was the primary handler of the food, and the nurse was capable by training. The longer she'd been around made her an even stronger contender, because she'd understand the Poe ways.

Ogden leaned back in his chair now, an ankle propped on the opposing knee. "I realize this is about who did whatever to Allan, but you best start with him. He lost his job after getting accused of killing someone in New Orleans. The family was giving him a fit at dinner."

That would be easy enough to chase down. "Allan Poe was accused of murder?"

He shook his head, like maybe he'd exaggerated. "Not exactly. Someone ate something then reacted and died. The restaurant got sued. Allan lost his job there as a sous chef."

"Nobody went to jail? Anybody charged?"

He was overly relaxed now, engaged in the quasi-gossipy air that the interview had taken on. "Not that I heard. Ask him. I only know he lost his job but didn't go to jail."

She would ask indeed. Her instincts told her, however, to take half of what this kid said with a grain of salt. "Any of y'all ever accidentally drop something toxic in a dish? To make someone sick? To win a bet?" She added with a tight grin, "To get even as kids?"

Ogden winked. "Sorry, Chief, but you struck out. We talk it; we don't walk it."

"Right." She dragged out the word.

He sat up straighter at seeing the jovial nature of his banter being taken too seriously. "Listen, Grandmother is the wizard." He rethought his words. "Or is that a sorceress?" Then he raised a finger, like he'd nailed a thought. "Witch, that's it."

"You call your grandmother a witch? To her face?"

"Hell no. She'd take me out like that." He snapped his fingers.

"Take you out? That's pretty strong."

His facial expression twisted. "A simple turn of phrase, Chief. Geez. She used to threaten to take us out of her will. And she would, too, so we don't push her too hard."

She'd heard enough not to accept as much as iced tea from any of them, and she didn't take much of what Ogden said at pure value, but she let him prattle on. This house teemed with suspects, assuming any of this was real and intentional. She could see them altering each other's snacks for kicks.

This boy loved to hear himself talk, so she let him keep going, learning more about the oddities of his relatives and confirming that his respect for any of them ran tissue-paper thin. By the time they'd concluded, she'd grasped a few generalities that applied to them all.

They sold real estate for a living, and a mighty fine living it was.

They catered to Grandmother, because she owned all the assets.

None of them understood where they ranked in the will today, known only to the solicitor.

They could all cook.

They all could talk toxins.

Could this get anymore Agatha Christie?

Chapter 5

Callie

CALLIE COMPLETED Ogden's interview. With Allan and Eddie at the hospital, that left six people to question, with time going on nine. She'd made a list, confirmed by Ogden, and after he left, she took a moment to prioritize the names. She would not get to everyone tonight. Allan's condition dictated whether she got to them all.

A medical professional would confirm or rule out poisoning. To accuse this household of a crime when Allan could've reacted to something much less benign than monkshood, was not terribly wise.

The grandmother would be last, and at this hour might be too spent to bother with. At eighty years of age, Grandmother Poe was probably in bed or too far faded to think straight.

Ogden's sister Kimi could wait for later. In her early twenties, she'd remain keenest the longest.

That left the eldest Poe sister Kimberly, the other aunt and youngest sister Lacey, Nurse Shannon and Chef Pauline. Yes, Chef Pauline.

Callie left the study and almost ran over Kimberly, Lacey, and Kimi waiting on two sofas within a few feet of the door, coffee in hand.

Lacey held up her cup. "Chief, would you like some? Freshly ground beans we order from a shop on King Street." King Street, of course, being downtown, upscale Charleston.

Not no, but hell no. Callie feared partaking of anything short of bottled water, and she'd want to unscrew the top herself. "Thanks, but no caffeine for me at night."

"We assumed we were going to be up late," she said, "so Chef put the pot on."

Callie took tally. "Grandmother go to bed?"

"Shannon tucked her in," Kimberly said. "Chef is working. Eddie is at the hospital. Looks like we are your choices at present."

That one sure liked to be in charge. . . especially with Grandmother not around, Callie bet. She moved toward the kitchen. "Honestly, I'll go get that water. Nobody goes anywhere." She disappeared before anyone could reply. Pots clamored and glassware clinked, so she followed the noise, preferring to see Chef Pauline without her employers listening.

"Hey," Callie said, hopefully not loud enough to spook her.

Pauline looked up from the sink, the humidity from the hot suds having beaded sweat on her temples. "Can I get you something?"

"A bottle of water. Assuming you have any." She waited until Pauline dried her hands and retrieved the drink for her from the fridge. "Care to let those dishes soak a while so you can talk to me?"

"Here or the study?" she asked, drying her hands more thoroughly. "Your choice."

Pauline winked like she had an idea. "Follow me." She led Callie to a door at the end of the kitchen that went to a small porch. Outside, the environment changed from the subdued muffle of the indoors to the wide-open span of the Atlantic, its rolling crashes of waves caught up by the wind and sending spray dancing, droplets reflecting porch lights of surrounding houses. Gusts whistled around the corners.

No porch light because of laying loggerhead turtles, which would be fine ordinarily, but Callie preferred studying her interviewee's reactions.

She peered over the railing. The tide rolled in on the other side of the dune, noisier than usual, and she wasn't sure how a recording would take out there anyway. Good idea to change from the study, though, where Kimberly and Kimi waited on a sofa together, and Lacey sat on the other side of the oval table between, eager to keep track of who, what, and when.

Maelstrom Manor was an awfully big beach house, though. "This isn't going to work," she said over the sea noise. "Any other suggestion?"

Pauline wasn't much taller than Callie but had thirty pounds on her. Guess chefs did a lot of taste testing. She pulled her guest back inside, adjusting her small brunette ponytail blown loose in the wind. "Honey, I'd go to the station for privacy, but I can't have these people seeing me do that." The chef peered around the kitchen, thinking. "What about the pantry?" Pauline grabbed a folded stool from the corner of the kitchen, opened a small door and disappeared inside, not waiting for affirmation.

Callie followed, expecting a four-by-four closet, and she wondered how the heck this was supposed to work. Once inside, however, Pauline was unfolding a chair that matched her own, extras used when chairs were short. Aprons hung on the door, helping with acoustics, and the room appeared the size of a tiny bedroom.

Shelving lined the space, from knee level up to the twelve-foot ceiling. Pauline turned on the overhead light and shut the door, giving a vacuum seal sensation, but without the claustrophobia.

"Okay, I guess this works," Callie said. "They'll be pissed if they find us in here, though. If they do, this is my idea. You don't need these folks mad at you."

The eight-by-eight pantry was sufficient in size and loaded with supplies, canned goods, and assorted small appliances. Clearly the house had been designed for entertainment. Callie pushed back a monster jar of baby sweet pickles on a shelf at chest height to rest the phone.

After the formalities of who Pauline Vitalis was, Callie asked the obvious. "How well do you know the Poes?" Pauline had seemed overly attentive to Allan, enough that the family had let her take charge of the man when he fell ill. Rather odd for family to concede to the newly hired chef nobody had met before, so there was somewhat of an assumption that Pauline and Allan had a past.

"Never met the others until this week," Pauline said. "Allan recommended me to the family. He and I go back to New Orleans when I took him under my wing. The restaurant owner there was a bit of a bully, and I'm not one to be bullied. I was sous-chef, and Allan was only a year out of culinary school, so I carried more clout. Allan's a natural in the kitchen, and he has amazing tastes. He performs beautiful work."

"How long did y'all work together?"

"Almost two years."

"I heard Allan got fired from The Red Lacey, though. Why weren't you? Also, if he was truly to blame, I'd expect him to have been arrested or sued. Instead, they hand him his notice and pretend he no longer exists?"

Pauline's expression shifted to something dry and somewhat disgusted. "The families of the two diners did their research and the restaurant thought twice, because something tells me the Poe attorneys led them to believe pursuing this wasn't in their best interest. The Poes could have closed The Red Lacey, and frankly, I'm surprised they didn't. The compromise was cutting Allan loose. Or so I heard." She gave a short snort. "Allan is now paying penance, which is how the Poes roll. He was still used as the scapegoat, though. . . probably with a Poe nod. They never liked him leaving Charleston."

"Wow," Callie said.

"Yeah. And I wasn't working that day, or I might have gone down with him."

Insane. Callie felt sudden empathy for Allan.

"After they canned him," Pauline said, "I started handing out resumes elsewhere. With those people showing their true selves, and me mentoring Allan, there was still the chance that the scandal would stick to me, so I launched out of that town. A very nice place in Atlanta scooped me up, and within a year, I was head chef. The owner came down with cancer and made me a decent offer to take over the business, an incredible turn of events for me. Allan, however, from what I hear per grapevine, has had a difficult time. Without references, you can't get hired. The restaurant world has a healthy network."

"You didn't vouch for him?"

"He didn't want to tarnish me, he said."

"The Poes didn't find him new work?" If they wielded so much power, why not?

"You'd have to ask them. Those people think differently than the rest of the world."

Pauline's use of the word penance made more sense now, and Callie couldn't help but wonder if retribution had continued via Allan's tainted tea tonight. "Where does he live now? Is he not working?" Callie asked. Someone whose life crashed around their head could find themselves making desperate decisions, but she wasn't quite ready yet to listen to Nurse Shannon and her insinuation earlier that Allan could have done this to himself.

Pauline shook her head. "Don't know exactly where he lives, but he isn't working. When he called to hire me for this, he at least said that. I haven't seen him, however, since New Orleans. Not until he arrived this afternoon, and I was too busy to talk to him solo."

Callie listened, remaining neutral for now. "He didn't discuss the menu, or advise how to cope with this type of . . . family?"

"No, he dodged talking about himself. Maybe he didn't want me to feel sorry for him, or he worried I'd turn him down. I have a sneaking suspicion, however, that he's going to ask me to give him work. But he got in tonight, twenty minutes before food went on the table. I didn't see him again until I set his plate before him. Then again with the dessert." She gave a mild scoffing laugh. "Yeah, I know him well, but then I don't really, do I, since we've not seen each other for over a year. The Allan I was close to was brilliant, enjoyable, and too nice for his own good. Too nice for the likes of these people. No wonder he stayed gone."

Allan wasn't the typical Poe per Chef, but Callie would get to the others in a second and judge for herself. "But Allan said he was poisoned and even named what was used."

"Monkshood," Pauline said. "Doesn't take much to be lethal, but light doses have their medicinal uses, too. Just like good cooks know how to adjust for nutrients and taste, they also know what *not* to cook with, especially those who like to cook clean. Some food seasoning is great in the right doses and not good for you in the wrong ones. There's a lot of toxic plants in gardens, in flower shops, in farmers markets, and even along the road. Hemlock for instance—"

"That one I know." Callie didn't say how, but a certain Indigo Plantation back up on the island and its employees taught her a little bit in a case where a food critic died from hemlock being added to his sandwich. She really had to make time to look up more about the island's flora. The fact that something so toxic could be common and beautiful unnerved her. "Does this monkshood grow around here?"

The chef discounted that quickly. "Maybe in the upper part of the state near Appalachia. Not a tropical plant, so not coastal."

Callie saw hemlock wherever she went and was grateful she didn't have to add monkshood to that list. "Someone who knew what they were doing brought it."

Pauline swept her hand wide, toward the main part of the house, her knuckle bouncing off the extra refrigerator against the wall. "Sorry." She rubbed her hand. "I was trying to say any one of them might know."

The grandmother would know from deep-seated experience. The youngsters could know from general knowledge of what made you high in addition to what they'd learned at their grandmother's knee. The siblings in between grew up cooking alongside their mother.

"Is monkshood fast acting?" Callie asked.

"Oh, yes."

Familiarity of toxins, venoms, whatever, would entail not just dosing. "Is there an antidote?"

Pauline shook her head.

Callie's eyes widened. "So, he's. . ." She tried to find the right words to avoid sounding so callous. Was he up the creek? Done for? Were his days numbered? "Is he going to be okay?"

Pauline scrunched the bridge of her nose. "It had to be a small amount, plus he had sense to gulp everyone's water, and I grabbed the charcoal from the kitchen. He'll probably come home tonight or in the morning." She thumbed toward Callie's phone recording all of this. "Google WebMD. You'll see who lives, who dies, and why."

Callie was relieved, but instead of her Googling, she had a serious question. "Why would he even come back here?"

Pauline inhaled long and deep. "Excellent question. Not sure I would in his shoes."

"And why would they hurt him? He's family."

"Again." She smirked. "Not my monkeys, not my circus. I'm quite glad they aren't my people."

"You say that, but answer me this. . . why are *you* staying?"

Pauline looked down at the floor.

Why dangerous for Allan and not her? Why stay in such a hostile environment? "You're the chef, for God's sake, Pauline. Blame can be placed on you easier than anyone else. The culprit might be setting you up for their deed, and if Allan comes home well in a few hours, they might not be happy that their plan fell through. They could try again."

Callie spoke to her like an innocent, but silently she still wasn't giving the woman a full pass. Pauline was trained and highly experienced. She would earn a pretty penny on this gig, but how much was sacrificing one's reputation worth? Whether being naturally nosy or owning a cop's sixth sense, Callie even wondered whether part of the chef's contract was to scare away a family member. At this stage, when Callie knew so little about everyone involved, anyone was suspected.

The chef stared at her inquisitor as if they'd strayed off the path. "Chief, I get why you asked, but I am here solely because Allan told his family to hire me. I respect him. And now that he's been harmed, I have even more justification to stay. I'll hang through this for him and keep a sharper eye on things. I'll ask them to stay out of the kitchen, for instance."

"It's their kitchen. And anyone can slip in at night."

Pauline flushed. "I'll ask them to stay out of the kitchen, and considering what happened to Allan, and your suspicions, I claim complete and solo control over the food. I'll put snacks out so they don't have to go through the cabinets. I'll stay present in the kitchen and dining area, on guard. If I get push back, then I'll threaten to leave. They'll back off."

Gumption. Callie liked gumption, but as admitted earlier, Pauline didn't know this family well enough. Someone could go after Pauline as well.

But the chef wasn't through. "Between you and me, I think someone's practical joke went sideways."

"That's some insane playfulness."

Callie would tell the Poes where to stick it and leave if she were in the chef's shoes.

The chef being chosen by Allan lessened the odds of the assassin being Pauline. Even if he wanted to off himself, not high on Callie's list of probabilities, he wouldn't do so in such a way that Pauline would appear suspect. He'd want to protect her.

Unless he had an axe to grind with her. Unless he held a grudge that he suffered the New Orleans scandal and she escaped scrutiny. She kept working while he got canned.

What if Allan knew how much of the plant to take to sabotage the chef's reputation?

This case could go in any of a zillion directions.

"I'd be leaving if I were you," Callie said. What she didn't say was, *What if someone wants this pinned on you? What if he asked you to come to this event to set you up?*

Callie wouldn't want to be in the crosshairs of any of these people.

But instead of appearing dismayed, afraid, or even lightly concerned, Pauline's facial lines relaxed. "Listen, I loved that boy. And, like I said, I suspect he'll be asking me for a job. Who's to say I won't hire him? No, ma'am, Allan Poe wouldn't come for me, and I'm not coming for him. Nothing you can say can make me think otherwise."

Admittedly, Allan wasn't Callie's first theory. She needed to talk to the rest of the family. Pauline had opinions with no personal experience to support them. Callie liked hearing Pauline's thoughts, and they'd help her in judging, but she'd feel these folks out herself.

Ogden had shown his true self when questioned alone, like this, under the promise of secrecy. Most people did become somewhat cleaner once alone and secure. Hopefully Pauline had, too.

Honestly, the most normal person Callie'd seen thus far was this chef. Then the nurse, even having hung up on 911. These were the non-Poe people. Their interpretation on how the Poes lived might help to establish a baseline. Now she wished she had the nurse at hand.

A knock sounded on the pantry door, then someone tried the handle and called out. "Chef? Are you in there?"

"Planning meals. I'm a bit busy," Pauline shouted.

"Wondered where you were," they said, the voice sounding like the youngest of the sisters. Lacey, Callie thought.

"I told the police chief to come in here with me while I worked." Before Callie could stop her, Pauline stood and opened the door. "I have so much work still to do, and all of this has set me back. The chief offered to talk to me while I kept going." She turned to look over her shoulder, making Lacey peer, too.

Callie waved. "Are you asking to be next?"

Lacey reared as if slapped. "No, no, just trying to see who is where. We'll. . ." and she paused, "we'll be waiting in the living room."

"Perfect," Callie said, wondering how long Lacey had been standing outside the door attempting to hear.

Lacey left, and Pauline almost left behind her.

"Shut the door, please," Callie said, motioning toward the recorder. Pauline wasn't getting away that easily. "Time to get to the point, Pauline. Out of all the people at dinner, who do you think would poison the other? And why?"

Pauline sat and gave a moan. "I Love Allan, but damn, I hate I took this gig."

Chapter 6

Callie

AFTER HAVING shooed off Lacey, Pauline shut the pantry door and decided to multi-task, grabbing onions out of a bin. "Forgot I needed these." She reached for a Costco size container of black pepper. "And we're out of this in the kitchen. . . What did you ask again?"

"Stop collecting ingredients and tell me about the family." Callie waited for Pauline to cease her movements. "Are they as wise to cooking as Ogden said? Did the grandmother really publish a cookbook? How much truth is under all this bragging?" There'd been a lot of general talk about how everyone was smart about all things toxic, but nothing to support the stories.

Mention of the cookbook, however, made Pauline stop and pay attention. "Don't discount what they know, Chief. The house copy of *Southern Silver Spoon* is out there on the counter with the others. *Pon Top Edisto, Gullah Geechie Home Cooking,* and a few church recipe books. My two favorites, however, remain in my suitcase, because the Poes specifically asked me to make all the recipes out of the one renowned cookbook." She lowered the monster Vidalia onions resting in her hands; hands she'd been trying to speak with. She'd be building biceps doing that for long.

"The book's that good?" Callie asked.

Pauline chucked the onions back into their bin. "I'll be right back."

The chef returned in seconds, a book in hand. She rebalanced herself on the stool and lay the cookbook in her lap, facing Callie.

"I assume you don't cook," she said.

Giving a pinch of her fingers, Callie indicated how little she did. "I live with a restaurant owner whose specialty is Mexican. He's handy with seafood and other stuff, but I'm no judge. I'm glad I have him around and don't have to plan the meals."

Pauline smirked at her in a *Bless Your Heart* way.

Callie peered at the cookbook, a handsome tome of over two hundred pages sitting open about halfway through. She flipped pages back to the front, seeing a forty-year-old photo of Grandmother Poe from her heyday. The copyright for this first edition was 1982. "She used to be a looker."

"Seems so." Then Pauline flipped to the back, to the last chapter before the index. "Look at this."

The chapter was labeled: "Southern Flora: Tonic or Toxin?"

Callie looked up at Pauline, a tad stunned, and the chef bobbed her chin, underlining what she had said earlier. Whether Pauline was familiar with the people or not, she was fully aware of the book that had trained this family.

"I use this a lot," she said. "They, however, can recite the pages. They had a great influence in a woman like Doris Woolf Poe, and per what I recall from Allan, she schooled them around the dinner table each night."

Callie read the page before her, the plants listed like a medical guide. She found Monkshood, aka Wolfsbane. Description, geographic location, what part was toxic, the reactions, who could die, the medicinal uses, the antidotes, the treatments if no antidote, what to tell 911. . .

"Did anyone do this when talking to 911?" Callie asked, pointing to the guidance.

The chef turned the book around to read what Callie meant. Then she peered up. "Not sure? The nurse made the call then went into the next room while I tended to Allan. Everyone else watched us. You'll have to ask her."

Callie thought, yeah, they had a nurse. Who wouldn't expect the nurse to handle a 911 call better? But then, Nurse Shannon called in the emergency and hung up. She hadn't hung around to do what 911 told her to do. She hadn't done anything, from what Callie'd seen and heard. She let Pauline take over.

"Chief," the chef said, bringing Callie back around. "Believe me when I tell you this. . . ice water runs through Poe veins. I'm not saying they have the boldness to slay people, but there's not an ounce of empathy in their bodies. I understand you must question me, and admittedly I've cooked for people I wanted to kill, but I have self-control."

Callie wasn't feeling the humor right now. "Why did you take the gig again?"

"Allan," she said.

"And he'll vouch for you?"

"All day long," Pauline said.

"How's his ice water veins running these days?"

"The Allan I knew was leery of judgment at first, but he grew into his apron. He became a more tempered version, and he enjoyed his new self. Why do you think he didn't want to come home for three years?"

"But he was fired, you say."

The chef nodded. "For something he didn't do."

"I would think that could regenerate the old Poe in him," Callie said.

Pauline gave her an arching brow. "Cut the kid some slack. Why wait until now to become some dark, scheming creature?"

Time would tell. Allan might come back in the morning with color in his cheeks and decide all was good.

"Look at things from a calmer perspective." Pauline counted on her fingers. "One, if they did anything, they only wanted to sicken him, not kill him. A joke maybe. Two, he drank enough water to dilute the effect, and I gave him enough charcoal to absorb the danger. I'm not seeing his life really threatened. Three, someone miscalculated what they were doing and are afraid to speak up."

"Tell me why you so conveniently had that charcoal?" Such a save seemed awfully opportune.

Pauline winked, a habit Callie had come to recognize. "Charcoal is used to decorate food, make ice cream, color dough, and give a smoky taste to dishes. The very reason it counters poison, however, is the reason it was banned from restaurants. Because of the absorption properties, charcoal sucks nutrients from food as well as active ingredients in a lot of medicines. I have used it a time or two at a private gig. But not only did I bring some, but I found a stash in the pantry as well. Chefs appreciate the need. These people consider themselves food savvy, so I'm not surprised they stock some."

"Fair enough." Callie sat there in the pantry, wondering what other oddities surrounded her, and a thought came to mind. "Seen any stashes of toxic items?"

Chef chuckled. "Getting paranoid?"

When Callie didn't chuckle in return, she sobered. "If this were my kitchen," she said, dragging the words out a little, "and I maintained a stash of herbals, said stash wouldn't be kept in the kitchen for accidental use. I'd keep it private, hidden, and carefully identified for no other reason than my own safety."

Interesting. "Do you travel with—"

Pauline almost looked offended. "An herbal collection? I prefer to buy whatever I need for a gig like this from the local markets and stores where items are fresher, the flavors more authentic."

They'd taken forty-five minutes with the interruption and the recipe discussion. The night was about to get too late to catch everyone.

Her phone vibrated, a text. Out of habit, and since most of the beach had her personal cell as well as the one for work, she checked the device after signing out of the recording with Pauline. Callie expected Mark, asking when she'd be done and if he needed to bring her home something for her to eat since she'd missed dinner. Anything else job related, she'd call on her night officer. Officer Wiley enjoyed the night shift.

But the message turned out to be from Jeb. *On my way. We need to talk.*

Okay, what happened to change his mind from spending the night in Middleton? She gave him a thumbs up and waited to see if he had anything else to say. Meanwhile, Pauline gathered ingredients and exited the pantry, leaving the door open. A coolness drifted in underlining how stifling the room had become.

Jeb texted again in afterthought, *I've about made up my mind.*

She reread the text. Made up his mind about what? He hadn't communicated in any manner about what sent him to his grandmother and his girl home without him.

What the hell kind of problem was this?

She started to text back for clarity when a voice sounded from the kitchen. "Chief? We're still waiting, and it's getting awfully late."

"Be right there," Callie called.

She'd rather pack up and leave. The pull of her son and whatever decision he'd made at whatever crossroads he was at, gnawed at her thoughts now. She formally didn't have a crime yet, but in case the medical verdict about Allan turned into something nefarious, she'd be wiser having done interviews tonight.

We need to talk tonight, Jeb typed again.

She quickly typed. *Thought you were spending the night with Grandma?*

Callie often called her mother by her name Beverly for reasons too complicated to explain, or the full-on formal address of Mother which stroked her mother's ego and kept the personal feelings a little bit at arm's length. Jeb, however, called her old-fashioned Grandma, and Callie went with that under the circumstances.

Grandmother and grandson had connected from the time Jeb could walk. Even with Callie living in Boston at the time, the once or twice a year treks down to South Carolina only underlined how easily they bonded. Jeb ran into her arms without hesitation.

Tonight, his girlfriend came home in her own car to her mother, Sophie, instead of sharing dinner. That alone had made Callie spin scenarios. On top of that, once Sophie had spoken to her daughter, Callie would've expected a call about whatever this was. If Sophie had been told to let Jeb tell Callie, and Sophie had honored that request, something ranked rather critical.

She was almost absolute about this being related to post-graduation. Beverly wanted to be number one in line to hire him, and Callie wanted her to have zero hand in his professional future. As mayor of Middleton, Beverly had the power to hire him in about any capacity, and with Jeb being part of the Cantrell heritage, he'd be widely accepted.

Beverly would put the mechanics into play, sway Jeb, then pressure Callie to get on board. But she didn't want her son in politics. He'd be taught the darker, despicable side of politics. Beverly could be brutally ruinous in her political schemes, and at twenty-one, Jeb was impressionable.

Callie knew this day would come but felt she had another year. She sensed a feud on the horizon.

Jeb texted. *We finished dinner. On my way home.*

She texted back. *I'm interviewing people on an urgent case that came up tonight. I might not be home until late. You said you'd probably spend the night, so I took this call.*

He always told her that she texted like an old person with too much punctuation. Who texted with noun verb agreement and complete sentences?

She did, she argued, to avoid misunderstanding. She hoped he would poke back about her texting and not argue that law enforcement deterred her from putting her family first.

The dots appeared, then stopped, then started again, then stopped. She waited until no more dots happened, but there was no more texting either.

She much preferred an old-fashioned phone call.

Jeb's dislike for her law enforcement profession was steeped in experience. The assorted criminal elements in Callie's life had taken Jeb's father, his grandfather, and a prior beau of hers who her son had come to respect. She often felt that Jeb saw her as an ill-fated soul, attracting criminal sorts and bad omens, but as negative as he felt about her career, she was equally as hellbent about remaining in the field.

Except for her son, nothing made her life richer. She'd had the badge taken from her once and given it up another time, but she kept coming back, each time stronger in a fuller understanding of what tapped her strengths and kept her sane. Probably sober, too. She hoped her delay tonight hadn't gravitated into the age-old argument about her being a cop.

Callie hopped off her stool, hoping to step out of the pantry before someone saw her, but she exited and almost ran into Kimi.

The young lady cousin made a pouty expression. "They told me to come check on you. Look at the hour. Our time means something too, you know."

"No doubt," Callie said, putting away her phone. "How about you and I head to the study and do this, Miss Poe?"

"But Mom and Aunt Lacey thought one of them needed to be next."

Callie gave a sly grin. "Yet they sent you to fetch me knowing full well I'd choose you out of convenience."

The girl stiffened as the comment made sense, and her pout deepened.

These people were not difficult to read, so Callie might as well use their insecurities against them. Especially with them so stuffed with arrogance.

Chapter 7

Callie

WALKING ACROSS the room in front of the mother and aunt, without a word, Callie and Kimi entered the study. Callie told the girl to shut the door.

"They're going to be pissed at me," the girl uttered, taking her seat as Callie walked around the desk and took hers. "You don't think they'll think I asked to talk to you first, do you?"

"Let them," Callie said, doing the recorder thing again. In a smooth motion, she had things set up and rolling. "Doesn't matter."

"Are you mad at me?" Kimi asked, like she was setting up a defense for what was about to come. "You're so . . . somber."

"It's not a party, Miss Poe, and I don't have personal feelings regarding any of you," Callie replied. "Now, who do you think took a shot at your cousin?"

"Wait, you think I know who tried to kill him?"

"Who said attempted murder? And I would think your first response would be that none of them would do such a thing."

Kimi shook her head, to rid herself of the sudden confusion and regain control. "Of course, none of my family would do such a thing. You're using wordplay against me, police lady. I won't be fooled. Nobody tried to kill him, period."

She wasn't quite back in balance, but she was steadier. . . and much more wary.

"I never said murder or kill, Kimi. You did."

"Why did you choose me to ask?"

"You know all the persons of interest," Callie said.

"So does everyone else."

"You were there," Callie continued.

"So was everyone else."

"You are closest to his age, and I've interviewed Ogden."

Her mouth opened for another quick retort, but she had none.

"I could go on and on with the reasons," Callie said, "but surely you have some sort of theory. At a minimum, a suspicion."

Kimi crossed her arms. "I don't like doing this."

"It's not everyone's cup of tea, pardon the pun, but all of this is quite simple. Accident or otherwise, who do you think did it, and why?" Then she let the recorder run . . . and run. Kimi even looked over at the device, recognizing the onus on her to fill in the silence. The longer the silence, the more guilty she would look. . . or at least that's what most interviewees thought.

Kimi turned and took a quick glance at the shut door, like she could mentally connect with her relatives waiting outside, sending them barging in to intercede.

"Do you need me to repeat the question?" Callie asked. "For the third time?"

"No . . . ma'am."

Callie waited.

"Allan is my favorite relative," Kimi finally said. "I would never hurt him."

"Who do you think would?"

Kimi studied her thumbnail. "I don't want to blame any of my family."

"Are you thinking non-family? The nurse or the chef?"

Kimi looked up quickly. "I didn't say that. I don't even know the chef. And Nurse Shannon has been with us for years. Not sure how many, but a lot of them. Loyalty and all that."

Loyalty and all that ran through Callie's mind. "Then cover everyone. On a scale of one to ten, how would each person in that room rank when it comes to going after your cousin?" Statistics made opinion less personal, putting everyone on the board on an even playing field, Callie removed the stress of singling out one. Maybe the girl didn't know who, but learning who was more prone than another would be helpful. "Start with your grandmother."

Kimi scoffed at the thought. "She'd have to give an order to someone else. Did you get a good look at her?"

"Yet she poured the tea."

Kimi's humor vanished. "Well, there is that."

"Scale of one to ten," Callie reminded. "Whether she did the deed or ordered it done."

The young woman hesitated. "Eight? Allan left the family business then sullied the family name with all that mess in New Orleans. Grandmother doesn't like tarnishing the name."

Nice to hear. Callie'd previously gotten the gist of the New Orleans story from the chef, someone who would know details better than Kimi. She'd learn more from Allan. Callie moved down the list. "What about your Uncle Eddie."

"I'd like to say zero, but I have to give him an eight, too."

"Even being Allan's father?"

Kimi made a deep throat clip of a laugh. "He shows no love for Allan."

"Yet he followed him to the hospital."

"Because that's his job. Grandmother would expect that for appearances' sake." A lot of sarcasm seemed rolled up in that last sentence.

Callie said as such. "Sounds a bit harsh."

"The truth isn't pretty. Uncle Eddie's little more than a sperm donor, in my opinion. He's not that proud of his son. Not enough even to visit him in New Orleans and see if he's okay after the mess that happened. Not enough to ask him to come home either. The Poes have enough clout to get him a job in Charleston. At least Beaufort or Savannah. Besides, my uncle loves Grandmother way more than he loves Allan." She held up a finger, like she wasn't through. "Worships the altar might be a better way of saying it."

"So, he's an eight, too?" Callie wrote the number down next to the name, like she had to make a record. "Your mother?"

"Again, I'd rather not," the girl said.

"Again, one to ten, Kimi." If Callie had to guess, she'd say a lump hung in the girl's throat from how she swallowed hard once, then again.

"Eight, I guess."

Callie waited for the why.

Kimi winced pondering her thoughts. "Mother would prefer I inherit. She thinks Allan is undeserving and worthless. She thinks I walk on water, only you'd never hear her admit that aloud. Genes carry more weight than love does around here, so don't go thinking sentiment clouds her vision. Like uncle Eddie, parenting is not part of her constitution, let's say."

Callie took note. "What about your brother? You're older, right?"

"Yes, ma'am. But Mother thinks Ogden is even more worthless than Allan. Ogden's easy not to like." She paused. "I really hate that."

"One to ten, for your brother," Callie asked, quickly gaining knowledge of how this family worked.

"Oh, an eight. He hates Allan, but I'm not sure he's got the guts.

He lives for the moment and annoys the adults. He's a screwup and works hard to master the skill."

The pattern became clear. Kimi wasn't going to finger one individual.

"Your other aunt." Callie looked at her pad. "Lacey?"

"Give her an eight, too."

That was a little more unexpected. "How so? She seems the docile one."

"She'll do whatever Grandmother tells her to do, so the number is the same."

"Nurse Shannon," Callie said, moving on.

"Eight. Ditto Aunt Lacey."

"And finally. . ."

Kimi raised hands up in the air. "What the hell, lady? I told you everybody. What more do you want?"

After fifteen minutes, Kimi thought she'd gotten away with what was asked of her, without incriminating anyone.

"Allan," Callie said, calmly. "Would he do this to himself?"

Kimi hung still a second then sharply shook her head. "No. I'm not answering that one. Nobody is in his head and can know what he thinks, and you are unfair to put me there to guess. He's been gone. He lost his job, and none of us has a clue what he's been doing with himself. On one hand he's here, facing us, honoring family obligation. On the other hand, he hasn't kept us up to date, not that I blame him. Who knows how healthy his thoughts are. I refuse to assign a stupid number to his odds of committing suicide. Cuff me, write me a ticket, I don't care."

Kimi huffed, going for anger to hold back tears.

Callie wasn't moved. "Who says he wasn't seeking attention? Who says someone you assigned a number to wasn't doing a thing but flexing their dominance, doctoring his drink enough to scare him away? Wouldn't that improve someone else's inheritance?"

Kimi listened, looking like she realized what Callie said held merit.

"Or maybe someone has a heart and tried to scare him off, so he doesn't get seriously hurt?" Callie said. "Because they care so much for him?"

"It wasn't me, Chief. How many times do I have to tell you—"

"Could've been you, though. You're the one most prone to protect him from what you said."

"Could've been any of us," the girl said. "We're all more than capable. God knows Allan didn't want to be here, and by him being here that makes him the best of us all." She stopped abruptly, wondering if she'd said too much. Callie could read her eyes.

"You two were close once," Callie said, laying her pen down, regarding her.

Kimi nodded, and Callie had to point at the recorder to make her say aloud. "Yes, we're close. I'd like to think he'd tell me if he was depressed to that level."

"But he hasn't talked to you in years. How does that make you feel? He left you alone with a toxic family that he escaped from."

She snapped her head side to side. "Nope, I don't hold that against him. He did the right thing, in my opinion. I wish I had the balls to do that. They educated me then hired me. I had no real dream to go after like Allan did."

Callie believed her. Not only about Allan but about everything said. She'd become passionate about Allan with maybe a hint of regret about her brother, but the rest? No love lost there.

But Kimi stayed while Allan didn't, meaning the odds were she held out for the sea of money and assets from the grand dame.

From what Callie'd learned about this family, and as had been underlined via the three interviews, any one of them possessed the savvy and desire to do the deed.

Maybe they hoped he'd stay gone, removing him from the equation, and his return was a kink in the works. Or what if Allan wasn't the first one they went after?

"Has anyone else been poisoned like this?" she asked.

"Nope," Kimi said rather quickly. "This is a first."

After a few more questions about timeline and specifics on what Kimi had seen, consistent with the other two, Callie cut her loose and told her to send in her mother.

Right now, she'd love to snare the grandmother, to be honest. If Callie were the old lady, she'd feign memory loss and slow-on-the-draw reactions all the way to the end. Who could prove otherwise? Especially if she were the guilty one.

About five minutes went by without Kimi's dear old mom coming in, the delay likely attributed to the little Poe educating her mother. "Ms. Poe?" Callie called.

Kimberly strode in, head back and chest forward as if nobody chose when she made her entrance. "Here I am, Ms. Morgan."

"Chief is fine," Callie said, understanding how much the correction would slip under the woman's skin. Never start an interview of suspects with them having the upper hand. "Shut the door, please, and have a seat."

She started the recording, making Kimberly aware, but also making Callie realize time inched up on eleven p.m. Jeb would be home at any time, depending on where he'd been when he texted. Talking tonight was fast slipping into the realm of *not happening*.

When she looked up, Kimberly sat stoic and poised, staring a hole through her. "Are we doing this or not. . . *Chief?*"

"We are indeed doing this, Ms. Poe. Thank you for talking to me." Callie nodded to her phone. All she got was a bobble of a brow from her new interviewee. Then Callie came out of the chute with a question the woman would not expect, to tip the scales. "Why are there no spouses in the family? I'm trying to get a grip on who and what the family consists of."

Kimberly's red, freshly lipsticked mouth opened, then closed, Callie finding funny her need to touch up image before coming in.

"My husband died," she replied, a perceived self-worth heavy in her words. "Ten years ago."

"So sorry. How did he die?"

Kimberly clouded up. "Heart attack, if you must know."

"Thank you, and the others?"

"I don't have to answer about them. That's their business."

There were better hills to die on than about this. Callie leaned forward as far as she could on the desk. "Is this how we're playing this? You as the hostile witness? I see no judge, no jury, and the information is on public record." She sat back. "You decide how to proceed, ma'am. I can take this any direction you like." Again, she nodded toward the recording, underlining the silliness of this obstinacy.

Kimberly lightly rolled her shoulder and batted her eyes twice. "Well, I hate talking about other people."

Callie said nothing, doubting she meant a word of what she'd just said.

"Um, there are no other spouses, if you must know," Kimberly continued.

Good, they were back in business.

"Lacey's husband died of an aneurysm two years after they married, ages ago. She remained with our mother and never remarried. Edgar's wife died of cancer when Allan was a teen. My grandfather passed twenty years ago. A stroke. Ogden, Kimi, and Allan never married." She expressed a big breath to say she was done.

Poe spouses sure didn't last long, and nobody seemed to want a second attempt at marriage. "Who do you think would want to hurt Allan tonight?"

Dramatically contemplating the ceiling, Kimberly replied, "I guess you have to ask, but I have no earthly idea."

"Sure you do. He ingested poison. Either something slower acting from the food, or something quicker in the tea. Seems all of you love dabbling in a kitchen, and I've heard talk that you used to compete in your knowledge of this sort of thing."

The woman released a shrill scoff. "Ha! Who told you that?"

Kimberly would ferret out the culprit upon leaving the interview. Kimi and Ogden had best expect second interrogations from dear old mom. "Doesn't matter who. You all have culinary skills. If you had to lay odds on someone who might've put that knowledge to use tonight, who would it be?"

"Nobody," she replied, hardly before Callie finished. "Allan lost his mother, his father isn't much good to him, he ran off to be a chef instead of making better money in the family's real estate enterprise then screws that up, loses his job, and remains unemployed to this day." With embellishment, she slowly stretched out her hands in a wide swoop, her crepey underarms swinging as she did. "Voila. Evidently the boy did this to himself. He hates us, so he waited to make a statement here, on display for everyone." She tsked. "I hope he comes back, packs, and leaves."

So, Kimberly was hanging her hat on attempted suicide. Trouble with that theory was that Allan would know how to follow through. "From the sound of things, he fought to avoid succumbing," Callie said. "I'm not feeling suicide."

"He got scared," she replied. "Unless he was showing off to scare us."

Callie pretended to take another note. "Did you try to kill him? You seem awfully anxious to see him gone."

Kimberly's eyes blinked as her red lips hung open then clamped shut. "How dare you," she finally pushed out.

"Hey, everyone gets the question," Callie said. "I would be wrong not to ask you."

"Did someone say I did?" came the reply, again wanting to identify a rat to pursue.

"Most people give me an adamant no first."

"No, then," Kimberly exclaimed. "No, no, no. I did not attempt to kill my nephew. Let there be no misunderstanding whatsoever."

She'd denied in every way possible, leaning in to be closer to the recording.

Then like the others, Callie asked a few more questions about what she saw, the timeline, how dinner was prepared, who assisted, and if she was familiar with monkshood.

"We all are," she said. "But we don't practice with poisonous plants. We only know about them."

The interview concluded shortly thereafter. The night was old. Lacey would have to wait. Besides, Eddie and Allan wouldn't be available until tomorrow.

Callie watched Kimberly sashay out of the room and couldn't help but think of her own mother, wondering how this mother would rank going up against Beverly.

Nah, Callie's money was still on Beverly.

Chapter 8

Allan

AFTER TWO IN THE morning, still laid up on an ER gurney, Allan felt considerably improved over a couple hours ago when he was certain dying would feel better. Now, however, his head spun at the who and what of it all.

Despite him telling the doctors no need to pump his stomach if the toxin was monkshood, or wolfbane, the name comic book writers used, they didn't want to take chances. Despite the fact he'd thrown up so many times he'd lost count before reaching the hospital, they pumped his stomach. Better safe than sorry, they said.

They hadn't seen the trash can full of black gunk back at the manor. If he'd had his wits about him, he'd have told someone to bring it in the ambulance.

His father relaxed in a chair in the corner. An unexpected pleasure came from watching his middle-aged father doze. Eddie's presence was more attention than Allan had received since his mother died, and he admittedly basked in the moment. Experience told him Eddie did little more than what society expected of him as a parent, and that he was no more than the eyes and ears of the family, but Allan could hope, couldn't he? Maybe distance and time had made a positive difference? His father had called on holidays and birthdays.

But Eddie's one promise to visit New Orleans never materialized.

At first he'd been disappointed that Kimi didn't visit, but he hadn't come to see her either. Aunt Kimberly and Grandmother kept his favorite cousin on a leash. She represented promise for the family.

Allan, however, paid a price for leaving without permission, pursuing a profession that hadn't been formally sanctioned and not accepting a position with the realty enterprise that had been saved for him since he was in middle school. Cooking was a sideline, an asset to give one's character depth, but not a Poe career.

His head still throbbed, and thinking about anything Poe-ish didn't help, so Allan laid his head back on the thin pillow, studying small stains on the ceiling, wondering what kind of human fluid had sprayed that far, and how. Closing his eyes, he emptied his mind and sought dull minutiae to give that headache a rest.

One LED bulb near the entrance of the ER bay flickered periodically, ten flickers per minute by his count, not yet worn out enough to be replaced by a frugal hospital budget. He thought ERs were loud and noisy, too, like on Grey's Anatomy, but this one wasn't. Time dragged.

After a half hour he had counted electrical outlets (five), light bulbs overhead (six), and curtain holders anchoring the curtain onto the ceiling (thirty). Twenty-five floor tiles lined up between the back corner and the bay opening. Sixty pairs of shoes had walked by in the last thirty minutes.

Unemployment had taught him to notice details, the little somethings to keep his psyche engaged, sometimes in lieu of rum. He'd learned quickly he wasn't an alcoholic, the hangovers not worth the nights before.

He shifted the pillow and sank back again.

Who the hell had dosed his tea?

Monkshood had a medicinal side. For anxiety and to regulate one's heart, but these days advice was don't. Even brushing up against the wrong part could cause health problems. Digesting it took those problems to another level, like his.

As jungle-like and inviting as the Lowcountry was to fast-growing plants, monkshood was not one of them. The habitat wasn't until you approached the North Carolina border.

Someone went out of their way to bring it to the beach.

He bet that the police chief scratched her head hard on this one.

The curtain was flung back, and a fireplug of a nurse flew in with way more energy than anyone ought to own this time of night. The physician's assistant from earlier trailed her. "Ready to go home?" the nurse asked, the decision made from the way she disconnected him from equipment and noted items on a clipboard.

Eddie Poe snorted and came back to life. "We're done?"

"Yes, Dad," Allan said, sitting up. "This stuff was going to run its course on its own, but I appreciate you coming along and hanging."

"Aconitine," said the PA. "Never seen that before. Definitely in whatever you ate. Not enough to do permanent damage," she added, not using the word *death*. "Between what you did to incapacitate the potency, and our pumping your stomach, you dodged anything serious." Her observation of him filled with suspicion. "Not sure where you got it from. You say the police got involved?"

"Not your concern," Eddie said, standing to stretch his back, then his neck before moving to the side of the bed. His khakis no longer held their crease, his shirt not tucked in to order. "What does he do now? Any restrictions? Any prescriptions?"

His Poe authority had mixed with stilted parental traits, and Allan didn't even try to get involved.

The PA, however, wasn't amused. "No prescriptions counter aconitine poisoning," she said, with a taste of condescension. "We can only treat symptoms, and all we see is that he's worn out. Nothing sleep won't cure." She raised a lone finger in warning. "However, if you feel heart palpitations, get yourself back in here. Right now, you're steady."

"That's it?" Eddie asked, like he wasn't buying the diagnosis.

"Unless he wants an anxiety drug to keep him from worrying."

"No," Allan said, sliding legs over the side of the bed. "I'm good. Let's get out of here."

Hand resting on the mattress, Eddie's stare held a little longer than necessary on his son, but he said nothing. The PA left.

Oblivious to all the nuances flying around the room, the nurse plopped a bag of Allan's belongings on the foot of the bed. "Need help getting dressed?"

"No, I'm good."

He signed three times on documents he didn't read. The second the curtain closed back, he reached for his bag.

Eddie remained standing, not assisting, his body language forecasting he had something to say.

Allan stood and dropped his gown. "Say what you're thinking, Dad."

"I've had a lot of time to think tonight, son."

Between snores, but maybe so. "Me too, Dad. Me, too."

The father hesitated. Allan backed off his sarcastic thoughts and silently prepared to leave. He'd hoped for some legitimate feelings, some empathy, even regret from his father for not having seen his son in so long, but Allan didn't want to appear needy. However, if Eddie reached out, Allan would attempt to meet him part way.

"Why did you do it?" Eddie asked.

Hope drained out of Allan, and the old, guarded sense of preservation filled its place. He buckled the belt on his slacks that he couldn't help noticing looked a lot like his father's. Very coastal Carolina.

"I didn't, Dad," he said, rolling up his sleeves out of habit.

A scowl clouded the elder's face as he caught a clean sight of the tattoo. "Surely you don't think any of us would try to make you sick, son. That's over the top. Even for you."

Standing there in socks, Allan paused, a loafer in his hand. "Care to explain *Even for me?*"

"I would not invite you here for someone to hurt you and neither would your family. That's hurtful, son. What's happened to you?"

Allan's hopeful remnants of reconciliation fell away. Eddie gave him no credit or benefit of the doubt. His words would soon be in every Poe ear at the house.

Allan ran fingers through his hair, made sure the bag was empty and all his belongings accounted for, then gave full attention to the dad who'd just disappointed the hell out of him. He was almost as disappointed in himself for giving his father too much grace.

"Dad, come on. Someone spiked the tea. Maybe it wasn't supposed to be my tea. Could be a prank." He gave a melancholy one-time laugh. "But the name Poe does reek of sinister."

"No, we're not going there," his father said. "You are not allowed to cast aspersions on this family, son."

Allan was fast developing an aversion to being called *son.* "There are five other people in the family, Dad. Not counting the nurse." He dropped his second shoe he'd been holding to the floor, satisfied at the plop echoing in the silence of the early morning hour, and he slid his foot in.

"What about your chef?" his father asked, way too much snide in his question.

"She's the one I trust most."

Heat rose into the father's cheeks. "I do not appreciate that."

"And I don't appreciate being treated like an embarrassment to the Poe name."

The father tried to act appalled, unconvincingly so. "Nobody thinks that." His eyes strayed to where the raven tattoo peered out from the sleeve.

"Haven't seen you in three years, Dad. What does that say?"

His father gripped the foot of the bed. "It says you avoided us. You chose to stay away."

Allan shifted his foot, repositioning the sock in his shoe. "The roads run both ways."

Eddie pointed. "That tattoo says you're proud of being Poe."

But Allan wasn't willing to cave. "More an ownership of being Poe, the details saying I do Poe my way."

The senior Poe took a breath of frustration and turned, slung the bay's curtain to the side, and left, his heels tapping the tiled floor until they echoed into nothing.

The nurse returned, her neck craned to where the father went. "He's a bit of a pickle, isn't he? Your dad?"

"You'd never guess, would you?"

Of course she didn't respond, having weathered tons of family drama in her ER duties.

"Can I go?" he asked.

"Yes, sir. Take care." Then she disappeared before he did.

His stomach ached from a night of forced activity. Now he had to ride back to *Maelstrom Manor* with his ticked-off father. . . for forty-five minutes.

Outdoors, the night rested comfortably in the fifties. Birds were roosted and silent, the time of year too early for frogs and cicadas to sing. The two men silently entered POE 2 and headed back. Finally, Eddie uttered, "Seriously, I'm glad you're okay, son."

To which Allan mumbled, "Me too, Dad."

Upon leaving ambient city lighting, the landscape turned too dark to take much note of the passing landscape. The occasional yard lamp pierced the black, nothing to see, so Allan fell into his thoughts.

Who did it?

And why?

And frankly, was he safe to go back?

If he returned, packed up, and left, would that not be the hoped-for result?

From Grandmother to Ogden, Allan couldn't exclude anyone from the list of culprits. Regretfully, he threw in the nurse, but still, he would not blame Pauline.

This week started off holding hope for employment or a better standing in Grandmother's eyes. Maybe both. Grandmother's thoughts about him remained in the air, but he and Pauline had been on good terms. She would simply tell him no if she couldn't hire him. As for Grandmother? Maybe tonight's incident would entice a word or two out of her in honest appreciation that he was safe and sound. Recognition would almost make the trip to the hospital worthwhile.

They crossed the big bridge sooner than expected, and his heart skipped a beat at the expectation of returning to *Maelstrom Manor.*

All of this. . . this, united family image, fortified in the public's eye by the infamous last name, didn't agree with Allan. They'd kept him from being sued in New Orleans, but they hadn't really stood by him. The posturing had been for name protection, not for Allan.

Their ensuing silence made him too ashamed to come home. Like this even felt like home. Technically, he had no home. He had addresses, none of them lasting much more than a year, like his two attempts at employment. Such history only underlined the family's opinion of his choices.

In his darkest moments, he reminded himself he was only half Poe. His mother had died when he was fourteen after a three-year illness. Those years were long and difficult, and he was often pushed aside, his father craving every last moment his wife breathed as his, almost holding a grudge against the son for remaining alive in her stead.

At least that's what it felt like for a struggling teenager.

At eighteen he entered a small culinary college with a propensity toward seafood, and there he found his joy. Then on to the Louisiana Culinary Institute thanks to an advisor who'd loved his way with crab, who'd heard of the Poes, and had visited one time to Edisto Beach.

Allan finished second in his class, snared three job offers, and thought he'd made his great escape, enroute to a legacy of his own.

But his last name led people to look up to see if he was a real relative of the author. There they'd learn the Poes had acreage in Charleston County, a house on the Battery, and a real estate enterprise that bragged forty seasoned agents and Eddie as Senior Broker, Kimberly officially at his side. . . on paper.

Then there was the bestselling cookbook, which still pulled well on a search engine. A bible of gastronomic advice direct from a blue-blooded Lowcountry matron with double ties to literary genius – Woolf and Poe. Branding from heaven.

They were people who shared blood and lacked sentiment. If Grandmother died anytime soon, tears would be shed from outsiders. The clan would stand firm, dressed in the appropriate haute couture, shaking hands and accepting condolences with stiff lips facing the public. . . and welcome relief after.

But in the meantime, Grandmother Doris dared anyone to cross her. Once upon a time she'd been a social animal with a busy agenda, friends, and followers. She loved to share her socialite stories at dinner parties, and until Allan was in his teens, he hadn't recognized the self-importance that she infused into everything she did, the same as she expected of everyone beneath her, family or staff.

The Poes loved their standards.

A drawer in the study held old clippings and social announcements about her catered, invitation-only signings, now in albums yellowing with age. The best of them, however, were formally preserved in rich dark walnut frames on the study wall. In one she posed after a television appearance with Paul Prudhomme in 1985. That one hung prominently in the dining room, matted ornately in black, the dark oak frame matching the dining room table.

She'd been handsome in stature and countenance. An eight on a scale of ten, but what little she lacked in beauty, she made up for in style. Money helped anyone make up the difference, and she possessed enough of that to level up well.

Poe life was about watching Grandmother Doris do her cookbook thing, while the real estate activities padded the family's pockets deep and thick. Power led her to the most brilliant chefs, dining in their signature restaurants, making the rounds to culinary schools where she autographed books, spoke, and relished kisses of her proverbial ring.

Still Grandmother knew her shit in the kitchen, and she made sure all of them did.

She'd come to Allan's graduation, only to be invited to speak at the ceremony, and Allan had spent his day answering the question, "That's your grandmother? For real?" He'd ended the day wondering if his degree was more for her bragging rights than his.

He was never sure whether that absence of affection back then was her flaw or him not performing up to the Poe par.

In the last three years, he'd concluded all this behavior congenital Poe flaws he could do nothing about. Pragmatism, apathy, and emotional bluntness beat in the heart of this family. He liked to think of himself as the exception.

He leaned his head against the window, staring into the dark. God, this would be a long damn week. He'd have to show how worthy he was to the Poes and pray he could team with Pauline well enough to land a job.

Pauline had been restricted to the recipes in *Southern Silver Spoon*. Good. Those he knew, but he could add a pinch of knowledge to a couple of those dishes that Grandmother would notice. . . and respect. Anything to give her a chance to remember him on a good note.

At four AM, Eddie pulled up to the house, the sky dark but the stars bright, the briny air medicinal. Waves seemed diminished, low tide close at hand making the breaks sound more like murmurs. Without a word, the two men entered *Maelstrom Manor*.

Allan thought he heard Eddie speak. "You say something?"

His father shook his head. "Sleep in tomorrow. The chef will prepare you something whenever you get up." Like Allan could not decide both of those things on his own.

Their bedrooms were on the second floor, and Allan held back for his father to climb first. He briefly scanned the dining room where all the hoopla had taken place. Spotless. No sign of the trash can.

"Night, son," Eddie said halfway up the stairs, as if they had exchanged words. Back to the Poe standard. Chin up and all that.

Allan changed his mind about bed, at least for a moment, and ventured into the kitchen. The cookbook was in its righteous place on the side counter, with a pad of paper. Allan dared to peek.

The pad contained the menu for tomorrow, or rather today being almost dawn. He studied breakfast, then lunch, but especially dinner. Good choices, but he could come in handy if Pauline gave him half a chance.

Chapter 9

Callie

CALLIE ARRIVED home moments after midnight and parked under the house between pylons, noting Jeb's Jeep on the other side. He was home, but at this hour he was likely in bed. There was a certain peace that came with knowing he was under her roof, under her oversight, but she'd promised him a talk. Those were fewer and further between the older he got.

Tomorrow she'd revisit the Poes, hopefully see Allan, finish with Eddie, the nurse, and so on, but she would let Jeb's availability direct the schedule. Tonight, she'd leave him a note to wake her up or call her. They could eat breakfast together, maybe with Mark. . . hopefully with Mark cooking. Omelets weren't difficult, but his beat the hell out of hers hands down.

The motion sensor popped on a light as she exited her vehicle and others followed suit as she rounded the corner to the steps. Constructing beach homes on pylons allowed hurricane waters to push through and avoid damage to the interior, but the downside was having to trudge up two dozen stairs after a long day. More lights snapped on at mid-landing, enough to illuminate Jeb waiting alone in a cushioned rattan love seat against the porch wall.

She smiled, so happy to see him. "Hey, kid. Where's Mark?" she asked, reaching him and taking the chair perpendicular to his, her back to the east end of the porch enabling her to see him better.

"Hey. Didn't want to wake him." He sounded spent.

But judging by the time of Jeb's phone call, he'd been there an hour. "What's going on?" she asked, pushing cases and law enforcement out of her mind.

He was dressed nicely from dinner in a long sleeve button up and slacks. No duffle bag, nothing other than himself. He sat slumped, arms crossed, legs wide, like he'd dug in and waited for quite some time. Normally he lit up when seeing her after a while, a sweetness in his eyes. Clearly, he was troubled.

Coming home unexpectedly on a weekend, leaving his grandmother earlier than planned, sending his girlfriend to her mother's instead of letting her accompany him. . . none of this was normal Jeb. His shoulders slumped, weighted with his thoughts.

Of course, Callie's mind gravitated to the worst, but a twenty-one-year-old brain saw the world in greater extremes, way better or way worse than reality, so she tempered her feelings. She had to remain steady, not imagine tragedy, and be the mainstay he might need in case he'd sat here long enough to overthink his life *ad nauseum*.

She'd follow her own advice as well. She was a pro at overthinking things, too.

"There is nothing we can't work through," she said, remembering when she was Jeb's age, still at the University of South Carolina studying criminal justice against her mother's wishes. Her future loomed, or at least the options for the future. Beverly had envisioned Callie in political science, like herself and had held tight to a plan that took Callie from a bachelor's degree to a master's then straight into a role with the town of Middleton.

Thanks to her own past, Callie had given Jeb distance in school. She'd help when asked. Very un-Beverly.

Not that she couldn't overthink things better than the average Joe.

She told herself Jeb was miles more mature than she'd been at his age.

"Start with dinner with your grandmother," she said, uncomfortable with the silence going on too long. "How did it go?"

He seemed to loosen up at the question. "Not bad. . . at first."

"Is she doing okay?" Callie asked, trying to hold onto the positive and bring him down off whatever ledge he stood on.

He nodded. "I listened to her go on about town council and a new sewer contract, then about permitting a new shopping strip along the railroad that butts up against the historic section. Nothing happens in that town without her nod, does it?"

Softly smiling, Callie replied, "Nope."

All that sounded like Beverly. She hated town council but loved butting heads with them, especially with two of them being men who'd dared run against Callie's father Lawton for mayor once upon a time. Negotiation wasn't in Beverly's nature, and she did not forget the simplest act against her or the family name. They saw the town's future through a whole different lens, and she wouldn't let a living soul unravel what the Cantrells had achieved.

Callie heard scratches on the big trash cans around back. This time of night the raccoons trolled en masse, testing everyone's bins for unlatched lids. Only took one to find success for the others to rush to the spilled treasure. From the sound of things, hers were secure.

Jeb heard, too, using the few seconds of diversion to go back quiet again. His jaw fretted a bit.

"I'll sit here till dawn if necessary, son." To show him, she eased back, emulating his posture.

"She wants me to work for her in Middleton," he said.

"Not a surprise to any of us. Doing what?"

His attention darted to the side, into the dark. "Public Information Officer."

Callie thought for a moment. Middleton wasn't that large, meaning there weren't that many town hall positions available for a newbie with a poli-sci degree, making the town not a bad place to start. "Assuming you want to work for her that's actually not a bad position." She almost added, *I wouldn't, though.*

"I suggested I start in another town to get my feet wet," he said. "So the nepotism wasn't so obvious."

Callie couldn't agree more. There was a reason she was proud of this boy.

He sat upright, more energy in his expression now, and began talking with his hands. "When I said that, *your* mother had the gall to want to approve which town I applied to. If I wasn't going straight to work for her, she wanted to have control over which direction my resume took. When I said I would make my own choice, to avoid riding her coattails, she laughed." He stared at Callie. "Can you believe that?"

"Why yes, I can," she said, her own face-off memories with her mother still vivid.

He inched forward. "She warned me that she knows every mayor in the state. Warned me!"

"She probably does, son." Callie wanted to drive to Middletown, wake up her mother, and chew her ass for upsetting Jeb. But on the other hand, she relished how Jeb was able to see that side of his grandmother. The side Callie had disliked for years.

His momentum picked up. "All I had to do was tell her which ones I applied to, she said, and she'd make my dreams happen. Then after five years tops, because of her age, of course. . ."

"Of course."

"She expected me to return to Middleton and assume my rightful role in the Cantrell legacy." He blew out hard from his nose. "Like I had zero choice. Like I had let the military pay for my school and now owed them my service."

Very good analogy. Beverly liked playing the general.

"Can you believe that?" he tacked on again.

"Yes, I can."

"There's more."

"No doubt," Callie said, settling in for the rant.

Jeb did the opposite and slid forward. "I was to eventually become mayor and serve out my years in that position until my own child could step in. I'd retire before sixty to make way for Junior. She'd have been long retired now except that you messed up the order of things, by the way, forcing her to remain in power until I came into my own." He blew out again. "Geez!"

Callie took his rant in, hearing nothing surprising.

Jeb continued. "My obligation is to serve Middleton and groom an heir to do the same. The encumbrance. . . that was the word she used. . . was on me, and I better not disappoint all these people. Generations have watched me from the time I was born, anxiously awaiting my adulthood, like I was to perform for them by slaying a damn dragon and saving the kingdom." His voice ran louder and faster, and Callie was glad nobody lived in the house on the east side of them for the time being. Sophie and Sprite were in the one to the west, and they'd leave well enough alone even if they heard.

The front door opened.

They'd forgotten about Mark.

Before Callie could apologize and send Mark back to bed, Jeb jumped up. "I'm so sorry, man. Did I wake you? I got in late, and I had a lot of my mind, and Mom came at the right time for me to unload, and life is kind of over my head now, and. . ."

With Jeb between her and Mark, and Jeb rattling on, she motioned for Mark to retreat and mouthed *thank you.*

"I'm good. Only thought I heard people and wanted to make sure who." Mark raised a sleepy hand of acknowledgment and returned inside.

Jeb returned to his chair. "You don't think he heard, do you?" he asked.

Callie grinned with a small scowl. "Doesn't matter if he did. Now, go on."

She remained level and motherly, wishing her son would listen to the soothing sounds of a beach night. How many times had she sat out here and made herself do the same, so that the sweetness of nature might overcome the turmoil inside. "What's really going on?"

Jeb had the jitters, like he'd exposed himself. Like people could see through his much-guarded wall. "I wanted to go to grad school," he said, taking himself down a notch.

"So go to grad school," she said. "Nobody's stopping you."

"I hadn't even decided whether to ever work for Grandma, you know? I wanted to wait until I really had to make that decision, like in another year or two."

She laced her fingers, leaving them in her lap. "And you don't have to decide now."

"But Sprite's getting involved. . ." He didn't complete that thought.

He said enough to plant an idea in Callie's head. Surely Beverly hadn't gone through Sprite to persuade Jeb. Surely not. Stirring the girl up, dangling potential, emphasizing responsibility that she might be robbing Jeb of if she didn't help him fulfill his future properly. That was Beverly to a tee.

And good Lord, they didn't need Sophie stirred up in the middle of this.

"Jeb." Callie reached over to take his hands in her own, and for a moment she thought his hands shook.

This poor kid of hers looked so strained. Nothing he'd mentioned was earth-shattering and nothing was urgent. He had strings he could pull. . . or not. Losing his father left him a small trust fund, and losing his grandfather gave him another. Also, Callie and Beverly had the means to see this kid through college and into a new life. Callie, however, wouldn't put the conditions on his choices like Beverly would.

He let his mother cradle his hands. "She wouldn't cut me out her will, would she?" he asked.

"Let her," Callie said. "Totally unimportant. There are other means."

He pulled his hands back. "No, I don't care about the money. I care about what she thinks of me."

"She didn't play the money card, did she? Or the disappointment card, either, for that matter."

"Not really. . ."

Meaning Beverly hinted enough. *Damn, Mother.*

Callie reclaimed Jeb's hands and inched closer. "You do what you want to do to make you happy. Not what I want, not what your grandmother wants. If you and Sprite get serious, then take her into account, but listen. . . your life is yours to plan. I don't want you to look back when you're my age, wishing you'd done your own thing instead of being coerced by Beverly. Or me."

Some tension eased. She sensed his hands relax, and she let them go.

"Do you regret what you did, Mom? Did Grandma influence your choices?"

Without a doubt Beverly had influenced her choice. She was just lucky that she'd rebounded from her mother into a career that suited her. "Don't do what I did, either," she said. "I made a choice to spite her. Remove your grandmother from the equation, son. It's not her decision to make, or influence."

More sighing, but Callie this time as a release.

"She wants an answer," he said.

"Tell her you can't give her one," she replied.

"She wants an answer by the end of this semester. If I don't reply, or if I refuse, the offer is rescinded. I don't want her pissed at me. I don't need her hating me, Mom."

Son of a bitch. Recollections of ultimatums from twenty-some years ago flooded back. "Damn her," she whispered.

This child was strong, but he was sensitive about family. He'd lost a father and a grandfather far too young, and now he was left as the only male, and with that reality came a duty of protectiveness. With his family half the size it once was, he couldn't afford to alienate either of them. He didn't have to say what was written all over him.

"She will always love you, Jeb," she managed to say. "Whether she hires you or not, whether she wills you her fortune or not, she can't stop loving you. And in the end, when her days are down to a few, she will understand you did the right thing being loyal to your needs, your wishes, and your desires. Always be true to yourself, son. She's lived her life doing just that, and she cannot help but admire you down the road for doing the same."

Tears welled in his eyes, making them well in her own.

He came out of his seat and wrapped her in a hug, the warmth filling her and making the silent tears come harder.

She hated her mother for putting her son through this. She'd do something about that tomorrow, but for now she'd welcome this.

Jeb eased back and wiped his cheek. "We'll talk about Sprite tomorrow. Right now, I'm whipped. Thanks for this, Mom."

Eyelids getting heavy, he turned to the door.

"Wait, what about Sprite?" she managed to say. "You can't leave me hanging like that."

But he'd reached the door. He waved at her. "Come on, Mom. It's nothing bad, or at least not now. Let's wait, please. I'm worn out after today." He disappeared inside, leaving the door ajar.

How was she sleeping after a bombshell like that?

At least not now, he said. What the hell did that mean?

Chapter 10

Callie

THE SUN SHINED yellow through her bedroom's northeast window, but Callie woke up groggy, a sluggish memory reminding her that Jeb was home after having a rough day with his grandmother. She popped awake remembering him withholding another piece of news he would tell her today. Something about him and Sprite, and about things being okay *now*. When wasn't it okay? Why wasn't it okay? What fixed it? Why did it need fixing in the first place?

"What time is it?" Mark mumbled.

She hadn't even looked. "Six thirty. Go back to sleep."

"You, too, Sunshine. You didn't sleep well. I know, because I didn't sleep half the night for you not sleeping half the night." He rolled over, and when he fell back into regular breathing, she eased out.

Brain now engaged, she threw on a robe she didn't wear unless Jeb was home or a guest in the house, and she tiptoed to her son's room. Peering in, a peace fell over her at how deeply he breathed, the quilt gathered in fists and snuggled under his chin. He wasn't a sprawler like a lot of guys; he was a cuddler. If he wasn't a grown man, she'd steal under that quilt, hug him like she did when he was five, and close her eyes to the sounds of his mellow snores.

No, she wouldn't wake him. He was tired from yesterday and last night and goodness how long before that for whatever reason she wished she knew.

Nothing bad, or at least not now. . .

At this hour, Sprite was likely sleeping, cozy in her old bedroom in her mother's house next door. Callie suspected Sophie was up, though. Her Circadian cycle ran in sync with the sun. Callie considered getting dressed and wandering over there, to see what Sophie knew since a daughter confided in her mother way more than a son did.

For a split second she wished she had a daughter. . . instantly prompting the memory of the daughter she lost seven years ago. This year's March birthday of the baby lost to SIDS came and went with only Callie taking note. Jeb might have recalled the sad anniversary but said nothing. The event well preceded Mark in Callie's life, so of course the date wasn't at the front of his mind, either, and she didn't feel the need to remind him of an event that never impacted him. Each year, and sometimes in the months between, Callie would go to the drawer in her bedroom, release the ribbon around a box, and sink her nose into the scent of the baby blanket. Not as often anymore, though, because the smell faded each time.

She glanced at the neighboring house. How long had Sophie known whatever this was? Or had she? She couldn't keep a secret to save her soul, as her daughter was aware. The roof next door would fly off if the topic held serious substance unless they'd been up all night in discussion, too, and Sophie hadn't had the chance to come to Callie. God, she came to Callie about any other gossip, social, or political issue. She might not even have all the facts, but she wasted no time being the first to spread what she knew to include her opinion about same.

Callie lassoed her thoughts back and tethered them.

Jeb had promised he'd tell her. Finagling the story out of someone else before he had a chance would betray his trust in her. Well, depending on what the deal was.

Dredging up patience and a personal scolding, Callie returned to her bedroom, tossed off the robe, and showered. A normal workday. Business as usual. Later, at a decent hour, she'd call the Poes and see what went down in the seven hours or so since she'd left them. She'd speak to Jeb when Jeb wanted to speak to her.

Once dressed, she looked in on Jeb again to find no change. A sticky note on his door told him to call at his convenience, promising him that she'd steal a few moments from work. She had to rewrite twice to fit all of that on the yellow three-by-three piece of paper and squeeze *Love Mom* in the lower right corner.

It wasn't until she'd settled into her cruiser that she gave her mother a second thought. That split second shift, however, catapulted her into frustration at the way her mother behaved. Her phone remained in her hand, having checked for any urgent messages. At the notion of her mother, however, she gripped tighter, then tighter still. She looked at the time. Seven thirty.

Mayor Beverly Cantrell's workday at Middleton Town Hall commenced at eight per public notice, but she'd be up and at her office already. Having been a morning person forever, despite her gin martini night caps, Callie's mother was one of the most functioning alcoholics she'd even known. She'd groomed her own drinking habit at the knee of that woman, so she ought to know. The thought of those years, and the yearning for Beverly's favorite top shelf gin, only underlined her irritation.

She looked up at Jeb's bedroom window, then over at Sprite's next door, then told herself to cool her jets. Maybe this wasn't her fight. Beverly had a plan, and the fact that Callie had interrupted the *natural* order of things by declining a role in politics sort of moved the bullseye-emphasis from her back to Jeb's. She wasn't about to feel guilty for that, because nobody ought to feel obligated to fill their parent's shoes. Or their grandparents', or great-grandparents', or however many ancestors there were, no matter how famous or noble. Any human being's commitment was to live their life well, in acknowledgment of others, in pursuit of happiness and the well-being of their family.

On their terms.

Well, hell.

She slouched in her seat, suddenly hit with the reality that she'd just defined Beverly's purpose on earth. Her mother was being the best human being she could be, wasn't she? From her perspective anyway. On her terms. The trouble was, she felt her offspring, daughter and grandson, were tools in her personal toolbox to fulfill said purpose.

Life, however, was not that black and white, and Callie wasn't so naïve to think Beverly thought it was, either. That woman understood all the shades of gray in the color spectrum, and she was using her grandson's loyalty to further her bigger cause of perpetuating the Cantrell heritage. She would get tricky, too, nursing the poor boy's naïve devotion.

Callie's thumb hovered over the button, and for the third time in her five-minute spin of contemplation, she willed herself not to dial her mother's cell and strike a match.

For the umpteenth time since Jeb got home, she chided herself for feeling responsible. Beverly pursued him on her own, and Callie's decline of a similar invitation yesteryear did not mean she failed her son today. On the contrary, Callie had taken charge of her own life and set an example for Jeb.

Beverly was sixty-eight. Not much time to groom a protégé, which meant she had to perform well and get herself reelected, remaining in office until Jeb became the only candidate that made sense to succeed her. Per the questions Callie received from major Middleton movers and shakers, the citizens still saw Callie coming around one day.

Callie quit trying to correct them, but Beverly wouldn't.

A text came through from Marie. A text meant an issue, but nothing urgent and likely optional. A call over the mic would mean something different altogether.

Johnny Scott seen on another street dumping trash.

She sort of wanted to wait until a homeowner lodged a fresh complaint. She thanked Marie and told her to hand the issue to another officer.

But the back-and-forth texting gave her momentum, and once done with Marie, she flipped into another text, shooting a blurb to Beverly.

Mother, lay off Jeb.

Nothing. Then she had to remind herself this was her mother, who hated texting almost as badly as she hated social media.

Beverly would let the thought sit a while, not wanting to appear reactive. She might even blow off the message, feeling such communication tacky. Callie had made herself known, though, which was enough to relieve her own pressure.

She felt better.

Until she realized Beverly wasn't responding because she'd go straight to Jeb.

Shit.

Putting the car into drive, she started patrol on her own street, then moseyed toward Palmetto Boulevard, driving by *Maelstrom Manor* to see if Poe 2 had returned from the hospital. From a distance, the number of cars had grown, and upon approach she spotted Eddie's vehicle. Hopefully that meant Allan was home and in decent enough health to be interviewed a little later. Being still early, she put that chore off for mid-morning and set out to cruise a few streets before heading into the office.

A ding sounded. A text. A tiny ripple slid down her spine. She pulled over, just in case.

You didn't want your mother involved in your choice of career path, dear. Let Jeb make his own decision. The message then spaced a line, then in all caps read, *LIKE YOU DID.*

Callie took three deep breaths, fighting not to see red, but she'd undeniably fanned the flames. Caps. That's about as angry as Beverly got.

You didn't hint to Beverly. You spoke your mind. In Beverly's opinion, you either let well enough alone, or you threw down the gauntlet.

Her mother was accepting a challenge. Not war per se; maybe more of a defiance. *Don't test me.*

Now, what was Callie going to say when her mother called Jeb? Beverly wouldn't think twice about waking him, using the abrupt interruption to demonstrate control and drive a wedge. She decided what was important, when it occurred, and how it went down in her life, and if you were in her immediate circle, that meant your life, too.

The mayor of Middleton loved being Queen, and if you accused her of doing so, she'd own the title to the hilt.

Damn, Callie should not have texted.

Callie decided to deal with Johnny Scott after all. His stupidity and defiance would take her mind off Queen Bee.

She wasn't a block past Dawhoo Street, where she'd seen Scott yesterday, the street on which the dumpster resided that he tended to *borrow.* No sign of the gray Dodge Ram, but between there and his house on Eddings, thirteen blocks ahead, she'd keep her eyes open.

By the time she reached Eddings Street, she hadn't seen him, and he wasn't at home. As he said yesterday, his dumpster was filled to the brim.

She continued down Eddings to Myrtle Street then turned on Murray to reach the station, her office not a third of a mile from Scott's house. She'd see him sooner or later. That or someone would be calling.

Johnny Scott, however, waited in the lobby.

Callie gave him a nod, continuing through the swinging door to behind the counter where office manager Marie pecked away on her keyboard.

"Um, I'm confused," she said in undertones to her office manager, giving a covert, heavy-lidded, sneak-peek at Scott.

"Came in about two minutes ago," Marie replied. "Said he had to speak to you."

"Did we get another complaint about him?" Callie asked, thinking maybe his visit was an attempt to get ahead of something, or file a claim to get ahead of someone else.

Marie never missed a keystroke. "Didn't say. And we have nothing new either."

Scott would be a good time filler until she could get back to the

Poes. "Mr. Scott? Come on back to my office."

The man wasn't hard on the eyes. No wedding band. Tanned and, other than his silliness with dumpsters, a decent dude. With nobody around to listen in, she left her office door open and let him take a seat across from her desk.

Better that she hear his side first before letting on she was aware of his early morning trash disposal that day. "What can I do for you?"

"There's a valid reason I use someone else's dumpster," he said.

"Do tell," she said, trying not to be the stereotypical uniform forming a premature opinion about the person before them.

"Believe me or not," he said, showing she'd failed at her effort. "But I found other people's construction debris in my dumpster. They filled mine up. I've consulted with others, asking if I could use theirs, but everyone turns me down. I'm trying to be the good neighbor. Share and share alike, you know? I was not pointing fingers, and I was not trying to film anyone." He took a breath. "Surely there's something in the rules about sharing dumpsters."

Okay, that was different. "Nice of you to ask them, but we do not dump on someone else's property without permission."

He started to speak with his hands, but then he rested them in his lap as if giving up on finding the right words. "I see."

Callie wasn't sure whether to take him seriously or not. "When do they empty your dumpster?"

"This evening. . . supposedly."

"Good. Then all's well then."

He looked pained. "But I have work to do today."

"All I can say is to make a pile in your yard until the container is emptied. Extra work, I know, but maybe you can communicate better with your service. People are beginning to complain about you, and you don't want to make enemies, much less hold up your work with an arrest."

He was listening, waiting for the name of the person, or the address, or something he could use to dispute or file a claim.

"For instance, I'm aware you'd been dumping on Eddings Street this morning," she said.

"Wonderful," he said, rolling his eyes. "That person is one of the several putting their debris in mine. Last week, when theirs was full—"

"I hear you, yet here you sit." Callie saw where this was going, which wasn't in a straight line. The circle of finger pointing would take them nowhere, but the Ring camera provided solid evidence with Scott's identity clear. Confirmation enough to ticket him, and if she contacted that owner again, she was ninety-nine percent sure she'd have Scott and his truck nailed on the record. . . again.

"Stick to your own property, Mr. Scott." She leaned on a hand, eyebrows raised, trying to lighten up the moment. "Everyone stays happier that way."

"Except me," he said, his voice having a tired edge.

"No," she said, quick to correct. "Everyone. I don't have to get involved and the neighbors stay happy. Win-win-win." She leaned forward. "How about this?"

He looked up, waiting.

"Ask someone in advance about using their dumpster if you get in a bind again."

"I told you I did that a couple of times. They always say no."

She leaned back, seeing he wasn't listening very well. "Try again. Apologize about before. Try someone new who you haven't violated. You have options, Mr. Scott. Manners go a long way. Are you repairing your house for a rental or for a residence?"

"Residence," he said.

"All the more reason for you to make friends, not enemies, with your neighbors." She tried to temper things with easy reason. "Take them, I don't know, a bottle of wine, plate of muffins, whatever, to smooth things and start over. It works."

"Whatever," he mumbled, seeing he was getting nowhere but where the chief wanted him to go.

He rose to leave but paused and turned back. "This is all new to me, you know."

Callie didn't ask about what *this* he referenced, but no matter. "You'll do fine."

"This house, this place. . ."

She waited for him to make his point, but he turned and let himself out.

Well, so much for her consoling him. She was going to say he'd make friends soon enough if he gave everyone half a chance to get to know him but so be it.

She returned to her seat to check pending paperwork and emails before hitting the road again. Something about Johnny Scott tugged at her, in a sympathetic way. All he had to do was go to happy hour enough times or any local public event and he'd start opening doors. Being civil gave you civil in return.

For the second time today, she felt a look-in-the-mirror moment. Civility with Beverly made sense to anyone on the outside of the family looking in, but damned if Callie was able to make that work. She'd told Johnny Scott to keep trying to get along and people would come around.

So why wasn't she able to exercise this lesson on Beverly?

Because her mother would see her coming a mile away and eat her lunch in the attempt to be civil and compromising. Such behavior screamed weakness, and when anyone showed weakness to Beverly Cantrell, they lost their soul to her. If you dared brace the mayor, exerting enough strength to make her think twice, she'd still suck you in and own you.

It's why Callie ran off to Boston after college.

It's why she wished Jeb would do the same.

Beverly would play the age card, but sixty-eight wasn't that old. She could have fifteen years left in her. That would make Jeb thirty-six or more before he came around, but working under Beverly's tutelage from the outset, for that long, might turn him into something more like her.

And that scared the crap out of Callie.

Chapter 11

Callie

BY TEN THIRTY Callie had tended to Johnny Scott, then one of the residents who did call to complain about him after all. There was a domestic involving a golf cart and one household lost their fishing poles, left loose under the house for teenagers to snag. Her uniform on the street, Officer Annie Greer, dealt with much the same. Typical Edisto calamities.

Noting the time, Callie returned to the Poe house, choosing to go unannounced in case anyone decided to disappear before she got there.

This case was quite unique for Edisto Beach. She wasn't aware of malicious poisoning in its history. And attempted murder by residents and renters wasn't anywhere near the norm. She hadn't opened a case, per se, but things weren't exactly concluded. The hospital would not speak to her unless she actively pursued on the record.

Counting cars as she approached, she parked strategically behind three of them. She reached the door, closed and not open like many of the other ocean-front houses to allow the breeze through, and rang the bell. No camera. She saw more of those lately, and she would've thought this house to be one of the first.

Nurse Shannon answered. She backed up a step recognizing the chief. "Oh, nobody said you were coming." No welcome whatsoever.

Callie remained polite. "I mentioned last night that I would return today. Maybe you weren't in the room." She waited to be let in.

Instead, Nurse Shannon held up her palm. "Hold on, if you don't mind. I need permission to allow you entry." Then she disappeared.

Allow you entry. That was a first.

It didn't take long for the nurse to return with two people in tow. Eddie and the oldest sister Kimberly. They didn't invite her in either.

"May I help you?" Eddie asked.

But then Kimberly spoke before Callie could. "We told you what you needed last night. Nobody knows how this happened, and we assume an accident on somebody's part. Nobody tried to commit murder or suicide. There is no crime; therefore, no need for you."

The brother did a little push thing in the air with one hand. "Hold on, let's see what the chief has to say." He unlatched the screen door and allowed Callie to enter. Nurse Shannon disappeared. Eddie led Callie to the living room, the same one the ladies had occupied with their cups of coffee last night. Kimberly followed, and Callie swore she heard tsking behind her back.

"Have a seat," Eddie said, then left. Kimberly stood guard in the arched entry. Callie remained standing in front of an upholstered chair, trying to shake the unnerved feeling in her bones.

He returned with Allan, and in a whispered aside, sent his sister away. "I assume Allan is your focus, Chief Morgan. I trust Allan to give you the information you need to satisfy your. . . curiosity." When Callie didn't immediately say anything, he grinned and left.

If this had been Jeb being interviewed by a cop, she would've stuck around until instructed to leave, and the uniform would've had to explain themselves more than once. Eddie left like Callie was there to plan a Friday night pizza party.

Allan, however, wasn't fazed, either.

"How are you feeling?" she asked. He didn't look worse for wear. He appeared rested, color good, not unstable when he walked in, unlike last night.

"A little weak around the edges, but good," he said. "Thanks for asking."

She had her notepad out, leaving the recording app alone for now. "What did the hospital say? I thought you said monkshood, and Pauline told me after you left that's what you both thought messed you up. I had to have her explain that plant to me, and I was so happy to hear it doesn't grow wild in this part of the state."

He nodded, like nothing was unusual. "Yep, aconitine poisoning. I told them at the hospital the incident was an accident. At first they wanted to know how that could even happen, but I told them it was a long story, completely innocent, and I really didn't want to embarrass anyone."

Say what? "They showed no more curiosity than that?"

He gave a one-shouldered shrug. "Might have something to do with the name? Dad was there, you know, so no telling what he told them outside my room. The name thing happens all the time. Part of why I moved to New Orleans. Family. . . they are who they are." He tried to chuckle, not mastering the effort well.

"So, you're fine," she asked, wanting to hear him say the word plain spoken and clear.

"Perfectly," he assured her. "Who have you spoken to?"

Guess there was no reason not to tell him. "Your aunt, your cousins, and Pauline. I learned you people are good cooks and know ingredients, to include toxic plants."

"I see," he said. "I can see how that might make you wonder about us, but let me set things straight, Chief. This was no more than a joke. I'm fine. Chalk one up for that person. We're an odd lot. The family tale will be told around the Thanksgiving table for sure."

"But you haven't been to the last three Thanksgivings. How would you know?"

His smile waned. "Touche, Chief. I hope to attend the next one though. My trip here was to make amends with a couple of people. I have no intentions of ruining that chance. So let me be frank . . . I am not filing charges."

Was this by personal choice or family collusion? "I still must ask who do you think spiked your tea, your food, or whatever. Everyone seems to lean toward the tea being tampered with."

He seemed to have to think about that. Callie would wonder about what was said behind his back if in his shoes, too.

"Who may have done this. . . as a joke," she asked.

"Don't know," he said.

"Take an educated guess. Some of the family ranked others on a scale of one to ten as to who might be so prone to such a hoax."

Allan scowled briefly. "Not sure who would say that, but I have zero idea." His mood shifted, an attempt to be more jovial. "I bet someone claims the win before the week's over, though. The trick was quite the coup."

Callie looked at him warily.

"Yeah," he said, with a lone laugh. "We're not normal people. I guess you can see now why I won't be filing charges, and you can move on to the real lawbreakers on Edisto Beach."

"Mr. Poe," she said, using the formality to show she wasn't amused. "It's not up to you to file charges. This possibly meets the criteria of attempted murder. I can pursue this with or without you."

"But wouldn't this be more like involuntary manslaughter?"

"Not in South Carolina. Intent has yet to be established plus nobody died. There is no *attempted* manslaughter," she said, aiming to kill the smugness that had inched into the conversation.

But Allan didn't give in. "You're assuming they tried to kill me, when I argue they have the knowledge to understand the proper dosage, which defines intent."

"And who would be the most knowledgeable as to get that right?" she asked, pushing back and away from arguing legalities with a very uninformed civilian. He was mistaken as to legal terms and charges. She was just glad nobody died. . . this time. And she was beginning to sense that this event wasn't a first with this family.

"Even Kimi?" she asked, throwing out the one who seemed to like him best.

"Any and all of the Poes are fully capable," he answered. "A twisted sense of humor. A strong competitive yearning to win. Call it what you will, but yes, even Kimi. As you probably learned since you talked to her, I am her favorite. No way on this planet that she tried to kill me though. A prank? Yes. Murder? No."

Thus far, Allan was Callie's favorite, not Kimi. His sense of Poeness wasn't as ingrained nor actively brandished. And he'd run off to escape them.

Time to change gears. "How about the non-Poes? The nurse and the chef."

His regard strayed past the entry way toward the dining room, as if they might be in there. "Sure, lump the nurse in. She's been in this family for over a decade, ever since Grandmother started needing assistance. Going to urgent care doc-in-a-box doesn't suit Grandmother, and her regular doctor died, so she hired her own RN with a direct line to specialists and a new GP. The nurse has proven her loyalty."

"To whom?"

He seemed to feel the answer obvious. "To Grandmother." Then he thought. "Guess that means to Aunt Lacey, too, since she's the family member in charge of Grandmother's care."

Precisely as Callie thought. "You keep mentioning how close your family is. Does that extend to Nurse. . ." She waited for him to fill in the name.

"Shannon Kirby."

"Nurse Shannon." In hindsight, Callie remembered hearing the name last night. "Doesn't that mean that Nurse Shannon had to show loyalty to the entire family to remain employed? You keep reiterating how the Poe name is gospel, so after all these years wouldn't that have embedded in her?"

"I guess so."

Pauline walked into the room, and both Callie and Allan sat back in their seats. Allan seemed to welcome the interruption. Callie wasn't exactly happy.

"Thought y'all might need something to drink," she said, placing an informal tray on the coffee table containing two bottles of water, two cups of hot coffee, two sweeteners, and what appeared to be real cream in a small china pitcher. A saucer held what looked to be oatmeal cookies, four of them.

Pauline backed up looking from the tray to each of them, hands rubbing down the front of her chef's smock. "I wasn't sure hot or cold drinks. Last night you wanted to open your own bottled water, Chief, so there's that." She motioned like they couldn't see the items themselves. "And I made the cookies only this morning." She motioned again, this time toward Allan. "He's had three of them, so he can attest to their. . . goodness." Then she spun and fast walked out of the room.

Callie watched until she disappeared, to see if she looked at anyone en route, but she seemed to beeline back to the kitchen from the appearance and sounds of things.

Allan went for the coffee, black, then a cookie. "It's perfectly safe," he said. "Who in their right mind would poison a police chief investigating a poisoning?"

"That's the problem," she said, choosing the water, passing on the cookie. "I wouldn't be the one investigating. I'd be the one incapacitated. . . or dead."

He was not amused, but they took a second for a couple of sips, and before Callie could launch back into another question, Allan spoke, attempting to lighten things. "Grandmother would despise this." He waved his coffee cup over the tray. "Bottled water? Seriously?"

Callie wasn't amused.

"Speaking of Grandmother," he said, and Callie wondered if he'd segued into her over the tray on purpose. "Can you see her doing this? She can barely take care of herself. Surely you've ruled her out."

"She served the tea."

"With help."

Callie raised a brow. "So now Pauline is a potential suspect? Thought she walked on water."

Realizing his mistake, he set down his cup and the last bite of cookie. "This is etiquette. Last night she was simply doing her job. She didn't request this family assignment. I asked for her because she's good, she's trustworthy, and she respects Grandmother and her cookbook."

"And you need a job," Callie added. "That or you resent her for not getting in trouble when you did in New Orleans. She escaped and evolved. You stagnated."

"Who told you all that?"

"Everyone has motive, Mr. Poe. You can speak for them, but you don't really know them. Any of them. Having sequestered yourself in New Orleans, having missed corresponding with Pauline and avoided holidays with family, you honestly have no idea who would take issue with you and why. Therefore, how can I believe anything you say?"

"I—" and he stopped. He hadn't seen that coming, and he had no smart response to compensate.

"Someone's listening," he finally said, no covert tone at all, and he looked at the entry way where Pauline had gone.

Callie took in that he'd spoken loud enough for anyone eavesdropping to hear, which meant everything they'd said had been heard. She should have taken him to the station.

Which also meant that everything he'd told her was for anyone else's ears, too.

"Chief Morgan," Allan said, in the same level voice. "What I tell you here, in ear shot of anyone else, is what I'd tell you in secret. There was no attempted murder. Maybe you've proven to me that my hand is rusty about all things Poe, but the fact that I am Poe takes murder off the table."

The next part, however, came out firm. "As for Pauline, don't you ever think she's malicious, or that I'm deceptive regarding her. We weathered New Orleans. We are comrades. She came here for my sake, and nothing else."

They were getting nowhere, and honestly, Callie had reached the point she couldn't prove anything one way or another. The Poes had closed ranks, and they were quite adept at doing so.

She made another effort. "What if you eat a bacon and egg breakfast tomorrow morning and drop dead because someone figured out the right dose? What if they doctored everything you ate in small doses for a cumulative effect?" She looked purposely at the cookies.

"Stop," he said, frustrated. "You're wrong."

"That cookbook is awfully damning," she said, pushing on. "Are there prior poisonings in this family?"

"No. None."

"That you know of," she said, reminding him of his unique distance from the family.

"No. We don't act on what we know."

She eased forward for effect. "Any other health issues happen I should be aware of? Something short of attempted murder?"

"I'm not giving you my family's medical histories. No Poes have been murdered."

She gave him the time to take three breaths then retorted, "What about the spouses?"

He had to ponder the why of the question.

"Nobody seems to stay married," she explained.

He took on a redder hue. "What the hell are you saying?"

"I'm saying the spouses die young in this family." She hated making him a culprit in lieu of the victim, but he was as bad as any one of his family the way he defended them. "And your aunts shed their married names to reclaim Poe. What last name do your cousins use again?" She knew but she wanted him to appreciate how clannish they appeared to people on the outside.

"Poe," he said. "The family likes unity. Things are cleaner that way."

Who renamed their children after the mother's family when the father died?

He didn't reply to the obvious, and, admittedly, she hadn't voiced a question. "You keep claiming family ties for everything, yet they ignored you for years. Why didn't they run you down?"

He gave no answer.

"Tell me," she continued. "Is that why you were the one chosen for the prank?"

This time he spoke with a whisper. "It isn't like it looks."

With a light touch, she slid the tray forward, so she didn't bump it as she scooted to the edge of her cushion. "Educate me."

"I sort of stepped out of line in their eyes," he said.

She admitted he didn't come across as conniving as the others. "In everyone's eyes, or just some, or maybe one in particular?"

He moved the tray totally out of the way, then moved a couple of other trinkets to the side, like he wanted nothing between him and her and what he had to say. "Chief, we're here for Grandmother's eightieth birthday. The unspoken here is that we're being judged and measured."

"For what?"

"For the right to rule. For money. For everything after Grandmother dies. Everyone thinks she's having a new will drawn."

"Thank you for that," Callie said. "But why not divide the assets equally?"

A look of disbelief creased his brow, his chin, the lines around his mouth. Genuine, not a mask. "What's the fun of that? That's what normal people do."

With her own expression of doubt, she said, "You call this fun? Fun for whom?"

He rolled his eyes. "Grandmother, of course. That's how she's always rolled. The older she gets the more her legacy is all she's got."

Callie almost asked again how he would know that. "Are you fearful of her?"

"No."

But he'd spoken with a nanosecond of hesitation.

This family was performing for the grandmother. Callie could interview everyone else, but now saw no point, expecting nothing more than what she'd previously gleaned. No, she'd hold onto those interviews for another time, if there was another time. God, she hoped not. She preferred they disappear back into Charleston.

"Allan," she said, making like she'd finished her mission. "I hear what you say, but I'd watch my back. . . and my food if you choose to stay the entire week. That's advice from someone on the outside looking in who has seen a lot of situations go sour in the blink of an eye."

He shook his head. "I have to stay," he said. "Like the lottery. If you don't play you can't win. To bow out is to forfeit." He gave her a weary, cynical grin that didn't look too genuine.

She stood, thanked him for seeing her, and told him she'd let herself out, in hope of not seeing the others. As she stepped into the foyer, she turned to canvas the view.

Eddie sat at the dining room table with his mother and sister Lacey. Eddie started to get up.

"No, no, I'll see myself out," she called. "Tell Pauline thanks for the hospitality."

Outside, she made her way to the car, feeling eyes on her back, not anything she wasn't used to. Once in the car, however, she replayed her conversation with Allan.

These people chose heritage and name over health and sanity. Public image over self-preservation. No wonder their spouses died young. This was a level of brainwashing she'd hadn't seen since the mobs in Boston. She almost liked some of them better.

This was a level of indoctrination Beverly would be envious of.

Chapter 12

Allan

CHIEF MORGAN waved to whomever was in the dining room without reservation, confident in her skin. She'd made Allan almost feel like a co-conspirator instead of a victim. She'd made him make excuses, take up for his family, and deny things that someone on the outside looking in would think he might be lying about. He was talking out of his you-know-what most of the time, though, and she probably saw through him. He had no idea who the culprit was, their incentive, nor their intention for the future. She'd made him wonder about that last one. What more could he expect if he stayed at *Maelstrom Manor?*

She wanted him to think hard and maybe come back to her. She'd done a good job.

Allan wasn't fond of confrontation, much preferring a kitchen under pressure to such in the real world. He thought he'd done well for a few short seconds, until Chief Morgan backed him into a corner, and pretty damn fast, too. He'd tried humor, and he'd attempted lighthearted refusal of her theories, but in his heart of hearts, he kept hearing sense in her side of the conversation. She was much more adept at getting into someone's head.

And how stupid was he to talk legal terms with her? That was a losing choice from the outset, no different than her trying to tell him how much better her Beef Wellington would be than his.

Five minutes later he remained on the sofa in the living room. Family might be leaving him alone on purpose. He'd only spoken to his father and Pauline today. Kimi and Ogden were on the beach.

When nobody seemed to leave the dining room, reality hit him. He was supposed to report to *them*, not expect them to come to him. His *Poe* was rusty.

From his aloofness and non-existent concern this morning, poor old dad had used up his reserve of empathy last night in the ER.

Allan finished the last bite of his cookie. God, Chief Morgan must have found him easy to read. He didn't blame her for settling for the safe bottle of water, either. He might have too if he'd been her. This family had to feel like something out of a Hitchcock movie, yet he had defended them when he totally related to how abnormal they seemed.

No doubt kin had listened in on the interview. When his father had brought him in to see the police chief, Grandmother was seated at the dining room table, coffee before her. Allan bet the balance of his bank account that his father returned to sit with her, and either Shannon or Lacey wouldn't be five feet from Grandmother. Any of them likely stood on the opposite side of that wall, listening. He replayed what he'd said, wondering if his remarks had passed muster in their eyes.

He'd backed his family, discounted the tea event, and not contributed to the chief's pursuit of anything hinting at criminal. Sounded good enough to him.

His coffee had turned cold, but he drank to wash down the last of his cookies. What was he to do now? Was everything beyond repair with his people? Was the inheritance totally out of his reach? That talk to Chief Morgan about the lottery, *you have to pay to play*, was bullshit that popped into his head, the cockiness an overkill effort to show he had his shit together. . . when he was anything but collected.

Again, she'd made him think.

She'd be wary, though. She'd see nothing patrolling streets when all the Poe action took place quietly under this roof. If Nurse Shannon hadn't called 911, Chief Morgan still would have no clue.

Should he watch his back, though? Stupid question. Of course he should, but he was more interested in the why. Was the monkshood a warning that he was not in contention for the inheritance and assumed too much by returning? His father wanted him to come, or at least he presumed he read his old man correctly. Kimi seemed to love having him back. But the others. . .

Had he burned his bridge going to New Orleans, or was contaminating his food an invitation for him to play? *Tag. You're it.* And if he were to retaliate, against whom? He didn't come here to piss off anyone.

He'd returned seeking the family's good graces. Admittedly the inheritance wasn't far from his thoughts, but he seemed to have stumbled into what might be a competition. Was that it? Was grandmother watching to see who did what to whom, and he'd been the easy first shot for someone to take?

A small headache crept up the back of his neck, to behind his eyes, and his stomach did a little gurgling thing that he assumed was reminiscent of last night. He wasn't sure how long the side effects of the monkshood would last, and while he'd slept about five hours, he awoke weary and dull. Yesterday's twelve-hour drive didn't help. But he had to get a grip and decide how he would play the rest of the week.

His next step was to get his bearings, and from there develop a strategy. The only two people he felt comfortable approaching were Kimi and Pauline. He might sound like an idiot to them with his suspicions, or appear weak in asking their assistance, but there was no moving forward otherwise. Speaking to anyone other than them would be like talking to all, since they operated with a hive-mind.

If Allan packed up and left, he was a hundred percent sure he would be cut from the will. To abandon Pauline to this crap was in essence to toss out that job, too. He'd invited her. She'd accepted for his sake. He had to stay and play.

He nabbed another cookie, a stupid little reason not to get up yet, but he wanted to think before making an appearance in front of whomever sat in the dining room. He finished his cup then lifted the other, drinking the coffee meant for the chief, hoping the caffeine might push the small headache away.

Was everyone in the family doing threat assessments, too? Did last night's event only forecast to the others that the game was afoot? In any competitions you knocked out the weak links first. Were there extra points for getting one over on an elder? Surely nobody would touch Grandmother. She probably watched this week's behaviors to dictate how to finalize her last wishes.

He went for another cookie. He didn't have much to eat this morning, his stomach wary of eggs and bacon, so when Pauline made cookies, the fact they were oatmeal labeled them close enough to breakfast food. This made his sixth. Three earlier then these three. She'd toasted the oatmeal, something he would've done, and the cinnamon wasn't the grocery store kind. Ceylon in lieu of cassia. Kudos to her.

Quit stalling. What next?

What if alliances were being made? Or worse, had already formed? He was the last person to arrive plus they lived with each other. Clearly that left him solo, unless he could get someone to play double-agent.

The eldest siblings could band together to cut out the three young cousins, thinking they would have a second chance of being in their parents' wills. But Kimberly could also partner with Kimi and Ogden, protecting her own, the kids accepting whatever power the eldest sibling had as theirs. Lacey and Kimberly, however, the ladies jealous of Eddie running the real estate show, might team up, thinking the kids not an issue and Eddie being the biggest threat.

Lacey and Shannon took care of Grandmother. Allan could see a union of sort there, because who hadn't heard of a favored hired help earning a place in the will?

His mind raced, and he willed the spinning thoughts to slow.

Which made him wonder if Kimi was safe. No, he best start with Pauline, clearly the one most loyal to him.

He indulged in the last cookie and the last half of the second cup, shifting to another theory, one that sent a chill through his core.

Was last night even a prank?

Then worse, was this one person or collaborators?

Was Pauline at risk? They could easily pin a crime onto her. Collateral damage in the effort to elbow him out of contention.

Eddie was so thrilled accepting Pauline because she was a part of Allan's life, he said. Yet she'd make the perfect scapegoat, or target, or excuse to take Allan down.

What the hell was wrong with him? His family was weird, but not to this degree.

His head spun in contemplation.

Stop. Slow down. The bigger question was the simplest place to start. What was he to do today about smoothing things over in his reinvention of himself in his family's eyes?

He stood and his stomach made a noise, a hint of nausea coming back, so he sat back down.

With his gut having taken a beating last night, he may have overdone the cookies. Butter and sugar weren't the best to throw at a hungover belly.

Hand on his stomach, he froze.

Son of a friggin' bitch. Surely someone hadn't gone after him again when he hadn't fully recovered from the first round.

His headache grew worse.

He dropped the cup onto the saucer, partly out of spite, partly because his grip slipped. Then he did his best to stride into the dining room, trying not to put a hand on the entryway arch as he rounded to avoid looking compromised.

Eddie, Lacey, and Grandmother sat at the table, each with coffee and plated oatmeal cookies neatly set on quilted placements, black with gold designs of moons, stars, and suns. They reminded him of witches.

"Who spiked my cookies?" he said, reaching the far end of the table from the others.

The two youngers frowned, Grandmother with no reaction whatsoever.

"Son," Eddie said, releasing an exasperated breath. "What is wrong with you? There has been this you-against-us thing since you arrived."

"Because I was poisoned yesterday, and I'm a new kind of sick now," he said, pulling out a chair and taking a seat to keep the room from spinning. "Y'all have a track record."

Lacey sat wide-eyed, a side-peek at her mother before responding. "No, we don't. Nobody does that in this family."

"Bullshit. . . sorry Grandmother," he said, elbows on the table. "You might not have spiked the food before, Aunt Lacey, but we have talked and schemed, competing around the dinner table about the hows of doing so, for our whole lives. The proper and improper ways of toxins." He did a sharp finger jab toward the other end of the table. "Our matriarch there taught us how to kill people from the time we could spell CAT." He sat up straight like he used to do in his recitations of recipes. "Toxic mushrooms: death caps or *Amanita phalloides*, inky caps or *Coprinus atramentarius*, false morel or *Gyromitra esculenta*. Henbane, dog bane, flea bane. . . wolfsbane. . ." He nodded at that last one, a cynical look at the three since that was another name for monkshood.

His stomach cramped, his head throbbed, and he craved a cool pillow.

"The lessons taught us how to avoid those plants, son." Eddie paused, coating his words with parental sympathy. "Are you all right?"

He asked to do the right thing. . . not because he cared. Allan closed his eyes, then struggled reopening them. "What the hell did you add to the cookies?"

"You tell us, Allan," Grandmother said, almost sounding like years past when you were schooled before being allowed to pick up your fork and start eating. She held up her own cookie. "Mine taste fine." She took a bite to show him. "The Ceylon cinnamon was an excellent choice."

"Whatever it is, it was sprinkled on after baking so the potency wouldn't be affected by heat," he said, realizing those were the first words Grandmother had spoken to him since he'd arrived. She was coherent after all.

He took note of his vitals. His heart rate wasn't up, nor was his breathing encumbered. This was something minor and more gut reactive than neurological.

Sifting through the years of meals where they'd been quizzed and made to prove themselves, he searched for the answer. No doubt this was a test, a re-indoctrination into the Poe circle.

Way back when there was homework for school and homework for dinner, but the purpose had always been about knowledge. Nobody dared follow through and cook something to see how someone else would react. As a matter of fact, they'd been warned as children not to. Just knowing was good enough. Anything else was dangerous.

This time the substance had no flavor, the cookie tasteful enough to mask. The coffee had tasted fine, and its simplicity made the taste more difficult to disguise, especially drinking it black. His rote memories finally managed to tag a couple of items with potential.

"Ergot," he said. "The flavor of the oatmeal covers it up." His first choice made perfect sense since ergot was a fungus that grew on grains. During the Salem witch trials, contaminated grain made some women act crazy and get mistakenly labelled, then hunted, then killed.

His stomach flipped again.

Ergot. Higher doses caused hallucinations and in some cases convulsions. But the more common usage was for women, causing abortion, then stopping the bleeding. Along with that came nausea, dragging a person down, making them want to lie down and sleep, and in extreme cases, cause unconsciousness and death.

Someone could have chosen much worse, making this time even more a prank. . . or a statement.

He wouldn't have reacted as much if he hadn't eaten all four cookies on the platter. And from the way he felt, there hadn't been much to begin with.

Good Lord, Chief Morgan.

"You could have harmed a police officer," he said, flustered but yearning for bed. A weakness came over him.

"We didn't make the cookies," Lacey said, a half-eaten one on her saucer. They all appeared to have tasted the cookies. That only meant one thing.

"You may not have made the cookies," he said, pushing himself back to standing. "Yours are clean. Mine were the only tainted ones, and don't you dare hide behind Pauline. Own your cunning, people." Thank goodness Chief Morgan had not eaten any. Maybe they assumed she wouldn't, being suspicious of food from the night before.

He looked at his aunt. "I wasn't the one to tell the chief about our odd ways. I didn't tell her about the cookbook. I didn't tell her about Grandmother's prowess in the kitchen and how she'd taught us. Several

of you schooled her well enough on that, so you can't pin that on me."
He went to turn then remembered, "Or Pauline."

He ought to tell Pauline to pack up and go home, but he needed to lie down so badly that he wasn't sure he had enough reserve to climb the stairs.

But he would. And he'd sleep. Then he'd awaken at whatever time and come up with a strong defense. . . an offense, if necessary.

He had too much to lose to walk away.

Chapter 13

Callie

CALLIE WASN'T SURE what to do with the Poes. Allan Poe said the poison was aconitine. What was she supposed to do with that?

The how wasn't as difficult as the who. Everyone was a suspect. Allan called the incident a joke that went awry and wouldn't press charges, not that she needed him to, but she had to have a name to do anything without him. Allan was physically fine and protective of his family, in her mind akin to an abused spouse taking up for their abuser.

He was cut from the same Poe cloth, too. She had a niggling feeling there would be more troubles, for want of a better word than *prank*.

She'd met some odd sorts on this beach, and she'd heard rumors about the Poes. She'd heard the family walked this earth differently than normal folks. But seriously? Damn. She wished they took this genetic anomaly back to Charleston, sooner rather than later. Let them kill each other in someone else's jurisdiction.

Officially, she didn't want to force feed this situation into a case. A one-time mistake. Odds of recurrence were slim if that was true. She hoped her having been up in their business twice would be enough to make them behave like regular human beings.

She left the Poes' place and headed east, toward the entrance of town, to cruise through the commercial district which happened to include El Marko's. She would then drive down Jungle Road past her home, which would take her back to the office to check in and write up the morning.

But she hadn't even come around Food Lion before she received a call. She picked up expecting Jeb, but instead got her second guess, Sophie. "Hey, Soph. Nice having the kids home for an unexpected weekend, huh?"

Sophie, however, held no mood for pleasantries. "The kids and I are having an extremely important three-way conversation at the moment, on your side porch."

Her neighbor paused, like that lone sentence had said all that was needed to send Callie home.

Callie had been expecting such a call after the dropped hint by Jeb about Sprite having gone through something but was fine now. Atop the worry about his grandmother that Jeb carried like a weight.

Last night Jeb had shed some of that weight, thank goodness, but he'd gone to bed with the bombshell about Sprite. Not a bombshell to Jeb, because he said all was good on that front, but one to Callie because she had no idea there had been a dilemma to solve. She was growing to dislike being the parent of an adult child. They could tell you what they wanted, after the fact, cutting out the scary parts, with the parent none the wiser.

"Get over here if you want a say in guiding these kids." Sophie was tense. "They aren't listening to me."

Ah, Sophie. She wasn't asking Callie's presence; she was demanding it.

"I'm a block away," Callie said, not wishing to dialogue on the phone. Hanging up, she radioed Marie to show her at home for a family issue, but to interrupt for an emergency.

Callie parked in her drive. Upon exiting, she heard the reverberations of a high-pitched voice, Sophie. Then came the muted one of her son, with Sprite following. A lot of back and forth, but nobody spoke faster and more over the top than Sophie.

Callie hoped an hour was long enough.

Letting her steps be heard, she expected to be met at the top of the fourteen-foot climb of twenty-four steps. Yes, everyone knew how many stairs they had. Come home too tired to put one foot in front of the other, and you'll know. Or carry fifty pounds of groceries after that same long hard day. How quickly you learn where the halfway point is and how many more steps you have left to take.

"All I am saying. . ." Sprite's voice carried louder as Callie reached the top, nobody having heard her arrival which demonstrated how deeply they were mired in this conversation. Jeb interrupted, saying something unintelligible.

That only raised the decibels of what Sprite was trying to say. "Listen to me, Jeb. Grow a pair of damn balls. This is our future."

Whoa. This sounded like something the kids needed to address privately, without the moms, but no way was Callie letting Sophie sit in on this and her not be there to balance things.

Callie eased inside and through the house to the side door leading to the screened porch. She wasn't sure why they chose this location to hold their debate, but at least nobody saw them from the front or the back. But if they didn't take the sound down a notch or two, the whole beach would be aware. "Your grandmother is way out of line!" Sprite yelled as Callie walked through to the porch.

"I got a call about noise disturbance?" she said. "At my own home, no less."

Jeb looked questionably, missing the humor.

Sophie beamed at her call having produced Callie so soon. "No, you didn't. I called and told you to get here."

Callie didn't confirm or deny as she pushed past her friend to her favorite seat on the porch, wide enough to take in her utility belt and all its paraphernalia. "Anyone care to fill me in? I'm taking off work for this, so bring me up to speed quickly. I'm a uniform down because of y'all, so if an emergency happens, I'm gone."

All three spoke at once, Sophie adding some slinging arm movements. Sprite tried talking over the other two, and Jeb only spoke louder.

"Stop, stop," Callie said. "Let's start over."

They shifted chairs around to be closer together. Sophie grabbed the chair on the other side of Callie, the result giving the scene a kids-versus-parents sort of vibe.

"Jeb," she said, giving her son the nod to start.

But Sophie started instead, with Sprite seeing her mother's interruption as permission to do the same.

"Y'all, hush." Callie reached into her pocket and retrieved a pen. She handed it to Jeb. "He's holding the talking stick. All of you understand what a talking stick is, right?"

Everyone nodded, Sophie saying yes.

"Good." Callie nodded to Jeb. "Your turn."

"I was recapping to them the conversation with Grandmother last night. How she wants me to come work for her as soon as I can. I could work for her and still attend graduate school, she said. The job would be public affairs, which would let me learn every aspect of town government, even sitting in for her sometimes."

"Grooming you to be her clone, you mean," Sprite said.

Callie looked to Sophie who laid a hand on her daughter's arm. "You don't have the talking stick, sweetheart. Shhh."

Callie tried not to crack a grin, but having a small snippet of humor in this turmoil could be medicinal if everyone took a breath.

Jeb went on. "When I said I wanted to start working somewhere else before deciding about Middleton, she wanted a hand in that, too."

"Unbelievable," Sprite uttered under a heated breath.

"Right? Then like the five generations before me, excluding Mom, I'd groom my child to fill my shoes."

"And a wife has zero say-so." Sprite spoke without the talking stick, filling in tid-bits she felt Jeb missed. They'd certainly had this discussion a time or two before now.

"And you told her what?" Callie asked, wanting him to repeat what he said to her last night.

"That I'd have to think about. To tell her no right then felt wrong, Mom. I need to mull this over then come back to her with my own plan and the logic for my way versus hers. I cannot say no just because. I need to have reasons and purpose."

Callie couldn't be much prouder at that explanation. But Sprite didn't look very satisfied. Before Callie could tell Jeb to pass the pen, Sprite leaned over and snatched it out of his hand.

"I was about to do the same thing, sweetie," Sophie said. "That right there. . ." She pointed at Jeb, "was a conversation full of crap. That bitch—"

"Mom!"

"Sophie!"

"Miss Sophie!"

Sophie conceded, waving palms in the air. "Sorry, sorry. That was wrong. At least I admit when I'm wrong." She inhaled down to her belly ring and regrouped. Sprite tried to hand over the pen, but Sophie declined, motioning for Sprite to continue. She still had the floor.

Callie looked to Sprite. "Go ahead." Hopefully she wouldn't have to stop any more name-calling.

"Nobody has asked me where I would prefer to live. Nobody has asked me about my career aspirations. And who says I want my child groomed at the knee of Jeb's grandmother to be crowned king or queen of Middleton?" She swallowed, took a moment, then summed things up. "Who the hell does she think she is sculpting my life? Or Jeb's life, for that matter. Much less our offspring?"

Sophie cut a look at her friend. Callie understood fully what she was thinking. Who said these two kids were a permanent item? They hadn't even talked about marriage, much less raising the heirs of Middleton, South Carolina. At least they hadn't told their mothers if they had.

Sprite turned hard attention to Jeb and continued. "Your grandmother seems to think we are a forever thing, Mr. Morgan. Are we? Do we need her royal nod for you to feel you have permission to broach the subject?" Her voice escalated. "Do you have to have your ducks in a row before having said conversation with me? Can you not think for yourself?" She huffed, and Sophie reached for the pen. Sprite pulled it to her chest, not through. "Will she set the date, the place? Will she pick out our home? How would she feel if I kicked your ass to the curb because she butted into our business and I wanted no part of it?"

With that, she thrust the pen at her mother.

Sophie gently accepted. "You made your point, sweetheart. Now you're just kicking the carcass."

Snatching a look at her mother, Sprite's brow knitted tight enough to hurt. "What the hell does that mean?"

"Language, daughter."

The girl got even louder. "Language doesn't mean crap right now, Mother, or you're missing the whole damn point!"

Sophie waved her pen. "I thought this was mine right now."

But that only catapulted said daughter's attitude. "Screw the pen. I'm twenty-one years old. That's legally an adult. I can speak my mind when I desire, and curse words are there for my choosing." She scrunched up her nose. "Carcass?"

"Don't kick a dead horse," Callie said calmly. "She meant make your point and move on, don't beat the subject to death."

"Seriously?" Sprite said. "We're talking about the wicked witch of the South, and that's where you go?"

Neither mother was sure who Sprite meant.

"Back to the topic at hand," Callie said, reaching for her pen back. "Beverly overstepped. She tends to do that. She likes to control. She gets even when she can't. You two," and she pointed to one child then the other, "need to talk. You do not have to do what she dictates or even suggests. She will lean on you. She will make you think her suggestion is your best option out of all the options in the world because she's worldly, wise, and shrewd. But through all the caustic bullshit, try to understand where she's coming from."

"We're all she has," Jeb said.

Partially correct. "She loves us, and we love her. But that does not allow her to use that relationship to get her way. Screaming at her, cursing her, butting heads with her isn't the way to reach an understanding with her. While tempting, you'll only make yourself mad and make her want to get even."

Music wafted through from somewhere inside the house. Callie's radar went up at recognizing "The Gift of Song," one of the lesser-known songs on an early Neil Diamond album. Callie's vinyl, Callie's turntable, but her mother's favorite tune.

"Shit," whispered Sophie, looking to her left, making the others turn toward the porch doorway as well.

"Continue, please," Beverly Cantrell said, having slipped up on them and listened for who knew how long. "Though I could hear everything down below, so you might lower your voices."

Chapter 14

Callie

EVERYONE FELL silent instead.

Beverly pushed herself from resting on the doorframe and entered the porch, choosing one of the most uncomfortable chairs to sit on. Callie guessed the height of the hard back chair had more to do with displaying her mother on a higher plane than the rest of them than comfort. The woman lived for strategy.

"No, everyone, don't continue," Callie said.

The kids should handle this. It was their dilemma, and their decision to make. Callie went quiet and looked at Jeb, praying Sophie would keep her mouth shut. "Your show, son."

Seemed Jeb had the question on the tip of his tongue. "Did you contact Sprite before you invited me to dinner last night, Grandmother?"

All looked to Beverly for an answer, but Callie couldn't help herself. "You did what, Mother?"

That lit up Sprite. "She has been calling me, being nice, like she's getting to know me *in a new light* she said, which I assume is as Jeb's significant other for the long haul." She turned to her beau, but for a brief second. "Not that we'd even discussed that possibility. All this sort of ruins that, don't you think? We become a business decision, not a personal one." She swept her hand around the group. "Puts pressure on Jeb and sucks the spontaneity and a hell of a lot of enjoyment out of the occasion. . . assuming a proposal even happens." She let out a clipped laugh. "Y'all chew on that a while." Then she sat back in her chair, arms crossed, clearly done with verbally smacking everyone around.

Callie hated this. Sophie probably hated this more. Sprite was a hundred percent correct.

No doubt Beverly heard the words and received the message, but Callie understood her mother well enough to know that Sprite's words, as steel-edged as they were, hadn't scratched the grandmother's surface. Beverly's innocent let's-get-acquainted chats had motive from the outset, and familial duty trumped anything else. Beverly didn't waste time with lightweight banter that held no purpose. She wasn't swayed if you felt hurt by the effort, because all she'd done was enlighten you so you could best address life.

In other words, she'd suckered Sprite in to use her to get to Jeb, and now both kids felt used and backed into a corner.

Callie stared at Beverly. "What the hell, Mother."

Unfluffed, Beverly recrossed her legs, the pastel turquoise pantsuit crisp, making her careful not to cause wrinkles, seeing that the creases fell properly toward the toe of her low heels. Then she sat back straight. "I briefed dear Sprite on the pragmatic reality of the Cantrell blood line. What is your major again, dear?" she asked.

"Italian and Spanish. Double major," Sprite said, yet Beverly would have asked this question prior and tucked the fact away for future reference.

"And what would you do with that?" Beverly asked.

"A thousand things," Sprite answered. "And teaching high school isn't going to be one of them."

Callie took a quick glimpse of Sophie out of the corner of her eye, enough to see her friend wink proudly.

Jeb was a political science major, a line of study that lent itself to a graduate degree. Yes, Sprite could teach school, which is what Beverly's generation would assume, but these days Sophie's daughter could land all types of positions with corporate and business entities needing interpreters. Tourism, business, media, government, but the pickings would be much less in the confines of Middleton. Charleston, an hour's drive with such congested traffic, provided better potential, but Beverly would prefer the future first lady of Middleton to be at the ready and employed in town limits. Assuming she worked.

"None of this is fair to Sprite, Grandmother," Jeb said, the most collected of the lot. That's what Callie was most proud of.

"Life is short, sweetheart," Beverly said. "Mine, yours, your mother's. You can't ride it out and hope it takes you somewhere. You seize opportunity. I did so at age twenty-two, like you two. I married your grandfather, and we took off, enjoying life, making strides, and doing good things for good people. We left our mark. Being closer to the end of my life than the beginning, I have to make the best use of the remaining days." She did a limp-wristed motion at her grandson. "And if I have the power to pass my gains on to someone I love, well, I'd be horribly remiss not to follow through."

"Please stop, Beverly," Callie said, using the name to show just how un-family her mother's plan was.

Her mother swiveled slowly, giving her daughter full attention. "I don't want him to become another cop, for God's sake."

"Hell, I don't want that either, Mother," and Callie wished she hadn't slipped into the familiar. "Just like I wanted to have my own life, under my terms, Jeb and Sprite are entitled to that as well. Whether they wind up together or apart, where they live, how and when they get their degrees. . . all of that is none of your business. You can be happy for them. You can say how you did it your way. I'd hope you'd congratulate them regardless but giving them a timeline is not your responsibility."

Beverly turned to Jeb. "She's right, you know. She made her choice. You make yours. But my offer is not indefinite. If you settle elsewhere, in another direction, you lessen your chances in Middleton. Without you there, the citizenry will believe you made your decision not to perpetuate the lineage. The next election will open to the masses, and no telling who will step into my shoes once I'm gone."

Beverly waited for the guilt to set in.

"Not my problem, Grandmother."

"My efforts are woven in love, dear. Weigh your options. I'm not saying ignore Sprite. I'm saying include her, dear."

She'd said *dear* twice. To think Callie thought *dear* was reserved for her. She used to hear that sarcastic endearment in her sleep, for God's sake, and it took her leaving South Carolina and being in Boston for several years before she shook it from her dreams. Some would call that a level of PTSD, her husband used to say.

"Grandmother," Jeb said, his eyes wandering a moment like he needed to regroup. "I'm to graduate at the end of next year and work for you. Step up to the throne."

Beverly subtly smiled.

"Or I could graduate and try to work on Edisto, under Mom's tutelage."

Rearing from the unexpected, Callie bit the inside of her mouth to remain hushed. She'd never ask that. She'd never thought that. Edisto couldn't afford him anyway. They could barely afford her.

"Or I could graduate and then go to graduate school," he continued. "Or graduate and take a job elsewhere."

Beverly scowled.

Jeb continued. "I can accept the perks of family or turn my back on them and learn from professionals who aren't promising me the moon."

Beverly uncrossed her legs. She'd heard enough. "Most people—"

"I'm not most people, Grandmother. But I am also not royalty and not entitled. If the time comes and I decide to take you up on the offer, fine. But if—"

She interrupted. "My offer has an expiration date."

Jeb didn't ask what that was.

Sprite's fingers slid over and eased into Jeb's hand. "Can we go?" she said almost too faint to hear.

"Yeah," he said, squeezing her hand back, rising from his seat and gently pulling her up. "See y'all later."

Callie stood to follow them out, making Sophie go wide-eyed at the idea of being left alone with Beverly. "I'll be right back, Soph. Promise."

She met up with the couple and escorted them to the front door. "Where are y'all spending your day? I'm sure you aren't eager to hang at either house after all of this."

Sprite held back to answer, while Jeb was antsy to leave.

"I like knowing where you are. No problem. But put all this out of your head," Callie said. "Visit friends. The beach is perfect today. Make Zeus take you out on the water." Sprite's brother was quite laissez-faire and could make them chill easier than anyone.

At the head of the outside steps, Sprite glanced in the direction of the side porch, unable to see the two other women but now keenly aware of how easily one could be heard. She shook Jeb's hand once. "You may get mad at your mother about her career, and the impact her choices have had on your life. You've said people you loved died because of her being a cop and having to relocate here, which turned out nicely if you ask me."

Callie fought not to wince at the honesty and waited for Sprite to reach whatever point this was.

"But she's never tried to dictate your personal life decisions. She's always supported you." She gave his hand another little shake. "Your mother's cool." Then before Callie could embrace how good that made her feel, the young woman tacked on, "While your grandmother's a bitch."

"Okay," Callie said, wanting to change the subject and see them off. Sophie had to be trembling out there alone with her mother. "Where are you. . . never mind. At least tell me if you leave town. . . never mind. Just don't make me worry."

"We're meeting friends to eat, then who knows?" Jeb said.

Their normal friends were at school, and she wanted to ask who they were so badly she could taste it.

"Kimi graduated last year," Jeb explained. "Her brother has a year and a half to go."

A chill traveled through her. "Kimi?" Callie knew all the residents. Kimi wasn't one of them.

"She and her brother," Sprite said. "They're fun. They're in town for a family vacation and wanted to get away from the adults for a while. Them being here was part of why we scheduled things with y'all now."

They were all adults, and Jeb had tried to emphasize how adult they were on the porch, but Callie caught on. One generation needed to get away from the other for a while.

"The Poes?" Callie asked, words zipping through her head on how to advise these two but without telling them what to do.

Don't go in the house. Don't eat anything from that house. Stay away from Allan Poe since he seems to be the lightning rod for Poe intentions.

But she calmed herself. First, like they didn't want to be here at *Chelsea Morning*, they wouldn't want to be at *Maelstrom Manor*, either. Secondly, Allan wasn't mentioned, probably a good thing. But finally, Callie remained silent, deducing that the Poes only ate their own kind. Her two kids would be fine.

Callie told herself three times the kids would be fine before they reached the bottom of the stairs and left in Jeb's Jeep.

"Crap," she said, spinning around to go back in. Sophie and Beverly still waited on the side porch. She had run through the house to that side porch and was about to place one foot over the threshold when her phone rang. She reversed herself, holding up a finger to tell the ladies she'd be a moment. Sophie gave quick mini shakes of her head to show she wasn't doing this much longer. That or Callie should not take the call. Callie didn't know which.

She'd been away from work longer than she liked. The pause, however, would give her a chance to think straight before properly asking her two guests to leave. Sophie would welcome the opportunity to bolt. She'd call her later. Beverly, however, might make herself at home and wait until Callie got off work. One was never sure with that woman except that she had to feel like the one who made the rules.

"Chief Morgan," Callie answered. "Can I help you?"

"Pauline Vitalis here," whispered the caller.

Unexpected but not a total surprise since Callie had left six of her business cards with assorted residents of the Poe household. "Pauline.

What's up? Why are you whispering?"

"They did it again," she said in a forced, raspy whisper. "They used me as a tool. Allan's still lying down, but he's not saying much. Nobody will admit anything happened, but something did."

Callie removed herself further from the porch, into her bedroom, wondering what being used as a tool meant. "Are you safe?"

A humph sounded over the line. "Of course, I am. But Allan's feeling under the weather. . . again. . . from something they did. I'm ninety percent positive."

"Does he need the hospital again?"

"He says no."

This was odd. "How is the rest of the family behaving?"

"Business as usual," Pauline said. "One said Allan was still feeling the effects of last night. I had finished feeding them lunch and asked why he wasn't there. No sympathy in this lot at all. I went up to his room, but he said he'd be good after a nap." She hesitated. "Wait a minute."

Callie waited, hearing scuffling and muted voices.

"Okay, I'm back," Pauline said.

Unsure where this was going and what Pauline expected her to do, Callie point blank asked, "They poisoned him again?"

"Probably. Ooh, gotta go. We need to meet. When and where?"

"My office in a half hour. Can you do that?"

There was hesitation, then more voices in the background. "I'll take Allan something to his room in a couple minutes," Pauline said to whoever was there. "Dinner should be around six."

Callie waited. Pauline came back. "Sorry. That was Kimberly. She wasn't there when it happened."

When what happened exactly? Pauline's half-finished sentences and incomplete thoughts left Callie dangling, but they couldn't do this over the phone. "My office. Thirty minutes."

"Yes. Yes. You have a great day." The chef hung up, the odd salutation either a habit, or said because someone could hear.

Callie wasn't fully sure Pauline would be free to appear at the station from those constant interruptions, but she would be there. Great reason to excuse herself from her own family drama, too.

She scurried to the porch entrance to add urgency to her departure. "Y'all, I've gotta run."

Relief washed over Sophie. However, Beverly, ever astute, noticed Sophie's itch to escape. "I was rather looking forward to spending time with you, Sophie. I'm not as bad as all that, my dear."

Wide-eyed, Sophie stiffened. "I didn't mean. . . I just. . . I have . . ."

Looking at her watch, Beverly let Sophie stutter, hem, and haw until she ran out of steam.

"Let me take you to lunch," she said, standing. "You name the place, but I'd rather not eat outside. I'm not fond of gulls snatching my food or bugs on the table."

Sophie looked to Callie with a silent plea for help.

"Whatever y'all do, I've got to go. Lock up the house, please." Then in afterthought, Callie told Sophie, "Practice your own preaching, Soph," reminding her neighbor of her own advice to the kids. Say no to Beverly if you need to.

"When do you get off work?" Following her inside, Beverly had asked before Callie could reach the front door.

"When people quit calling me," Callie said, and this time she left.

Taking her twenty-four steps down like a double-time tap dance, she reached her cruiser, cranked the engine before her belt was buckled, and aimed west with one last note of the house. Poor Sophie. Beverly would win. She always did. Callie wouldn't be shocked if she got off work and Beverly had kept Sophie in tow for the entire afternoon.

Chapter 15

Callie

CALLIE PREFERRED being at the station before Pauline arrived, and tending to the chef as quickly as she could to avoid the Poes missing her.

She passed Marie, her office manager, seeing no messages that couldn't wait. There was one about Johnny Scott. . . again. His service was supposed to have emptied his dumpster, so what was his problem?

"Marie, tell Annie to go ticket that man. . . again."

"Gotcha." She reached for the radio.

Callie heard the ding on the lobby door about the time her butt hit her desk chair in her office. She bounced back up and returned to the outer office. Pauline reached the counter and leaned on his forearms.

"Come on back," Callie said. "What, no snacks? I missed lunch today thanks to a bit of family drama. That family you're wrapped up in ain't got a thing on mine."

The chef froze. "I'd have brought you something. . ."

Opening the swinging door, Callie laughed. "I'm kidding, Pauline. Come on through to my office where we'll share a couple of protein bars."

With a grimace, Pauline followed. Callie hesitated with her hand on the door. "Open or closed?"

"Closed," she said. "They think I'm at the grocery store. And pass on the protein bar."

Time was short and Pauline was nervous, so Callie let the recorder slide and slid her chair under the desk, hands where Pauline could see them. "So what's going on?"

"They messed over Allan again."

"The Poes."

"Yes. And they did so with my cookies. At least I think they did. Allan won't commit."

"They sabotaged cookies?" Callie clarified.

Pauline nodded, her chest up and down, heartbeat up.

"Take a breath and talk to me in complete sentences," Callie said.

"Start from the beginning." She exaggerated an inhale to demonstrate, which always made the person opposite do the same thing.

Pauline did as instructed, seemingly better, then launched into her story. "I made cookies this morning. Oatmeal raisin."

Motioning to herself, Callie reminded her. "I was there. You served both Allan and me. Brought us coffee and water, which I greatly appreciated, by the way."

Leaning forward, Pauline looked worried. "Did you eat a cookie?"

Callie shook her head. "After last night? No, ma'am. Nothing against your baking, chef, but I wasn't too keen on sharing any food stored, baked, boiled, fried, or refrigerated under that roof."

Pauline gave a huge sigh. "Well, thank goodness for that. The plate was clean when I collected the tray, so that means Allan ate all four cookies. Might explain why he felt bad."

"You baked them?" Callie repeated, confirming.

"Yes."

"Was the substance cooked into them or sprinkled on them?" She could not think of any other way to taint them.

"If he's right about the substance being ergot, then sprinkled."

Well, that was creepy. "What the hell is ergot?"

"A grain fungus. Not normally lethal."

Callie was learning more than she cared to about Mother Nature's bad side. "Who happened to be in the kitchen as you took them out or placed them on the plate?"

She mashed her lips once then twice. "Been racking my brain on that. It might be easier to say who wasn't in there, which is the sum total of one. Old Lady Poe."

Callie went to ask for a tighter timeline, but Pauline was ahead of her. "Ogden asked to lick the beaters, which I'm not too crazy about, so I gave him the mixing bowl and a teaspoon. When a batch was in the oven, Nurse Shannon came in wondering when they'd be coming out because Grandmother had smelled them and asked. Kimberly took a spoon and sampled the dough. Then came Eddie as the first batch cooled, and he swiped two. When the others saw them, they asked if I could serve them a late morning snack with tea. That would be Eddie, Lacey, and the grandmother."

Callie had seen them when she left, still seated at the table. "What about the kids?"

With some eye rolling, the chef answered. "They breezed in, snatched up one each, then disappeared, without so much as a thank-you. They left the house."

"Then Allan. . ."

"Allan did like the cousins. After losing his dinner last night, then breakfast this morning, he grabbed several cookies and a glass of milk while he talked to me about what was in them."

"And nobody got sick?"

She shook her head. "Nobody. Including Allan."

Good measuring point. "At what time did you leave the kitchen in all this?"

Staring down, her whole demeanor sliding into almost one of shame, Pauline mashed her lips. "After Allan had his snack in the kitchen, I walked out with him, went up to my room and took a moment to check on my restaurant back home. Don't know where he went. Didn't see him again until after you arrived."

Wonderful. The offender could have been anyone. "What makes you think the cookies were tainted?"

"After you left, Allan sat in the living room for quite a while. But while doing so he ate the two cookies you didn't eat. They were enough for him to feel the effects. When he finally reacted to them, he walked to the dining room, or so they tell me. Eddie, Lacey, and Grandmother Poe were seated there, probably trying to listen to what y'all were saying, having their cookies and tea. Allan came in and fussed with them enough that I peered out from the kitchen."

The same three family members who Callie had seen when she left, even waved at and thanked as she left this morning. If she had eaten the cookies. . . Were they surprised she walked out unscathed and unaffected? "How is Allan? What are his symptoms?"

"Some nausea, a mild headache."

"That could be a lot of things, right?" Callie asked.

But Pauline stood firm in her belief. "The fact he ate three cookies earlier and had no reaction, then the latter four gave him a reaction, someone certainly pulled a stunt on y'all. But with just two cookies intended for him, his symptoms weren't meant to be anything but minor, I think. How do you feel?"

Doing a little self-analysis from head to toe, Callie felt fine. "But I ate nothing. And the water bottle was sealed. Are you sure this isn't residual from last night?"

"He was good when he ate the first batch," she reminded.

It couldn't have been too dangerous, but that only told her someone had the ability to dial things as dangerously or as innocently as they wanted.

Pauline came forward, elbows on Callie's desk, lowering her voice. "Took me some heavy-handed arm-twisting to get him to admit today was a second attempt. He's already better, but still, I felt you ought to know. Especially since you might've been targeted as well."

Exactly. That was damn bold. Clearly not deadly, but who does that?

Everyone but Allan appeared rather emboldened in that household. Who the hell were these people? Maybe Callie wasn't even a factor in the equation, correctly assuming she would know better. But one of her less seasoned officers would not have.

The conundrum was that they kept things under their roof, nobody admitting anything gone wrong, and nobody wanting to get anyone in trouble.

Someone was kicking Allan while he was down, giving them the excuse that he was still getting over the night before. Was this a team ganging up on him or a lone adversary? "Do they dislike him that much? He called this a game, but damn, Pauline, who does this?"

"The Poes don't believe they fall under the normal rules of humanity, Chief."

Callie scoffed. "So, I've gathered." She made a mental note to speak to Beverly about these people, for a second even hoping she'd stuck around with Sophie after all.

Difficult to believe she'd wished such a thought, but Beverly could shed some light on the history of these people. Even if she'd never entertained them, she'd have done her homework on the name.

Beverly had knowledge of Edistonians going way back. The Poes had never lived there, but they'd owned their house for decades, making them kin to a resident. She was older than the siblings but younger than the grandmother, so could have brushed against any of them in social circles. And if the cookbook was that famous, Beverly would know. Callie'd even wager her mother had the damn thing, regardless that neither she nor Callie had ever been too creative in the kitchen.

Pauline spoke up, jerking Callie back. "I may love Grandmother Poe's knowledge and respect the cookbook, but this other crap is over the top." She looked at her watch. "They're going to miss me."

"Let them," Callie said. "To be honest, why don't you pack up and vanish?"

Pauline repeated the very reason Callie expected. "Allan. If he's here, I'm here. The boy needs someone in his corner."

"You can't win if you don't play," Callie uttered, recalling his words.

"Pardon?"

"Just something I heard, never mind." Callie gave the chef a slightly skeptical look. "That's some kind of loyalty between you two considering you haven't seen each other in years. Especially under the circumstances you two parted."

Chef rubbed her nose, then pushed a strand of hair back out of her face. Callie recognized the motions of buying time to get one's story straight.

"I stayed gone too long," Pauline said. "That's totally on me. I should have reached out. He took the fall for whoever hurt that couple in New Orleans." She sat still, reminiscing. "In afterthought, I should've seen he wouldn't come to me. Shame, fear of rubbing off on me, call my distance what you will. Our industry is fickle and judgmental, Chief Morgan, and the slightest whiff of disgrace makes you a pariah. He wouldn't want to discredit me." She cleared her throat. "No, the onus would've been on me to reach out to him. If not for his grandmother's birthday, and him trying to reenter the Poe fold, he wouldn't have reached out when he did."

"And you couldn't say no," Callie said.

"Precisely," she said.

A fresh school of thought surfaced. Had the Poes reached all the way to New Orleans to tarnish him? They possessed enough clout to do so, and they damn sure possessed the nerve.

"Did they have a hand in screwing him over in New Orleans?" Callie asked.

But Pauline shook her head. "On the contrary. They stopped any lawsuits. Not sure if the concession was that he leave The Red Lacey or not, but everything sure got quashed with a lot less shrapnel than there could've been."

The family had saved his neck while still making him pay a price for the fallout. That tracked.

"Do they know you're aware of this morning's deal with the cookies?" Callie asked. There was still the chef's safety to consider.

"Maybe. Depends on what they think he would tell me."

"Assuming someone added extra spice to your cookies, how can we prove any of this?" Callie asked.

"We can't. All evidence is gone. He's the only one who appears to be affected. Besides, a light dose of ergot is easily digested and passed through. He is still claiming it's a prank, and he could be right, but damn,

I don't know which way to turn in my kitchen right now. I'd like to believe they need me more than I need them." She gave a cold laugh. "I'll be fixing my own meals separate from theirs, though."

This was an insane definition of family unity.

"And before you ask, he's still staying," Pauline said. "Which means I stay with him."

That didn't make the chef much smarter than Allan, in Callie's opinion. She didn't understand these people, but she had lots of history about human nature.

The Poes could be setting Pauline up for a fall if all this went sideways, especially after what had happened in New Orleans. She got out of one incident, but she'd never escape two.

What the hell was the end game here? What didn't she understand about the relationships of these people? "How long is everyone scheduled to be here?" Callie asked.

"Leaving Saturday."

That was five whole days away. Allan was on his second day, not even twenty-four hours into the birthday week, and he'd been *challenged* twice. Or if you were Callie, open to all theories, this could be Allan's second warning to leave. Whether he was too tainted for Poe tastes or being challenged to see if there was enough Poe left in him to be accepted into the inner circle, Allan played a dangerous game here.

Even from outside looking in, Allan appeared the weak link in that family. Maybe their aim was to cull him from the herd. Or maybe to teach him a lesson so he'd never leave again. But looking at Pauline across the desk, Callie worried where she fit in. Had she been a tool of Allan's to worm his way back in? Or had the family used her to get at Allan?

There wasn't enough for Pauline to file a complaint, and Allan had vowed not to report on his family. "My suggestion is to leave Edisto, Pauline."

Pauline started to speak up.

"Don't bother," Callie said. "I know you won't. Since you won't, would you mind updating me periodically?"

"I guess so," she said.

"And don't wait until someone is in the hospital."

Puffing out her chest, the chef put a hand on her hip. "And how the hell do you expect me to see them coming?"

Callie exhaled at the impossibility of all this. "Stay sharp, Pauline."

This week couldn't be over soon enough.

Chapter 16

Allan

MONDAY MIDAFTERNOON, after a nap that had not come easily with the activity in his head, Allan came downstairs, wishing the grogginess would leave. He had to confront this family other than over a meal or puking in a trashcan, and he hoped he didn't look too worse for wear when he did.

Eddie waited at the bottom, probably having heard the second and third steps groan. They'd creaked as long as Allan could remember, and as a child he would leap and half slide down the banister to skip those steps when slipping out to the beach in the middle of the night.

Why didn't Eddie bother coming up to the room to see his son?

The elder cleared his throat. "Forgot to tell you, but we decided the birthday party is Wednesday night. Midpoint of the week. A long enough build-up then a couple days of decompression. That agenda would give each of us personal time with your grandmother either before or after. No point waiting the entire week in case something comes up with work. She still holds me responsible for the business, you know. Then there's her health. She wears out easy these days." He gave a dark, humorous breath. "But hell, she might outlive us all, you know?"

"Is she ill?" Allan asked.

Eddie scoffed. "She can't run sprints, but her insides keep ticking."

She was still tough. Allan wondered how everyone liked that.

"Wednesday work for you?" As if he didn't like Wednesday they'd consider a change.

"Um, sure, Dad. You told me to be here all week. Doesn't matter which day to me."

Eddie pondered his fingernails. "Well, one never knows. Had to ask, son, to take a head count."

No, he was issuing a directive in case Allan pondered leaving early after the two incidents. Everyone else probably already knew when the party was. Did they want him here or not? If his father wanted to ensure Allan stuck around, he should advise the others to lay off the prodigal son.

A taste of temper rose, and Allan warned himself that spouting off won him no favors. The family had to be as awkward around him as he was around them. Having left on a somewhat sour note, launching into the world instead of putting down roots in Poe territory, he didn't have that great a reputation amongst them. Maybe these were trials and a bitter-sweet welcome. A reminder of who he was, who he belonged to, which made him wonder again if he was to play the game back.

He wasn't keen on doing so though. Not after New Orleans. Nope, he wasn't going there.

"How are you feeling, son?"

Damn, he finally asked. "Better," Allan said.

"That's good."

"So, Wednesday, huh?"

"Yeah. Seems to suit everyone."

Awkward silence.

This was Monday. Whoever left early would lose points in Grandmother's eyes and earn gossip credits with the others. Kimi had already made a remark about the inheritance being up in the air. "Where is Kimi?" he asked, much preferring conversation with her.

"She's out with her brother meeting someone from college." Eddie turned and disappeared into the dining room, towards the kitchen. Guess bonding time was over.

Allan had seven years on Kimi and nine on Ogden, so for them to seek out others their age made sense. He wished he'd been up and about so that he'd been invited, though. Now he was stuck with the elders unless he wanted to walk solo along the water.

Maybe he could go out and grab something a hundred percent safe to eat.

Eddie waiting for him at the stairs seemed odd, and while maybe a coincidence, Allan wasn't feeling too trusting these days. How long had Eddie been waiting? Why not come up, maybe with a cup of tea or coffee?

I feel fine, Dad. No, must've been something I ate, Dad. Maybe I'm still feeling whatever happened last night, Dad. Crazy couple of days, right?

Maelstrom Manor felt cavernous. Standing on the bottom step, listening to the sounds of the house, he heard two female voices somewhere in the vicinity of the study. No way he was interrupting that.

Grandmother occupied the ground floor bedroom, the master. Ground floor as in the lowest to the ground because the house was fourteen feet off the sand for times of wind and water. He hadn't gained the nerve yet to approach her solo. He needed to. The key was how to do so without other ears in the room . . . or hovering behind a door.

That one time she spoke this morning demonstrated she had her wits about her. She used to love making you underestimate her, and he'd forgotten. His Aunt Lacey, one of the voices off in the study, probably with Aunt Kimberly, was the least savvy, so fooling her as to Grandmother's acuity wouldn't take much. Nurse Shannon was more nursemaid than RN. She'd hung up on 911, for God's sake, and let Pauline take over in the middle of an emergency. What was she going to do when Grandmother stroked?

Two women under Grandmother's thumb who didn't even know it.

He wished to find Kimi and talk family, but he still needed to speak to Pauline. . . alone. The most time he'd had with her was when she held his head over the trashcan yesterday. She had thrown him a wink here and there in front of the others, but where was she now? She wasn't in her room, a small bedroom at the top of the stairs. Maybe at the grocery store, or out at King's Market for something fresh. He strolled to a window and peered over the parking area. Her vehicle was gone.

That left nobody protecting the kitchen, and despite him starving, he wasn't eating anything in there without Pauline's safety blessing. The chief of police had asked for an unopened bottled water for a reason. Was he too hungry to walk two miles up to McConkey's?

A small piece of him wanted to drive up there, eat, then keep going back to New Orleans.

Nobody else had turned ill. Nobody seemed to care much that he'd become ill. They seemed to wait on pause to see how he would react. The worry he kept chewing on, however, was what if he didn't? Would they try harder? Was he supposed to give as good as he got? Prank or no prank, he wasn't looking forward to an entire week of this.

Mission, dude. Get back in Grandmother's good graces and consummate a solid position in Pauline's restaurant.

Talk to Pauline. Talk to Kimi. Grab alone time with Grandmother.

Paranoia flickered just out of reach. This family had carte blanche to treat him as they wished, and after two episodes, the police chief had done nothing. She'd said she could file charges without him, but she hadn't because she faced an uphill struggle without him being on board. After all, he'd be crucified by the clan. He bet Chief Morgan realized that, too.

He'd forgotten and quickly been reminded of how testy things were before he left. He'd graduated, become a chef, and Grandmother had expected him to remain in Charleston, embellishing the Poe name and, therefore, rejuvenating the cookbook. Maybe even co-writing one with her. He'd been the only Poe to attempt to match her culinary skills, and the only one to defy her wishes. While the other family might've thought of following their own vision once or twice, they hadn't. That made him the enemy. They'd love to see him fail.

His gut twisted as heartburn churned deep down his throat.

Was an inheritance worth the animosity?

Was an inheritance worth the requisite reconnection to the others?

If he could inherit liquid assets and maybe the intellectual property of the cookbook, he'd be gone and be happy. But these people weren't known for appeasement. Case in point, kin poisoning kin.

He wondered if the inheritance came with a chain to the business and remaining in Charleston?

Still standing on the stairs, he literally feared entering the Poe world again.

Stupid. He was a grown-ass man. He stepped down and strode through the dining room toward the kitchen. He had to act like he belonged here.

Eddie was rummaging through the refrigerator, opening covered dishes, smelling, appearing to judge what dishes were worth the sampling. For a second, Allan thought he'd hang and see exactly what Eddie was willing to eat, then eat the leftovers. Safe.

"Anything good in there?" Allan asked.

Jerking barely enough for Allan to notice, his father answered, "Hey, son. Hunting for a snack."

Allan had passed three plates of snacks on the dining room table en route to the kitchen. Pauline's effort at keeping people out of her business was to give them over-the-top snacks they couldn't pass up, after a warning that she couldn't have her other food bothered.

"You didn't like what was out there on the table?"

Eddie looked past Allan, like he misunderstood. Then his forehead smoothed. "Um, no. Didn't see anything I really wanted out there."

"Pauline laid out a nice variety," Allan said. "You didn't even taste the pickled shrimp? That used to be one of your favorite things."

His father shook his head, suddenly eager to get by his son, leaving the refrigerator door ajar. "No. But I've got no business snacking." He rubbed his belly, which wasn't huge but not exactly washboard material.

"Guess I'll pass."

Eddie patted his son on the shoulder as he pushed by. "You, on the other hand, could afford a couple of pounds. You eat my share." He finished sliding past. "Think I'll go check emails. Can't stop thinking about work, you know?" He left the kitchen.

Allan watched his father repeat his tracks past the dining room table, past the snacks laid out on the table, then up the stairs.

Eddie had walked by the three appetizers without notice.

And not one of them was pickled shrimp.

Nope, Allan wasn't eating anything out of the fridge now. He was walking, no, he was driving down to Coots.

Eddie had mysteriously waited for him to come down, then led him into the kitchen, touching some if not all dishes. Paranoid that this was phase three of the family game, Allan made a command decision to order extra takeout when he went out.

But where was he to safely store it?

His stomach grumbled. With nobody in sight to ask where he was going, he exited the back door, scooting under the house to reach the front and his vehicle. Pauline's car remained gone. He wished he'd gone with her.

She took her job seriously, ever choosing fresh over frozen, and God forbid, in a can or processed. Processed food was a lazy short cut and detrimental to health, one of the many habits he loved about Chef Pauline. Cooking healthy ranked first and foremost. Fish right out of the water. Vegetables right out of the field, and organic. Herbs never came out of a bottle or tin unless they were the last resort. Honey in lieu of sugar. The list went on and on.

He wanted to visit with her so badly.

In short time he had covered the two miles to Coots in no time, the small restaurant/bar at the back of the Pavilion.

Known for its laid-back air in both the gift shop and Coots, the Pavilion had been a hopping venue back in the fifties. The restaurant's 1,200-foot pier was swept away in 1959 by Hurricane Gracie, then rebuilt and a rejuvenation attempted with a motel and bowling alley across the street. More storms, construction issues, and financial worries hurt the landmark, and the building's ownership passed around until informally restructured to today's structure. Simple and overlooking the Atlantic, the pier was much shorter.

Pulling into the sandy parking area at three in the afternoon, he scanned the old place, remembering all the history Grandmother had drilled into their heads. Just like the Poes had a legacy, anything within an hour's drive of Charleston merited study, per her orders. History mattered, especially regarding affluent families, famous lineages, and historic events. Every mayor, representative, and senator. Natural flora and fauna, monuments and bodies of water. If they crossed paths with the well-off, at least they were informed and, therefore, respected.

Of course, she expected anyone in those reaches to reciprocate and know them as well, and if they didn't, she made sure they wanted to. The responsibility of a generously endowed family, she'd say, was to be aware, be seen, and be well thought of. Allan seemed to recall that his great-grandfather had donated to rebuilding this very pier. Only once, though. No Poe threw good money after bad once another hurricane hit.

As Allan exited his car, truth hit him that he couldn't venture anywhere around here without Grandmother's voice in his ear, telling him who and what was important, and how incredibly appreciative he ought to be.

In New Orleans he was a nobody, the anonymity refreshing after growing up in Charleston. At least until he became the somebody who might've injured that couple at The Red Lacey.

With all the Poe cars accounted for back at the house, his fit cousins must have walked the beach. He called Kimi. There were only a handful of places she would meet friends, with Coots the most likely.

She answered after the first ring. "Hey, Cuz. You still puking or are your guts intact now?"

"I'm better and I'm starving. Where are you?"

"Coots. You remember, right? You go all the way down—"

He bypassed the long ramp entrance and fast walked the stairs. "It wasn't like someone kidnapped me as a child, brat. I'll be right there."

Took him about thirty steps to reach the door to the place, but Kimi wasn't inside. He went to the bar. "Kimi Poe been in here?"

Allan figured she'd be recognized, and, sure enough, the bartender pointed outside to the pier. Before leaving, he ordered a grilled shrimp BLT wrap, fries, and a nonalcoholic beer to be brought outside. He had to restrain himself from ordering two of everything.

As soon as the door opened, Kimi squealed, "Cousin!" and waved for him to come over.

The tables and benches were blocky wooden picnic type structures with umbrellas in the center, built to withstand the weather and breezes. The wind wasn't bad and the sun comfortable, so they had the umbrella down.

They being four people, all close to the same age.

"Sit next to me," Kimi said, scooching over. "Finally, we can talk without all those ears."

Amen to that.

A complete opposite of his sister, Ogden showed no feelings, much appreciated since he could be an ass. Allan still nodded in greeting, but his boy cousin was too busy taking note of the strange new girl, seated adorably close to the unfamiliar boy.

"Allan," Kimi said, in her dramatic manner that never seemed to be too much. "These pretty people are Jeb Morgan and his lovely honey Sprite Bianchi. And friends, this is my long-lost cousin Allan. He's a chef."

He nodded. "Nice to meet you." Jeb reached over to shake his hand.

Something rang a distant bell about Jeb, but Allan wasn't into thinking too hard at the moment. He'd escaped that house and could sit in the sun enjoying a meal where he didn't have to fret over alien ingredients.

"Y'all go to college together, huh?" Allan asked, unable to stop himself from eyeing up the coast toward Charleston. The pier allowed you to see a few miles in either direction, and the waves rolled comfortably and mesmerizing. Gulls called overhead. A vee of pelicans glided past, their shadows gracing the tables.

The girl spoke up first. "Miss Priss here had to graduate and get all adult on us, but we still see Ogden." She winked at him. "He gives us our dose of Poe. Y'all are a rather unique lot." She winked again, this time at Kimi. "Or so I hear."

Allan looked to Kimi for a hint as to what that may entail. Surely she hadn't talked the tea last night, or the cookies this morning? Wait, was she even aware of the cookies this morning?

But Kimi gave him a quick wink, and he chose to read that as she kept quiet about all that.

"Our clan is rather unconventional." Allan groaned comically. "Next you'll be expecting me to recite *Annabel Lee* or something."

"No, not something so common," she said, her look teasing. "How about something more obscure, like *The Bridal Ballad.*"

Jeb rolled his eyes.

Kimi grinned in her impish manner. "I do not see a ring, but are you trying to tell me something?"

Jeb suddenly set his attention on a cold French fry, dragging it through ketchup. Not a lot of fiancé light in those eyes.

"This one here," and Sprite elbowed him lightly, "has a grandmother who is trying to hire him, groom him, then force-feed him into the role of mayor of the town where she happens to be the current mayor. I'm to marry him, spit out babies, and train them to be in politics, too. She doesn't ask. You would not believe the conversation we had earlier today about this . . . crap."

"It's not crap," Jeb said. "And she means well, so don't paint her as the devil."

Kimi's eyes widened. She threw a stare at her brother, then another at Allan. "Hey, Jeb, trust me. We can talk this talk." She leaned in. "You do remember who our grandmother is, right?" A quick sarcastic laugh punctuated her point. "Look who I'm working for." She pointed to her brother. "Who he will be working for once he graduates. You think we've got a choice?"

"I had a choice," Allan said.

Kimi laughed. "And look where that choice got you. Didn't you just get out of the hospital this morning from eating something. . . unexpected?"

Sprite sobered. "What does that mean?"

Allan gave a hard stare at his cousin to shut up.

"It means he ate something that seriously disagreed with him," Kimi said, reading Allan well enough. "Now, what is this about your grandmother, Jeb?"

Jeb shook his head. "Sprite's talking too much."

"What?" Sprite said. "Whoever their grandmother is, I still speak the truth." Taking one of Jeb's fries, she dipped up ketchup and licked, not willing to be ashamed.

Seated directly across the table from her, Ogden finally spoke. "If his grandmother is evil, Sprite needs to know up front. In-laws can be a lot to take in."

Kimi gave him a squeaky, "Ha! Listen to you."

"Don't start," her brother warned.

"Let's turn this back on you, bro." Kimi started counting off fingers. "You're not married. You don't even have a girlfriend." She patted herself on the chest. "I'm not dating and see no redeeming qualities to being married, honestly."

"Kimi," Allan warned.

"Oh, no." She shook her head. "This sage brother of mine opened this conversation. He doesn't even know what an in-law looks like. Our family kills them off." She pointed to her brother. "Do you have a dad? No." She pointed to Allan. "Do you have a mom? No. And the other aunt has no husband anymore and had no children. Grandfather died ages ago. The entire family is pure blood kin with no plans to dilute the gene pool."

Allan was remembering the downside of his favorite cousin. Opinionated to a fault, except in front of the Poe elders.

Jeb frowned. "Please tell me you speak figuratively. Poes talking about killing people sort of raises eyebrows."

Ogden gave a dreary laugh.

The group went quiet at the sudden seriousness of things.

Chapter 17

Callie

CALLIE CALLED Beverly before the station door had a chance to close behind Pauline. Odds were her mother remained on the beach, harassing Sophie, killing time until she could then harass Callie when she got off work.

The woman was on a mission.

But this time Callie preferred to pick her mother's brain. Callie's resources for all things Edisto were, in this order, Marie, Deputy Don Raysor, the deputy on regular loan from the county, Sophie, and her mother. Marie specialized in the beach, with crazy historic knowledge of islanders, too. Deputy Raysor had fifteen years on Marie, and a more rural knowledge of the island as well as the entire county. He was related to enough of the people to have serious dirt knowledge. Old family secrets were their specialty.

Sophie was more social in nature, but not a smidge of gossip left anyone's lips without making its way to Sophie's ear by nightfall. She had a network that consisted of people who might not realize they belonged to it.

Beverly, on the other hand, traveled in the more affluent beach circles, not bothering with anyone who didn't own a house in the town itself. No renters. She'd been around the beach for longer than Callie had been alive. Occasionally she socialized with islanders, if they strayed to the sand, and if they owned exclusive homes on marsh, sound, or the Atlantic. There were always conditions with Beverly.

Since Callie's concern was the Poes, Beverly won hands down this time in terms of potential expert knowledge. To ask anything of Beverly meant you had to barter, though. She gave nothing without something in return. Even with her family. That was how life functioned to her, as natural as breathing.

"Hello, dear," her mother answered on the second ring. "Your friend and I are having a lovely lunch at Pros and Cons. My first time since they opened."

Callie gave a controlled, silent sigh. She had to play the game or Beverly would balk, refuse, or make life utterly irritating when she realized she was being pumped for information. Simply Callie calling Beverly gave her mother the red flag that something was up.

"I haven't eaten there yet, Mother. How is it?"

"Well," Beverly started. "Keep in mind we're at lunch, not dinner. There are a lot of fried things, though I admit they look enticing. But I had a very pleasant wedge salad. Dinner looks quite appealing though. The wine is excellent. Beautiful wine list."

"At ninety dollars a bottle it ought to be," Sophie said in the background.

Wonderful. Her mother had bought the whole bottle. For two normal wine drinkers, that wasn't terribly extreme if consumed with a decent meal and ample time to consume both, but Sophie wasn't much of a drinker. Her vice of choice was pot, and not too often at that. That meant Sophie nursed one lone glass to satisfy the lady paying the bill and probably out of curiosity to see what a bottle of that price tasted like.

That meant Beverly would take care of the rest.

"Who drove?" Callie asked.

"I did, silly."

Wonderful again. She should be thankful Beverly hadn't gone the martini route. "Y'all going to be there for a while?" She couldn't ask them to come to her and put Beverly behind the wheel, and nothing Callie had to discuss couldn't be heard by Sophie who might even supplement things. "Y'all order dessert, and I'll be right there. I have a few questions for you ladies and talking there is as good a place as any."

"Sounds good, dear. I'll order you the house salad since I remember how you're not too fond of feta."

Callie would eat whatever Beverly put in front of her. Deciding what her daughter ate without asking was a tiny power thing. Callie had lived her entire life recognizing these mini moves. Beverly was a pro at them, and she exercised that power relentlessly at her favorite eatery in Middleton. Oscars. She told guests, coworkers, and political rivals where they'd eat when sharing a business meal and what not to eat when they arrived. Which wine was worthy, and which dessert the most exquisite. In the back and forth, she inevitably got her way as she wore out whoever sat across the table. Lulls were not allowed.

Callie told Marie where she'd be and headed over. One mile as the crow flew, driving took two miles to go around the Wyndham resort then enter through the gate.

The guy at the resort gate waved her through, a nice older gentleman who'd been there forever. Winding her way around roads named after golf terms, she reached Fairview Drive and parked.

Nobody asked her for her reservation, and nobody had to direct her to the table. Lunch was over, the place mostly empty except for a couple of heavy middle-aged guys at the bar ogling a local lady ten years younger who'd claimed the stool to their right, the three into their conversation, cocktails, and sweet potato fries.

Of course, Beverly had chosen a table in the middle of the floor, not unlike her beloved Oscar's back home only this eatery proved way more formal with its rich wood and black décor contrast. The woman had to be seen, and she had to see everyone else's comings and goings. Sophie, on the other hand, looked captured.

Sophie was probably the most fit female on the island if not the top one percent of Charleston. To meet her alone for the first time guaranteed being impressed. Her self-assurance was admirable, her charisma enviable. Men and women alike wanted to be her, be with her, or be admired by her. On Edisto, people took doses of Sophie any way they could get them. Her children rolled their eyes at her power, with Zeus, her son, calling her a witch. Almost the pot calling the kettle black since he inherited more of her ways than the daughter, the son being a long-haired hippie-type who had dated a fortune teller twice his age. He promised customers successful fishing ventures on his charter because he professed to have a gift reading the stars.

Beverly, however, overshadowed Sophie, even on her own turf. One could recognize the alpha dominance at first glance, and it pained Callie seeing her best friend diminished by her mother in such an unearned way. Beverly radiated power and control, and the sight of her made one think twice about exchanging hellos. She used her behavior to *cull the world*, as she described herself once, removing the unnecessary from her circle before she had to deal with them.

The house salad awaited Callie, along with a ginger ale. At least they didn't have to argue about Callie sharing the wine. Abstinence wasn't something Beverly cared to fully understand, but she wasn't going to offer a drink to someone in uniform.

The mood at Pros and Cons was calming. Aromas weren't heavy with the small crowd, but they were alluring. Callie appreciated the turn of events bringing them here so she could get a feel of the place and relay an opinion to Mark. She tried to hear the trio's banter at the bar and was grateful she couldn't make out the words. Good acoustics for talking and not being heard.

"How was lunch?" Callie asked, shaking out her napkin.

Only the wine glass and a few butter crackers sat before Sophie. Had she even eaten?

"Oh," her friend replied, seeing Callie's scrutiny of her plate. "I had them fix me a shrimp cocktail." Sophie got what she wanted wherever she went, too. At least on Edisto.

Callie spotted the irony at the whole hierarchy thing taking place here, on this beach. This was Sophie's territory. Beverly used to be more well-known, but this restaurant was too new to recognize her. Callie would've liked watching the dynamics of them placing their lunch orders, each woman flexing. Except for the tab. Beverly would pay, and Sophie would let her.

"Looks good." Callie dove into the salad, hungry, glancing up once at Sophie to judge how she was weathering this luncheon date Beverly had forced her into. Sophie tried not to look like a child confined to a chair in the principal's office.

Three bites in, Callie began with her own mission. Sometimes the simple task of dining diluted any wariness in the air. Even in her own office, when people were sequestered for questioning, she at least offered them water and protein bars.

"How well are you familiar with Doris Poe?" Callie asked her mother after washing down her lettuce, letting the glass of ginger ale hang delicately in her hand like a wine goblet.

One brow raised, then another. "Doris Woolf Poe?"

"The one and the same. Quite the literary statement in her name alone."

"She's considerably older than I am, dear. Could be my mother."

Bless Beverly to touch upon the negative first.

"Do you know her?" Callie asked, continuing to eat. Sophie watched with interest.

"We've met, but not for years. Why, dear? That's a name I haven't thought of in a while."

"The family is staying in their Edisto house this week," she replied, not feeding too much information, but enough to see where this went.

Beverly took a sip, thinking, probably trying to remember the last time she'd seen these people, or that would be Callie's guess. Beverly hated to be caught ignorant. "All of them?" her mother asked. "Together?"

Callie didn't expect that. She named off the family members she'd waded through the other night, not mentioning the nurse or the chef.

"Curious," Beverly said, lifting the bottle and refilling a glass still a third full. The pour almost emptied the bottle.

"Why is that curious?"

Beverly set the bottle down without a sound. "That's the entire family. They don't normally gather in a unit. And I thought that one boy was blacklisted."

Callie finished her drink. "How do you know all this?"

One would almost miss the miniscule shift of her weight, slow and elitist. "I keep up, dear. Part of the occupation. And I may have been to their events over the years."

Everything Beverly said was understatement. Callie hated the woman's games but spotted them from a mile away. That's how one danced with her.

But the curious thing was that in her lifetime as the child of Lawton and Beverly Cantrell, the mayor and tsarina of Middleton, South Carolina, Callie had never seen the Poes. Her parents hadn't had them over, and they'd never had Poes to any political events Callie'd ever attended. Middleton was only twenty-five miles from Charleston. "How well do you know them, Mother?" Maybe things had changed since those earlier years.

"More from reputation than anything else." Beverly swirled her wine. "We've met a dozen times over thirty years. That matriarch is intimidating, and she wields it. They don't come to your function. You get invited to theirs." She gave a breathy scoff. "I don't have much time for that."

Which to Callie meant they had nothing Beverly needed and vice versa.

That family had control written all over them. It only made sense that they impounded themselves here at the beach. Nobody lived here impressive enough to woo them, so their vacay was pure getaway so they wouldn't be disturbed. Callie bet nobody local called when the Poes came to town, and the Poes called nobody on Edisto when they arrived.

"How do you know about the one guy not exactly fitting in?" Callie asked, attentive to her meal before this conversation raised to the point she couldn't get a bite in between words. That's how most of her working meals went. One started with good intentions to consume a few calories before you gave up having to address the work.

"The Poes don't do Edisto," Beverly said.

"That I can agree with," Sophie added, Callie giving her full attention since she'd been so overshadowed up to now. "I hardly hear about them coming to town, and if I don't catch wind of anything, nobody does."

Beverly passed a knowing look at Sophie, like she got that. Sophie beamed.

The waitress approached, and Callie smiled at her for being attentive, the police chief being the perfunctory public servant who tried to be inviting to any and all. Beverly's glare, however, pushed her off like bait fish avoiding a predator.

Callie reached across the tablecloth. "Mother, come on, be nice. Some of us must live here."

But her mother ignored the chastisement. "As for the Poes, good luck cracking that inner circle. Better people than you have tried." Then she shifted gears. "Why exactly are you interested in them? Is your concentration of a criminal nature? That would be intriguing."

Ignoring the question, Callie continued. "You said somebody, a boy, you said, was blacklisted."

"You named him. Allan. Son of Eddie. Edgar and Allan Poe." An eye roll. "Who does that?"

People who owned who they were plus some. Callie tucked that thought away to keep Beverly from slipping into a theoretical pissing contest about the qualities of society's upper crust. Her mother was a big fish in a small pond. The Poes, however, splashed loud in the big pond of the Holy City. She didn't care to hear her mother embarrass herself.

"Allan Poe is in his thirties, right? I met him earlier today," Callie said.

Beverly nodded. "He ran away from them. I'm surprised they allowed him to come back. What has he done? Or maybe he's broke. I assume he has the issue since the others would be toeing the proverbial line. Or," and Beverly held up a finger, "is someone terminal? Doris Poe is rather ancient."

"Beats me," Callie said, not feeding the question. "Allan seems innocent enough, but since you brought her up, tell me about the grandmother."

But Sophie piped up first. "She's noted as a witch."

Beverly hesitated, then with a grin nodded her agreement. "As silly as that sounds, I have heard that said."

"Oh, that's funny coming from you, Mother." Callie said, wolfing down another bite, spearing the last of the cranberries, chasing all with a sip. Wiping her mouth, Callie leaned on the table. "Two witches calling out another. That's choice."

"Hey, I totally own my title," Sophie said.

"I know you do."

Beverly's delay said she teetered on whether to own hers, too.

"Mother's one, too, whether she admits it or not," Callie tacked on. "She's atypical, though, just not out of the closet. But y'all tell me about their culinary skills. Or any nefarious reputation they may have."

Sophie gasped. "You're wanting gossip?"

"Any and all of it," Callie said, pushing her plate back. "Sling away."

Her mother had to hold herself back from leaning on the table in kind with Sophie, who launched her two cents first. "The old lady has been known to kill people for a deal," Sophie said. "They're too rich to get caught."

Beverly laughed. "That rumor came from someone who had a heart attack while in a high-powered bidding war over a piece of Mount Pleasant real estate. Had to be twenty years ago."

Sophie pointed at Beverly like she had one better. "Hey, remember when someone else died who tried to smear the son's name in the Charleston *Post & Courier*? A week after Eddie was accused of falsifying papers, the accuser had a stroke. About that time people started calling Mrs. Poe the witch."

"There was another, wasn't there? About one of the husbands dying."

"I believe so. Not as flamboyant, but still, Poe magic."

"But," Beverly said. "That second one you mentioned, the one that threw the spotlight on Eddie, is when her cookbook took off for the second time. Accolades to her agent, or whomever, who initiated a second edition and a PR coup because of the noxious plants listed in the back. They took full advantage of the bad press that said they were capable of killing off their adversaries, then spun the media attention into gold. They are masters, I'm telling you."

"I didn't know that," Sophie said, breathless.

"You wouldn't have been traveling in those circles, dear. I, however, rank a little higher on the social ladder. Not your fault."

"But I cook. Or I like to," Sophie said. "The Italian in me, I guess."

Callie gave her an atta-girl in a small attempt to offset Beverly's irreverence. "You make great sweets at Christmas, Soph. And your lemon bars are to die for."

Sophie puffed up bright and happy. Beverly regarded her like she'd make an exception for her this time.

Typical arrogance, but Callie bet Beverly wasn't in too many of the Poe circles, either. If Beverly did any elbow rubbing with those blue bloods, she'd have bragged and at least have invited them to one of her fundraisers.

Beverly was surfing on pure bullshit.

This was what Callie had hoped for, though, chatter that covered ground she had no clue about, so she sat there and listened and gave everyone grace to embellish.

When the waitress came by to refill water glasses and bring Callie another ginger ale, she offered to open another bottle of wine. Thank God Beverly refused. But the waitress remained.

Callie looked over the table trying to figure out what she was waiting for.

"I heard you mentioning the Poes. I hope you don't mind," she said, more so to Beverly than anyone else.

"Oh, honey," Beverly said, "do pull up a seat."

But the waitress waved her off. "No, sorry, not allowed. I only wanted to say I heard they only eat food they can control. They've never eaten here, for instance, and this is the most upscale place on the beach. People say they hired their own chef for the week."

Sophie gasped. "Ooh, that makes sense. Their adversaries might strike back, and people of that caliber make a lot of enemies. I wonder how they scout their chefs, though. How do you trust that a chef hasn't been bought by some nemesis?"

Nemesis?

"Money does buy loyalty," the waitress said. "I've seen it."

Whatever that meant, Callie didn't want to ask.

Beverly didn't add to the topic, but she listened. "I bet I could make some calls. . ."

"Okay, okay," Callie said, not needing the restaurant staff to start the grape vine buzzing about what she might be investigating, nor did Beverly need to take on a project. "We might be taking this out of bounds, y'all."

The waitress shrugged apologetically and left.

"Well," Sophie said, energized at the camaraderie, "seems the witch is well known. She has potions and herbs and venoms and God knows what else."

Sitting back, taking in the hypocrisy, Callie crossed her arms. "Nobody said any of that, Soph. Good heavens, y'all."

"What?" Sophie said.

"I shouldn't be surprised that two witches could identify another."

Beverly rolled her eyes. Sophie scoffed. Not for the first time, Callie wondered how Doris Woolf Poe would fare against Beverly Cantrell.

Sophie and Beverly had given Callie an inkling of what to expect of these people. They considered themselves exclusive. The Ravenels and Pinckneys, Calhouns and Legares, Villepontoux and Manigaults, the foundation families of Charleston and Mount Pleasant held comparable bloodlines. The Poes, however, were renowned from Boston to Philadelphia, from New York to Baltimore, with year-long stints in places like Charleston, thanks to the nineteenth century author. Long enough for Sullivan's Island to have a restaurant named after the original patriarch's short story, "The Gold Bug." The famous "Annabel Lee" was supposedly inspired by his stay there.

Time to go. Lunch was entertaining, to say the least, and to some degree educational. She'd confirmed what she suspected plus some. The Poes held tight ranks and penalized family members who violated family code. They held a reputation of money, real estate, cooking, and toxic plants. They never lost.

Maybe she ought to let them destroy each other. Not like she could stop them.

"Wait a minute. Have they ever killed anyone?" she asked as the others laid napkins on the table to rise. Both sat back down. "I mean, seriously. Any talk of charges?"

"Pardon?" Beverly said.

"Y'all have all these stories of the Poes, most of them quite nefarious," Callie said. "The question stands, does anyone think they killed anyone?"

The two said nothing.

"Y'all are talking awfully big and powerful about stories, but how about in real life?"

Beverly rummaged in her purse for lip gloss. Sophie's eyes darted.

"Well, that's a no," Callie said. Pure gossip. Well, she'd asked for that, hadn't she?

All she had were hints of pranks in the guise of family discipline, and unless she could prove malicious intent or serious bodily harm, there was nothing she could do about them.

But her son and his girl had gone out to meet two of these Poe people, and she couldn't ignore a small degree of discomfort in her gut about that.

Chapter 18

Callie

SHE WASN'T TELLING the other two women about Jeb and Sprite meeting the younger Poes. Beverly and Sophie took the silence to mean they could leave. "Wait, one more thing," Callie said, before they fully stood.

Beverly settled back and tiredly asked, "What's that, dear?"

"Lay off the kids. Both of you. Trust me, it's all I can do not to get involved either, but to do more will chase them away."

"Hey, I'm on their side," Sophie said, with a side-glance at the woman who'd paid for lunch, as if she hoped she hadn't crossed a line.

"Pardon me, dear, but I am on their side as well," said Beverly. "Maybe not in the same way, but if you two would step back and take things seriously, you'd recognize I am their future. What I can do with that boy will catapult him into success. And your daughter as well, if you let me. She's bilingual. Do you know what I can do with that?"

Sophie's fists went to her hips, a signature move Callie knew too well. "No. Tell me, pray tell. What exactly will *you* do with *my* daughter?"

"Alongside my grandson, she will flourish."

Callie would let Sophie tackle this.

"Flourish how?" Sophie asked.

"As the first lady of Middleton, she'll be introduced to—"

"Beverly," Sophie interrupted, a coolness having infiltrated her pixie manner. "You said you'd do something with her being bilingual. Let's hear that. Not how she could be a good wife. I've been the good wife before, honey, and it ain't all it's cracked up to be if you aren't fulfilling your own needs."

Whoa, listen to Sophie.

But Beverly wasn't affected. "Dear, she can interpret for her husband in dealing with industry coming to the area, or with dignitaries who also speak other languages. She can represent Jeb–"

"Jeb, Jeb, Jeb. You want her to be some administrative assistant to a spouse. Is that what you're saying?"

Beverly winced in her highbrow manner. "First lady is way more than that, dear."

Uh oh. A third *dear*, which carried unmistakable condescension.

"Why can't Sprite run for mayor?" Sophie threw out.

Callie didn't see that coming. This could be interesting.

"Bloodline, pure and simple," Beverly replied. "None of that is her fault, so let her contribute in the next best way, through her husband."

Sophie held up a finger. "Let's say they get married. That hasn't even been discussed except by you, so even that's still a leap, but let's play this out. Then they have kids. Sprite could be mayor and groom her son to fill her shoes. That would make everyone happy."

Excellent, Soph. While that might be a game changer for anyone else, with no surprise to Callie, the current mayor of Middleton didn't miss a beat. "We cannot risk the skip in generations."

"Why not?" Sophie asked. "Jeb would still be running around town being Public Relations or whatever you called the offer you made him. He'd be running point on a lot of things. And Sprite could impress by being the bilingual mayor who can communicate without assistance."

Ooh, Callie was enjoying this.

"I can work better with Jeb," Beverly said. "I'll involve your daughter in everything, making her presence in essence his presence. The power behind the throne. Then if something happens to Jeb, God forbid, she'll be prepped to run in his stead. How about that?"

"This isn't a business deal." Color had spread in Sophie's cheeks. "They aren't yours to manipulate."

"It's called opportunity. They'll see that in ten years."

"And make them miserable in between. No," Sophie said. "You'll ruin them, *madam*."

"I'll make them golden, *dear*."

Holy Bejesus.

The three at the bar and the guy behind it were beginning to watch after no doubt having heard the energy building in the middle of the restaurant floor.

Beverly lifted her purse from her lap and dropped it on the table, enough to make the girl at the bar jump. "Don't tell me how to do my job."

"Don't tell my daughter how she'll live her life."

"Then maybe she's not ready for my grandson, *dear*."

Sophie had been swept up into Beverly's world for the duration of lunch, as per her mother's plan, but Beverly had taken things too far, allowing Sophie to remember who she was. "Don't *dear* me, you bitch." Sophie stood.

O-kay. "Let's take both you witches outside," Callie said, to lighten the moment enough to remove them from the restaurant before punches were thrown or management requested they leave.

Beverly snatched up her purse. Then after a dramatic, exaggerated measure of Sophie, replied, "If I can't visit with the kids, I need to return to my office." She pivoted and strutted out.

Sophie's mouth gaped open. "Who the hell does she think she is?" She stared at Callie like she'd let some of this fallout happen.

"Don't look at me, hon. This was a hundred percent the two of you. Come on."

Sophie took a few slow steps, her get-up-and-go still stuck in her thoughts. "I thought I knew her. I thought I could see her coming. I thought since we spoke of our kids, she'd be. . . What the hell, Callie?"

Callie patted her on the back with a slight nudge to keep moving. "Need a ride back?"

Sophie moved on, talking over her shoulder. "How the hell did you not become her?"

"Beverly's not my biological mother, remember. My real mom is your next-door neighbor." Sarah had only revealed herself as Callie's mother two years ago, during a dire time in both their lives, making a lot of sense about things Callie'd never fully understood before.

"I know who your mama is, Callie, but Beverly raised you. How did you grow up under her roof and not absorb all that. . . evil?"

She stopped in the doorway, unable to make her legs move with a question stuck in her head. "Callie, what just happened in there?"

"You got sucked into Beverly's vortex, Soph. Her goal was to get you on her side, and trust me, she would've come close to making you think her plan had merit if I hadn't come along. My presence sort of shifted things. You might've walked away thinking her plan for the kids was for the best for all of us, totally indoctrinated. Eventually, she'd have had Sprite as the power behind the throne, like she said, like she always perceived herself with my father. And she'd have made you love the concept once she planted images of you at fundraisers, dignitary dinners, and ribbon cuttings, like some Queen Mother."

Sophie's scowl took a moment to form as she pictured those scenarios in her head. "But Sprite wouldn't have gone along with all of that," Sophie said. "I know my daughter."

"Beverly was tweaking you so that you would try to convince Sprite what was best for her."

"Hmmm."

Callie kept playing the situation out for her. "But if Sprite had heard you were scheming with Beverly, how would she have reacted?"

"She'd hate me, hate her, hate all of it."

"Yes," Callie said. "And Beverly doesn't care about that part. She's ruthless."

"Oh my God," her friend whispered as they moved outside. "Wow, I never saw that coming. I mean, I thought I could read your mother."

"You held your own well enough." Callie didn't want her friend belittled by all of this. "You pretty much disliked her before the lunch, didn't you?"

Sophie's mouth formed a little O. "Jesus, Callie, I did, didn't I? That's universe-rocking-scary how she manipulated me. You're lucky you weren't corrupted beyond redemption."

There was no need to respond to that. Truth was, Callie had her father to thank for tempering things between his wife and daughter, but still, Callie had run away. But not until Beverly had taught her how to be an alcoholic.

Neither of them as mothers wanted Beverly to play director with Jeb and Sprite, potentially forcing them to move away and escape the pressure. They'd come back years later as different people, mature in ways they didn't get to share with their parents, a bittersweet that never really loses the bitter.

Sophie moved like she'd stripped a gear. Visual in everything she did, her feelings usually spilled out in color for all the world to see. Some of those times, she provided comic relief for Callie, who this time had been allowed to escape worry through corralling the two women. Now her beloved Jeb rushed back to the forefront of her mind.

She still didn't know the thing Jeb had mentioned on the front porch last night. The unknown thing that Sprite had overcome.

Bad grades. A sexual encounter? She'd almost been snatched by a predator on the college campus back in the fall. A pregnancy lost? That last one she didn't want to think about. The thought of those kids enduring solo something that life-altering gave her stomach a flip.

Standing in the middle of the parking lot was not the right time to ask Sophie either. Nor alone in Callie's cruiser, and of course, Sprite's personal issue had been a topic not for Beverly's ears. For a split second, she'd thought about asking Sophie to chat right after Beverly left but asking her in the middle of a dining room floor if she was aware of some issue her daughter had gone through, only to learn that Sprite had not told her mother, would create a rebound tornado. Sophie would implode.

That daughter was everything to her.

Callie tried to tell herself that whatever *it* was, must not have been much if it hadn't seemed to unnerve the kids. Sophie would've told her if she knew. Jeb spoke like they were on the other side of whatever it was. At this point, did she even have the right to know if all was well?

Assuming all was well.

Assuming Sprite wasn't scarred by any of whatever *it* was.

Mothering adult children was harder than herding toddlers. You couldn't out-maneuver them anymore. If she were meant to know what they'd overcome, she'd have been told, right?

She preferred thinking about Beverly, honestly. The master manipulator. Callie couldn't stand the thought of hearing Jeb announce they were relocating to Michigan or Oregon to make their own life choices.

As much as she tried not to, Callie despised her mother. Adopted mother, she reminded herself. No shared DNA which in a small way was a relief. A very small way.

She pulled up to Sophie's house, having driven the couple of miles in silence, something Sophie unnaturally tolerated.

"You didn't say much," Callie said.

"Because your brain is on fire about something," Sophie said, hand on the door. "Care to share?"

"No time, girlfriend. I've wasted enough rescuing you from Beverly. Gotta get back to work."

Sophie kept on, though. "So, your mind's on work?"

"For sure."

"Well, thanks for the rescue and the ride." She suspiciously eyed her friend.

"Trust me, Soph. Let me run."

Callie pulled away with a wave, unhappy at herself for lying.

In a weird way, the mental struggle segued her into work. Another aloof, entitled grandmother challenging a grandson who struggled to be his own person, too. Only Callie's family wasn't so weird that they tried to prank one another, who might at any time make a mistake and take the prank too far. A family who'd make national news if they did.

But the families were way too similar.

She made a circle around the beach town, hunting for a Poe tag out of place. In a beach town this small, anyone in decent health, and especially the young, walked everywhere. She hoped someone had been lazy enough to drive.

The eateries on the beach were somewhat limited, and for young adults, desire narrowed that down even more. After having called El Marko's, asking if her kids were there, she realized they wouldn't go there precisely because the place *was* El Marko's, belonging to Callie's guy. Next she checked McConkey's, whose occupants could be seen simply by circling outside. Nothing.

The next was Coots, and, frankly, the popular place would be her first guess except of its location being third in her line of march. There was no checking for those occupants from Palmetto Boulevard. The secluded spot on the back facing the ocean meant one had to literally go inside to look. You couldn't even see who dined on the pier without walking through the indoor area to the outside door or standing far enough outside on the sand to be seen by all the diners. With her being in uniform, she'd have everyone wondering who she was hunting. No clandestine way to handle this.

A dozen cars filled the parking lot. A couple of those would belong to people in the gift shop, but the majority would be dining around back. Pulling off the road, she remained in her vehicle, taking a hard mental note of each car. She'd have preferred a few trucks or vans in the mix to narrow things down, but no such luck.

Ten cars down the line, an instinct told her to go back and review them again. Most were white, the trend these days. One red, another gray, then black, one blue. Color wasn't working for her, so she studied the plates. Six from South Carolina, none of them Jeb's or Sprite's. Georgia, Florida . . . there. An older model Honda.

She'd seen that car at the Poe house, with a Louisiana license plate.

She chose the indoor route and let herself into the small eating place. The wood was a deep stain, and despite windows on three sides that framed the bright beach and sparkling waves, the room held a grip on that darkness. Particularly at night.

The place was half full, popular with natives and tourists alike. In the mornings, Sophie had been known to hold yoga sessions here, propping the windows and door open to snare the ambience of waves. She recognized regulars at the bar, and half the tables held the stereotypical out-of-towners. Halfway through the room, however, she stopped and gazed through the windows to the sunlit pier.

The second table down on the left. Five people. Her two kids and the three Poe kids.

"Get you something, Chief?" asked the bartender who doubled as a waiter for the food.

Diners had quit talking when he'd asked the question, wondering if this was lunchtime for the police or someone on a mission.

What was she to do now?

Chapter 19

Callie

STANDING IN THE middle of Coots' dining area, Callie declined the barkeep's request to take her order, then eased from the center of the dining room toward the door leading to the pier. The air conditioning ran with light music in the background, while outside, hair danced in the wind, the roar of waves competing with conversation.

Sea gulls hung in the air, wings outstretched, gazing for the right diner to hold a French fry a little too long in their hand. Sure enough, one dove in for the win at the table furthest out toward the pier's end. Natives actually had names for these gulls. One was half black and crippled, unable to fly, but he stayed stout enough from sympathetic handouts.

The four young people Callie had hunted for looked safe enough, with Allan Poe making an unexpected fifth. He was too old to be a college friend, and if all accounts had been accurate, he hadn't been in the state for at least three years. Lonely came to mind.

Though kids in her mind, the ages encircling the table ranged from twenty to thirty. So much life ahead of them and little idea where their choices would lead, something Allan could probably preach if the subject arose.

For the life of her, Callie couldn't come up with an excuse for being there or the right questions to ask without the others overhearing. Others who had no need to hear. She wanted to interrupt, but her better judgment advised otherwise.

But as she was about to turn, Sprite spotted her. Callie read her lips, holding no doubt as to what was said. "Hey, isn't that your mom?"

All five turned. So did about eight others at neighboring tables.

Guess Callie was joining them after all. She exited, the sun making her squint after the dark interior, and she approached the table, retrieving shades from her pocket giving her even more of a cop appearance.

"Mom?" Jeb said, standing as he was taught to do for a woman entering the room, especially an older one, and particularly his mother.

"She's your mom?" Allan asked, but he quickly put two and two together. "Right. Morgan." He looked unsure whether he ought to dislike this revelation, and he turned to his female cousin.

Kimi shrugged. "I didn't know either."

"We don't exactly brag about it," Sprite said, like Callie was her own blood.

"Sucks to be you, dude," Ogden uttered under his breath to Jeb.

Callie pulled up a bench and joined them, taking a harder glance at Allan for signs of illness. Wearing a tee, his intricate forearm tattoo would give anyone the sense he was proud of being a Poe between the knives and the raven. He'd hidden the tat under a button up shirt at the house.

Jeb sat back down. "What are you doing here, Mom?"

Exactly. What was she doing there?

"Someone asked me to come by on something I really can't get into," she fibbed. "Had no idea y'all would be here."

Jeb gave her a questioning look, but all signs pointed to her having stumbled across them. But then, she was a cop, and this was her town. Callie read him like a book, but he had nothing to go on. She was safe.

"Did you eat yet?" Sprite said, pushing her plate of onion rings over to share.

But Callie remained true to her healthy salad from lunch. Plus, she wasn't comfortable eating at a table with Poes seated around. She wasn't pleased her kids were either. "Thanks, but I can't stay long," she said. "I had lunch with Jeb's grandmother. She returned to Middleton, so the coast is clear."

Jeb held his reaction, but Sprite gave a dramatic sigh of relief.

Kimi noted all. "Wish my grandmother could leave. One would think I live with her the amount of time I have to be around her."

"I love my grandmother," Jeb said.

Jeb did love her, and Callie respected that.

"Not that she's easy to get along with," Sprite threw in.

"But does she control you?" Ogden asked.

"Odd that you say that," Sprite started, but Jeb reached over to squeeze her arm.

Everyone either ignored the move or didn't see, because the discussion went on for a few more rounds, talking grandmothers in general. The pros and cons were tossed around of how both mavens were healthy, wealthy, and supposedly wise.

Sadly, nobody had experienced one who had read bedtime stories, hugged them tightly, and loved without measure. That weighed on Callie. There was magic in grandparents, or supposed to be. She'd loved her father's mother. Callie would find a piece of candy and a small gift on the bed whenever she spent the night, at least once a month. The items may have come from the dollar store, but the small gentle gesture always made the visit special. Around Christmas, she was gifted a holiday nightgown. Grandmother Alison did that until she lost her health, about the time Callie reached tenth grade.

"Were you looking for me, Chief Morgan?" Allan asked, which shut down the grandmother chat and brought Callie's thoughts around.

"Heck, I assumed she was looking for us," Sprite said.

Kimi laughed. "Maybe we're all in her crosshairs." She narrowed her eyes. "I bet she keeps everyone guessing. That's her superpower."

Callie asked Allan, in an attempt to determine whether she had permission to speak openly. "I usually catch people alone," Callie said, mostly directed at Allan. "Don't like airing certain matters in public."

"Here's totally fine," he said, catching her toss. "My cousins were present during my, um, incidents, and your kids here seem to be all right. I imagine you tell them what you do anyway."

"She really doesn't," Jeb said. "Trust me. My mother's full of secrets."

Callie didn't respond. He spoke truth.

That got bobbled brows from the girls. Allan gave her a reluctant thumbs up to speak in front of everyone seated at the picnic table.

Before Callie could break the ice with small talk, Allan dove in. "Ask away. What I can't answer maybe the cousins can. Our family is rather eccentric, and honestly, transparent about the fact we are weird."

"You think?" Ogden said, rolling his eyes.

Sprite chuckled. "Gotta live up to the Poe name. Otherwise, you disappoint people. Like my last name is Bianchi. Everyone thinks I speak Italian, cook spaghetti, and solve algebra."

A scrunched-up look deepened Kimi's porcelain complexion. "Algebra?"

"Some guy named Bianchi came up with a certain kind of algebraic equation," Sprite explained, downplaying the trivia.

"Which means you understand who he is and what he did," Ogden said, admiration in his eyes. "You probably know more than you admit. I love Italian, by the way. I hope you've mastered that one. Maybe one day you can teach me—"

"You're right. I know all three," she said, Ogden's interest having prompted her to brag. "I bet people have expectations about the Poes, too. You write, you're dark, you keep a crow in a cage, but I hope you don't do opiates. And you were made to learn how to cook if she's like Jeb's grandmother, only her forte is politics. Ugh."

"Yep, ours damn sure made us learn our way around a kitchen," Ogden said, enjoying the repartee with the girl that accented the sparkle in his eye. He flicked the tattoo on Allan's arm. "And that's a raven, not a crow. Ravens are more wicked."

Allan ran a hand over the ink, uncomfortable. He brought them all around with a clearing of his throat and a shake of his head. "Back to the Chief."

Callie didn't mind if he opened the dialogue, and she wouldn't ask anything that was too terribly personal. Jeb and Sprite might hear enough to make them appreciative of keeping more of an arm's length distance from this crew.

"Wait," Kimi said, eyeing her college friends. "Ogden and I were interviewed by you after the first. . . incident. Now that there's been a second, you're retracing steps, aren't you? Why not ask us whether we mind talking about it?" She gave a side-glance. "You followed us, didn't you?"

Jeb gave his mother a questioning gaze that she pretended to miss.

"No, I didn't know you guys were even here. But since you two were around for both incidents against Allan, were you involved?" Callie asked. "Do y'all really poison each other for fun?" If Allan was making this public she would oblige him with answers. If the cousins left, that said something, too, and she'd follow up later.

"Wow," Ogden said. "You're really trying to narrow down the criminal in our family."

"Is there one?" Callie asked.

"Might be all of us."

"One or all, my ears are wide open. Care to share?"

"Mom," Jeb said low, warning.

But Kimi took the reins. "If there is an evil villain in our family, they haven't informed us. And if said villain was either of us, would we tell Allan? Would we have hurt him and showed our hand in front of Jeb and Sprite?" she said, pointing to Allan's plate, moving her hand like she held a saltshaker.

Callie leaned on the table. "Nope, too public. But we're apparently being rather open now. Did either of you hurt Allan?" She stole one of

Sprite's onion ring pieces and held it high to let the most daring of gulls have a bite and to make him quit hovering over her head. Air poop drops were a real thing.

"No, we didn't," Kimi said.

"Not here," Allan warned.

Callie pointed with another onion piece. "Y'all opened the door, not me."

Everyone remained silent, so she lowered her attention to Ogden. "If there is a criminal, I'd appreciate your assistance. Better than being innocent and getting painted with the same brush. Family or not, crime is crime." She motioned at Allan. "It's not like you guys are all that loyal to each other."

Ogden's previous starry-eyed persona slid into one of annoyance. "Chief Morgan, look at you turning into a badass cop. Bet we're a welcome change from sunburned drunks and people dodging their tabs."

"Hey, dude." Jeb interceded. "I'm not letting you insult my mother."

"She's a cop, and she pretty much insulted me. Sort of gives me the right, don't you think?"

But Jeb stood fast. "Are all real estate people crooks then? Is the whole Poe family a snake den of con artists? Taking advantage of buyers and killing them off if they get in your way of a million?" Each word rose in volume.

As much as Callie wanted to temper Jeb, he didn't need to be lectured, scolded, or chastised by his mother. Everyone around the table presented themselves as adults. She'd let him be whatever shape he desired right now.

"Have a civil conversation or get the hell out of here," Jeb continued. "But that's my mother."

"Sucks for you," came the reply, an echo of a moment ago.

Jeb stood. "Excuse me?"

Nearby diners stopped talking and waited to see where this went.

Sprite laid a hand on Jeb's back. Kimi took a handful of her brother's shirt sleeve. Allan instead studied Callie, who studied him back. *Here or somewhere else?* her gaze asked.

His back rigid, Ogden took a long deep breath, not rising to meet Jeb's challenge. "I didn't agree to this open-air discussion, and I don't like being suspected of poisoning someone."

Jeb eased back down.

"Someone in your family was seriously poisoned?" Sprite said, studying her college buddies in a new light. "Jeb? Did I hear that right?"

Callie let the talk play out.

"Listen," Allan said. "My first night here I got sick from something I ate. I went to the ER but came home in the morning. Crap happens."

"Someone said twice," Sprite reminded.

"I think someone played a joke sprinkling a substance on my cookies this morning. But I'm good."

She scowled, judging one person after the other, ultimately settling on Callie. "Are you investigating here?"

"Nope," she replied. "Nobody filed charges. Nothing has risen to the level of me forcing my hand."

The answer didn't appease Sprite. "Kimi, y'all poison each other for fun?"

"No, for God's sake, no," she said. "We know this stuff because of our grandmother. She's rather peculiar, which I guess makes us that way."

"Except for now," Sprite said, pulling her plate back closer, then in a brief hindsight pushed it away. "Sounds like a vacation ritual or something."

Ogden shoved back from his plate. "Now look what your bitch of a mother has done, Jeb. She's—"

Jeb leaped back to his feet, the force pushing the table into Ogden. The force took him backwards, then losing balance, he went down. His head bounced off the pier's plank floor for all to hear.

The nearest table of diners left their seats and moved toward the door. Callie shoved benches out of the way and went down to her knees to check the boy, Allan doing the same across from her.

"Don't get up," she said, studying Ogden for head trauma.

"You don't tell me what to do." He sat up, embarrassed. He might have seen the deck spin a bit, but he positioned himself to his knees, then his feet.

Callie reached toward the back of his head, but he pushed her away. Allan checked instead, shaking a no toward Callie that there was no wound.

"Are you okay?" she asked, truly concerned. "Sit a minute and let's see how you feel." A glance at Jeb told her he wasn't happy at how things had gone awry. She made a nod at him to do the right thing.

He came closer and leaned at the waist. "Man, I totally didn't mean for that to happen."

"Hey," said a new voice, the deeper older tone of the barkeep, arrived to do damage control. "You all right, son?"

Callie tried not to let her irritation be noticed. If Ogden wanted to make a stink about being injured on the restaurant's property, he could. She'd be a poor witness as mother to the party who caused the fall. She shuffled the what ifs that could occur if such a well-heeled family pursued charges.

But Ogden stood, with no sign of physical injury other than his feelings, a different person than went down. "No, I'm fine. Tipped back too far." He reached for his beer bottle and took a swig. "Only had one, so my own clumsiness, I guess."

"Let me bring you another then," said the barkeep. "And y'all relax and enjoy yourself as long as you like. Be right back."

Every soul looked relieved. Callie wanted to check Ogden one more time before leaving. Her presence had only muddied issues she'd hoped to clear up, at least a little. She waited until everyone sat back down. "Are you sure you're good?"

"I'm sure," he said, riding a middle line she couldn't read.

She looked to Jeb. "How about you?"

"I feel horrible," he said.

"He shouldn't have disrespected your mother, Jeb," Kimi said.

Ogden's right brow arched in irritation. "Thanks for the support, Sis."

"Shut up, *Bro*," she said. "You don't go around calling someone's mother a bitch. Get over yourself."

About that time the barkeep reappeared, an assortment of snacks from the appetizer menu on a huge round tray. He set another beer in front of Ogden. "Take your time. On the house. Anyone need a drink refill?"

Appropriately impressed by the added food, the kids settled, no damage done to their friendships. Callie took that opportunity to stand, wish them a good day, and leave.

On the way down the long ramp toward the parking lot, she debated on how much damage she'd done but more importantly, she hoped she'd opened the eyes of Jeb and Sprite enough to be wary.

Chapter 20

Allan

ALLAN WATCHED Callie's back disappear down the ramp at Coot's until wind and distance put her out of earshot. "Now," he said, loudly enough for only their table to hear. "Who the hell is contaminating my food?"

Kimi reared back at the unexpected, then hunched in to avoid being overheard. "Don't even think of me. I am still in your camp, cousin, and you should know that. Never ever assume me. I am the one—"

"You never came to New Orleans, Kimi. Actions speak louder than words unless you want to count a few texts on birthdays and Christmas."

"I sent you presents, too."

"Yeah," he said. "Books."

"You always liked to read. . ." She peered down to her plate, playing with a fry. "Pressure, I guess. And the longer the time the harder it was to reconnect." Then she forced herself to change tones. "But you know how our elders roll, Cuz. I was still in college, and this year they won't give me a minute's peace as I try to learn the business."

His sarcasm rang through in the lone, clipped laugh. "Wow, Kimi. And to think you *were* my favorite."

That popped her head up. "But I still am. Your favorite in the family, I mean, just like you're mine. Trust me."

"Appreciate being second fiddle, Sis," Ogden said, draped over the table with his beer, picking through the free platter of snacks they'd received from management thanks to his tumble.

Kimi smacked his hand. "Quit touching everything, you idiot. Nobody wants your germs."

Ogden waved her off. "Yeah, real deep sibling loyalty," he grumbled.

"Well, you can't say one nice thing about me, so you can keep hanging in my shadow till hell freezes over."

"I have my own talents, thank you very much."

"Who could tell? Again, my shadow." With a dramatic turn, she gave him her back.

Allan might miss a little of the family banter, but this different, adult version of his kid cousins had turned caustic. This side of them he didn't miss.

Kimi had changed the subject, though. She had people skills, nurtured at the knee of her mother, uncle and grandmother, and she'd been on the debate team in high school. She loved controlling conversation, and she'd launched into a whole other direction.

"I'm older and working now," she said, and continued bragging about how she'd sold five properties on her own without the elders, tacking on how she'd collected ten listings that would pay in the upcoming year beating the first-year record of anyone in the family.

Allan, however, wasn't about to let her off topic so easily. "You didn't answer my original question, Kimi. Who is messing with me? I came to Coot's to eat without fear of another damn trick, assuming that's what it is. You claim to be all devoted to me, so talk. Why aren't you sick? Or Ogden? Or any of the elders." Not Grandmother, though. Nobody had the balls to take her out. Even the smallest of playing around with her meals could push her over the edge at her age, resulting in total family alienation. "Better to tell me what's going on than for me to figure out later that that you knew all along."

Her eyes darkened. "I don't appreciate the scolding. I have nothing to admit," she said, jaw tight, muscles twitching beneath.

"Then rat on the person."

"I have no idea." She darted a look to her left to see if the ladies near them heard.

Meanwhile, Sprite and Jeb remained solemn. She exchanged nervous visuals with him. "We probably need to run."

"Shit," Kimi said, waving a hand at her college friends. "Look at them, Allan. Look what you've done. They think we're on FBI's most wanted now." She reached for Sprite's hand, who tried not to draw back.

"You must admit this sounds rather sinister." Jeb reached around her waist as Sprite edged closer.

"This is how your family functions?" Sprite asked, a touch of the adversarial in her voice. "And I thought our people were dysfunctional."

"Well, if not for Jeb's mom. . ." Ogden started, but Kimi smacked the back of his head again.

"Shut up, you idiot! Damn, don't you ever learn?" She pointed to her friend across the table. "I like Sprite. Now she thinks I'll put something in her drink. And you'll mix mandrake in their food."

Jeb and Sprite stiffened. "What's mandrake?" she asked.

Allan gave a small shake of his head in disbelief at his cousins' stupidity. They couldn't dig themselves out of this.

"It's a common enough looking plant, but the root can make you hallucinate and nod off," Kimi said.

"Or worse," Odgen added. "You're supposed to be able to hear it scream when you yank its roots out of the ground. Look up your history. Hannibal, Shakespeare, the Greeks—"

His sister's slap aside one ear stunned him into silence. "How many times do I have to call you an idiot before you register, idiot?"

Ogden's voice turned deep and Jeb's word *sinister* took on fresh meaning. "Hit me one more time and you'll wish you hadn't."

Jeb had searched on his phone for mandrake, the eerie noise it made coming off his phone when he found the right site. His eyes went wide as silver dollars. "How do you even know this crap, dude?"

Sprite's mouth hung open. "Did Ogden just threaten to poison you?"

Ogden ignored Sprite, and Kimi avoided looking at her.

Allan could see a friendship's foundation crumbling.

"It's just history," Ogden explained. "Our grandmother knows this shit and makes us learn. I told you. It's only botany, Sprite. Nothing more."

"Jeb?" Sprite said, nervous.

Kimi rubbed her temple. "This is scary to them, moron."

Allan took measure of the non-Poes beside him whose discomfort shined for all to see and could easily be misinterpreted as exposure for who they really were. Jeb and Sprite touched shoulders down, in a sort of protective union. Allan bet Jeb held her hand under the table.

"And to think people call *my* mother a witch," Sprite whispered.

Kimi did a smirk thing. "You've mentioned that. Is she a good witch or a bad witch?" She gave her best Glinda voice from *Wizard of Oz*.

"Good," came the reply.

"Do tell," and Kimi rested elbows on the table, chin in hand. "Does she have spells?"

Allan's question had died unanswered, with Kimi taking everyone in a different direction. She wasn't as big an ally to him as he'd expected, a major disappointment. Ogden didn't care. Never had. Nobody answered who laced Allan's food.

Kimi waved her hand in a *spit-it-out* motion to her girlfriend. "Go on. The witch?"

"My mother," Sprite started, but her voice failed her, belying how unsettled she felt. "My mother talks to the occasional spirit and believes in crystals. She sages the house and smokes pot to better connect. She teaches yoga because she believes in the mental effect, the gentle life path taught, not just the exercise."

"She's a psychic, too?"

"To a degree."

"Wait, that's it?" Ogden asked. "She smokes weed until she sees dead people?"

"It's not like that." Sprite pushed on to justify her words. "She's a good witch, but even more, she's a good person."

Ogden switched attention to Jeb. "What about your grandmother? She sounds like bad witch material."

Jeb's teeth clenched from the look of his jaw. "Not up for discussion."

Ogden ignored the hint. "We talked about her mother, why not your grandmother? Hell, I'll tell you all you want to know about my family, as messed up as they are."

Jeb reddened, but Sprite spoke up for the save. "My mother owns who she is and what she believes. Jeb's grandmother doesn't travel in any sort of spiritual circles. She's just a strong woman. She's mayor of Middleton, which says something."

Kimi teetered sideways, directing herself at her brother. "Wait, shouldn't our family know all the mayors around here?"

"Only if they're notable," Ogden answered.

Jeb's complexion reddened at the implication. "Forget my family. I want to hear the answer to Allan's question. Which one of your family is a saboteur?"

When nobody answered, he looked to Kimi.

"I've not touched anyone's food," she said. "But I speak for no one else."

"Me either," her brother echoed then scoffed. "My bet's on your chef. Back her ass in a corner and interrogate her. She has firsthand access, and she uses Grandmother's cookbook. Plus, she's a professional, which means she learned which plants do what, or she isn't worth a damn."

"How sick were you?" Sprite asked Allan.

"ER, stomach-pumping sick the first time. Nauseous and tired the second." Allan chose to remain mute about Jeb's mother being there when he ingested the cookies, and how easily she could've also been affected.

He reached for the free food the owner had brought out and no one but Ogden had touched. Grabbing a sweet potato fry, he dipped into the ranch and appeared to savor the taste as though *duck a l'orange*.

Inside, however, he was disappointed. Maybe out here on the pier hadn't been the best place to question his younger kin, but he thought they'd be more comfortable away from the others.

Honestly, he didn't trust them anymore.

Kimi once again tried to steer the talk back to something non-lethal, literally and figuratively, but her two college friends had lost interest. Ogden turned introspective and dark.

It didn't take long before Kimi realized she was a one-person show, the only one talking and nobody listening hard.

"I think we need to go," Jeb said, standing and not waiting for anyone to agree, pulling Sprite up with him. "I'd like to say we had a good time, but I'd be lying."

Ogden gave a breath of resignation. "Hey, man, I apologize."

"That's saying a lot for him," Kimi quickly said. "I do, too."

Their likenesses as brother and sister made their smiles come across as practiced, but Allan felt they meant the regrets.

"Thanks," Jeb said. "See y'all another time." Then after waiting for Sprite to step clear of the benches, they walked off hand in hand, not giving the Poes a chance to say anything else.

Kimi's smile faded. Ogden turned his attention back to the food.

"Hope y'all are happy with yourselves," Allan said, feeling like the parental figure at the table.

But Kimi didn't accept the rebuke. "You started all this shit by asking who came after you, so don't dump on us. I have no idea who is playing tricks and right now don't care. It didn't happen to me and I didn't do shit, so leave me out of this altogether. Whoever won't tell anyone anyway. They'd be dumb as a rock if they did."

She had a point.

Even as hungry as Allan had been, he'd eaten enough to satisfy, and with the company being so sour, any place was better than here. He started to collect some of the food for later, but he'd have to refrigerate which only exposed him again to everyone in *Maelstrom Manor*.

"It's been real," he said and rose to leave.

"Damn sure has," Ogden said.

Allan left, not needing to explain himself. He needed peace of mind since he'd damn sure not found such here with these two.

He reached the bottom of the ramp, exiting outside instead of winding through the restaurant, when a text came through. *Dinner at six.*

Two hours from now. Good. That would give him time to walk the beach. He wouldn't even take his car home, for fear someone would see him. Instead, he struck out toward the Edisto State Park side of the Pavillion, taking him toward Jeremy Cay and away from anyone at the Poe residence.

He stopped and texted the chef. *Got time to walk the beach? We need to catch up.*

Then, thinking she might only have a few moments before having to orchestrate dinner, he reversed course and headed back west toward *Maelstrom Manor.* Even ten minutes would be nice enough to open a dialogue.

But by the time he reached Access Four on the beach, she hadn't replied. At Access Six, she texted. *Sorry. Busy with dinner. Maybe later tonight.*

Don't forget I'm sous-chef for the birthday dinner on Wednesday, he texted back.

He got a thumbs up, then silence.

He'd made zero strides with neither family members nor Pauline in two days, with his attention focused on feeling ill. Five more days to go, assuming the week didn't end early. Once the birthday party was over, even Grandmother might be eager to forego the rest of the week with the way everyone didn't get along. He might even be the catalyst for that.

Getting back in their good graces seemed increasingly far-fetched.

He almost felt at an impasse, or maybe a crossroad, where he decided whether to give up. . . or take things to a new level.

He refused to grovel, though. He wasn't begging his grandmother to use her influence to land him a job in a King Street restaurant or even out on Mount Pleasant. Accepting that sort of handout would chain him to her, which meant to all the others as well.

He'd rather flip burgers.

So, what exactly was his plan?

Chapter 21

Allan

ALLAN WALKED TWO miles along the water to mute the worry in his head. One mile down almost to *Maelstrom Manor*, and another back to the Pavilion to retrieve his car. By the time he flopped into his driver's seat, his calves were tight as a tension wire holding up the Ravenel Bridge in Charleston. He'd lived on flat land at sea level his entire life between South Carolina and Louisiana, but New Orleans didn't do sand and beaches. The Big Easy sang of marshes and swamps, and nobody walked through those. He was out of practice.

When he pulled into the drive, all the other vehicles were accounted for. Inside, he heard people more than saw them. Someone in the kitchen banged around, speaking to someone else. Someone sang low in Grandmother's bedroom. Another walked around upstairs. Despite the door shutting announcing someone entering the house, nobody cared enough to come out and check.

A trace of sarcasm raced through his mind at the fact the front door wasn't locked. Nobody feared a break-in. Who'd want to mess with the epic horrors of the Poes? Or risk the consequences of messing with them.

Some days he wished his name was Jones.

He hadn't climbed halfway up the stairs before his father caught him. "Feeling all right this evening?"

Finally. Allan appreciated the concern and turned around with genuine gratitude, daring to hope for an invitation to share in a drink on the back porch or something similar. "All's good, Dad. Just got in a long beach walk."

"Good. I don't do much of that anymore. Prefer catching the waves from a chair out back and a bourbon in my hand, enjoying a good sunset."

I wouldn't mind that either.

He didn't bother reminding his father the sun set on the Sound side of the island, but the ocean was beautiful in its own right.

"Wash up for dinner," Eddie said. "It's a half hour from now, and you know how your grandmother is about a schedule."

Allan tried not to let his hope vanish so obviously. Disappointed, he waited for his father to leave. One always let the older family member leave first, eat first, make the first move, but Eddie remained in place. "Smell that?"

Oh hell, not this shit again.

Allan gave an exaggerated sniff. "Seafood."

"Surely you can do better than that."

He sniffed again. "Not just shrimp. A combo, I think." The mixture of seasonings leant itself to a sauce or a stew. "Seafood chowder."

Southern Silver Spoon contained four chowder recipes, and Allan hoped his father didn't ask which one.

Eddie did a light fist bump in the air, looking out of place for the man who never wore less than khakis, loafers and a button up. A man who'd never cheered at a ballgame, including one of Allan's when he was a child. Nobody'd seen the man's knees for decades. "Yes, you still have the talent," Eddie said. "Good job, son." This time he turned and left.

Was this the one-track conversation they'd share all week? *Name That Dish?*

Seafood chowder was an easy-peasy dish to contaminate with about anything. Looks like he'd fret all week about what toxic substance might be added to which food. Tea, cookies, and now maybe chowder. . . and God knows what else. What type of collusion had taken place in his absence? But then, everyone had a phone. One could plan a murder right under the victim's very nose with texts.

All four of the chowders in Grandmother's cookbook were pleasant, but if he were setting up someone, he'd go with the one titled Deeply Lowcountry, with its mixture of shrimp, clams, and crab. Sometimes oysters, depending on the time of year. In the cookbook's long history, that chowder had received the most and the loudest accolades. Cooking for this size group was expensive these days with the cost of shellfish, but then cost wasn't an issue, was it?

Cooking alongside Pauline for the birthday dinner was his present for Grandmother, along with inviting Pauline in the first place. A hundred miles out of New Orleans, he realized he hadn't thought of bringing his own copy of *Southern Silver Spoon,* but he had convinced himself no need with a chef on board and a copy permanently affixed to this kitchen. Now, however, he itched to study the toxins chapter. To steal the lone copy, however, would inconvenience Pauline since Grandmother wanted all meals for the week to come from that tome.

He had to be prepared if retaliation was in order.

Flipping into a bookstore online, he plugged the cookbook title into the search box. He halfway expected Grandmother to have forbidden an ebook format in the publication of her work, but the publisher must have won that toss because there it was. Twenty dollars. A bit steep for an electronic version, but he made the purchase and continued upstairs, noting the little time he had before dinner. Quickly, he located the chowders, scanned the ingredients, imagined the flavors, and stood by his first instinct that the choice would be Deeply Lowcountry.

His father didn't mention side dishes. Maybe Allan could ask for a smaller bowl or pretend to eat. His late lunch had filled him such that he could get by not eating.

Surely there was bread. Sourdough preferably. Homemade from starter, either Chef's or Grandmother's. One couldn't pollute a piece of a loaf and ensure the target got a specific slice. His mouth began watering about the time he caught a whiff of bread coming up the stairs.

Yeah, he could make do with bread, even enjoy a slice, only using butter after he saw someone else test first.

This was going to be a long, strategic, clandestine, watching-over-one's-shoulder week.

Upstairs, once prompted by the cookbook, his old habits gravitated to planning the menu, testing himself to see how close he would come to accuracy. For a salad, a Caesar would be his first choice, with coleslaw second, but the former would be more to Grandmother's taste. Cheesecake or fruit for a soft finish after the heavy entree.

As he dried his hands, he wondered if there would be anything else. Spring vegetables. Roasted broccolini. Nope, a side dish bordered on overkill. Salad, chowder, bread and dessert. Coffee and tea. That would do it.

He missed menu planning. He missed cooking at the hot pace required for a Friday evening crowd, easy jazz in the background tempering the noise. Trying to ignore the painful little tightness in his chest, trying to remember the good of being in The Red Lacey kitchen with none of the bad, he soothed himself with the reminder he'd get his chance at Pauline's side soon enough. They could talk and cook at the same time, possibly broach the subject of him coming to Atlanta.

Washed up, he returned downstairs, but at the dining room entrance, he looked in and stutter-stepped. At the head of the table sat

Grandmother, parked like before, which he assumed was becoming the norm now that she wasn't as stable on her feet. Not only did doing so give her caretakers freedom to do other things, maybe help with the table or tend to their own needs, but also enabled Grandmother to silently reign from her throne as family came and went.

Then like when he arrived that first evening, her gaze locked on him. The woman never seemed to blink.

He would have to be the first to appear, wouldn't he?

Or was he the only one who let her power affect them?

Her eyes didn't flash silver. They weren't gray like everyone else's, but instead held an heirloom hoary color, like antique silver, barely holding onto its polish but respectable enough to retain serious value.

Still striking.

Still dominating.

Still proclaiming worth.

Like before, she wore a color that accented the white hair and silver eyes, and tonight the gentle paisley print of her dress was pastel blue with threads of peach.

And here he was still wearing the slacks he'd worn on the beach. At least he'd changed into a button-up and shed the tee.

There was no way to walk past her without speaking, but he'd been wanting to speak to her anyway, right? Wasn't that the first of his two goals? He'd whined to himself since he arrived at not having the chance, yet here she sat available, so why not grasp the opportunity? Ten minutes until dinner. Surely he could do ten minutes. He could break the ice and make just enough strides then let the normal course of dinner interrupt them.

But he'd never decided exactly what to say.

Pasting on what he hoped looked like a loving grin, he approached, eased out the nearest chair with no noise, and sat. "We haven't had a chance to talk, have we, Grandmother? It's been a while."

She studied him, ear to ear, brow to chin. A way to intimidate, he assumed. She'd always been good at making people think twice about who they were and how they should express themselves without her saying a word.

"How are you feeling today?" he asked, going with a question that couldn't be deemed rhetorical. Anyone would ask this of someone her age.

She sat backbone stiff, hands clasped before her on the table beside a cup of tea. But up close, the veins in her hands, the folds of her neck, and the age spots on her cheeks gave the woman a less vibrant and less relevant persona Allan hoped he would never endure.

"I'm tolerable for an ancient lady," she finally said, as if she sensed his awareness of her vulnerabilities.

A mixture of feelings unexpectedly rose into his throat.

He'd never in his life experienced sympathy for Doris Woolf Poe, and he wasn't comfortable feeling such now.

She'd never given anyone a chance to think of her as anything but powerful. But age had a way of leveling the field.

"Well, you're looking good," he added. Another cliché, and he had no idea if she looked good for a lady of eighty or not, but etiquette mattered.

This was good. Silly, but her answering his question, one in no way directed at anyone else, gave him a sense of access, like she'd acknowledged his presence, and he was welcome to enter. Their separation these three years had labeled her as someone posed on a pedestal in his head, and while he'd rarely held long-winded conversations with her before, the honor of her spending one-on-one time with him was real.

In those few seconds, those few words, his mind had cast off into a whirl of second thoughts, uncertainty, and a hint of shame about the image he'd formed of her. He hated that this family didn't understand true feelings, because here sat alone the woman who'd raised, taught, hired, and enabled all of them. And nobody talked to her.

Up close, she wasn't the ogre he'd painted her as. Her humanity was solid.

"Still cooking?" she asked, ignoring his comment about how she looked. The tenor of her voice said she was way past that.

"I am," he said. "I'm not employed at present, but feelers are out. Something will come through." He sounded like such a teenager, promising he'd bring that C grade up to an A. "That ordeal in New Orleans did a number on me, Grandmother. I'm allowing the dust to settle." He almost held back the next comment but then figured what the hell did he have to lose. "And I don't want to ask you for a job. I'd rather succeed on my own."

Her expression was minor, but it did shift at that piece of information. He hoped he looked good. He didn't want to ask her to pave the way for him. That would make someone hire him for connection rather than his talent.

Should he tell her about his plans to pitch Pauline? No. She might talk to the others. Then talk would reach Pauline before he could query the chef directly.

He couldn't take that chance.

"I've missed you," he said instead, almost groaning how untrue that might sound being they hadn't spoken for years. Maybe the burden had been more on him to call her than vice versa since he'd been the one to leave, to remain distant. A small piece of him was hurt, however, at the family not reaching out.

Living in New Orleans, he learned to blame his upbringing and family arrogance when he got angry. When sad he blamed them for the alienation. When he was happy. . . he couldn't recall when that was. At least since the fiasco at The Red Lacey Inn.

"Have you now?" she asked, snatching him back. "Missed me?"

He gave himself a second. "Yes, I believe I have missed you." He was probably more surprised than she was at his answer.

"Why, pray tell? You're not just missing the name?" she added right on his heels. "The influence?" She stopped short of saying the money, though he'd rather slit his throat than sell real estate like the others.

"Um, the name sort of follows you around," he said. "No dodging it, trust me."

She would be aware of that more than anyone else. Touting both Woolf and Poe, her maiden and married names, both signed, printed, and exhibited on everything, she'd endured a lifetime of people asking about historic literary connections. Distantly related to both authors, she fully owned those branches of her family tree. People were always in awe, like sharing even small pieces of a certain bloodline enabled you with powers.

It made her memorable, he'd heard her explain more than once.

She'd gone silent, watching him.

"But out of everyone here, Grandmother, I've missed Kimi the most," he said, picking things back up. "Then I'd have to say you." He gave the wry smile used to win over people when he was working. "Hope you don't mind."

Her brow lightly rose. Her lips possibly lifted on one end.

He'd surprised himself. He seriously wasn't lying. He missed who she was, missed being a part of something bigger, and Grandmother was the emblem of that. While away from the family, the negative of being a Poe seemed to represent how he envisioned home, but back here in the thick of the Poe kingdom, he could acknowledge a positive or two. There was a sense of satisfaction in the Poe effect.

He just hated most of the Poes.

And from the way his food had been messed with, one or more of them wasn't too keen about him.

"Why is someone trying to hurt me, Grandmother?" he asked before realizing he'd spoken what was on his mind before giving the thought an edit.

"Why do you think that, Allan? What would make anyone even do that?"

Why did her using his name sound so good?

He voiced all the reasons easily since they'd taken up such a strong residence in his head. "Because I left Charleston and didn't call? Because I didn't follow in the family footsteps and go into real estate? Because I shamed the name with that scandal in New Orleans, and y'all had to come to my rescue? I didn't do what they said I did. They fired me to say they addressed the tragedy, and to pacify you. The police couldn't prove I did anything. I could have fought, but. . . well, you know how those days played out since you orchestrated everything."

Another brow rose in measure of him.

"Grandmother, I'm not belittling who the Poes are, but really, what did I do that was so egregious to merit monkshood and ergot in my food?"

"Could've been worse," she said, turning her head in wait for him to acknowledge same.

"Yes, I know, which is why I think this is a prank or a message. . ."

"Or what?" she asked when he trailed off.

"Or a dare," he answered.

"A dare, you say?" Her voice rose at the end, almost like she hadn't seen that remark coming, but he doubted that. She was too wise.

"Yes, like they are testing me, Grandmother. Infecting me to see if I still have the skills to not only identify but also to sling back."

"I see," she said.

"Do you have any idea who?"

"You asked that," she said, meaning she was not inclined to answer the question. Slow and deliberately, she lifted her cup, a slight tinkling as the cup tapped the saucer before she achieved full grip.

Maybe he'd gone too far. Who was he to ask questions when he was the prodigal son? A grandmother loved all her family, the good and the bad. He hoped so, at least.

"Sorry, of course you wouldn't know," he said.

But he bet she had her guesses.

She sipped, not bothering to answer one way or the other.

Lacey flew out of the kitchen like she'd been ejected. Mumbling to herself, she drew up short at Grandmother and Allan. "Almost time for dinner," she said, as if that was her duty. She commenced inspecting the table straightening place settings, each of them, adjusting every fork, napkin, and water glass.

"Thanks for the talk," Allan said to his grandmother. "I enjoyed our time together, and I hope we pick this up again."

Pauline whooshed out, kitchen scents blowing through with her strong and savory, her hands full of dishes. "Bet y'all are getting hungry, huh?"

Lacey left without a word.

Ten minutes had come and gone. The dinner hour had arrived, and the chef was keeping pace.

"Mind if we talk later?" he asked his grandmother.

"Don't mind at all," she said, then removed her forearms from the table as Pauline began setting for supper.

Kimi entered, winking at him. Breezing past into the kitchen, she slapped him lightly on the butt, like nothing had happened at lunch.

Lacey scurried back in. "Anything you need, Mother? You haven't been too lonely out here, have you?"

Grandmother didn't bother to reply, and Lacey didn't wait for an answer.

In waltzed Aunt Kimberly, then Nurse Shannon.

Then the doorbell rang.

Everyone peered at each other, looking for who was to blame for a visitor at this inopportune time. None of them made a move toward the door.

Until Allan did.

He opened as the visitor rapped knuckles in her second announcement.

"Oh, sorry," the small woman said. "Saw all the cars, but when nobody answered right away, I wondered if the bell was broken."

She held a basket. Middle-aged, she capitalized on her attractiveness in the colors and draped fabric she wore, all of which accented her eye color, a distinct shade of aqua. Coral nails carefully tended. A dozen thin bracelets on her wrists.

"Let's see," she said, giving him a side-eyed look. "Could you be Allan?"

Reluctantly, he extended his hand. "I might be."

Eddie came up behind him. "Who is it, son?"

"Not sure, Dad." Both waited.

A hand went up on her collarbone in Southern belle manner. "Honey, I'm Sophie Bianchi. Here." She handed over the basket to Eddie. "These are mystery cookies. They are much beloved by my family, and I wanted to see if the infamous Poe palate could identify the mystery ingredient."

The Bianchi name piqued Allan's memory, reminding him of the lunch conversation centered around speaking Italian, spaghetti, and algebra. "Are you related to Sprite?"

"Absolutely. Her mother. I am the unofficial welcome wagon around here, and since I heard all y'all were here, which never happens, I felt the need to bring you goodies to help you celebrate whatever has brought you together."

In handing over the basket, she had nudged Eddie and Allan back, so she proceeded to cross the threshold in typical Sophie fashion. "Mind if I come in?" Then she halted. "What is that I smell?" Twisting back around, she feigned embarrassment. "I'm not interrupting dinner, am I?"

Allan saw where Sprite got her spitfire. Clearly Sprite had talked to her mother about lunch, and mother had decided to check out the Poes. Maybe to make sure that Jeb and Sprite weren't in the doghouse for Ogden's fall at Coot's. Maybe because that's just who she was, the nosy witch of Edisto Beach.

"Of course you're not interrupting," Eddie said, offering his arm for her to take. "We were about to sit down to supper, but I'm sure we can find another chair for one of Edisto's finest ladies. Come with me, and I won't take no for an answer."

Well, this was opportune. Chances were less that anyone would alter Allan's food with an outsider in the room. Maybe he'd get a decent meal after all.

He'd taken the basket from his father when he'd taken charge of the guest. Nothing looked odd about them. Still warm, too. He hadn't had a chance to ask why the cookies were a mystery, and these days, he wasn't too big on taste-testing food for what it might contain.

Chapter 22

Callie

CALLIE LEFT COOTS and returned to patrolling the streets. The three young Poes held a sense of entitlement, but not too terribly more than most of the affluent visitors to Edisto Beach. They weren't overdoing the beers. More importantly, they'd overlooked Jeb's table nudge that took Ogden to the pier floor.

Allan had looked out of place, but age difference and her previous interview with Pauline explained that. He'd just returned to the fold. Of course, he'd pal around with the younger Poes versus his father's generation.

Kimi acted the most privileged. Ogden, however, held a nastiness that didn't set well with Callie. A boy who tugged against authority but didn't have the intestinal fortitude to fight very hard, therefore, painting him as a bully with no teeth. Callie tried never to judge quickly, but she never ignored her gut either. With no purpose, he appeared too weak to test his tethers and seek a future of his own liking. An assumption, sure, but there was an unsettling aura coming off that boy.

Then a thought came to her. Monkshood and mandrake were two of the mentioned poisons in the Poe repertoire. They could be little more than sugar or a cousin to ricin, for all she knew. She pulled over to the curb on Palmetto and placed a call.

"Callie, how nice," Donna Baird answered.

Callie listened to see if she could tell whether the woman was outdoors or in, because she lived for walking her Great Dane. This time of year was made for such long walks. She heard a car go by, then taking the phone aside, she told Horse to heel.

"You two out for a stroll?" she asked.

"The three of us," Donna replied. "I'm standing here while Stan jabbers with people. Horse is getting restless. He likes to move."

"Where exactly?" If she wasn't far, no point in a phone. Phones made her cut sentences short, and that often came with misunderstanding.

"Dolphin Street," she said. "Thought the two boys would prefer walking on silted roads for a change."

Which meant Stan. The dog could go for miles. Stan, after his broken leg last fall, still managed a challenge or two.

Callie covered the two blocks in no time, finding them still standing in front of someone's full-time residence, Stan leaning on a cane with one hand and accenting his words with the other. Callie parked the car in the drive of an empty rental.

"Chicklet," Stan said, welcoming Callie for a hug. She loved this old boss of hers. He was one of few on this beach who understood the depth of her experiences, both personal and professional. Even more than Mark, her fulltime guy.

She gave Stan a second squeeze, apologized to the neighbor he was talking to, then asked, "Mind if I borrow your girlfriend?"

Stan quickly returned to telling his story to his friend, and Donna wandered further away for privacy, accustomed to having these professional talks with the chief of police. A completely different relationship than Callie used to have with another councilman until he tried to show up Callie and do her job, getting himself killed by making the wrong traffic stop.

"What's up?" Donna asked, motioning for Horse to sit.

"What can you tell me about monkshood?" Callie asked.

A surprised look flashed across the other woman's face. "Gorgeous flower. Looks like a delphinium. Toxic as hell. Contains an alkaloid called aconitine that affects nerves, blood pressure and heart rate. Tingling, vomiting. Featured in Harry Potter to help Remus Lupin in his shift to a werewolf, in case that interests you. I love that series." Then of course, she had to ask the obvious question. "Why?" Then curiosity made her ask, "Is someone sick? Are you needing me right now? Is this urgent?" Donna might be a veterinarian, but she'd come in handy a time or two when that's all the medical help they had for forty miles.

Callie pushed down the air before her. "It's done and over with, so no emergency."

"Thank God for that."

Callie rubbed Horse around an ear. "Can't really say the who, Donna. Have you seen monkshood much? If someone tastes any, does the residual wash on through the system or is there a long-term residual effect?" Callie could've asked Allan, but that opportunity had passed, plus she wanted an answer from someone who'd only divulge facts, not a slanted opinion.

"Assuming the dose wasn't a lethal amount," Donna replied, "monkshood can have some residual in the liver, and effects can harm the heart. But a small dose gets eliminated within a few hours. But I've never had firsthand experience, but I just used to read up on these things because pets are more prone to accidentally ingest something like that."

"Thanks. So," Callie began, trying to word this properly. "If the patient was given charcoal and lots of water, and the dose was small, they'd recuperate. I mean, they'd go home from the hospital and maybe not even spend the night?"

Donna looked skeptical, trying to fill in blanks. "Correct. Callie, what happened? Anyone I know?" She paused then asked, "Was this intentional?"

Thumbs hooked on her belt, Callie peered back at Stan, picking what to say. "The scare is over and the person is fine. I was only worried about long-term effect, and you answered that."

"I'd certainly follow up with my doctor to make sure, but yes."

"Hmmm," Callie said, then moved on. "What about ergot?"

Donna's frown deepened. "That one isn't nearly as much of a problem. LSD used to be extracted from the fungus, and years ago it was used to cause abortions. You find it on rye, and farmers are wary, sometimes rinsing a harvested crop in a salt solution." With a concerned expression, she exclaimed, "What the hell is happening? This isn't spreading to restaurants or anything, is it?" As council woman, she had a genuine concern.

"No. All contained," Callie said. "Someone played tricks with the stuff."

"What?"

Callie laid a hand on her friend's forearm. "All is contained, Donna. Please don't spread anything. You answered my questions."

But the retired veterinarian looked distrusting.

"Had a case involving hemlock a while back, and I learned it grows in ditches everywhere," Callie said. "I didn't spread that news around either, because people freak when they realize they don't know what they don't know."

They'd also freak if they were aware of the harsh crimes that she'd averted under everyone's noses. To include murder.

"I need to get back to work," she said. "Y'all have a good walk. Keep Stan happy and healthy for me." She turned to leave.

But Donna wasn't satisfied. "We don't want this sort of person on the beach, Callie. I feel I need to know more."

"They're leaving by the end of the week. I say disaster averted," Callie repeated, seeing where this was going. She could tell Donna that worse cases than this had been kept quiet from the population, but that would push the council woman to ask which cases, when, were they closed, and were those dangers removed from Edisto Beach.

"It turned out to be pranks," she added, kidnapping Allan's word for things. "I wanted to be wiser for the future. From what you've told me, nothing to be concerned about."

"Still. . ."

"How many cases of monkshood did you treat?"

"None."

"And ergot?"

"Maybe one. The farmer wasn't wanting the word to spread so he swept his concerns under the rug."

Callie held out her hands in a shrug. "You just certified why this isn't a situation."

Donna didn't speak but one could see her mind still churned.

"Gotta get back to work. Thanks," Callie said. "Didn't mean to upset you." Then she yelled over at Stan. "Bye, old man."

Without another pause, she entered her cruiser, waved to everyone and left. No, escaped was more like it.

Shit. She should've kept that to herself. Also, that conversation went far in justifying when to choose to open a case. An open case meant more ready access by town council. If she'd opened this case, and no Poe wanted the family's dirty laundry aired, the town might find itself up against a lawsuit, too.

And to think Beverly thought law enforcement wasn't politics.

Once back on Palmetto Boulevard, she instinctively headed to check Dawhoo Street and the house with the dumpster that Johnny Scott seemed to be so fond of these days. Funny how this was a case on record. These were the types of situations town council preferred. They could nod as Callie informed them, then nod again when she said she'd handle matters. Anything more controversial, and they stuck their heads in the proverbial sand, ever willing to point fingers of blame on her practically for allowing such behavior in the first place.

The dumpster was still on site. Its house stood on the eight hundred side of the street, the other side being in the seven hundreds, considered a separate block. Halfway down, the dumpster remained, and while not filled to the brim, bits of old lumber poked up on one side, warranting needed relief soon.

The repairs ought to be almost done here. Mrs. Chester was sixty-five. Callie's office manager life-long Edisto resident Marie guessed Mrs. Chester had lived in that same house for as long as she and Callie had been alive. Mr. Chester died a decade ago, and their two children loved being able to visit the beach for free, so they'd pressured their mother to remain there. For her own good, they'd said, even if Mrs. Chester wasn't as spry running up and down those stairs as she used to be. Said children had also suggested an elevator, one of those simple ones big enough for one person and a bag of groceries. None had ever come forth and offered to pay, though.

Yeah, Marie was a goldmine of intel on this beach.

Instead, Mrs. Chester's fixed income and mediocre level of investments paid for living expenses, medical bills, the extravagant amount of taxes and insurance required to live on a beach, and repairs. Beach houses warranted repairs that inland folk couldn't fathom. Right now, her contractor was finishing up a new roof, having replaced boards on the porch and a few stairs, two items that quickly wore out on every house in town.

But being that she was alone, didn't rent the residence, and the job was considered minor per your average beach-focused general contractor, the length of time had stretched beyond the norm. She was high and dry and didn't need the rent to live on, so she became the job tended when others were through.

Age pushed others of a lesser age to take advantage, brush off, and ignore. And these elders could do little about being discounted, because to fuss was to be labeled a curmudgeon. But there were no laws broken in any of that to draw Callie's attention.

Not unless you counted Johnny Scott taking advantage of Mrs. Chester's dumpster as a crime, which Callie did. What good was a cop unless they stood for the underdog? She liked to believe someone would be there for her when she reached that point and lived alone with limitations.

For good measure, Callie pulled into the Dawhoo Street address. The trim around the eave remained unpainted and the outside stairs unstained. Caution tape draped across stair access, top and bottom, so she walked around to the back entrance, taking those stairs up to the screen door.

"Mrs. Chester?" she called, the nice weather allowing the owner to leave her main door open for the pass-through breeze. Not something she'd do as someone older and vulnerable, but Callie and her people attempted to police the area well enough to allow residents like this to enjoy where they lived.

Gentle footsteps sounded from sneakered feet. The homeowner appeared, wiping her hands on a rag, an end tucked in the belt of oversized cargo pants. Her hair had given up the ghost to total gray, and she kept it long and bound on top of her head. Tendrils fell around her face that wore not a drop of makeup.

"Can I help you? Oh, Chief Morgan. Is there something wrong?" Mrs. Chester paused. "Is that man using my dumpster again? I haven't been notified of new picture on my porch camera, but I can double check."

Nobody used her first name Abigail. She'd been Mrs. Chester as long as anyone could recall.

She reached up and unlatched the screen door. "Come on in, if you don't mind. I'm in the middle of making cornbread, and I've got tea about to boil on the stove." She turned and strolled back the direction from which she'd come.

They hadn't reached the kitchen doorway before Callie figured out the meal. The cornbread helped. A crockpot did its business on the counter, the timer indicating three hours, the smell indicating chili. Jalapenos were half diced on a cutting board shaped like the state of South Carolina. Cheese sat shredded in a bowl covered with plastic wrap.

Mrs. Chester flipped off the burner under the pot of water and left the tea bags in the almost-boiling water to steep. "You're invited to stay, if you like," she said. Then to Callie's surprise, she dumped the jalapenos into the cornbread mix instead of the chili, then in rote habit, she grabbed a well-worn, a bit scorched, potholder and lifted a cast-iron skillet of sizzling butter from the oven with unexpected strength. In went the cornbread batter, the sizzle popping only for a few seconds before settling. She shook the skillet a bit to even out the batter, then shoved it back in the oven, setting the timer for twenty minutes.

"There's plenty to share," Mrs. Chester said.

Though the smell was lovely, Callie ate Mexican at El Marko's with Mark. Maybe she could do a taste comparison?

"You ever enter Whaley's Chili Cookoff?" Callie asked. The annual event took place in January with every eatery in the area throwing their hat in the competition, although oysters ran a strong second as enticement for a large crowd to show. Live music and a bar helped as well. "If this tastes half as good as the smell, you'd be a contender. When will it be ready?"

"Half hour," she replied.

Too long to wait. "I hate to miss, but I'm on duty. I stopped by to ask if you've seen your dumpster guy of late."

"No," she said. "Sorry."

Callie chuckled. "Nothing to feel sorry about. Maybe he's behaving." Then she pointed to the back door. "You leave yourself vulnerable with the door open like that. Not necessarily from him but from others."

"The screen door's locked," she said. "I can exit the front if I hear anything." She clicked her tongue. "I have a concealed weapons permit. Had the thing since when Jordan was still alive."

Cocking her head at the surprise, Callie asked, "What kind of weapon?"

"Snub nosed .38. Just enough to work. Small enough to be manageable. Easy enough to reload."

Like she would need to reload a weapon if anyone broke in. "Where do you keep it?"

"In my bedroom. It'd be stupid to keep it anywhere else, don't you think?"

Mrs. Chester hadn't been precise, but Callie wouldn't either if she were asked that question. "Any other weapons? If I need to come to your rescue some night, I'd like to know what I'm up against."

Mrs. Chester snickered. "Only the one weapon, locked up safe."

If Johnny Scott only knew which he didn't need to, of course.

"I wanted to let you know I've stopped Mr. Scott twice and left him with tickets once. I'm hoping he's done, but sometimes stupid isn't selective. Call if he comes again."

"You don't think he's casing my place, do you?" the older woman asked.

Good question. "No, I really don't, but one can never be too safe."

Mrs. Chester was a long timer here. Johnny Scott was new. She'd earned the community's trust, but the jury remained out on him.

Callie stood. "I've really got to go. Again, only checking on you."

"I'll make sure the gun's clean."

That was not quite the response Callie wanted, but she couldn't tell a gun owner not to keep their weapon clean. "The responsible thing to do, but please don't tell anyone you have it."

Mrs. Chester scowled. "I might be approaching senior citizenhood, but I'm a long shot from dementia, Chief." Then her expression fell into humor. "You should see yourself. If I couldn't be trusted, I'd have shot the bastard. Don't worry yourself, young lady. I have never been a problem for you before. Don't intend to be one to you now."

"Enter the cookoff," Callie said, heading to the door. "They need new competition."

After ensuring the screen door was latched behind her, Callie left, still unsure why Johnny Scott chose this address to steal dumpster space from. Without hardly thinking she could list four more houses under renovation, all of which the owners weren't occupying. Johnny could dump his stuff in those dumpsters, at night, after the contractors had gone home.

Maybe he was casing the place, but for what serious reason? He wasn't lacking economically, not considering the house he bought and what he was doing to refurbish the structure. Nice vehicle. Plus Mrs. Chester wasn't exactly rolling in assets. Being old enough to be his mother, she wasn't any other kind of attraction either.

With Mrs. Chester warned, Johnny Scott ticketed, and the other officers aware, hopefully this situation was moot now. Callie hadn't ever spent much time with this particular resident, and she was glad she had this evening. It never hurt to collect karma credits.

Her phone rang. Jeb. "Hold on, son. Give me a sec."

She didn't want to hang in Mrs. Chester's front yard without explanation, so she cranked up the cruiser and moved two houses farther to an empty rental and parked off the road. "There. What's up? Ogden's still okay about the fall, isn't he?"

Jeb blew a nonchalant breath into the phone. "Oh that? History, Mom. I feel bad, but a small piece of me wasn't. Especially after the rest of the conversation."

Okay, he had her attention now.

Chapter 23

Callie

JEB WAS STILL getting over the incident with Ogden at Coots. Callie might see him as close to perfection, but even through the rose-colored glasses of a mother, Callie raised a boy to do for others and not seek revenge. His shocked look of regret was real when Ogden hit the floor at Coot's.

What had changed?

"Care to share your concern?" she asked. She'd played hooky off and on most of the day between Beverly, Sophie, and then the kids. A face-to-face with Jeb might have to wait until she went off duty.

"That family messes with poisons," he exclaimed. "Did you know that?" But he didn't wait for an answer, the question clearly rhetorical. "Allan thinks he's already been poisoned. Kimi tried to prove to him she wasn't involved, but he wasn't sure he trusted her. Ogden says he didn't do anything, but who can tell with that dimwit. Then he launched into talk about how you use mandrake root, almost respecting the stuff because of ancient Greek history. At that point, Sprite and I completely lost our appetites. We left them arguing." He moaned. "We never saw that side of Kimi at school, Mom. Not at all. I'm not shocked at Ogden, but, geez, he was way too knowledgeable about something people shouldn't be."

If Callie had stayed longer, or Jeb had left earlier, the kids would be ignorant about their friends. Good thing the conversation unfolded like it did. The Poes had a demented sense of humor and an air of dominance she preferred her children not experience.

Not so much Allan, but he'd been away from the drama long enough to dilute his behavior. He had returned to the fold, though, so his Poe behaviors might fall back into play.

Callie didn't share what she'd gathered about *Maelstrom Manor*. Jeb would tell Sprite who would tell Sophie, and the whole of Edisto Beach didn't need to think of the Poes as witches and warlocks. With the kids distancing themselves by choice, she was satisfied that they need not learn more.

"Grandma is less of a bitch in Sprite's opinion now after hearing about how the Poes roll," he said. "Having a comparison sort of diluted her feelings."

Good to hear. Callie had wondered whether Sprite and Beverly would smooth things out or continue to lock horns. In-laws were always an adjustment.

A blue light lit up to her right on Palmetto. Officer Annie had snared a speeder.

"Mom? You there?"

"Yes, son. Anything else?" She needed to return to patrol especially while Annie was occupied.

The seconds of hesitation told her he was about to say something she might not want to hear, though, and she waited.

"About the three moms," he said, halting again.

"Miss Sophie, me, and Grandma? Are those the three?" she asked, to be certain and to say something to help along whatever this was.

"Yeah." A brief pause. "Let's say that we'll ask for help when needed, okay?"

"Go on."

"Let us do school. Let us figure out what we want to do. Hell, Mom, let us decide if we are even a couple. Y'all have us engaged, married, having kids, and our kids running Middleton forty years from now. That makes us uncomfortable."

"I hear you."

"But do you think I'm right?" he asked. "We don't want walls going up here."

For a couple of years, she'd been telling Beverly to leave Jeb alone about where he took his career. Here lately, she'd been leaning on Sophie as well. Callie tried not to interfere, but on the other hand she wondered if they thought she ignored them.

"Yes, understood, son. I'll try not to butt in."

"Who says we're a permanent couple?" he said, escalating, almost like he hadn't heard her.

She hoped otherwise. "True that." The family head-butting could have made them think harder about that very topic. Families were so damn dysfunctional. She felt rather blessed growing up in a small family. In her experience more people only incited more problems.

"I thought you'd be more opinionated than this," he said.

"I'm only wanting you happy, son." What else could she say and not make a mistake. "Is Sprite with you? She okay?"

He let out a small laugh. Good, Callie liked hearing him laugh. "Sprite went straight next door after lunch to vent and bake cookies with her mother. Miss Sophie said she had to deliver them to someone this evening. I didn't want to sit around and listen. I'm playing a new video game that came out a week ago, enjoying the solitude."

Sophie hadn't said anything about cookies. She spoke openly about her daily plans and who might be involved and her impact on others' lives. If she wasn't in someone's business, she was talking to her friends about what business they were in so she could join.

Sophie didn't bake much either. Sophie didn't eat anything with cane sugar or white flour.

What was up and who was she trying to impress? Or better, whose business was she trying to insert herself into?

"Is that something they do?" she asked. "Mother and daughter baking cookies?"

Callie wasn't any more of a baker than Sophie, but the thought of enjoying such a afternoon tugged at her. The cozy thought left her empty while at the same time released a memory that she was ashamed had become more distant.

The daughter she could've shared such time with died of SIDS before her first birthday. The child had been an accidental pregnancy later in their marriage, having arrived when Jeb was in middle school, but that loss almost destroyed the marriage. Then her husband John had to go and get killed a year after that.

A knot filled her throat. Her daughter would be in elementary school now. A real person eager to crack the eggs and lick the beaters.

"You okay?" Jeb asked.

"I'm fine. Got a couple of cases tugging at me. The thought of making cookies sounded rather nice, making me wish I could do something like that."

"You want to meet me at El Marko's for dinner?" he asked, and the thoughtfulness drew tears to her eyes.

"Sure. When?" Her heart warmed at the chance to sit across the table at him. Once he got married, these types of moments would be rare. Sophie would want a piece of them, and so would Beverly. Their lives would grow fuller, and they'd forget about parents left in the wings.

"Mom? Did you hear me? I asked if in an hour would be good."

"An hour. Yeah, that works."

"See you then." He hung up.

She kept threatening to record their conversations so that one day, when he was too busy adulting to share time with her, she could listen to the once-upon-a-times when it was only the two of them.

Slipping her phone into her pocket, she pulled back onto the road, paused at the stop sign and turned right on Palmetto.

Feeling like six, she started when she noted a quarter past seven on her dash. One tour around the beach town then she'd park at El Marko's, even if a tad early for Jeb. Marie had gone home by now, and the beach would be winding down. Her night officer should've come on duty.

She might as well take a drive past Johnny Scott's house up ahead. If all was good, she'd finish her route and be done.

Johnny Scott was loading empty paint buckets, insulation scraps, and a mishmash of trash into the back of his pickup. His dumpster was gone.

When he acted like he didn't see her, despite no other car on the small street, she rolled down her window. "Mr. Scott?"

He shifted things in his truck bed like they had to be dealt with first, then gawked at her like he didn't recognize her. What was he up to?

"Where's your dumpster?" she asked, pointing to the debris.

"Picked up," he said. "I'm about done, and I didn't want to pay that price with only the little junk left."

Patiently she sat, hoping he'd tack on the rest of his explanation, something along the line of where he was dumping this last load. "Bulk debris is picked up on Tuesdays," she said.

Regular house trash was picked up on Mondays, and the service had already been through the town. With no sign of his trash cans, he must have taken them in, unless he had his kitchen bags of trash beneath the junk in his truck. The scraps were allowed to be stacked on the edge of the road, ready for tomorrow.

She couldn't believe she was thinking this hard about trash. "Want me to help you pile it on the curb?"

"No, can't let you do that," he said and moved to the back of the truck as if blocking.

Her in the car, him leaning against his tailgate, they appeared at some weird unspoken stalemate.

"I just came from Mrs. Chester's house," she said.

"Who?"

She pretended he was serious. "The lady whose dumpster you keep using."

"Oh."

She almost got out of the car but told herself he wasn't worth the effort. He feigned ignorance, but she had neither energy nor reason to ticket him.

"I don't think you want to cross that woman," she finally said. "She's a handful, and I don't want to come save you."

He burst out laughing, forgetting he'd just acted unfamiliar with Chester. "I've seen her, Chief. I believe I can handle myself well enough."

Callie started to ask if he was armed but thought better. He didn't need to know Mrs. Chester had a weapon, and he didn't need to arm himself in case she was. A quick memory of Brice LeGrand being gunned down at his infamous traffic stop flashed back to mind for the second time this afternoon. "Well, you best leave her alone, Mr. Scott."

"Sounds ominous, but I'm happy to take your advice, Chief. Anything else I can help you with?"

Callie'd wasted enough time, enough maybe to make him think twice about where he dumped his trash and save her from some trouble tomorrow. "Have a good day," she said, and once he reciprocated the wave, she left.

It was close enough to dinner time to circle Palmetto to Dock Site Road then up Jungle Road to the restaurant and be done.

She made her lazy run along the all-too-familiar route, more slowly along the Sound side where sunsets could be mesmerizing. Hardly anyone stirred along the marina side. Finally, she came around Lybrand and turned onto Jungle Road.

A radio call gave her a small jolt since everything had seemed so serene, after she'd mentally slid into the end of work.

"Ambulances dispatched to Palmetto Boulevard. Two adult victims."

Dispatch relayed the house number. Callie took a split second to sync the road address with a house name, the latter more of how they kept up with activity in the town.

Maelstrom Manor.

Chapter 24

Allan

DESPITE THE VISITOR arriving unannounced, Eddie gushed over Mrs. Bianchi, escorting her to the dining room with a grin wide enough to pinch his ears. Allan followed behind holding the basket of cookies, guessing Sprite's mother was aware of the lunch debacle at Coot's, where Jeb all but knocked Ogden to the floor and Sprite worried the Poes were dangerous.

So much for talking to Grandmother any more tonight. Drama had stolen the show.

By the time they entered the dining room, the entire family was present. Kimberly was seated as was the nurse beside Grandmother in the same seat Allan had used. Lacey ran in and out of the kitchen trying to assist Chef while Chef tried to tell her to get out of her way. The two youngers hung to the side, clearly not wanting to sit until they had to.

"Everyone, this is Sophie Bianchi," Eddie announced, and all stopped to listen. "She claims she's the local welcome wagon and wants to make us feel at home." He motioned to Allan who promptly set the basket down on the edge of the sideboard against the wall.

"She brought dessert," Eddie said, then he lightly nudged Sophie. "Tell them, honey, what you said about the cookies."

Allan almost gagged at Eddie's awkward attempt to sound genteel, his flirtations rusty as hell. Even Kimi turned away, a hand over her mouth to hide the smirk. Unaware how unnatural he appeared, Eddie shined. God, the man couldn't be that lonely, could he?

"Well," Sophie started, pointing to the basket. "These are called mystery cookies, because they contain an unexpected ingredient. Nobody ever guesses it on the first taste. Even the first cookie. I won't tell you where I got the recipe, but the recipe was altered to my own liking. Don't you go Googling, either." She giggled, her whole body moving when she spoke, a bright yellow and cream exotic skirt dancing in her effort to absorb attention.

Allan now deemed Sprite Bianchi far less exuberant and spirited than he'd originally thought. She was slow motion compared to her mother.

Eddie was smitten. Allan had to admit the longer Sophie talked, sucking in each personality as she addressed the room, the more attractive she became. Her gaze was magnetic, her voice enticing, her movements easy like someone who knew her body.

Maybe that was the clue to the magic. She didn't care that anyone knew that she used herself that way, because it worked.

Grandmother broke the spell, of course. "Why don't we eat first, dear, before we judge your wares?"

Sophie stopped her antics. "You said *dear.* I know someone else's mother who uses that endearment, and she wields that word like a gavel." Sophie winked. "Am I right?"

I'll be damned. She's flirting with Grandmother.

But all Grandmother did was smile. Sophie smiled back, the silent exchange indicating they'd somehow found a commonality only the two of them understood.

Eddie seated Sophie in Allan's place, and the rest sat, with Allan shifting to the right next to Kimi.

Pauline walked in balancing four plates of Caesar salad, stopping in mid-stride at the addition of another diner. She didn't object, and she didn't stop and ponder what to do. She set the four salads in place then extracted another place setting from the sideboard stationed against the paneled wall.

"I, um had a rather large lunch," Sophie said, as a salad bowl was placed before her.

Eddie leaned over. "Don't feel you have to eat everything. You won't hurt anyone's feelings here. You didn't expect to be asked to dinner."

She leaned into him. "Are you sure I'm not intruding?"

Allan watched the dynamics between the two with interest, and from the kick under the table, Kimi did also. Peering down the table, Allan noted Grandmother studying the pair as well.

The Caesar dressing was from scratch, the croutons homemade and exceptional for some undefinable reason. For a second he worried he'd been handed another toxic prank. Or should he accept the possibility that Chef Pauline had outdone herself in concocting something unique to accent such a simple salad?

By now, at the end of the second day of celebration week, along with several notable meals, attention had morphed from Grandmother to Allan. Three bites into his salad, he caught everyone scrutinizing him.

He held up his bowl. "Hey, I'm willing to trade with anyone."

No one took him up on the offer, turning back to their own. All except Sophie who studied the table like she'd missed something.

"I'll trade with you," Kimi offered, staring with proud defiance at her family. "Anyone want to stop me?"

She reached over the traded salads with Allan and then took an obnoxiously large bite of salad and crouton. Again, nobody reacted.

"See there?" Kimi said to her cousin. "All's good." Then with embellishment she exchanged silverware with him. Finally with a snicker, she exchanged water glasses and drank.

Yep, she still had that crazy streak in her.

"Pauline did a grand job with this dressing," he said. "And these croutons, damn." He popped one into his mouth. Only then did he get a rise out of anyone, that being Aunt Kimberly scowling at him using his fingers.

Sophie, however, after watching the small performance, and probably after hearing what Sprite had replayed about the lunch conversation, pushed hers to the side.

"Something wrong, Mrs. Bianchi?" Allan asked.

"I'm not much of a bread person," she replied. "But the salad dressing is rather good from the bite I tasted. I've never made dressing from scratch, have you?"

The occupants around the table chuckled.

"What did I say?" she asked.

Eddie did a light *tsk* at everyone on her behalf. "Allan is my son, and he's a chef by trade. We all cook. Very well, I might add." He nodded toward Grandmother. "The Queen there published a cookbook years ago that's still on the must-have shelf of every Lowcountry chef."

Sophie laid a hand on her chest. "Oh, my. I'm totally novice here, aren't I? If y'all say the food is good then it must be out of this world!" A coquettish titter followed.

The diners laughed all around.

Then her concern replaced humor. "Heavens, I'm not sure my cookies will pass muster now. Remember what a newbie I am when you sample them. A little grace would be greatly appreciated."

Warm expressions told her she'd be fine when the time came.

Allan finished his salad, suddenly hungrier than he thought, grateful for any food not fried. Pauline couldn't mess up a meal if she tried.

The chowder arrived in individual deep bowls, the ones with

Portuguese markings in strong primary reds and yellows. Everyone sniffed the aroma in their own way, nobody with a negative word.

"Everyone sure is quiet," Ogden said after everyone had sampled the chowder.

Allan found the remark odd coming from the guy who sat and moped in the presence of the adults. But as he dove into his chowder, Kimi traded bowls with him. "Just in case," she said.

Aunt Kimberly scowled at her daughter.

"What are you doing?" Allan whispered once everyone returned attention to their food.

"Showing these people that you and I are united, and that they need to quit fucking with you. Here." She quickly sank a spoon into her switched serving.

"You're insane," he said.

"You're paranoid," she said back.

A sip of chowder, the crunch of a crouton, the combination of tastes pushed this meal to perfection.

Spot on, Pauline. She'd double teamed the croutons on the salad and the chowder, the little cubes of toast acting unique in each dish. Allan tasted a slight adjustment from the cookbook, so the chef had felt inclined to add originality to this event. Maybe a bit of mystery in her own right.

Sophie, however, like with the salad, nudged her bread cubes aside. Her distaste didn't go unnoticed.

"Oh, honey," Lacey said. "You've got to eat at least one. It might indoctrinate you into the world of bread once you've tasted something baked properly. Honestly, I'm not much of a bread eater either, but if you serve me something homemade, I'll sample. Especially toasted." She lifted one on her spoon, crunched down, and swallowed.

Everyone looked at Sophie. With pressure on, in a half dainty, half regretful manner, she hunted for the smallest and gave a try.

"See?" Lacey said.

Mulling the piece around her mouth a second, she then bit, slowly chewing. "Better than expected."

"See what happens when you don't cook with white flour?" Kimberly said.

Allan continued taking tiny sips of the chowder, moving small amounts around his mouth for signs of anything he felt didn't belong. He followed with a lone crouton, then a sip of water. Each bite was a test, a sampling, an exploration. Finally, chowder and a crouton together.

All seemed well.

Chowder was such a compilation of tastes and herbs that just about anything could be hidden in its savory blend, but thus far, nothing seemed amiss. To be honest, the meal was damn flavorful. Maybe if he ate just enough to say he'd eaten, he'd be fine. At the same time, he'd watch his family, noting who studied him more than others, who waited for him to collapse, throw up, turn purple, whatever.

The chowder was on the creamy side, and not the Deeply Lowcountry recipe he'd thought. Good thing Eddie hadn't backed him in a corner asking for the exact recipe. But there was only one chowder in *Southern Silver Spoon* that called for a hint of something especially unique, and this was it.

Everyone seemed particularly impressed.

Kimi tapped his arm. Sophie was finally enjoying hers as well, pausing after each taste wondering what was different.

"It's saffron," Allan said.

She sat back. "Isn't that insanely expensive?"

"Eighty dollars an ounce," Aunt Kimberly said, before taking another mannerly sip.

Sophie turned to Eddie. "Are you kidding me?" she whispered.

"All that means to us is that you don't hurt the chef's feelings by not enjoying her trouble," he said, with a barely noticeable motion of his spoon toward her bowl. "Eat. . . and enjoy."

Sophie did. They all did. For the first time since Allan had arrived at *Maelstrom Manor*, the room felt like family. Funny how it took a stranger appearing and a chef who knew her stuff to make everyone share food and act normally.

This kind of Poe life he could appreciate.

Small talk tittered for another twenty minutes before Chef Pauline cleared the bowls and brought in small crystal ones of fruit in a Grand Marnier sauce, served on a matching crystal saucer.

You hit this out of the park, Pauline. But still, wait until I'm sharing the stove with you.

"Well," Eddie said. "I think this calls for cookies as a side to the fruit. What do y'all say?"

"Absolutely," Kimi said, suddenly giving Allan the impression she might be catering to Sprite's mother to atone for lunch. "I'm itching to see who can guess the magic ingredient."

"Aren't we full of mysterious ingredients this week?" Ogden said, waggling a brow.

But everyone was talking, even joking, maybe even sliding back into becoming some semblance of a family to give him the attention he sought.

Sophie jumped up. "Let me hand them out." Grabbing the basket from the sideboard, she laid a hand atop the folded plaid napkin covering the cookies. "Good. They're still a little warm."

Walking the length of the room, she approached Grandmother first out of courtesy, allowing her a choice before anyone else touched them. The older woman studied Sophie, then the array in the basket, gingerly lifting the one on top.

"I'll wait for everyone to get theirs," Grandmother said, setting hers on her saucer that held her fruit cup.

One by one, Sophie made the rounds until she reached her own seat, setting one beside her plate after Eddie took his.

"Now, for those who didn't catch the story earlier, these are Mystery Cookies. They have a unique ingredient. Some say the secret adds to the taste, and others can't tell the difference. I believe there's a moisture factor involved that adds to the finish."

Everyone studied their cookies, smelled their cookies, using all their senses as if analyzing a newly opened bottle of wine.

Sophie snickered at everyone's curiosity. "Once you've all tasted, we'll go around. . ." She coughed. Then as she started talking again, she coughed again.

"You all right?" Eddie asked, sliding her water closer.

Clearing her throat after a sip, she nodded. "Yes. Just swallowed wrong." She shifted her shoulders, sitting taller." Now, I cannot take full credit for these. An author put this recipe in a story of hers, but many people tweaked the ingredients. The base is a spice cookie."

She lightly cleared her throat like a remnant from the meal remained. "Now, everyone. . . take a bite." She led the way, tasting her own to show she wasn't hesitant to eat her own treat.

"Hmm," Lacey said, taking a nibble, then another. She mulled the piece around her mouth, savoring, wondering.

With Sophie from outside the family, the cookie had to be perfectly safe, so Allan took a bigger bite, consuming a quarter of his cookie. Typical spices, yes. Cinnamon, nutmeg. . . maybe a modicum of ginger. Was that a pinch of cloves? One had to be careful with the overwhelming nature of cloves.

Ogden tapped on the phone hidden in his lap.

"No," Sophie said, voice raised. "Don't cheat, young man. Come on. Show me how that famous Poe palate works."

The words came out gravelly. She coughed again.

But then her eyes grew wide in fright. "What was in this dinner?" she said between coughs. "Wasn't my cookies," she added in a choked whisper.

"Why not?" Aunt Kimberly said, dropping hers on the table with a little toss while Grandmother rested hers on a napkin.

"Here," Eddie said, handing her the water glass again, but Sophie waved him away. "Can't swallow," she gasped.

No, no, no. Allan's father had placed Sophie where Allan intended to sit. Surely, Sophie couldn't have consumed what was meant for him.

"Who did this?" Allan hollered, snapping to a stance, his chair tipping backwards, almost keeling over. "Who the hell tried to do me in again? I was supposed to sit there." Then he called for who he trusted more than anyone under this roof. "Pauline!"

Everyone spoke at once. Some denied the accusation. Some yelled at him for spreading blame to the family with Aunt Kimberly even saying Allan shouldn't have come home. Everyone tried to tell everyone else what ought to be done about Sophie's inability to breathe.

Pauline rushed out, analyzed the scene and ran back to the kitchen.

As Sophie's fear escalated, tears escaped the corners of her eyes. "Call. . ."

"Shannon?" Eddie bellowed, jolting the nurse from her frozen pose behind Grandmother. "Do your damn job!"

Grandmother motioned for Shannon to get her butt over there and assist.

Sophie fought for air, wheezing replacing breaths, a squeaking sound demonstrating how tightly her airways had closed. She slumped, her chair almost tipping, but Eddie caught her and laid her out on the Old English dining room rug. Allan pulled aside the chair in an assist.

"Give her some room," Shannon said, plump hips shoving her way through. "For God's sake, Eddie, let her sit up. She'll breathe better than if she's laying down. Ma'am, are you allergic to anything?"

Sophie gave quick little shakes of her head.

"Shit," Kimi said, standing to the side, arms wrapped around herself, and Allan went to stand beside her.

"Call 911," he repeated, then he remembered how inept Shannon had been when he went down with the monkshood.

Like she hadn't heard him, the nurse fussed over Sophie, trying to register what was wrong, touching her and there, asking questions the ill woman could barely answer.

Until Sophie passed out and couldn't.

Allan dialed 911 himself as Pauline exploded back into the room.

"Middle aged female appearing to be having an allergic reaction," Allan said to the operator, giving the address, scared to say someone might be poisoned since they'd come there to for that before. "We have a nurse on site— Pardon?"

Eddie snatched the phone from his son and thrust it at Shannon. "You ought to be talking to them, damn it. Earn your keep."

Shannon crouched on her knees, phone gripped tight, but she appeared lost.

The operator raised her voice. "Hello? Sir? Can you tell me the address you're calling from?"

Pauline hustled through the throng. "Oh, for heaven's sake, talk to the operator Shannon, and let me take care of the lady." Thrusting Shannon aside, toppling her to her butt, Pauline got on her knees, opened an epinephrine pen, slid up Sophie's skirt, and jammed her thigh.

Everyone held their breath as tightly as the woman they'd watched trying to breathe. Not a person spoke, making the 911 operator's voice even louder. "Hello? I'm dispatching an ambulance. Authorities will be on site in a few minutes, the ambulance in twenty to thirty. Hello?"

If they hadn't been so silent, so intent on watching Sophie's eyes flutter back open, her breathing coming back in increments, they wouldn't have heard the second thud.

Shannon stood and screamed.

Pauline snatched the phone away from her and told the operator, "Better send two."

Chapter 25

Callie

CALLIE DROVE PAST El Marko's parking lot, flipped her lights, and sped up Palmetto toward *Maelstrom Manor*. Two victims?

Allan and who else? Had Allan retaliated once someone came at him again and maybe paid a price for doing so?

Was this time even poison? Most likely, because she didn't see the Poes as the stabbing, shooting, or fist throwing sorts.

God, she'd be glad when they returned to Charleston.

These people were proving to be both bonded yet combative by blood. They didn't speak of competition, but Callie read the rivalry in their interviews, in their tones, and in their choice of words. Being Poe meant everything to them, and while Grandmother Poe ruled the roost, each Poe possessed a unique opinion on how a Poe should properly carry themselves. And they ragged on the ones who didn't meet the standard. They didn't know how to be anything else but Poe, but none of them seemed particularly happy to be one.

Amidst all this family anarchy, Callie wondered if Grandmother's dominance was slipping. No doubt one or more counted their inheritance. Life never failed to dumbfound Callie how those with money could be so ruthless in obtaining more. And how those without money could be the most generous.

But with Grandmother being close to the end of her time on earth, why weren't they after her? And why were they hot and heavy after Allan, assuming his incidents weren't accidents, unless he was some sort of threat to plans for the fortune?

He was the oldest grandson, for goodness's sake, which carried weight in most families.

Where was the motive? Allan might call these incidents innocent, but she wasn't accepting that. Not anymore. This was her third visit to this house in two days. If somebody wound up dead, she wouldn't be surprised, but at the same time she would be asked by council and others why she hadn't stopped anything with all these warning signs.

She arrived at the house. The ambulances would be another ten to fifteen minutes at best, making her stop with a lurch as the first responder on scene. Distance from medical attention was the biggest reason people retired here, grew older, then changed their minds and sold to the next person, who would likely do the same.

Running in a zig zag around the cars, Callie took the steps two at a time, out of breath at the top, and prepared herself. Blood, fighting. . . death.

When Allan answered the door, however, her thoughts tangled a bit.

"No, not me this time," he said, flustered, waving hard for her to hustle in. "We've got one stable, but the other we're not so sure."

Seeing him healthy irritated her for some reason, and she bit off grumbling *What is with you people?* but held her tongue, following him with a scurry into the dining room.

"Soph?" she exclaimed, seeing her neighbor and best friend on the floor. "Oh my God, what happened?"

"Something I ate," her friend replied, and she weakly pointed to Pauline. "She realized and gave me a shot."

"Epinephrine," Allan said from behind Callie.

Pauline nodded. "I keep one or two handy for reasons like this. She must be allergic to something."

Sophie was more washed out than scary pale, and she shook her head in denial at the assumption. She seemed to be recuperating, which made Callie assume she was the stable one. Praying she was the worst of the victims, Callie stood and rushed toward the cluster of others not far to her right, hoping to find this one on the mend as well.

Nurse Shannon hovered over Kimi, fretting, not keeping the calm as one would expect a medical professional to do.

"Come on, honey. What's going on?" the nurse said, rubbing Kimi's arm, then the other, then patting her cheeks. "No, ma'am. Fight this and sit up for me." She kept trying to make Kimi take her hand, so that she could be pulled into a seated position, but the girl had neither the focus nor the strength.

"What happened?" Callie asked, kneeling. Unlike Sophie, Kimi's complexion waned ghostly and weak. Unsure of her surroundings, she could only sink back into herself. "Did you give her an Epi-Pen shot, too?" Callie asked.

Shannon startled at the new voice. "This child has no allergies yet that chef bitch used one anyway. The ambulance is coming, and there's nothing you can do. Give me space." The defensiveness in her tone belied the ineptness she felt.

"Like you took care of Mrs. Bianchi over there?" Ogden hollered. "You're worthless, lady."

"Shut up, child," Shannon said. "Let me work."

"And do what?" Ogden yelled.

"Get the hell away from my daughter," Aunt Kimberly said with a cold hardness, shoving Shannon off kilter. The nurse bumped into the leg of the buffet table, shoving the back against the wall. "You're a shit nurse, Shannon."

Then to Kimi, the mother cooed and eased hair from her child's face. "Baby, Mama's here. Just you and me. Come on around, honey. The ambulance will be here any time, and we'll get you better, but I'd love to see you wake up and talk. Please, baby? Do this for me?"

Kimberly's reaction underlined how the rest of them felt. This family could afford way more caregiver value than this nurse, but Callie tucked that away for now.

"Tell me what happened," Callie repeated to the nurse, accustomed to people acting outside their norm during emergencies, trying to push aside the fact Shannon was someone who should be trained to know better.

"That woman over there is what happened," Shannon exclaimed, pointing to Sophie. Her slight plumpness disabled her from standing very fast. "She comes in here completely unannounced, brings cookies with God-knows-what in them, then brags about the mystery ingredient to make everyone eat one and guess. Who says she wasn't trying to kill the whole lot of us?"

Her drama was embarrassing to watch. But Shannon wasn't done. "Who the hell does she think she is? The welcome wagon lady? Seriously? The Poes have owned this house for years and there's never been a welcome wagon visit." She released a sob. "Interrogate her. Make her tell everyone the mystery ingredient. What toxin did she hide in those cookies? What is her motive for even being here?"

"She probably came to get back at us after we talked to Sprite today," Ogden said.

"After I left?" Callie had to ask. "Why, what happened?"

"A spinoff of what you saw. Nothing to us, but Jeb and Sprite looked like they'd been contaminated by the time they left." He peered over his mother's head to see his sister again, his whole body tense. "And who says you aren't here to set us up? Charge us with some fabrication of a crime maybe?"

Allan stepped in. "Shut up, Ogden."

Callie would like all these questions answered as well.

Lacey came over and put an arm around Shannon's shoulders.

Eddie continued to keep Sophie company, and unless Callie read things wrong, he would entertain a private dinner with the likes of the yoga queen. And Sophie would take him up on an offer once, maybe twice, letting him feel obliged while not telling her on-again-off-again boyfriend Buck.

Speaking of the devil, Eddie spoke up. "Shannon, tend to Grandmother." No excess words, but they carried strong orders. Lacey and Shannon moved to either side of Grandmother. One would think Kimberly the nurse and Shannon the sister when Callie weighed the reactions.

"Can you tell me what happened without the drama?" she asked Allan off to the side. "Begin with Mrs. Bianchi showing up."

He shifted with her a few feet further from the others. "Mrs. Bianchi arrived unannounced right as we were sitting down to dinner. Maybe six-ish?"

Callie slowly retrieved her notepad.

"My dad, somewhat besotted, asked her to stay for dinner. Chef Pauline came in with salads, totally unaware, and altered the place settings."

"Where was Mrs. Bianchi seated?" Callie asked. "Tell you what, tell me where everyone was seated and what changed."

Allan started with Grandmother and named who sat where, going full circle around the table. Sophie was given Allan's spot, and Allan slid beside his cousin Kimi. Callie envisioned the table, seeing how far apart everyone was, and who sat on either side of Sophie, either side of Allan, then either side of Kimi. Eddie, Sophie, Allan, Kimi and Ogden, counterclockwise. Who exactly was the target?

From the fussing and finger pointing Callie had an inkling of an idea why Sophie came. Nobody messed with her baby girl Sprite. Add that to Sophie's natural inclination to learn about anyone and everything on the beach, the cookbook and poisons being so unique. . . tack on the fact she and Sprite made cookies. . . well, the evening more made sense. Sophie couldn't help but come over with all those question marks in the air, and impromptu was her style.

Did Sophie poison Kimi, did the Poes poison Sophie, or did someone go for Allan and get screwed up with the musical chairs? Plus, he could have dosed either one.

"Like the rest of us, Chief, Kimi listened to our guest talk about her cookies. Like us, she witnessed Ms. Bianchi choke, wilt, and go to the floor. With attention on Mrs. Bianchi, we missed Kimi passing out."

"And you," she asked. "What do you think occurred?"

"I have zero idea what the deal is here." Allan looked like he told the truth, like all this had grown beyond his grasp.

In her drive over, Callie had wondered if Allan had attempted revenge, but hurting Sophie made no sense, and Kimi would be his last target.

The medics were due in minutes. Sophie was stable. Kimi, however, was not. Her breathing was off, her color not returning. "Does Kimi have allergies?" she asked Allan.

"No, she doesn't."

"Why did she collapse, though?" Callie asked. She was fast coming up with a string of questions to ask each person.

Who served?

How was each part of dinner served?

Who had access to the food?

Who had a grudge she hadn't heard of yet?

Who was the one most prone to be underhanded?

Who had a record, official or unofficial, of doing harm?

Who had the most to lose with Allan's reappearance?

Who felt challenged and why?

How was Grandmother's will set up and how did each person feel about her choices?

Who was power of attorney when she became incapacitated? Callie assumed an attorney would be the executor over an estate as large as this one, but she'd ask that as well.

Allan looked lost. "If someone came at me and mistakenly got to Kimi, I'll never forgive myself."

"What is there to forgive?" she asked.

He seemed uncertain how to phrase his response. "For leaving. For coming back. For expecting to be welcomed into the fold like the prodigal son while everyone else tolerated the toils of being a Poe." His hand ran through his hair for about the sixth or seventh time. "I feel responsible."

"Could still be you," Callie said. "Or could be that mistakes were made." She let her comment sound more factual than a ponderance.

Pauline came over. "I have no idea what could have done this to her, Allan. Do you?"

He shook his head, legit pain in his expression.

Pauline sighed, more of an angry sigh than one of exhaustion or even exasperation. "Well, I'm damn sick and tired of all this happening on my watch as chef. I'd leave except. . ."

"For me," he ended for her.

She rubbed his arm. "Sure, that, too.

"She looks guilty if she takes off," Callie chimed in for clarity.

Kimberly jumped up and pushed Pauline aside. "Listen to me. I see what you're doing over here in the corner, Chief Morgan. You'll talk to this cook and start weaving some sort of motive and intricate plot together about the Poes and their skills in taking people down. You'll paint us as evil and the press will move in, and we'll take a monstrous financial hit. All this must be a mistake."

"Or not," Callie said, as tranquil as she could. "I'll talk motive with you later."

Kimberly's mouth fell agape, no words spoken. To speak could blemish them all. Callie could see it in her eyes.

Where were the ambulances?

Callie went to the grandmother. Nobody had spoken to her since Callie had arrived, only peered at her once in a while. "Mrs. Poe, do you know what could have hurt your granddaughter? Or Mrs. Bianchi?"

Grandmother Poe remained in her seat where she'd probably been since before they ate. And while everyone else had spoken over each other at first, everyone was silent to hear what the matriarch had to say to the police. For being the head honcho, she sure hadn't said much.

The matriarch's demeanor wasn't the cold, stoic nature Callie saw before. She had melted to a degree, and worry filled the wrinkles of her eighty-year-old complexion. "She was fine through dinner," the woman said firmly but not loud. "So was the guest. They went down within seconds of each other." From where she sat, she'd have had a clear view of both ladies, probably paying more attention since she seemed one to observe and not mince words.

Callie didn't feel this the time or place to press her, so she returned to Kimi, noting how she breathed quickly and shallow, her color pale but not at death's door.

She looked over at Sophie. Her color sure was better. The allergy pen worked for her.

"You did try a pen on Kimi?" she asked Pauline, having been rebuked by Shannon when she'd asked before.

"Yes," Pauline said. "No change. Tells me we don't have a reaction to food, Chief."

There was nothing Callie could do for either ill woman. Frustrated barely brushed the level of her ire right now. She was fed up with the behaviors in this household, and it was all she could do not to lecture the whole damn lot of them. Again, not the place or time.

How was she to break this impasse when the Poes, as much as they rubbed each other wrong, still circled wagons and maintained a tight perimeter? They could drop dead, one by one, and those remaining would continue to cover. All for the God-damn name of Poe.

But there was one thing she could do in the few moments left before medics arrived.

She walked to the far side of the room and dialed Jeb, in lieu of Sprite. Jeb was the most levelheaded of the two, and with this being Sprite's mother, Callie worried the daughter would only want to leap into a car, speed over, and throw more emotions into the fray.

"Son, just listen."

"Um, okay."

"Try not to react, too."

"Yeah."

"Sophie came to the Poe house to bring her cookies, the family invited her to stay for dinner, and she reacted to something she ate. She's stable, but an ambulance is on the way to take her to St. Francis. Collect Sprite and follow them there."

"I'm at Sprite's," he said. "She's bragging all about those special cookies." His voice lowered. "You don't think someone laced them, do you?"

Sophie had her own wealth of knowledge about all things mysterious, but nothing of this level.

"Hold on Mom." He turned aside and told Sprite to hold on. She'd heard her name and the reference to her mother and was wanting answers, her words fast, her manner taking on a panicky pitch.

"I helped make those cookies," she said loud enough for Callie to hear. "Is someone coming down on Mama for something? Ogden I bet. I swear, she only went over there because. . . well, I'm not sure why. What the hell is going on?"

Callie heard. She relayed her reply through Jeb. "She just collapsed at the Poe house. Unsure why, but Jeb, if you want to drive Sprite here and wait outside, that's fine. Do not come up and create a bigger furor than there is. The medics will need room. Follow the ambulance to the hospital."

"She wants to see her mother, Mom."

"Of course she does. That's why I'm expecting you to control her, son. It'll just be y'all and her at the hospital, so tell her to wait for privacy there. If anything happens in the interim, I'll call you back. She's weak but okay. Ask Sprite if her mother is allergic to anything."

He did. "Nothing she is aware of. Wait, what?" Again, he spoke to Sprite.

"Hey," he said coming back to his mother. "She says her mom doesn't eat peanuts. She's never had a full-on reaction, but she has had hives, so she avoids them. Does that help?"

The menu. Callie had to get that menu.

Sophie loved being seen as gorgeous, fit, and invincible. She kept weaknesses under wraps. She'd never told Callie about the peanuts. "Okay. The ambulance will be here any second. Tell Sprite to throw together a bag for her mother and a few things for herself in case she wants to stay the night. Keep Sprite calm, Jeb. If she flies off or melts down, she's worthless to her mother."

"Yes, ma'am. Got it."

Callie hung up. An observation of Sophie and another few steps over to check on Kimi revealed the first was better, the second worse. Kimi had thrown up on the rug beside herself, unaware of doing so. Someone had brought a cool damp cloth that Kimberly held on her daughter's forehead. Like Eddie and Kimberly had expressed so clearly, their nurse wasn't worth much.

"Why no charcoal this time?" she asked Allan, Pauline beside him.

"None left," the chef said. "And she's unconscious. Not sure how we'd get it in her." Then she mumbled. "You don't ever expect to use the stuff, you know?"

Allan exhaled, lifted his phone, and scrolled. "I've been researching. Kimi's symptoms could be any of twenty plants or herbs, Chief Morgan. Mrs. Bianchi's reaction is textbook allergy to me."

"Well, I just got off the phone with Mrs. Bianchi's daughter. She doesn't have a defined allergy, but she has gotten hives from peanuts." Callie looked at Pauline, waiting for any suggestion as to the ingredient.

Pauline's eyes widened. "Shit," she whispered.

All three turned their backs to the rest of the room. Callie leaned close. "What?"

"The croutons," the chef said, barely audible.

Allan frowned. "We all ate them. The only person who could have doctored them would've been. . ."

"Me," Pauline said.

Callie was confused. "What are you saying?"

"I used lupin flour."

Recognition crossed Allan's eyes. "Oh man," he said, like the pieces had come together for him.

Meanwhile, Callie had no clue. "What?"

Allan explained. "Lupin flour is made from the lupin bean, a cousin to peanuts. Reactions can be severe and can include anaphylaxis for those sensitive to peanuts," he said, conspiratorially and hushed, not wanting the others to start blaming the chef, who let him do the talking beside him. "Pauline made a point of learning preferences and what ingredients to avoid this week. She can't be held responsible for someone dropping in unexpectedly who just happens to be allergic." His whispering voice had gotten harsher.

"Then hush," Callie said. "We'll talk later about her. What about your cousin?"

Turning the phone so she could read, he explained. "I downloaded *Southern Silver Spoon* this afternoon since I don't have a hard copy, and the only copy in the house is being used in the kitchen. I've been trying to second guess what could have hurt Kimi."

Callie drew out her phone. "Forward to me."

"I had to buy it so not forwardable."

Going into an online bookstore, she promptly found the cookbook and paid for the ebook version. The unspoken agreement amongst the three of them was that someone laced Kimi's food. Or maybe Allan's plate, glass, or silverware.

Callie could afford to wait and speak to Sophie at the hospital. She lifted her phone and texted Jeb. *Tell Sophie not to openly talk about tonight. Say only enough for the doctors to treat her. I'll need to talk to her later.*

She got a thumbs up in return.

Knocks sounded at the door. She trotted to let the medics in. Four of them, which meant two ambulances.

"Wreck on Highway 174," one said. "Who's worse here?"

The three of them pointed to Kimi.

They'd been told toxins or allergic reactions. They went to work on vitals, ensured the two were stable enough to transport, and quickly whisked them away.

Their red lights bounced off the fronts of beach houses, and Callie watched Jeb pull in behind them, then Aunt Kimberly in POE 3, the small parade taking Palmetto Boulevard east.

Spinning on her heels, Callie braced herself to confront the remaining culprits. Yes, that's how she saw them. They harbored secrets. In her opinion, they were guilty until proven innocent at this point.

"Everyone gets a chat with me tonight, and I don't care for how damn long," she said.

"Do we need attorneys?" Eddie asked, reaching deep for some broken piece of bombastic pride.

"I don't know, do you?" Callie didn't care how she came across. She didn't have a partner to play good cop/bad cop, so bad cop it was. Her good cop side had vanished some time ago.

Chapter 26

Callie

WITH THE AMBULANCES gone, *Maelstrom Manor* shushed like a funeral chapel. Sophie would likely be fine, per the medic. Nobody cared to forecast Kimi's recovery; she looked too fragile to predict. The vibrant young lady Callie had met at Coot's was too close to death's door.

This didn't feel like a prank anymore.

Callie shut the front door and returned to the dining room. "Now we talk."

Eddie cleared his throat. "Maybe I need to go to the hospital. I sort of feel obligated since I invited Mrs. Bianchi to dinner. And my sister will need someone with her." He didn't wait for an answer, walking toward the living room before he finished talking.

Callie stepped in front of him and put up a hand. He stopped short of bumping his chest. "No, sir. Kimi has her mother and Mrs. Bianchi has her daughter. Leaving will only make me suspect you more."

He froze, then attempted to appear tough, looking down on her, like she'd stepped too far. His stare dared her to push. Hers dared him to ignore her direction. "I beg your pardon," he said, droll and firm.

"Sorry, but no. You do not get my pardon. I've danced around your household and given you the benefit of the doubt one too many times," she said. Then to everyone, she announced her demands.

"First, nobody leaves this house. You are all people of interest. Secondly, you will be interviewed tonight. Third, if you want an attorney with you when I interview you, knock yourself out calling them and getting them here ASAP. Fourth, if you ignore my request, you will rise to the top of the suspect list, and I can't help but see guilt in your actions. And last, nobody touches anything on the table or in the kitchen."

Ogden scowled, maybe due to immaturity, or maybe from being told what to do, but in Callie's opinion, he was mostly facade. With the incident having injured his sister, his only sibling, he had to be shaken. Not quite as polished as his uncle. If he didn't have motive before, he damn sure did now for the future. If Callie didn't get to the bottom of this now, this serial criminal activity would continue.

Eddie returned to his seat, texting. "I've told Kimberly to keep us apprised."

Callie viewed him as totally opportunistic, and not a father who would do anything for his son, or for family, honestly. He held little empathy, his priority being family image.

Pauline pulled a chair away from the table, distancing herself from the evidence all over the dining room table. Crossing one leg over the other, she waited. She'd been thrust into a family that made her look amateur, and by simple acquaintance had made her a suspect. Callie understood that the chef would have to ride this all the way now.

Allan mirrored what the chef did in distancing himself to the side, and Callie appreciated them setting the standard, but they remained on her list. Both chefs had means and motive.

Lacey and Shannon had positioned themselves behind Grandmother but left her at the table, finally slipping the chair back to align with theirs once they saw Pauline and Allan do so. They exchanged a lot of looks behind Grandmother, which Callie took note of. Their simple-minded behavior didn't ring a hundred percent true.

Changing tactics, Callie decided to direct questions to all of them first, versus one on one, to see the responses they'd give in front of each other. If she interviewed one alone, the others would collaborate, and she'd come back to established stories and an obstinate wall of defiance. Here she could watch reactions, then take that knowledge and pick them apart in private later.

"Everyone has a seat, but away from the table. Again, don't touch anything." She couldn't say that enough.

While they maneuvered, she called the Colleton County Sheriff's Office. Lacey started talking to those around her, and Callie evil-eyed her to silence.

The forensics on this was far over her department's head. Her office could do little more than take fingerprints and collect evidence. Therefore, she wanted the people doing the testing to see the uncontaminated setup and take samples accordingly.

With time being late, she was told forty-five minutes, which was about as good a time as Callie could expect. If the evening warranted a step-up to the state's law enforcement team SLED, she'd only do so at the county's suggestion. The further you allowed a case to expand, the more people and levels involved, the higher probability of error, and the more a lead officer lost control of a case. She held the closest and deepest knowledge of these people. Other detectives might let the Poe name get in the way.

Lacey and Shannon had assumed places near Grandmother, Shannon having moved her chair beside Lacey. Eddie sat a couple yards past them, beside his son Allan. Ogden sat solo with both his mother and sister gone, so Pauline nicely slid a chair next to him and patted the boy's shoulder like she had his back.

Callie positioned herself, standing, in a location to keep them all in her vision. "People. . ."

"How disrespectful," Lacey said. "*People*. Like you gathered us off a city street."

"I don't know you from anyone I *could* gather off a city street, but don't read too much into this, Lacey, or I might take your comments as distraction."

She huffed, and Shannon laid a hand over on her forearm in a silent *be quiet*.

Grandmother cut her own disapproving glance at Lacey, and while Lacey acted like she didn't catch the look, Callie did.

So did Allan. The slow simmering anger in his eyes said he'd had enough.

Allan was still a catalyst. People would behave differently with him there versus if he wasn't. He'd been victimized twice, and with him at dinner seated next to Kimi, the darling of the family, he could only conclude he was the intended. He talked about playing pranks yesterday. Callie assumed, like her, he no longer believed that.

"County forensics is on their way." Callie turned to Pauline. "That includes the kitchen. Nobody goes in there. If someone feels they need sustenance, we'll order out."

Pauline nodded, Allan doing the same. The others, however, expressed strong discontent, but held their voices in check.

"You all know poisons," she said. "That makes you all suspects."

"I'm not one of them," Shannon said.

"But you're a nurse, and you've lived with these people for. . . how long?"

The nurse looked to Lacey then Grandmother for support and received none.

"Thirteen years," she finally said, withdrawing her hand from resting on Lacey.

Callie looked down her nose, an action she couldn't do with her diminutive height when others were standing. "You've lived with them long enough to be included, Shannon. You've read that cookbook, so, no, you don't get a pass. If anything, your profession enables you better to assist or enable even if you didn't do anything directly yourself."

Nobody in this room would go to the mat for another.

Lives were at stake, and these people continued to live like they weren't. Time to amp this business up to a level that snared attention. "Somebody in this house, this room, is responsible for these. . . and let's call them what they are. . . poisonings. Not jokes, pranks, or tomfooleries. Cooperate or I'll lock up every damn one of you."

Some eyes widened. Some narrowed.

"Tell you what," she continued, pacing a little bit on the English designed rug that had no business being in a beach house. "Let's have a lesson here."

The puzzlement was almost comical.

"Kimi is young and healthy. What would take her down that hard and that fast? Draw from all that expertise which y'all profess to be dripping with. Of course, if anyone wishes to confess, I'm all ears."

Discomfort passed around the room like a wave. Feet shuffled, eye contact shifted. All except for Grandmother who seemed perfectly content watching this play out.

But nobody wanted to be the first to reply.

"What were her symptoms?" Pauline asked, breaking the ice. "I wasn't in here."

Nobody spoke.

"Hey," Callie said. "Answer the lady." She pointed at Grandmother. If she talked the others would follow suit.

With all eyes on her, Grandmother Poe obliged. "She paled, her breathing increased, but she couldn't get enough air. She passed out. Then she threw up. Then she passed out again." She took a deep breath. "That could be any of a dozen causes, if you are assuming she ingested something." Her eyebrows told Callie she waited for some sort of acknowledgement. "Is that what you wished?"

"Do you mind naming a few plants or herbs or whatever that might cause those symptoms?" Callie asked.

"Be happy to. The ones I mention will be available in the South," Grandmother replied. "The more exotic would be more difficult to obtain. Is that satisfactory?"

Callie nodded. "That would be a good start."

The old woman was neither tense nor addled, and she performed well. With her age came confidence not confusion, making her more difficult to read.

"Start with the mushrooms," Grandmother said. "Death Caps, *Amanita phalloides*. False mushrooms, or *Gyromitra esculenta*. Fly mushrooms, or *Amanita muscaria*. Nothing in the *Psilocybin* species. They are more hallucinogens."

The room watched without correction. As the queen of *Southern Silver Spoon*, she would know, and as their mother, she would have trained them all.

"We can forego the Latin names, ma'am," Callie said, and waited for more.

Grandmother thought a second. "Not henbane. Too strong an odor. But oleander is all over this island. They line our drive like many of the houses out here. Not blooming yet, but any part would suffice. Jimson weed, or *Datura stramonium*, and I mention the Latin name because the seeds are called datura seeds and can inhibit respiration and cardiac activity. Coma as well. Any other nightshade could have the same reactions, and it grows wild on Edisto."

That one made a lot of sense. Readily available and easy to hide in this type of dinner. She had seen the chowder. Its many ingredients gave opportunity to hide most anything.

The elderly woman mentioned castor beans. "And lastly, don't forget azaleas and Carolina Jessamine."

Jesus. Callie had no idea that everyday flowers she'd pruned, weeded, and admired in her own mother's yard held such hidden power. At this rate, she'd be afraid to touch anything green.

Grandmother waited to see if the officer wanted more. No boasting, no grinning, only a woman who knew her stuff.

"Anyone care to add?" Callie asked the others.

Allan waited to let his dad and aunt reply first, a pecking order clearly in place.

"That's about it," Lacey said.

"Nobody knows better than Mother," Eddie tacked on.

"Ogden?" Callie asked.

"No idea."

"No idea as to. . .?"

He glowered at the request. "I'm the least knowledgeable, and everyone in here would vouch for that. I hate cooking. While they made me learn some of this stuff, I chose not to retain it."

Allan's expression darkened. "You were sure bragging at lunch when you were trying to impress Sprite talking about mandrake." He pointed to Callie. "Don't discount yourself, cousin. Tell the chief if you have any other ideas. This is your damn sister we are worried about."

Ogden yelled back, "I can't add to what Grandmother knows, so shut the hell up."

"Ogden," said Grandmother, her voice only a few decibels louder than her earlier recitation but enough to tell that she didn't speak up often.

The young man immediately wilted, his body language showing his subservience. "I seriously can't add anything, Grandmother."

That left Allan. Nobody else wanted to upstage the matron, so would he?

"The nightshades make sense, Grandmother. They would be my choice."

Callie liked his courage, and she watched the irritation on the others as Allan showed them up.

"Maybe a yew, a Florida yew," he added. "I've seen them in yards here."

Callie would look that up later. She never cared what plant she brushed up against before, now wishing she was still ignorant. She started to speak.

"White snakeroot," he added. "That's pretty common in the jungle around here."

Okay, okay, she'd heard enough. She'd rather shift to the staging and order of everyone and everything. Seems the poisoning possibilities were many, and identification would take serious testing by professionals other than she.

"Y'all, Kimi didn't injure herself," she said. "Mrs. Bianchi was in the wrong place at the wrong time. Who ate the cookies?"

Nobody spoke.

"Raise your hand if you ate a cookie," she reworded.

"I just took a small bite," Lacey said.

"Oh, come on, people. Bite, nibble, mouthful. . . I don't care if you ate a crumb or shoved the whole damn thing in your mouth. Let me see some hands."

Everyone raised their hand except Grandmother. Seemed Kimi reacted before Grandmother had a chance to taste test. That or she wasn't planning to taste in the first place.

"Any of you feel differently after you did?" Callie asked.

Heads shook all around.

"So, not the cookies. Unless she gave Kimi a particular cookie, but did she?"

Allan spoke, having realized nobody else in his family would volunteer. "She let us choose our cookie from the basket."

Callie didn't mention that Sophie had been informed by Sprite of the family's nature and would be leery of the entire family. Still Callie would tell forensics to analyze the cookies.

"But she kept saying there was a mystery ingredient," Shannon said, as if reading Callie's mind. "She clearly was testing the Poes. I do not trust her walking into this house unannounced and daring them to test something she baked. Nope, I don't trust that woman."

"Okay, enough of the cookies," Callie said. They'd all jump on the blame Sophie wagon to distance themselves. "Let's deal with the people in this room."

Lacey raised her hand. "You don't seem too concerned about Mrs. Bianchi as a suspect."

"Lacey," said Grandmother, and the entire room straightened up. "The mystery ingredient was tomato soup. . . out of a can. I know the recipe. I know the mystery writer. I know the book. Let's move on."

That was. . . impressive.

Callie nodded at the matron. Grandmother's address of the room was much appreciated, because Callie's annoyance was riding the cusp of her thoughts right now. "Thank you, Mrs. Poe."

Tension rose in an undercurrent, though. Grandmother held a stoic expression, like she couldn't believe her family had come to this. Eddie fumed, pretending to be in charge. Lacey's frustration coated her from head to toe in her movements and glares at each individual, but particularly at Callie. Ogden pouted much like those his age. Allan simply waited, but being the first victim had made him less suspected. He could keep playing that card yet clandestinely retaliate.

Callie hoped he hadn't though. He would be more unsettled if he'd accidentally harmed his cousin. . . unless he had done so on purpose for reasons hidden to Callie.

The outsiders Pauline and Shannon were not removed from consideration. Pauline was all business, attempting to console Ogden here and there, but Shannon seemed about to come undone. Clasping her hands, she rocked in a chair that didn't rock, and after a while, Callie realized the brief moments of clipped grunts she kept hearing came from the fretting nurse.

"Kimi didn't poison herself, and Mrs. Bianchi didn't poison any of you," Callie said. "While I don't believe anything malicious happened to Mrs. Bianchi, I do believe that her unexpected presence skewed the evening's events. Once again, I lean toward someone having once again tried to harm Allan."

"Why is he exempted from suspicion?" Lacey said. "He goes away because he hates us and is forced to come back for this birthday party. He has a grudge. Taking out any of us would improve his chances of inheriting. Who's to say he wouldn't take us out one by one?"

Eddie blurted, "Good heavens, Lacey, you've lost your damn mind."

Lacey stood. "Don't pretend you give a damn about Allan. How many times did you go to New Orleans and check on him? Especially when he got in trouble. Once? And why? Because you hated him for what he was doing to the Poe name and your own reputation. Your only child ran away from family responsibility and killed people, and all you did was save the family from a lawsuit." She pointed at him with a shaky arm. "I heard you say he'd burned his bridges with us. We all heard you. Don't pretend you didn't say it."

Eddie looked mortified.

Allan couldn't hide his pain.

Lacey had accomplished her mission. Everyone else pivoted toward Allan, human nature being what it was. Like a volley, the ball was now in Allan's court.

He had paled.

Eddie pondered his lap as the room went still.

"You are a Goddamn bitch, Lacey," Pauline said, catching everyone by surprise.

"Shut up," Lacey said. "You're not family."

"You don't have to be family to see the rot in you. You think being caregiver makes you the martyr, and everyone should count their blessings that you have to deal with the old woman instead of them."

Pauline had said what everyone thought, and Callie scanned the audience turning on one another under the stress of scrutiny. Secrets and resentments came out of hiding during times like these. Self-preservation was one word. Each had to protect themselves, saying and doing things that would make law enforcement look at anyone but them. They wouldn't necessarily be guilty, either, but they didn't want to be seen in the spotlight.

Ogden seemed to collapse into himself, turning aside. Maybe ashamed. Possibly realizing these people wouldn't fight for him either.

Shannon's wide eyes belied fear, and Callie wasn't sure from what.

Allan was clearly hurt but not shocked. Three years was a long time to come to the realization family wasn't like Saturday night sitcoms where everyone spilled their flaws and feelings then made up and hugged, lesson learned by the end of the show.

The chef remained red-faced. Pauline had the personality to come back at someone like Lacey, but she was also intelligent enough to see that Lacey was her own worst enemy. Her look traveled to Allan out of concern for a second, but the fury about the others never left her eyes.

Callie let them sit there stewing in their own juices, reflecting on who they were and how they came across to her. She kept an eye on Grandmother, though. This mess would be a strain on any eighty-year-old with intense disappointment rising to the surface. Probably aware of her family members' faults, no one likely spoke of them. Tonight, they'd revealed themselves in all their glory.

"Are you all right?" Callie asked her.

The woman nodded, but she wasn't exuding the strength of before.

Eddie's phone rang. Callie prayed the caller Kimberly, stating Kimi had come around and was on the mend. After all, Allan had always bounced back.

"Kimberly?" he answered. "What's the news?" He listened hard, never flinching, never wilting, never relaxing. Callie couldn't tell what was being said on the other end of the line.

"I'll be right there," he said and hung up, standing.

"How is she?" Allan asked, his eyes pleading.

"Kimi died," he said. "I have to go be with my sister."

Someone knocked at the door.

Chapter 27

Callie

OGDEN TURNED TO the wall, crying aloud. Allan rushed to him.

Lacey turned to the nurse beside her with whispers, Shannon wrapping an arm around her to console.

Eddie stood alone, phone still in his hand in shock. "I need to go to her." he said about three times, yet he didn't move.

Knocks sounded again.

"Take me to my room," Grandmother said, a little break in her voice.

Nobody had come to her. She'd been left alone seated near the head of the table, her reputation of strength expected to hold herself together.

Callie felt sorry for her most.

Eddie waved with his phone hand toward his younger sister. "Lacey, tend to Mother, dammit." Then he checked himself. "No, someone else do it. You and the damn nurse are two shallow, worthless human beings good for nothing but sucking off the Poe teat."

"How dare you," Lacey exclaimed, choked with tears. "Kimi was my niece."

"Mine as well, but you don't care, Lacey. You live off our coffers and contribute nothing to this family. We have a nurse, yet you hang around like you're still needed. Your damn instinct should have been your mother, yet you consoled the nurse. Seriously? What does that say?"

Lacey gasped.

Shannon blushed.

Callie left to answer the door.

Forensics had arrived. Maybe opportune because the family had fallen apart at the news of Kimi's demise. Seconds earlier and the team would've been engulfed in a round-robin of anger and accusations.

Callie led the six guys sent from the Colleton County Sheriff's Office to the dining room. A forensic team. Everyone Poe remained in place in the dining room, afraid to defy the chief, awaiting Callie's orders.

"Eddie, if you feel you need to get to Kimberly, go ahead," she said. "Lacey, tend to your mother. Please, nobody leaves without telling me. This is a case of murder now, and if you didn't see anything malicious before, you damn well better take murder seriously now."

"Well, that's harsh." Lacey hadn't shed a tear.

"We're suspects for. . . murdering Kimi?" Shannon asked, shaken, like that couldn't be.

Her naivete prompted Allan to turn toward her, and he took a few steps closer, making her take one step back. "What do you think? How stupid are you people?" he screamed to all. Then to Lacey, he shouted, "Yes, I said *you people*, because the name Poe means squat right now. You are no better than the stray on the street. I swear, Edgar Allan Poe would be laughing his ass off in his grave about this. You're all disgusting. Kimi died because y'all didn't want me back here, or feared I'd take a piece of Grandmother's money, leaving less for you. Kimi probably died instead of me. How insane is that?" His voice screeched by this time, and tears rolled down his cheeks. "Unless you killed her on purpose, which only makes you sicker human beings. Kimi was the best of us. Didn't you see that? Whoever did this is unforgiveable. Maybe that means nothing to y'all, but this is a forever promise from me. And yes, I hope Chief Morgan identifies you and locks you up so we never have to deal with you again. I don't care which Poe goes to jail."

Forensics waited for the hoopla to be over, avoiding the line of fire in case anyone threw something, pummeled someone, or brought out weapons. This was not their first rodeo.

Callie rushed to Allan's side. "You're making things worse. Go to your room. Take Pauline with you, if you like, but you're scaring these folks. They need to preserve the crime scene, so we find out who's responsible. Okay?" Then she leaned in and mumbled, "Don't put the attention on yourself, follow me? You're only fueling someone's fire."

He hushed, his body still trembling. Turning, he approached Pauline with an open arm and pulled her in. He said something to her. She said something back, and they gently herded Ogden to accompany them, disappearing up the stairs.

Lacey and Shannon tended to Grandmother as ordered, in an overtly expressive manner. Eddie was gone to the hospital.

Callie indoctrinated the team of six as to what lay before them. There was a lot to analyze, and if this hadn't been the Poe family, Colleton County might have balked at the expense. While this case fell far short of a New York City or Los Angeles crime, this crime ranked top shelf in the Lowcountry.

Callie took a moment to slip around the corner and tuck herself in the living room, to collect herself. She had to remain on site. Sophie weighed heavy on her mind. Worse, she needed to inform Jeb and Sprite about Kimi, who'd been a close friend from their behavior at lunch.

She also needed to let Mark know she might not be home tonight.

And she preferred another uniform here.

She was equally disappointed and pissed that this case became murder. The silliness, the childishness, all this unnecessary behavior angered her. Plus, these people would collect themselves and order each other to lock step into the same story.

They had pranked themself into something deadly. She wasn't ruling out Kimi, either. An inopportune mistake could have shifted a hoax into something deadly.

Callie was pulling out her phone when a big hand rested on her shoulder. "Hey, Doll. How's it going?"

Deputy Don Raysor.

If there hadn't been so many others in her presence, she'd have hugged the big goon. "God, I'm glad you're here, Don."

He had way more experience than any of her officers. On loan from Colleton County to the Town of Edisto Beach, Deputy Raysor worked almost full-time at the beach, a loan that had lasted most of his thirty-year career. His knowledge of all things Edisto and Colleton made him invaluable. So did his size, booming voice, and gut-sense of how to be an old-school cop, something she highly respected and often needed more so than the don't-insult-don't-hurt-anyone-training of the modern recruit.

"Can you be in charge while I call my son?" she asked. "He's at the hospital with Sophie."

His brows rose. He'd known Sophie for ages, and like most men on the island, would date her in a heartbeat. "Sophie? How bad?"

"Not bad, thank goodness, but I'll explain in a minute." She left to make her call.

Jeb answered after the first ring. "Mom?"

"How is she?" Callie asked.

"She's really good," he said, and the spring in his words went far in making her feel lighter. "She's putting up a front for Sprite," he said, "but she's been having Sprite mess with her hair and makeup and stuff."

Callie envisioned all that girlishness loud and happy on a stoic hospital floor this time of night. No doubt they'd been shushed a time or two. "I'm thrilled to hear that. Any talk of when she comes home?"

"Tomorrow," he said. "They want to observe her overnight, but from the looks on some of the nurses, they'd prefer the earlier the better. Sprite and I will spend the night here, Mom, rather than come home and return in the morning. That okay with you?"

Considering she'd be busy most of the night, she couldn't disagree. "Sure, son. And thanks for being there for her. A lot of parents wish for what you are doing right now, tending to them in time of need."

"Wouldn't behave any other way, Mom." He paused, and Callie heard him clear his throat. "I'd do the same for you, but. . . but we need to also keep that in mind for your mother, too."

A gut punch bullseye. "I'll keep that in mind," she said, meaning it. Tonight, she'd watched a family cannibalize each other and consume an old woman with disappointment, even as she fought not to show harm. *Take me to my room* from Grandmother Poe had said a lot, and the fact nobody had immediately listened to her said even more.

"I'll be here most of the night, son, but I called for a second reason."

"First, how's Kimi?" he asked. "I heard she collapsed like Miss Sophie. Sprite has been asking, and I said you'd let us know when you could. Know anything yet? Any chance she's here in the same hospital?"

"That is what I wanted to discuss. Listen," she said, collecting the right words. "About Kimi. . ."

But despite her best effort, he read her. "Oh no," he said, almost in a whisper.

"Honey, Kimi passed away," she hurriedly filled in to give him space to digest it.

After a sniffle and slight cough, he asked, "How?"

"She reacted to whatever she ate."

"How does that even happen? She was with family. They would know her allergies," he said, his voice unconsciously rising. "Miss Sophie is one thing, but not somebody who you know like your own skin." His lack of acceptance of something so inane registered with Sprite in the background, and she asked, "What happened?"

"I'll tell you in a minute," he told her, then returned to Callie.

"Not an allergy, son. And I can't say anything else."

"What?" This time he didn't control how he sounded or who heard. Both Sprite and Sophie asked what was wrong.

Jeb ignored them. "Who did it? How did they do it? What exactly did they even do?"

Here was where she had to stonewall. "Open investigation, son. Can't tell you anymore, so please don't ask. I assume you would rather inform Sprite than I?"

"Yes, ma'am."

"Okay. I'm sorry, son. I know y'all were friends."

"Yes, ma'am," he said again, and she gave him a moment. Then in an afterthought, Jeb asked, "How's Ogden?"

"Torn up, as you could imagine. I ask you not to call him right now, okay? Let's let the dust settle. This case is quite active, and the less I have to worry about the better. Maybe late tomorrow at the earliest."

"Yes, ma'am," he rotely replied.

He was dazed, and she yearned to hold him, to be with Sprite and with her best friend Sophie. The distance from Sophie, however, was wise and opportune as Callie deciphered what the hell went on in *Maelstrom Manor* tonight.

She texted Mark that coming home was open ended. He texted back no problem. As an ex-SLED agent and now a restaurateur, he was accustomed to irregular schedules. He'd have food set aside for her when she arrived. She seemed surrounded by foodies right now.

Callie returned to Deputy Raysor, who did little more than hold up the living room doorframe, but his gaze continually took in the rooms and exits.

"To answer your earlier question," she said, hand on his arm to tell him she was back, "Sophie had an allergic reaction to the croutons, we think."

His big ol' mug scrunched up like nobody else's could. "How can a damn crouton take you down?"

"It's a hoity toity one homemade from lupin bean flour."

He gave slow nods. "Good, then I don't have to worry. Hoity toity ain't my style." He paused. "What the hell is a lupin bean?"

"Nothing you'd find in your mother's backyard garden. Where is everyone?"

"Saw two ladies leave one room downstairs to go somewhere up there." He pointed from the room to the stairs.

Callie described Shannon and Lacey for confirmation.

"Yep, that's them." He asked their names again, to be aware.

She then identified all the others and where she'd left them. Then she attempted to explain what had happened, what might have happened, and what they had left to determine happened.

"Don't let them leave," she ordered. "Except for Eddie." She described him versus the other two males. "He's headed to tend to his sister who just lost her daughter to these shenanigans."

He looked at her sideways. "That's what we call murder these days?"

"Better a serious joke that went sideways, Don. In a sad, sad way. So yes, shenanigans are murder this time."

He peered around, seeing the house in a different light. "I thought this house felt creepy," he said. "What do you want me to do?"

"Guard this area," she said, realizing what an opportunity had been handed to her in his arrival. Her other officers could keep the rest of Edisto Beach covered. "Did the grandmother get moved into her bedroom?" The only downstairs bedroom was behind Raysor, the door about five feet away.

"Yep. By the first two who went upstairs."

Seemed the entire Poe family had the habit of situating Grandmother Poe someplace then leaving her to herself, but this concept was not a Poe original. Callie had watched families bring their seniors to the beach only to set them on a porch or on the sand in a chair with an umbrella, and venture on to enjoy activities their elderly could not keep up with. Patting themselves on the back for even bringing them, they abandoned their elders half the time. The seniors learned to sit and watch, and think, and not complain for fear of being made to do less.

Like now, Lacey and Shannon had left Grandmother in her bedroom and moved on, probably anxious to corroborate the evening's events without being overheard. Maybe determine between them who might be guilty. But their concerns for Grandmother clearly ran second fiddle and shallow. They'd only moved her when yelled at to do so. Callie hadn't been on the phone long enough for them to have relocated her to the bedroom, soothed her, and tended to her properly.

God, she was glad Beverly remained mobile and sharp. Her wit and sharp retorts wouldn't cut so deeply anymore.

"See you in a bit, Don. If someone tries to come into that bedroom over there, stop them. Tell them I'm speaking with Mrs. Poe, and I don't care who they are or what authority they say they have, hold them back. Got it?"

"Easy enough, Doll," he said, using the endearment again that had once years ago been a slur until they'd had a meeting of the minds and learned they didn't hate each other.

"Let's go easy on the Doll reference, Deputy. At least in front of these people. Neither of us needs that to give anyone a complaint to muddle things."

"Got it. . . Chief Morgan."

Callie almost laughed, but the setting was too morose. She moved around the big man to the short hall leading to the downstairs master and lightly rapped on the door.

"Yes?" came the reply.

Callie eased the door open. "Mrs. Poe? Chief Morgan. May we chat?"

When the grandmother said nothing, Callie took that as approval, entered, and shut the door behind her.

Mrs. Doris Woolf Poe sat in an upholstered chair in the corner, a footed pedestal table to her right, a Tiffany lamp turned on beside a cup of what looked like tea, half drunk, the rest likely cold. No heated pot on a tray to replace it.

This old woman was terse, having earned a certain degree of respect in her lifetime. . . way more than she was receiving tonight. She'd raised them and financed their lives. She'd taught them manners and cooking and so much more. Callie felt as if in the presence of some level of royalty.

Callie pulled up another chair, lighter and not padded. She sat close enough that she almost touched Mrs. Poe. Head stationary, the woman moved only her eyes, watching Callie's every move in a scrutinizing manner, but Callie chose to take that scrutiny as curiosity versus judgment.

Those silver eyes, however, were unnerving.

"First, I am so very sorry about Kimi," Callie said, noting not a tissue in reach. She rose and nabbed the box across the room from a dresser and returned. "I had lunch with Ogden and Kimi only today. She was smart, vibrant, and full of personality. She bragged about how much she had contributed to the Poe enterprise in her short time of being out of school. She was a force, for sure."

Those silver eyes tried to blink back a tear but failed. Callie handed her a tissue from the box.

"Mrs. Poe, I don't have grandchildren, so I cannot imagine your loss. I do have a mother, however, who thinks the sun rises and sets over my son who was friends with Kimi, by the way. Mother and I have even argued over how protective she can be over him, and how much she wants to control his future."

That was the best way she could describe Beverly's ways.

Admittedly, Beverly's persistence was about promoting her grandson, not inhibiting him. Nothing malicious. Doris Woolf Poe wasn't two steps different than Beverly. Maybe on a higher level, something best not said to Beverly.

"Would you mind answering a few questions for me? I sensed out there in the dining room wasn't comfortable for you. Do you mind talking to me here?"

Mrs. Poe dabbed at her nose, pulled the tissue back, refolded the moist side down neatly, then dabbed again. Despite the tissue box being within reach, Callie half rose, freed another and handed it to her.

"No, I don't mind," Mrs. Poe said, taking the offered tissue, sniffling, dabbing once more, then righting herself to sit straight. "Go ahead."

"I noticed that they seem to seat you someplace and leave you. Is that common?"

Mouth flatlining, she waited a second. "I'm afraid so. While I cannot keep up, of course, nobody goes out of their way." She stopped, trying hard to state a fact, not a feeling. "My energy can't keep up with theirs. They often interpret that as mentally limited as well, but they err in that regard."

Callie nodded. "This week, this birthday week," she began again. "It was your idea, wasn't it?"

"I might have suggested it," she said.

Callie gave a light chuckle. "I'm pretty sure your suggestions and hints are perceived as commands, ma'am. In that regard, you remind me of my own mother."

Mrs. Poe nodded, accepting Callie's analysis. If Callie had been recording, she'd have asked her to speak, but this was informal, an information gathering venture that might assist Callie with grasping the bigger picture.

"And you wanted to use this week to analyze and judge your heirs. Unless I'm wrong, and apologies if I am, you're pondering how best to divvy up the estate."

When Mrs. Poe said nothing, Callie worried she'd indeed misread the situation. "Nobody is present, and the reasons for this week factor into this evening, ma'am." She gave the woman a kind look. "It's why Allan is here, isn't it? First, you could see him again. Secondly, you could see them all together, watch them react, hear them talk, note how they behaved with one another, because when you leave this realm, they will be rudderless. That weighs heavy on you, doesn't it?"

The night, the dark paneling, the maroon comforter on the bed, and the wooden floors gave the room a deep cave impression. They were sequestered in secrecy far away from anyone, and Callie hoped this would make conversation easier for Mrs. Poe.

She nodded in the affirmative, and again, Callie didn't make her speak. She'd confirmed the will was in play.

"Tell me about your mother."

Callie's head lifted with a small jerk at the unexpected request. "*My* mother?"

"Yes. She sounds admirable."

Callie wasn't sure quite how to take this swing from the Poe family to hers, and whether the move would do either of them any good. "My mother's a force of nature, ma'am."

"How so? You've mentioned her twice, which means she's important in your life. Sounds like she is a close parallel to me, or she's heavy on *your* mind. Let me help you with that. Tell me about your mother."

Wow, where to start?

"She's mayor of Middleton. She'd want me to start with that."

That perked up Mrs. Poe. "Have I met her? Surely I have. If I haven't, I'm sorely remiss."

"I think you've met, but nothing memorable. At least to you. Or that's what my mother says."

"Give me a name, honey."

Not Chief, not Callie, not Mrs. Morgan, but *honey*. They had connected. Callie hadn't expected this, but she wouldn't run from it.

An uneasiness swept through her. She'd been forced and somewhat mastered an ability to compartmentalize her worlds. Work apart from family. Social apart from professional. Private versus public life. The mental practice was how she stayed sharp and maintained walls so that she didn't shirk responsibility for either side. It's how she'd learned to tuck away the darknesses of her past, so they didn't infiltrate the present.

She had to admit; this was not comfortable allowing the categorized versions of herself to cross paths. Especially to someone she'd met two days ago.

But there was something about the old woman that drew her in, and to pursue this case, she'd have to take the risk and show some of the underbelly of her own life. Connecting, she guessed, and she didn't like doing that with just anyone.

But then, this wasn't anyone. This was Mrs. Doris Woolf Poe.

Chapter 28

Callie

CALLIE COULD not see any way around discussing her family life with Grandmother Poe. She'd asked about Callie's family, which brought up Jeb, but more so, Beverly. Hearing Callie came from a political background intrigued the old woman, even in her mourning.

"Her name is Beverly Cantrell," Callie said. "Husband, my father, was Lawton Cantrell, also mayor before his death. She assumed his seat."

Mrs. Poe's head rose a notch, impressed. "I'm aware of your father. What was her maiden name?"

"McCants. Beverly McCants Cantrell."

She gave a short nod. "There was a short story author from South Carolina named McCants. From the town of Ninety-Six," she said. "Any relation?"

Such literary connections mattered to Mrs. Poe. "Not that I'm aware of, ma'am. I'll have to ask her."

Mrs. Poe softened, liking that last part. "How long has your family been in politics?"

"Four generations. I was to be the fifth, but I'm afraid I disappointed them in that regard. I prefer the enforcement side of things. I've seen too much foreplay in the other. Too many unkept promises. The public deserves to see wrongs dealt with. Guess I can't play the games I grew up watching."

"And her grandson, your son. Is he interested in politics?" she asked.

How far were they going with this being about her family instead of the Poes? Southern repartee meant talking family lineage or at least did for Mrs. Poe's generation. Negating such a discussion was deemed rude. Between etiquette and the need to keep the conversation flowing, Callie felt obliged to answer the matron's question to earn her respect. She'd be more inclined to reciprocate, or so Callie hoped.

She replied, "Yet to be determined as to my son's political interests.

Him entering politics is a rather sore spot."

"With. . .?"

"All three of us."

"How old is your mother?" Mrs. Poe asked.

"Sixty-eight."

The elder woman laughed. Callie liked seeing her laugh. Maybe this dialogue had serious merit after all.

"You may not see this from your perspective, but your mother is still young and still learning," she said. "I was once like her, forcing everyone's hand, believing I knew better than they did what was good for them. The result was a group of minions who can't think for themselves." Her laughter had disappeared.

The conversation had come full circle.

But Callie still needed answers. "Excuse me if this sounds abrupt, but I believe you understand the importance of my question in the bigger scheme of things," she said. "Were you preparing a new will?"

The woman peered toward the desk on the opposite wall, tired of talking.

Callie followed her gaze. "Mind if I look?"

"Feel free." Exhaustion hung on each word.

Walking to the desk, Callie noted papers in piles, marked up with handwriting, and a notebook off to the side.

She used the pen from her pocket to slide the papers around. There were multiple copies of the old will, which upon closer scrutiny showed assets distributed equally to the three siblings, Eddie, Kimberly, and Lacey. A ten-old year will. Allan would've been twenty and in college, with the other two just children.

Various edits showed assorted ideas on how to redistribute Mrs. Poe's holdings differently.

One showed dividing assets equally amongst the six of them. Another left more to Eddie than Kimberly and Lacey. Notes on the pad talked about leaving out Ogden, dumping on Kimberly to mold her wayward son and then decide in her own will whether he was worthy. Another left money in trusts for the grandchildren until they were thirty.

Then there were notes that would prompt everything to take place this week. Notes that made Callie inhale sharply at how much of a catalyst this would be if anyone sneaked in and pilfered through this.

She found a draft leaving everything to Kimi and Allan. Half to Kimi because she could handle the real estate side of things, giving her mother, aunt, and uncle what she felt they were worth. Half to Allan for perpetuating the culinary side of the family, something near and dear to Mrs. Poe. Something nobody in the family appreciated despite the time and effort she'd exerted to make them love cooking as much as she did. *Only Allan listened to me*, was underlined.

Based on this last scenario, Allan would get everything.

Callie turned around. Mrs. Poe watched as if measuring her reaction to the assorted scenarios that would stun the circle of Poes.

Callie started to ask if Mrs. Poe had decided. No, not her place, or was it? How many of these people had read these papers and felt the need to nudge the probability of them inheriting. . . or inheriting *enough*.

But Mrs. Poe spoke first. "Before you say anything, Chief, let me educate you. I've made up my mind. But what you might not be aware of is that we Poes have a history that my spoiled offspring have chosen not to remember. They needed reminding."

Returning to Mrs. Poe's side, Callie was eager to hear the logic of her family's heritage. "Before you explain things to me, I need to know if anyone has gone through these papers."

"Most likely," the old woman said.

The revelation was clear. "You baited them?"

"My papers, my desk, my room. I didn't ask for advice. Nobody knew what I was doing. If anyone learned about my affairs, they pilfered my room. I'm in such a state at my age that I cannot stop them."

Yep, the papers gave ample potential for motive by everyone but Mrs. Poe. Callie made herself comfortable. "You left the papers out on purpose, though, in order to help you make up your mind."

"Doesn't make me guilty of a thing, Chief."

"No, ma'am. Do you know who?"

"Lacey rummaged while I was supposed to be asleep. And again, when I'd been *parked*, as you said, in the living room. She slipped in under the guise of straightening up once and getting me a sweater I didn't need. Shannon did similar, but she's a snoopy sort. Not being family, she's less likely to be concerned with the will."

Callie gave her a sideways look. "Unless she's snooping on behalf of a family member. Also, she's been employed long enough to hope for inclusion. I can see Lacey and her in collusion, ma'am. When one has you in their care, the other studies your notes and peeks at your options. They share knowledge."

Mrs. Poe seemed aware. "I know." She had lived long enough for life not to shock her anymore.

"What about the others?"

"Kimberly. . . possibly."

Mrs. Poe was being too gracious. Callie could envision any one of these people hunting for opportunity. Who they shared the information with, who they collaborated with, was another story.

"Who would Kimberly share this with?" she asked.

Mrs. Poe didn't skip a beat. "Eddie. She loves her brother, and he does a lot of work for her so she doesn't have to. If not her brother, then her daughter. Kimberly would protect her children one way or another. She's the best parent in the whole lot of us." She choked on those words since the best parent had lost the most capable child in the family tree.

Kimberly had been rather obnoxious in a previous interview. Callie still hadn't interviewed Eddie, though. Or Lacey.

"So, what's this historic Poe deal you said makes a difference in wills? What could be so important yet so obscure for your children and grandchildren to have forgotten?"

Mrs. Poe came a little forward in her chair. "I told my attorney to tell everyone I had voided the existing will."

Callie wasn't sure she heard that correctly. "Currently there is no will?" Nobody with an estate of this magnitude would do that. And could one void a will verbally? For a second she questioned not only this woman's sanity but the worth of an attorney who would honor such wishes.

"I'm perfectly sane, Chief. And I directed him only to tell people the old will was voided. He was not to talk about the contents of a new one. He'd text or call me if anyone contacted him so I could be warned who actively prowled for answers."

"Has he called you?"

"Three times," she said.

Wow. What did that say about family loyalty other than being more a devotion to reputation? Her offspring were counting down her days.

"Mind if I ask who they were?" Callie asked, overtly nice. She needed the information for the investigation. It went to motive.

"Eddie, Kimberly, and Lacey," said the old woman.

The obvious. That still was sad. Would the siblings tell the grandchildren? Callie's guess was Eddie would not tell Allan; however, if Kimberly told Kimi, she'd tell both Ogden and Allan. So, everyone knew. . . or should know.

Mrs. Poe tipped her head in full understanding. "They behave abysmally don't they?"

"Behind your back."

"Correct. They'd be coercing me right and left to decide except they don't want to reveal they spoke to my counsel. At least they still fear me. They are afraid things won't come around to their liking." A grin slid up one side of her wrinkled mouth. "Gives me damn pleasure thinking about their mental dilemmas while I'm seated with little to do. I've enjoyed not telling them, to be honest." Then the pleasure melted away. "But there's a fine line here. They'd consider me incompetent given half a chance. Once deemed demented, I'd lose all say-so." Sadness resumed its place in what Callie had come to recognize as her stoic expression. "*May you live through interesting times* is a mythical curse that gets more powerful the older you get," the grandmother said. "The elderly lose dignity in the Western world, however. I have mere months until they yank everything from me. I prefer to have one established that means something to me. You learn to think that way as your days dwindle."

Each comment became melancholier.

Callie understood enough about estates to forecast generally what would happen if Mrs. Poe had no will. Dying intestate meant assets would be divided equally amongst the three children since there was no spouse, like in the old document the adult kids thought disposed.

"Why change at all?" Callie asked, having her own idea. All the grandchildren had become adults since the old will was created. "Did you ask Eddie to invite Allan back?"

"Yes," she said. "If I didn't prompt his return, nobody would."

A little bit of a cat and mouse game took place here with Mrs. Poe playing ignorant to everyone's games.

"I see this impacting everyone, ma'am. Maybe even impact what happened to Kimi."

The old woman had escaped grief for a short while until Callie's mention of her only granddaughter. On the brink of tears, Mrs. Poe fought hiding her attempt to stabilize her feelings, but she wasn't doing a great job.

Mrs. Poe loved her grandchildren like most grandmothers. Even Ogden. On the exterior, that poor boy seemed to exist on everyone's crap list, but Callie hadn't seen a grandmother who didn't love her grandchildren regardless of their flaws. Same went for Allan leaving home for a few years.

After a deep breath, Mrs. Poe sat rigid with forced potency. "Back to what the family has overlooked. Historically one hundred percent of the assets used to go to the one most deserving, usually the oldest male.

The practice drove most of the Poes in history to have no more than two offspring. One to inherit, the other as insurance in case one died. Those who didn't inherit often lost everything or had to marry up to financially exist. I was a Woolf before I married, and our family practiced the same convention. Virginia Woolf inherited and lived quite comfortably while enabling her to write. I inherited over my brother. My husband, a Poe, inherited everything, giving his younger brother a stipend to avoid destitution. My husband and I were both single when our parents died, and once we married, our combined assets took us far."

Callie couldn't help but do the math which took her back to the seventies or early eighties, more recently than she'd first thought, but the literary names gave everything a Victorian feel. Mrs. Poe's father was likely born in the twenties. History and its habits, while fading a bit, were alive and well and continuing into another generation. Callie wondered what happened to both families' brothers and what each thought about a Woolf and a Poe combining such wealth and leaving them dry, but that curiosity wasn't germane to this investigation.

"Lacey was a surprise," Mrs. Poe said.

Had Callie missed something? "Ma'am?"

"I'd planned and delivered two children, two years apart. Lacey is eight years younger than Kimberly, and unplanned."

"Does Lacey know that?" Callie asked.

"She does," she said. "We're not often savvy with our secrets in this family."

Says the woman who currently hid her intentions for a will.

"Everyone assumes Eddie would be the one and only," she said with a slight grimace. "Don't get me wrong. I love him, and he works hard, but he's not. . . bright. Innovation is not his strong suit, and this level of wealth is best not handed to the simple minded."

Well, that was plain enough, and Callie loved the opening to her next question. "Are you skipping a generation?"

Another sigh, like her decision was obvious. "Kimberly is lazy. She'd turn everything over to Eddie, and with him being *hired help* under Kimberly's thumb, I'm not sure how hard he'd work or how much he'd care to play second fiddle. His heir would have been left out, because she would bequeath everything to her two. Kimi I have no problem with, but Ogden's potential falls woefully short without a mentor. Kimberly couldn't be trusted as to who she would leave things to."

Earlier she'd stated the family was plain-spoken, and she'd just proven the fact. But now she stopped speaking. Callie waited to be told about Lacey and began to think the silence of omission stated the obvious. The facts lined up clearly enough.

Lacey was a childless widow and had never pursued success. She settled to be a caregiver for her mother, whether lazy, loving, or conniving enough to think staying close garnered her a seat at the inheritance table. No schooling, no second husband, no participation in the business.

"No point in mentioning Lacey, Chief Morgan. She's obvious."

"She might consider herself a contender because of her sacrifice for you."

"And such thought only underlines how unsuitable she is to inherit."

Damn.

"Her choice. Not mine," Mrs. Poe continued, tone harsh enough to have a sharp point. "I hired a nurse thirteen years ago. A strong hint to Lacey, one would think, but she never did a damn thing to further herself despite me freeing her up to do so."

She waved a tired, veined hand. "Enough. All this exhausts me. No matter. Little matters anymore." That last sentence dwindled off into a whisper. Surprisingly, she fell into a silent weep. Callie wasn't about to interrupt.

Whether unintentional or strategic, the matriarch hadn't revealed her final decision. While the inheritance particulars weren't her mission, identifying motive was, and damned if she didn't have a basket full of options now. Any of them could have infiltrated that bedroom. Mrs. Poe had pollinated a slew of potential murderers.

A tap came at the door.

Mrs. Poe's weeping had diminished into a light nap, her chin resting upon her chest, a limp hand holding a tissue in her lap.

Callie eased closer to the door. "Hold on a minute," she whispered.

Returning to the desk, she gathered the papers and tapped them together, including the notepad, and scanned the room for a hiding place. In a flash of inspiration, she slid them beneath the base of the nightstand next to the bed. She tidied up the desk then returned to the door.

Deputy Raysor stood there. "These two ladies claim they need to check on the old lady."

"How dare you call her old lady!" That was Lacey.

"Shhh," Raysor said, mocking.

Lacey tried to peer around him to see.

"They are absolutely right, Deputy Raysor," Callie said, for their sake more than the deputy's. "Her name is Mrs. Poe, and sure, the ladies can come in." She backed away, letting the door swing open. "Mrs. Poe fell asleep while we were talking, so I let her be. She's only been sleeping for five minutes. I had hoped she'd awaken so we could complete our chat, but she's quite weary, I'd say."

Lacey rushed in but took note of the desk, causing hesitation in her steps. On her heels came Nurse Shannon, who did the same, only more obviously.

"She must be beside herself," Shannon said.

"Yes, I saw a tear or two, but that's a solid woman seated there," Callie said.

Lacey threw a dark cloud of expression over her shoulder. . . and a touch of drama. "You could've at least moved her to the bed and removed her shoes."

"Or called us," Shannon said, like Callie was too stupid to walk and talk at the same time.

Callie let herself out and motioned for Don to follow.

She waited until the bedroom door shut. "Watch this room. Forensics will call you if they need you. If they come up with anything worthy, let me know, but I'm not holding my breath. This will take tedious work back at the lab. I only pray our people in Walterboro analyze for enough things to hit the jackpot. The hospital will test Kimi's stomach contents. Between the two of them I hope they identify the substance."

"Can't be too hard, Chief." Deputy Raysor could speak little of toxic plants but was full of supportive phrases.

Callie slowly shook her head. "I listened to the grandmother list all the possibilities once they took Kimi, and I bet there are more. This family is shrewd. Keep an eye on anyone who as much as walks through. They are used to bluffing; not used to killing. Your uniform might make them act weird enough to earn our interest."

But Callie also knew some were accustomed to putting on fronts for boards members, venture capitalists, and bankers. She could only pray like she said that the uniform threw them off their game. "Look for the ones who are overly confident, too."

"Stand guard, help forensics, and look like a badass deputy who can read minds. Got it, Chief. Traits I was born with."

She tried not to chuckle, left him in charge, and ventured upstairs to question two potential heirs and a cook who could've put God-knows-what in everyone's food.

Chapter 29

Allan

OGDEN SAT IN A chair in the corner, fists banging his thighs. "I want to kill somebody." His high-pitched emphasis on kill raised the hair on Allan's arms. Chill bumps traveled down his back when he heard his cousin's teeth clench, slide off, and click.

Ogden had gone upstairs at Allan's insistence. They went to Ogden's room, the biggest guest room on the floor, and gave the cousin the most comfortable chair, in a position where he and Pauline could keep eyes on him, with nothing close enough to throw.

Kimi's brother was in a dangerous state of mind. Losing his only sister, someone he looked up to and thoroughly admired, left a gaping hole in his life Allan didn't think could be filled. She had kept her brother out of trouble. She redirected him when a Poe edict went against his grain and all he could envision was sullying the family name without ruining his own, over time souring his general disposition.

He was completely unmoored now. When Allan returned home to New Orleans after this fiasco, there was no telling how Ogden would behave as the only grandchild left under the Poe thumb. Or he might disappear. . . which germinated a thought in Allan's mind. Maybe he could take Ogden with him.

He felt he owed Kimi, for reasons he couldn't quite put a finger on, but his personal compass sure pointed in that direction.

Allan was angry, too, but watching the anger flash out of his cousin stemmed his own. Someone had to babysit this guy. His mother was too busy mourning her daughter. The other aunt and uncle didn't know how and would not bother. And Ogden was way too much for Grandmother Poe.

"Who the hell did this?" Ogden yelled, repeating the phrase for the third time. His gaze lasered Allan, then he gave Pauline a glower that almost carried heat.

Pauline wrapped arms around herself. "We don't know, honey."

"You have not helped any of this," Ogden yelled, his hand jerking out as if to smack the chef wherever he could land a blow.

Allan grabbed Ogden's hand, the grip showing his relation that he wasn't the only one with feelings. With a tighter grip, Allan let him know he could lose that hand if he harmed Pauline. "Settle your ass down, Ogden. She is here to help."

The boy studied the redness on his wrist a second before tucking it under his other arm.

He was listening to a degree, but his rage still ran deep, his body balled up in a knot. "I'm killing who did this," he hissed. "Don't care who; they're dead."

"I get you, man." Allan missed Kimi with a pain he needed to explode about somehow. . . yell into the wind on the beach, swim out into the dark and shout under a wave, clobber a pylon beneath the house. He needed some way to blow up and tell the world how pissed he was, too. How in the hell had someone so intelligent, charismatic, and full of potential fall prey to her own family's horrific ways?

Damn these people!

"Allan," Pauline said low.

He hadn't realized he'd wadded up the bedspread on both sides of him, his own teeth grinding enough for the chef to hear.

"Sorry."

It had to be a Poe, though. Otherwise, the culprit was Pauline or the nurse. Both had skills to kill, but no motive he could define. He'd bet on Kimi's own mother before he'd suspect Chef. She was solid while the Poes were dark and demented. They slathered themselves with the concept they could be challenging yet always win. Don't cross them. Don't try to undermine Doris Woolf Poe. She'd eat you alive, and you'd never see it coming. That pressure, that stress, and that level of expectation were what sent him packing years ago.

But could he seriously suspect Grandmother? She'd been nothing but silent or gracious to him. She was old. She rarely walked unassisted. Yet she'd served the tea the first night. . . the tea that sent him to the hospital.

And the harsh reality was that she spawned them all. She groomed them. She coerced them. She managed them, ultimately molding them. He wasn't so sure she was happy with the results, though, but the end product was indeed all hers.

He liked to think he was different because he had escaped and allowed the world to reshape him, indoctrinate him into a more open mind.

Despite Pauline's little warning, he still caught himself emulating Ogden, fists on knees, but he had to remain the adult for his cousin. The cousin who needed to chill before he bolted downstairs and took a swing at the first person he met, and there weren't just Poes in the house anymore. "Ogden, let the police do their job," he said. "We have no idea who hurt her, man. Maybe they can figure things out."

"Hell, Allan," the boy said way too loudly, and Pauline shushed him with a glance to the open doorway. But Ogden continued regardless. "Were they after you? Why didn't they get you, Allan? Or was she the one they went for?" He hit his thighs again. He'd have bruises in the morning. "I think she tried to save you in switching dishes." A growl boiled down his throat. "They should've gotten you. Live with that, Allan. She died for you, man."

"We don't know that, Ogden," Pauline said.

The boy loosened his arms and inched to the edge of his cushion, ignoring the chef, laser-focused on his cousin.

Allan spoke hesitantly. "Do you think she staged something for me, as a joke. . . you know, and screwed up on herself? Some of these plants don't have to be ingested. The worst ones damage via touch." He paused. "You were taught that as I was."

Red-faced, Ogden gained energy again. "She wouldn't do that."

Allan strongly felt otherwise. "Yeah, she would. To thwart someone else from succeeding. In case someone was coming after me." He choked up. Kimi dying for him. . .

"You son of a bitch!" Ogden sprang from the chair and rammed into Allan's chest, shoving him onto his back. Grateful for the mattress beneath him, Allan didn't see the punch coming.

Knuckles hit his jaw, connected like Ogden had done this before. Allan, however, hadn't.

He tried to roll out from under Ogden, but he was trapped half by the sunken mattress and half by Ogden's weight.

He forecasted the second hit, though. He jerked, and eyes shut, he waited for the second fist to land.

But it didn't. Pauline had wrapped herself around the young man's arm, eyes squinted shut, holding on to stop the hitting,

Ogden reared back to strike her, but the shift in balance was enough for Allan to sit up and clutch his cousin's free arm. Now he was captured on both sides, Pauline wrapped like a spider monkey around one and Allan double-gripping the other.

"Stop it," Allan yelled. "We didn't kill Kimi."

"Why did you even come back?" Ogden yelled.

His youth and strength underestimated, he fisted the hand Pauline thought she controlled and bent downward, taking her with him until she lost her hold. Then, coming back and around, he cut loose from the chef and struck Allan on the side of the head.

Allan, however, refused to let go, and somehow, despite the stars in his vision and the ringing in his ears, he latched tighter. With a hip thrust, Ogden flew off balance, putting both onto their sides on the bed. Bedding dampened the hits.

"Ogden." Laid back flat, hands up in surrender, Allan tried not to shout. "This solves nothing, man, but if you must, go ahead. Hit me. Take your anger all out on me. Finish what you started."

Ogden remained straddling his cousin, breathing hard. "What?"

"Finish. Do whatever you feel you need to do."

Removing himself from the bed, Ogden stood, breathing still rapid but not like before. Blotches covered his neck and cheeks. "Beat you up? Kill you? Or do you think I tried to poison you?"

Allan's breaths came heavy as well. He sat up. "Hit me, shoot me, poison me. . . feel free. I did not hurt Kimi, but if you want to blame my presence on everything today, this week, do it." He couldn't catch his breath enough to openly admit he wished Ogden would just do it.

He wished to God he'd never come here.

"Now you make me feel like shit," Ogden said.

"Only you can dictate how you feel." More heavy breathing.

"I hate you," came the reply as the boy returned to the chair and fell into it.

Allan resituated himself on the bed, spent. Pauline returned to her chair, her breathing up some, too.

"You okay?" he asked her.

She nodded, and they all went silent.

He prayed Chief Morgan was damn good at her job. He had no idea what happened tonight. He was still confused about the tea and the next day with the cookies. After tonight, Kimi's death meant police and forensics would scour the place. They'd do an autopsy on Kimi. . . God, they'd cut open his beautiful cousin.

Someone had made a mistake killing her. Surely someone made a mistake.

It took him a while to register the hand rubbing his back.

"Someone's going down for this," Pauline said. "No more in-house mischief."

One could only hope, but did he want family hauled to jail? And not for a little while, either. This was life-altering. Someone would spend decades behind bars. Anything intentional meant the rest of someone's life.

"Hello?" came a call from the hallway.

"Chief Morgan," Pauline whispered.

"Shit." Ogden repositioned himself in the chair, straightening his shirt.

Allan tried to flatten out the bunched bedspread. But in looking over at Pauline, she seemed scared. So did Ogden. The three locked stares, uncertain and uncomfortable.

Chapter 30

Callie

CALLIE HAD JUST poked her head in the first bedroom, but the thumping and bumping sent her trotting further down the hall to the last room on the left. She spotted the chef first, then Allan and Ogden.

All three carried stricken appearances, but Allan wore large red welts on cheek, jaw, and chin. Callie recognized them for what they were, the results of a fight that would swell and bruise before the day ended. Pauline's cheeks flushed red as well but with excitement rather than harm.

In a corner chair, Ogden mashed crossed arms into his chest, his true feelings stifled. Whether from Callie entering the room or from what happened before, it didn't take an astrophysicist to read who threw the punches, but he carried no exterior wounds. He did, however, reveal sadness, a telltale broken heart, and a frustration at not being able to do much about either.

"Found you," Callie said, not high spirited but not gloomy either. "Mind if we have a chat?"

Pauline gave a weak yes.

Allan started to rise. Ogden unfolded his arms, clearly prepared to escape whatever this was. After all, Pauline had been the one to volunteer.

"No, all three of y'all can stay," Callie said, with half an eye on Ogden who dropped back into his seat and turned toward the wall, hands kneading the arms of the upholstered chair.

She scanned the room. "Y'all have a fight in here?"

Nobody answered.

"Let me rephrase that. Anyone care to file charges?"

"No," said Allan and Pauline, which labeled Ogden the instigator.

"Ogden?" she said, moving closer but slow and easy since he still bore signs of the wrath of whatever had happened. She wanted to avoid a physical reaction, and he looked of the mind to do so. His type, those ripe with anger and no place to dump, often spotted uniforms as good spontaneous targets.

"Go away," he said, almost too gruff for her to understand.

"Ogden," she said, using his name again to ground him and help him feel heard. "We both know I'm not leaving." She peered around for a place to sit and talk to him on his level. Pauline sacrificed her small wooden chair, noiselessly sliding it over.

Callie sat, her heart aching for this boy near to her son's age, but tonight wasn't the time for motherly sympathy. At least not by her. The big shame, however, was that nobody seemed to be consoling him. A cool draft of callous insensitivity clung to the walls of this house and all the people inside, with one of them a potential murderer. Could the other two blame Ogden? Could one of them be the culprit, and they fought to convince Ogden to remain silent?

She would speak to each one in *Maelstrom Manor* and give each a chance to contribute to solving this crime. No one was willing to talk thus far. Except the grandmother, maybe, and Callie wasn't sure she had told her everything or if what she did mention was truth. She'd fallen asleep conveniently quick once Callie had flipped through the assorted wills.

Callie wouldn't bet on Ogden being the killer, not as close as he was to his sister, but he might be aware of actions gone wrong. He might know the murderer, devastated that whoever would go this far, his brain frantic at the idea of family being arrested. He wouldn't want to be the one to rat.

Kimi could've accidentally killed herself, though. Callie kept hanging on to that.

Ogden could've accidentally killed her, too. "Ogden, any idea who might have done this to your sister?"

"Do you think I'm guilty? Who told you I might be guilty?" He spat his words like released bullets.

"Nobody named you," she said. "I don't even think it's you, but I must find reason to omit you. Therefore, I must ask you certain questions. The first is obvious and is one I will ask of everybody. Either intentionally or accidentally, did you hurt Kimi?"

A darting look to Allan and Pauline told Callie he preferred not talking in front of ears.

"Can y'all leave for a moment?" she asked. "Go to another bedroom or downstairs. Don't enter the dining room or the kitchen, but I'd prefer you not leave the house since I have questions for you."

"Doesn't really leave them many options," Ogden said under his breath. He was adversarial, and Callie hoped to dispel that.

Allan slid off the bed to the other side. Pauline, already standing, left quickly on his heels, pulling the door closed behind them.

The bedroom turned tomb-like. Ogden remained coiled, prepared to react in whatever manner appropriate.

Callie checked her phone, a commonplace move, but in reality she engaged her recorder, hoping she came across simply answering a business text. To tell Ogden he was being recorded would shut him down. In South Carolina one could record if they were a party to the conversation, and while she rarely recorded in this manner, sometimes, like this one, doing so best served the situation.

She replaced the phone in her pocket. "Now, we're alone. First, I want to say I am terribly sorry about Kimi. I liked her when we met at lunch today. She's sharp."

"Not anymore," he replied.

"Her death is a huge loss," Callie continued. "That's why I want to identify who did this to her. On purpose? Maybe. An accident? I hope so. But help me, please. As her brother, you seem the best place to start."

He studied her, measuring. "Who do you believe did it?"

"I have no idea, not yet. But you tell me since I assume you knew her better than anyone in this house."

"Ask your questions," he finally said. "Get this over with so you can focus on who really did it."

She winged this without much preparation, but sometimes that's how these cases went. "Care to answer my first question? Did you kill her? On purpose or accidental?"

"I did not kill her," he said. "I don't cook, don't care to, and I despise the Q&A that goes around the table when we're tested on things." He gave a disgruntled grunt.

At dinner, he sat on the other side of Kimi, the opposite of where Allan had been scooted to make room for Sophie. They'd sandwiched her. Both cousins had the opportunity to contaminate anything on her plate without her noticing.

"Did anyone else seem suspicious?" She itched to ask *Like Allan*, but she needed his unadulterated answer.

"No. We had a normal dinner with nobody enjoying themselves except Uncle Eddie drooling over the new lady, so my attention was on my plate. I talked with Kimi, but once Allan moved beside her, her attention went in that direction. I was counting down the minutes until I could leave."

While Ogden was twenty-one, he sounded younger. Teenage. As the baby of the family, he'd likely been treated as the youngest, so he behaved accordingly. That or he preferred acting out which was sort of the same thing.

"Do you recognize the symptoms as relating to a plant or toxin?" she asked.

His forehead creased, and he looked at her like she had horns. "I told you I don't care for that stuff."

"Tell me about mandrake root," she said. Sprite and Jeb had spoken of him bragging over lunch.

He stared, as if trying to drill the thought out of her head. She stared back, waiting.

"It's one of dozens in the cookbook," he said.

"You seemed to know more earlier at Coots."

His breath quickened, jaw tight.

"You know how I know. You know more than you want to admit. Do you know who or what killed your sister?"

"No!" His dander rose back up. "You have no right—"

"Let's change direction," she said, tamping his ire. "Is any of this about the inheritance?"

He released a dark laugh. "What isn't about inheritance around here?"

"I thought the will was to leave everything to the three children," she said, baiting him.

"How would you know?"

"Your grandmother," she said right back.

He breathed faster, through his nose, loud enough for her to hear. "That was the old will. My mother confirmed with the attorney that Grandmother cancelled that one and is writing a new one. I laughed my ass off watching her lose her mind while still on the phone. The attorney must think she's nuts."

Callie acted like all this was news to her. "Changed to what? Are you receiving a share?"

He scoffed. "They'd never include me." He scoffed a second time. "My mother didn't even ask about us. That ought to tell you something."

"If she didn't ask then what makes you think you're excluded?"

He looked her over, analyzing, showing arrogance in gauging her. "You said you spoke to Grandmother."

"It's your family. What's the talk, because once your mother called, I'm sure the news spread like a brush fire."

He chuckled once in affirmation. "Okay, smart lady, let's assume the grandchildren are included in this new will. Kimi is smart. Nobody disputes that. But while we were equals in intelligence, she had charisma and sex appeal. I'm dark, like Grandmother, plus I don't cook." He gave a sarcastic shrug, a sneer to go along. "No assets worth rewarding."

This poor kid's self-assurance had been whittled down to nothing. "Surely you cook even a little," she said.

The sneer remained, but Callie spotted the sadness peeking through.

"If you can run the business, sell real estate, or create recipes like that." He snapped his fingers. "Then you have a chance. I choose not to cook, and they've given me little exposure to the business. Kimi finessed her way into the real estate side, warmed up to Uncle Eddie since Mom isn't very active in the business, and won over Grandmother."

Callie perked up at the last remark. "Maybe your grandmother likes you being more like her."

He shook his head, the dejection front and center. "You have to make money or make food around them, and you can't be half-assed doing either. That and promoting the Poe name. You see, that's where Allan messed up. He hated being a Poe, and he ran off to do his own thing." A groan belied his next thought. "Kimi was the best Poe. I would not be surprised if Grandmother hadn't left everything to her." He gave a humph. "Probably go back to the original will unless one of *them* killed Kimi."

Certainly, that screamed motive for someone. "Would you have liked that? Your sister inheriting so much?"

He thought for a second. "I'd have been fine with that. She'd do right by Grandmother, and my grandmother is no dummy. And Kimi would likely do right by me."

The thought of his sister no longer being in that position seemed to seize him. Tears filled his eyes, and he turned away.

"Ogden," Callie said.

He turned back, the anger returned. "This is bullshit."

"What is?"

"Your using me." His voice bounced off the wall beside him. "You're a piece of shit thinking I might even consider killing the best person in my life." He stood.

"Sit down, Ogden."

"We're done!"

She'd give him one more chance. "Please, sit back down."

Ogden, the youngest and least informed of the clan saw where Grandmother was going with a new will, which made Callie wonder about the others, too. He needed to keep talking.

"You said Kimi cooks?" She spoke about the sister in present tense in hope of striking a chord.

The shift in topic messed with him as she'd hoped. He remained standing. "She can cook enough to pass muster with the adults, but that's still better than the average person. The serious cooking gene fell to Allan, but when he left he broke the code."

Good. "Any chance he's considered in the new will? If he's that good of a cook, I mean."

Ogden's darkness returned. "Why do you think he showed up? Grandmother has several drafts of a new will in her room, though," he said.

"Yes, I know," she replied, shocking him back.

"How would you know?" He sat back down.

"I spoke at length with your grandmother, remember? I've read them all."

He hadn't expected that.

Chapter 31

Callie

OGDEN WASN'T happy, which put Callie on guard. Grieving individuals easily lost control of their emotions, blinded by the love they lost. The small upstairs bedroom was feeling smaller by the minute.

He spoke harshly, making Callie wonder if he could be heard downstairs. Surely down the hall. "Why would Grandmother tell you about the changes in the will before telling me, or Kimi, or anyone?"

She remained calm yet primed. His feelings of betrayal only underlined his feelings of being the underdog. A stranger outside the family had been informed before he had. Even if he wasn't a major recipient, he deserved to know, or such would be his thoughts. Callie could read the tension in his shoulders, the way his feet planted flat against the floor.

"Ogden, anyone sees how incredibly crystal clear y'all vie for. . . something. Attention maybe. Validation possibly but not only about money. Regardless, your family wields a noxious vindictive bearing toward one another." She watched him. His unsettling balance between curiosity and ire had become unpredictable. "Plus, I saw the papers," she continued. "She trusts me because I don't have a dog in the fight, and my mission is only to find out what happened to Kimi."

He seemed to understand that.

Shoulders easing, he cooled himself down but still gnawed the inside of his bottom lip. He was simple to read. She gave him the time to put pieces together.

She could perform a similar interview with each family member, with few adjustments, and wind up right here in the same place. Each of them would want to know who was in the will more than who killed Kimi. She bet if the tables were turned, Kimi would be the same way. She just loved more than all the others. That gave her the strength to be who she wanted to be while all the others were too busy pretending and putting on airs.

Ogden hadn't mentioned who he suspected killed Kimi, but he had asked about the will. That was so sad.

"What did the different wills say?" he asked, disappointing her more.

Callie had really hoped to eliminate him from the suspect list. "You said you assumed you weren't in any of the wills."

His blood pressure rose a bit. "I said I probably wasn't."

"Let's go with that. Does excluding you make you upset?"

He gave a clipped laugh. "That's what detectives ask in a Netflix movie to rattle whomever they are interviewing."

"That's because a good line works. Are you angry for being excluded?"

"I don't know. Am I?"

"You act like it," she said.

"Am I in any of the drafts?" he said, evading, verbally dancing, trying to joust in return.

She pointed to the door. "When we get done here, go ask your grandmother. Or your aunt, or your uncle. Surely they'll tell you."

"The others know?"

"Why wouldn't they know?" Callie could do this all night. "Are you mad that they know and you don't?"

He exploded. "Hell, yeah I'm mad. I'm stuck riding the coattails of whomever is in power. If Kimi had won out, she'd have treated me decently. Any other scenario and I'm screwed. Guess what the wills say doesn't matter, does it?"

"Son, you haven't even suggested who might have killed your sister. However, you have tried for. . ." and she looked at her watch, "a half hour, to find out if you get any money when Grandmother Poe dies. If that doesn't make you suspect material, I don't know what does."

A flush fled up his neck into his cheeks. Hands gripped the chair again, fingers digging the tufted material. The veins in his throat pulsed hard enough to see.

Callie pushed on. "Any chance your anger made you do something you might not otherwise? Did the will send you down a bad road? Maybe you messed up and took your sister out by mistake instead of Allan." She waited before saying, "Unless you did so intentionally, fully aware your sister would take the pot. . . maybe leave you out."

He leaped to his feet. Callie rose to hers, still having to angle her neck up to address him.

Limited space between the bed and chairs gave little room to maneuver. Callie stood braced on the balls of her feet, right hand on her belt with barely three feet between them. And he stood eight inches taller and fifty pounds heavier.

"Who's guilty, Ogden?"

"Shut. Your. Mouth. Chief," he said through clenched teeth, each word enunciated in a sentence of its own. "I'd have to kill them all to inherit a dime. Kimi knew she was favored and Allan knew he wasn't. I, however, knew my future depended upon my sister." Tears traveled down his cheeks, and he didn't bother to wipe them.

"Who did it?"

"Grandmother watches and judges, those crazy silver eyes ranking us," he said. "What we say, what we do. You'd think she'd throw her grandson a fuckin' bone." As hard as he spoke, he didn't stop the break in his voice.

He was such a sad soul.

Callie thought of Jeb and hoped he didn't feel this anchored to a need to appease his elders. Young adults needed guidance, not restraint. They were supposed to look forward to the future; not think they didn't have one to pursue.

She struggled to find anything that could be deemed a bright side. "Your mother is in the will. She would—"

"No, she wouldn't."

Callie hushed and waited to let him explain.

"My uncle and my mother are tight," he said, holding up crossed fingers. "Mother doesn't like the business, but that doesn't mean she doesn't understand it. Uncle Eddie enjoys managing, but he isn't as smart as my mother." His sad chuckle and loss of contact spoke of certain memories Callie doubted she'd be made privy to. "It takes the two of them," he said. "They wouldn't waste their investment in the name of inheritance. Especially to me."

Callie still wasn't seeing the point. Surely parents wanted to leave assets to their offspring.

He thrust his arms out to the side, reeking of desperation. "Wake the hell up, Chief. In a united front, they'd leave the business to Kimi. Sure, I might be given a stipend for appearances, like Allan would, but my sister would be the star. If Allan and I received more than five percent, I'd be shocked."

No wonder there were multiple drafts of the will. Kimi made sense, both in the inheritance and in the poisoning.

"Who would you speak to next, if you were me?" she asked, attempting to lower the temperature of the conversation.

"The one most suspected or the one most knowledgeable?" he asked, and she admired the question. "Allan," he continued. "In case Kimi warned him about any danger or discussed the will. She'd tell him things she'd tell no one else."

"Over you?"

"Yes."

"Over your mother?"

"Without a doubt," he said through a look of disgust. "My mother was beside herself at Allan coming home. She thought he would ruin things in play." His chuckle was dark. "She might've been right."

"What about your uncle?" she asked.

"Uncle Eddie's who I'd talk to next. Or Aunt Lacey."

Interesting. "Why them?"

"My uncle liked being the Poe face. No doubt he heard from my mother about the will change, but while he'd be pissed, he's a sissy."

"Meaning?" she asked.

"Violence is not his thing. Poisoning? Maybe. He did make a fool out of himself doting over Sprite's mother tonight, in my opinion. Too much of a fool. Like he hid his involvement behind his showering of attention over Mrs. Bianchi."

Good for you, Odgen. "And your Aunt Lacey? Why her?"

He cleared his throat, noting the door like someone could be listening. He lowered his voice when he hadn't before. "Because she's sneaky, greedy, lazy, jealous, and worthless. Uncle Eddie would confirm that, which is why you should talk to him before her."

"Would she kill anyone?" Callie asked, not fond of the woman from her own experience.

He leaned over, and in a deep, sardonic voice said, "She'd kill someone in a fuckin' heartbeat. She's spent the most time at Grandmother's side over the years, watching how to cook. . . and what does and doesn't go into dishes." His nostrils flared. "She acts silly, but she's pure bitch."

Little comments like this showed he could still talk herbs and such. "Explain the toxic plants y'all studied again?" she asked, like she hadn't before.

But he saw through her. The spotlight had turned back to him.

He shoved her in the chest, hard enough to take her off her feet and onto the bed. Then he mashed against the side of the bed, and against her, using his weight and thighs to pin her in place. "You're pushing my damn buttons on purpose. I have zero to confess to. I did nothing to her, don't you see that?" He leaned over her, panting.

"Raysor!" she screamed as Ogden's arms stretched out on either side of her, coming down to shift his weight to the bed. Confined, she expected him to pounce and flail into her, unleash that temper that had come and gone, but now wanted to stay.

"Any of them could have killed her!" he yelled.

She could smell his breath, and two drops of his spittle landed on her neck.

"Uncle Eddie thinks the inheritance is his and my mother's. My mother thinks the same. Aunt Lacey expects a share for her sacrifice." His long deep breath scared Callie. She attempted to wriggle back, but he only moved with her, gripping the sides of her shirt to make a point. "The family is screwed!" he yelled. "I'm screwed."

He didn't hear the heavy footsteps coming up the stairs.

"Ogden, back away," she ordered.

But his complexion darkened. "Do you know how easy any of us could kill someone though? All you have to do is—"

Raysor plowed into the room, the doorknob banging against the wall. He rounded the foot of the bed, snatched Ogden off, then pinned him against the wall so they looked evenly eye-to-eye. A framed picture fell and bounced off a chair. Glass pieces scattered. Ogden's toes barely touched the floor.

"What's your problem, boy?" Raysor usually reserved this caliber of his voice for someone about to be perp-walked to jail.

Callie rolled off the bed on the other side and came up beside the deputy. "He just lost his cool a second, Deputy Raysor."

"Is that what we're calling assaulting an officer of the law?" he roared again for the boy's sake, not hers.

Ogden's rage had dissipated, though, and tears filled his eyes.

Raysor let him down. "Son, I'm sorry for your loss, but you do not touch the police."

Ogden crumbled into the upholstered chair he'd been sitting in most of the time. . . and sobbed.

"You hurt?" Raysor asked Callie under his breath.

"He shoved me onto a mattress, so no, Don."

He could've done more, but he didn't. "Ogden," she said, squatting to his level. "Who do you think killed your sister?"

"I don't know. I don't know," he cried, his elbows on his legs, his palms cupping his face and catching tears.

"If you had to guess," she said.

He sucked in hard from all the crying. "I don't want to incriminate my mother."

Surprising. "Your mother?"

He wiped his cheeks with wet hands and sniffled again. "No, not what I meant. She could not kill her daughter. My guess is Allan, Uncle Eddie, or Aunt Lacey.

Half the clan, then.

"Are you sure about Allan? You went to lunch with him. You were in here talking to him. . ."

Cheeks blotchy, he blinked through the tears. "After three years I don't know him enough to rule him out." The young man dissolved again, doubled over to where his head almost touched his lap.

"Better return downstairs," she told her deputy, moving toward the door. "This family is unpredictable as hell."

"Want me to take him with me?" Raysor asked, loud enough for Ogden to hear.

"Nah. I'll leave him here. Did you see Allan or the chef come down the stairs?"

He shook his head. "Nope."

"Then they're up here in another bedroom. I'll find them. You go on," she said pulling out her phone.

He left and Ogden remained in his chair despondent. She went into the hall, shutting the bedroom door behind her.

A revelation had occurred to her when Raysor was diffusing the boy. She'd blown the thought off earlier as crazy, but sometimes crazy found its place in a plan.

She turned off the app recording, then held the device for a moment longer. She dialed a number in her favorites. Not a top favorite, but one that dragged the bottom of her top ten.

"Mother? You still up?" Her watch said nine thirty. "More importantly, are you sober?"

Callie couldn't believe she was doing this. But she'd learned to listen to her gut and some of her random thoughts forged in the heat of a case.

"Yes to both, dear."

"How many martinis did you have tonight?" Four was not an unusual number.

"One about two hours ago. I found a new brand of coffee. A crème brûlée flavor I'm growing fond of. Is everything okay? Is Jeb good? He's still not mad is he? I certainly have his best interest at heart, and the sooner he realizes that the better we'll all be."

"Mother, remember me talking about Doris Woolf Poe today at lunch?"

The quick turn of conversation stunned Beverly, but she recovered quickly. A dignified scoff came through, likely from some memory that the Poes had not been very welcoming to her. "I remember her, yes. Why?"

"She just lost her twenty-two-year-old granddaughter tonight. I'm on the case at their house. You remember *Maelstrom Manor* on Palmetto, don't you?"

"Of course."

"Mrs. Poe is eighty and being overlooked here by the rest of the family who seem to be losing their minds. She's feeling rather sad and forgotten. I thought she might like to have someone closer to her age to help her through this. Are you up to it?"

Callie barely heard the inhale of surprise. Beverly could've been snide about the ages not aligning or comment about being called so late, but she didn't. "Why Callie, I'd love to. I'll be there in forty minutes."

"Don't speed. Those oaks along the highway are unforgiving."

"Quit talking, honey. You're delaying me."

Callie tucked her phone away, wondering what the hell made her make that call. She could have called Councilwoman Donna Baird. She had people skills, b ut she had zero in common with Grandmother Poe. Beverly, on the other hand, had people skills in spades. She could talk Grandmother's world.

Suddenly a part of her found the gesture rather wise.

Beverly was a tough old woman. Few could intimidate her, and if Callie told her to watch over Mrs. Poe, she'd do so with pleasure. The fact that her daughter was police chief would make her stop God from coming into the room. The Devil as well, and under this roof, the chances of the latter occurring were much higher amongst these folks.

Chapter 32

Allan

ALLAN DIDN'T know where to go and yet remain in the house as the chief ordered. The last thing he wanted was to be seen, questioned, or scrutinized by family. They'd blame all of this on him for coming back. Hell, he even thought so. Kimi might still be alive, and yes, he felt the two were connected.

Tears welled again at the thought of her.

"Where are we going, my friend?" Pauline asked, standing at his side at the top of the stairs.

"No fucking idea," he said in barely a whisper.

She rubbed his back. "Let me simplify, then. Upstairs or downstairs?

Peering downstairs enough to scan the dining room and a little more, he saw a deputy on guard at the base of the stairs. The forensic team still milled around. "Upstairs."

"My room good enough for you?" She led him there without waiting for his answer since the police chief currently occupied his room with Ogden.

Her bedroom was neat to a fault. Stacks of reading material which he assumed were recipes and cookbooks. A thick yet small suitcase rested on a chair, a suitcase which could contain something cooking related. Herbs maybe. Or toxins if he leaned toward impugning her.

He reached to move it, and Pauline rushed in. "Some of the things inside are breakable. I'll take care of that."

He let her move the case. Then she moved an unholstered chair a few feet closer, so they weren't yelling across the room.

"What's in the case?" he asked.

Her leery look gave him a small chill. "Why?"

He hadn't the patience left to let doubts go by. "Because I can't trust anything and anyone anymore."

The empathy she'd been showing disappeared. "Now you suspect me?"

He didn't really. . . yet a smidgeon of doubt hung there, plus he no longer felt entitled to give anyone a pass. He wasn't sure of his own judgment anymore. "May I see inside?"

"You're pissing me off, kid."

He gave a one-shoulder shrug. "If you're not guilty, you should have no qualms about letting me see inside." His imagination strayed to vials of dried herbs, packed in case there weren't natural fresh items at hand wherever her employment was.

But what if. . .

Not waiting for her permission, he reached over and unlocked the case. The lid was deceptively weighty, and upon opening, he saw why. Strapped in were bottle after bottle of herbs and seasonings. He peered questioningly at her, and she held disdain in her expression.

Jimson weed, oleander, and yew had already been mentioned as local items. Hemlock grew in ditch banks on the island. A jungle environment thrived with plants that could take someone down. But coming from Atlanta, she might've wanted to make sure.

"Go ahead. Open one. Any of them," she said, droll and annoyed.

Labels indicated sage, three types of oregano, and so on. The C's alone. . . cinnamon, chervil, chives, coriander. . . nothing saying cyanide. Allan randomly opened and smelled some bottles, his nose telling him the labels were correct. But he handled barely a tenth of them, and a dozen of them had no labels at all. He debated whether to ask her about those, but he still remained in hope of a job. He just didn't want to work for someone who might've killed his cousin.

Coming up short finding anything nefarious, he shut the case and felt guilty.

"Sorry, Pauline. I'm a hammer in search of a nail."

"I see that," she said, benign in her behavior.

He hated himself now.

Kimi was all anyone ought to be discussing. Her bright light was wasted by some sorry son-of-a-bitch. . . or bitch. He wasn't the type to beat the shit out of the person, but he was all for the chief of police finding them. Other than Pauline, he didn't care who. He could tolerate Kimi toying with his food, but not anyone else. She'd have been the only one playing innocent games with him.

Pauline watched him tripping through thoughts.

"I don't believe you did anything," he said, feeling her attentions.

"You don't say. You smell my herbs, notice those not labeled, then wonder how far you can afford to insult me."

Looking up at the ceiling, he inhaled, held the air and then released loudly. "I'm sorry. Give me this, please. Three food contaminations in as many days. All probably meant for me. I'm scared to brush my teeth, for God's sake."

Yelling traveled down the hall, heard even through closed doors. Theirs and the one Ogden occupied with the chief.

Both hushed, listening. Ogden seemed to be on a roll. Then someone heavy pounded up the stairs.

"Don't go out," Pauline said, listening harder.

A man's voice commanded attention, but they couldn't make out the words.

Then all went quiet.

"Maybe I ought to—" Allan started, but Pauline shut him down with a quick shake of her head. Quiet, quiet. . . then sobbing. "That's Ogden," he said.

"I believe so," Pauline replied, then pointed to the herbs. "I've kept my door locked because of that suitcase," she said. "And I haven't needed to use the contents. The kitchen here is well stocked. You're welcome to sniff the bottles downstairs, too, if that makes you happy."

Damn, he couldn't afford to alienate her. "I don't blame you, Chef. Let forensics investigate the kitchen." He gingerly locked the case. "I have no desire to tell them about this."

He needed Pauline on his side, and he hoped he still had her as an ally. He damn sure couldn't trust the family.

"Who do you think did it?" he asked her, hoping to rebuild a connection. "I mean to Kimi, not me. Personally, I expect the person to wind up being one and the same."

"I'm not assuming anything." She chose a comfortable position to wait.

He did the same, the closed door giving him some sense of peace. He shut his eyes but kept seeing Kimi. She was so perfect, prettier than when he left. . . the least flawed of the family. Surely someone mistook her plate for his.

He turned to Pauline. "She ate off my plate. Drank from my glass, Chef."

"I wasn't in the room," Pauline said, eager to hear more. "Y'all swapped place settings? Drinks, plates, what else?"

"Found you," Callie said, coming in before they had a chance to hear her knock.

Chapter 33

Callie

CALLIE PEERED AT the two chefs, as she'd come to think of them.

Allan seemed to be the catalyst and common denominator of this drama. Pauline had had her hands on every food item in question.

"Let's talk," she said to both.

"Not separately?" Allan asked, and from Pauline's expression, he'd beat her to the asking.

"Nope."

Unsettled at the unknown before them, the two shifted in place, her in an upholstered chair and Allan on the bed. They projected as a united front. Understandable since they'd had ample time to collaborate.

Callie started with him. "Allan, did you notice anything different between your food, drink, place setting, silverware setup, anything, and Kimi's?"

He shook his head more than necessary. "I noticed nothing, and nothing came to mind later. She didn't talk about the food. She didn't act like our settings were off base. She was her usual cut-up self. To show up everyone, she swapped her bowl and glass of water with mine." The memory turned up the side of his mouth. "She rather embellished the move, too."

Callie could see that. "Was this one of her tricks gone bad by any chance?" This had been one of her working theories from the beginning, underlined by the playful nature of the girl.

Allan exchanged looks with Pauline, which only proved to Callie that they'd spoken about the possibility. "If she did, I didn't see it.," he said. "She was being beautiful, smart, fun Kimi." Tears filled his eyes, then fell.

"I keep thinking someone came for me again," he said, "and she got in the way." Emotions overwhelmed him, and he released a sob.

Reaching over, Pauline rubbed his knee in consolation. "I'm here, hon."

Callie remained stable, letting Pauline be his consoler. Nobody in the family was beyond suspicion. Nobody could claim innocence. Not yet.

Allan, for instance, could've attempted retaliation. He could have even toyed with his cousin for pranking him first. Speaking of the original tricks, Callie asked, "Allan, any chance that Kimi owned up to the first two episodes with you?"

He shook his head.

Pauline looked honestly pained for him.

"Chef," Callie said, sliding herself a few inches forward. "Explain step by step from the time you cooked this dinner to when the event happened."

"Sure, I can do that," she said, as if grateful for a question she could easily answer. "I started prepping dinner right after lunch, except for the seafood which couldn't go in until a half hour before serving time so it wouldn't overcook and turn rubbery. Ever have overcooked shrimp? Or clams? They're worse."

Callie ignored the questions. "Did you leave the kitchen at any time? To go to the bathroom, or your bedroom?"

"I used the half bath off the kitchen. Two minutes tops. Stepped outside on the porch once when the kitchen got a tad hot, but I kept an eye on the stove through the screen. You and I had spoken about how vital it was to guard the food, so I did."

Callie nodded in remembrance but let Pauline continue.

"It got close to supper time, and when I poked my head out the kitchen door Allan was talking with his grandmother." She was animated with her words, her head bobbing. She turned to Allan. "Only the two of you, right?"

They might be in the same room, but Callie didn't want them to compare her account to his. "Please don't ask for validation, Pauline. Give me your take. I only want what you saw, you heard, and experienced, even if nothing like Allan's interpretation."

That made the chef stop and think. "No, that's what I saw. I gave Allan and Mrs. Poe about ten minutes, but then I had to set the table. The family likes its meals on schedule. When I came out with items in my hand for the table, Allan rose, and Mrs. Poe remained seated." She blushed. "Well, of course she remained seated. She doesn't walk much unassisted."

Then her mouth tightened. "They are always *depositing* her somewhere. I've talked to her a few of those times. While she's not one for many words, I figured listening to me prattle on about recipes and flavors was better than her being alone. God, that woman was such an icon once upon a time. I find it ridiculous how people discount seniors, particularly ones with talent. She still can master croissants and a smooth Bearnaise sauce. From scratch," she tacked on.

"Pauline," Callie said, interrupting the nervous chatter. Mrs. Poe would be Pauline's favorite short of Allan. She would have been aware of *Southern Silver Spoon* before she even met Allan. "You placed the settings on the table. How many?"

"Eight," she said without missing a beat.

The table could accommodate twelve, dating back to when there were spouses, Callie assumed. "Did anyone else come into the dining room or kitchen? Where were Lacey and Shannon, the people in charge of Grandmother Poe? Where were the kids? Did you not see Eddie or Kimberly?" Funny how nobody ever spoke of the last two.

With sarcasm, Pauline gave a *humph*. "Don't know where the kids were. Other times they blew through to eat something I'd fixed for snacking. Today, however, they vanished after breakfast. I take that back. One time Ogden wanted a drink. I stopped him at the door, pulled his bottled drink from the fridge, and shooed him away with orders not to return until called. Around four Eddie looked in to ask what time dinner was. Kimberly asked if she could help around three, but I told her no, and that you'd told me to keep the cooking area off limits thanks to all the mishaps of late."

Chef's accounting wasn't half bad. All could be confirmed or denied.

"Now," Pauline said, as if leading to the pinnacle of her presentation. "Lacey, being the witch she is, blew into my kitchen while I was setting the table. Right past me! I threw down the last utensils on the table and ran back in to stop her from touching my food."

"Did she touch anything?"

"Not that I saw," she said, with a slight squint of irritation. "She would've had to be darn quick to do anything. But how could she have doctored something that only Kimi touched and nobody else?"

"You tell me," Callie said.

Giving someone a free rein to speak led them to say more than they needed to. They preferred filling in the silence, showing how they cooperated a hundred and ten percent. That way they felt less scrutinized when the behavior did the opposite.

She let Pauline prattle on. With a dead girl and a family versed in macabre cooking, she needed any information she could get from a person skilled in the latter.

Pauline frowned. "That woman. . . I ordered her to get out. She told me it was a Poe kitchen, not mine. I told her as long as I was under contract to cook, the kitchen was mine to rule."

Callie envisioned her fussing at Lacey just like that.

"But she kept throwing the Poe card. I said pay me and cut me loose. The birthday dinner was on her. Please let me explain to Mrs. Poe before I leave. That shut her up. Grandmother is a strong trump card around here. Glad to see the old lady still has clout."

The chef's enthusiasm left her almost breathless.

"What did she say then?" Callie asked.

"She didn't say anything. The idiot turned and marched off. She's the least powerful of the brother and sisters, and she can't fire me." With a snort she waved a hand. "I have no idea what she did from there." Then she motioned that hand toward Allan. "He might be able to fill in the gaps."

Might as well. "Allan," Callie said. "You were in the dining room talking to your grandmother. . ."

"Yes," he said, repositioning himself on the quilt. "Lacey came busting out of the kitchen, but since we were about to sit down to supper, she stayed. Huffing about Pauline, she traveled around the whole table mumbling to herself while she repositioned silverware and turned the crystal glasses of water so that they all faced the same way, like she just had to do something to correct Chef. Thing is, nobody was watching her, so why?"

"You were her audience." Callie took special note of Lacey's actions at the table. "Was the water in crystal or glass?"

"Pardon?" he asked.

Callie had weathered enough of Beverly's fetes and galas to know the difference. "Crystal has no side. Glass, however, often has a slight seam you can see. You can't *face* crystal."

Pauline knew that from her expression, but she remained hushed.

"Well, then maybe she wanted the glasses the same distance from the plates, or the edge of the placemat, or the silver. She went around adjusting them."

"Then what?" she asked.

"Mrs. Bianchi arrived and we all sat down to dinner," he said.

He'd skipped a lot. "Fill in the gaps, Allan. You had to move places to where you wound up sitting. Did y'all pass the food or get served? Go back to when Mrs. Bianchi arrived. Did anything unusual happen?

Once you began eating, did some people eat one thing and not eat something else? Details are important."

"I didn't poison anyone," he said.

"Didn't say you did. Why are you defensive?"

"Why are you pushing? I've been the victim since I arrived." His voice hardened. A lock of hair kept falling in his eyes, making him mad to keep nudging it away. "You sure as hell can't believe I killed my cousin. She was the only one worth a shit."

Callie remained firm and level. "Who says it was intentional? Maybe someone else was trying to get to you, and again, the table seating change spoiled the plan."

Allan ran both hands through his hair, anxious. "This is my fault."

Pauline's hand went over her mouth, but Callie had heard victims and accused alike say this when meaning something totally different than they did the deed. Callie, however, wanted to hear Allan explain further.

"Allan," Callie said when he appeared to have gotten lost behind both hands. "Tell me exactly what you mean. How is this your fault?"

From behind those fingers, he trembled, and Callie gave him a minute. Impatient, she timed that minute, because she had little time for scattered feelings right now.

He spoke muffled. "Just me being here has caused all of this."

Whatever. He did not mold these people. Their dark, selfish peculiarities didn't happen between the time he left and when he returned the other day. Whether they preferred he remain gone was unknown. Each person held their own feelings regarding that. To some he might've been a motive to act. To others, he was a nuisance. She'd always been right, though, as to him being the catalyst.

Shouting and wailing rose up the stairwell. Striding into the hall, Callie spotted Ogden bolting down the stairs.

Wailing, Kimberly shouted, "Where's Mother? I need Mother."

"Kimberly," said Eddie, wrapping an awkward arm around her shoulders. "She's likely in bed. Let her be. She's hurting, too."

But the sister keened on. "I need her, Eddie. God, how am I supposed to go on?"

Bawling, she headed toward the downstairs master bedroom only for Eddie to hold her back. "I said let Mother be. She's too frail, Kim."

Callie reached midway down the stairs in time to see Ogden reach out to his mother, eager to console and be consoled. But he hugged way harder than he received.

"Why Kimi?" she cried into his collar.

Ogden reared back. "You mean instead of me?"

But his mother didn't answer him, which seemed as painful to her son as if she had. "Kimi held promise," Kimberly said. "She was the future of this entire family."

Ogden pulled back, stung, fighting not to show weakness through tears.

Callie felt someone at her elbow, catching a glimpse of Allan. Kimberly caught the movement and flashed red-faced anger.

Almost guttural, she didn't identify which person she addressed, but the entire house heard. "It's your damn fault."

She lurched toward the stairs, at Allan. Before Raysor could intervene, Eddie did. "Where's the damn nurse?" he shouted. "She needs a sedative."

The entire forensic team had huddled on the other side of the dining room.

All passion and no sense, Ogden shouted, "How can you say that Kimi was worth more?"

"Because she was!" Kimberly shouted.

Good heavens.

"I'm finding Shannon," Allan said, pushing around everyone. She hadn't been seen upstairs, and forensics kept her out of the dining room and kitchen. Either she was outside, where she'd been told not to go, or holed up in the study, probably with Lacey.

"She's in the grandmother's room," Raysor said, stepping forward. "Saw her take something to her to drink."

"The kitchen is off-limits, Don. How did she fix something to drink?"

The idea he might've erred stiffened him a bit. "A forensic guy wouldn't let her in the kitchen, but he nuked a cup of water for her when she explained the old lady's health."

"What about the tea bag, or whatever?" she asked, not liking where this was going.

The deputy shrugged. "Pocket? Purse? Hell, I don't know."

Not too thrilled about a one-on-one taking place between Shannon and Grandmother Poe, especially in light of this chaos, Callie pushed through, following Allan.

He knocked, but Callie reached for the handle and pushed her way into Grandmother's bedroom, just in time to see her hit the cup and saucer being pushed at her in her place in bed propped on pillows. The china pieces flew against the wall.

"Do not defy me," the elder woman directed. "I said I did not want it."

"That was to help you sleep," Shannon said, tight-lipped at being caught, being bested, who knew?

But Grandmother was tight jawed, her white brow furrowed, eyes narrowed, sinewy neck drawn tight. "You do *not* argue with me, Shannon. Know your place."

The nurse didn't back down. "I know what's good for you, and you need to settle down. You listen to me, you shriveled up old—"

Allan shoved himself between the two. "Don't talk to my grandmother like that. Nothing gives you that right."

But Shannon wasn't deterred. "I have every right as her caregiver. Lacey tells me—"

"You stupid cow," Mrs. Poe said, her words dripping with condescension. No volume and no rush, just a finite point.

Allan stepped aside to give his grandmother a view of her adversary.

"Shannon Kirby, I have paid your salary for thirteen years. Not Lacey. . . me. When I say no, I mean no."

"Now Mrs. Poe—"

"You're fired."

Shannon's condescension shined bright. "Now, now. Lacey—"

"Lacey didn't hire you. You're fired, I said."

Partly shaken, maybe still in disbelief, Shannon headed toward the broken saucer, liquid on the floor and wall, even puddled in some of the pieces. Some sharded had slid under the nightstand where Callie had hidden the assorted copies of the will.

"Leave it," Mrs. Poe said.

The nurse ignored her yet again. "No, let me clean this up."

Callie rounded the foot of the bed and took Shannon by the arm, raising her firmly to a stiff-legged posture. "You're leaving the room."

Shannon's expression carried a sense of trepidation, then defiance. "Look at me," Callie said. "You've been relieved."

Fear deepened in the woman's eyes. By now people had gathered inside and outside the bedroom.

"Raysor?" Callie called, and the deputy's head popped up over those of the family.

"Chief?" he replied, his voice carrying.

She tightened her grip on Shannon's arm. "Go get forensics." She watched as Shannon's eyes widened. A man from the team appeared. Callie pointed out the saucer and liquid splashed everywhere. "Pictures and testing. We need to know what was in that cup."

He peered around. "Where's the cup?"

"Probably rolled under the nightstand," Callie said. "And salvage those papers hidden under there. Nobody touches them but you and me. Is that clear?"

The family appeared clueless, but Shannon didn't. Lacey showed, and nobody could miss the silent exchange between the two women.

Bless her, Lacey tried to demonstrate some sense of power. "You don't have the right, Chief Morgan."

"Oh, but I do," Callie said, doing a finger wave at Raysor. "Take this one," and she gently rocked the nurse's arm, "to the study. She speaks to nobody. Stay with her until I relieve you."

"Got it, Chief." He moved his wide girth through the small crowd, replaced Callie's grip with his own, and disappeared with his charge.

In passing Lacey, Shannon tried to shake loose, as if Raysor's hold was anything less than solid. "Let me speak to Lacey."

But as told, the deputy continued walking, forcing Shannon to trip and keep moving, Lacey following. "She wants to speak to me, deputy. Stop where you are. I demand it."

Raysor kept on. As he reached the study door, Lacey hollered, "Shannon, don't say a thing without an attorney present. You hear me? Don't talk to anyone!"

The study door shut, leaving Lacey alone in the middle of the living room, everyone else standing outside Grandmother's bedroom.

Forensics returned with their kit to the bedroom.

Remaining in the bedroom entry, Allan spoke up. "What the hell is going on?"

Kimberly burst into tears again.

Ogden tried not to.

Lacey stomped her foot. "For God's sake people," then she cried as well. "Shannon and I are a couple. I have spousal rights."

"Shut up," Eddie said. "You're not married."

"How would you know?"

"You're an idiot," her brother said under his breath, giving her his back.

"I'm not believing this," Allan said, a low tone rising along with his temper. "Shannon abuses our grandmother, your mother, like that and you care more about her than what she might be doing to her?"

"Shut up, Allan," Lacey said. "You have no damn right—"

"What kind of misplaced concern is that, Aunt Lacey? What don't you want her to say? Or are you trying to protect not only her but yourself as well?" He gawked at his other aunt. "Aunt Kimberly. What if Lacey and Shannon killed Kimi?"

The room's occupants gasped collectively, including forensics who had no idea who anybody was.

By now the family rumbled in full chaos mode. Callie was inclined to watch and listen. Releasing some of the pent-up steam might likewise reveal clues.

Kimberly pummeled Lacey with screamed questions. Eddie shouted for someone to help his sister, then both his sisters, then realized nobody cared to help either of them and there wasn't a nurse anymore.

Allan held back Ogden, and Ogden yelled at Allan to let him loose. Pauline retreated up the stairs to the landing, took a seat and watched, mouth behind hands, elbows on her knees. The drama was downright magnetic for forensics, particularly belonging to the family of Poe.

Callie, however, called in Officer Annie. She and Raysor needed another set of hands to keep this group contained.

Chapter 34

Callie

WITH RAYSOR guarding Shannon in the study, Callie feared leaving the crowd. Emotional aggression could turn physical in a heartbeat. Voices still rose and fell with everyone seeking someone to blame.

She had inserted herself at Grandmother's doorway, wary of any member slipping in there to hunt wills, wipe up the spilled tea, or even back the old woman against the headboard of her bed for real answers. Nope, none of that was happening, which meant people would be antsy now, because the whole house felt like a tide was turning.

People suspected one another, and the cops kept showing up. Any guilty party would be nervous about how all this would pan out.

Officer Annie Greer must not have been far, because she knocked on the door less than five minutes after being called. Thank heavens for Edisto's small footprint.

Callie gave orders. "Annie, relieve Raysor in the study. If Shannon needs to use the bathroom or whatever, accompany her. Eyes on her at all times. Send Raysor to me."

The family held their breath long enough to hear what she had to say, to include why she'd called for a third badge. Even forensics had paused. "Y'all keep doing your thing," she said.

Raysor reappeared

"Deputy," she said. "Manage these people. Use your cuffs if you need them. Need mine as well?" she added purely for effect.

Voices quieted at the mention of cuffs.

"Sure," the deputy said, enjoying the theater and holding out his hand. Callie passed over the cuffs then entered Grandmother's bedroom. When Kimberly and Lacey tried to follow, she motioned for them to back up and shut the door.

"We have a right to be in there!" hollered Lacey.

"You cannot lock us out of our own property," Kimberly added, pounding the door.

"That's our mother in there!" Lacey cried.

"She can't be left alone. One of us needs to be with her!"

Callie snatched open the door. "Raysor? Are you even there? You can use the cuffs any time now. I don't need this interference in my mission."

"Mission?" Kimberly said, her tone dropping. She looked at her sister who looked equally clueless.

"You have no right," Lacey said, not sure what else she could say.

With as much clanging as he could muster, Raysor extracted the cuffs. "Who's first?"

The ladies hushed. When the men in their family didn't come to their defense, their mouths flat-lined.

Callie shut the door, going back to do what she came in for. Grandmother remained in bed appearing a bit more wan than before. "Mrs. Poe, are you sure you don't need medical attention?" she asked, the room wonderfully quiet after all the ruckus outside.

"I'm sure. I'm old but I'm not frail."

She reached Grandmother's bed. "I was thinking more along the line of losing Kimi."

"I know. I know," Mrs. Poe said, talking down into her lap and smoothing the covers around her.

"Would you like a family member with you?" Callie asked, not mentioning that she reserved the right to limit who.

"No, Chief. I want nothing to do with them right now." With a big inhale, the older lady steadied herself. Callie wasn't sure Mrs. Poe was as stable as she believed. "Can you speak to me while I'm in bed?" the woman asked, patting the covers.

Callie agreed with that plan. "As to having someone in here, what about Allan?"

He was the most settled, plus she wasn't allowing Ogden, Lacey, Kimberly, or Shannon. Pauline. . . no. Not yet. Eddie maybe. He was a dope. But she didn't want to question this woman without giving her a chance of having someone at her side. Eighty was an awfully big number.

"No one, Chief." The sadness hung on her. She was surrounded by family yet unable to trust even one of them.

Callie got to the point. "Then tell me about Shannon." Mrs. Poe might start fading. "What was she doing alone with you here in the bedroom a little while ago?"

But instead of wilting at yet another disappointment in her group, Grandmother fired up. "That bitch told me I had to drink whatever was in that cup. *To calm my nerves*, she said. *No*, I said. *Where're the wills*, she asked. *Hidden*, I said. That's when she tried to force the cup on me. With all the noise out there, nobody could hear, so I fussed, shoved back, then smacked the cup." Her long snort of a breath carried indignation, and Callie admired her.

"That's when I came in," Callie said, very happy she did.

Mrs. Poe pointed at the desk, and Callie peered over. Papers were stacked neatly. Papers that seemed all too familiar. "Forensics put those there?" she asked.

"At my request."

Callie couldn't stay long. With Shannon locked up and waiting in one room, family trolling outside this door, and a forensics team at her disposal, Callie had a backlog of matters to tend to. The woman before her looked tired.

"Anything you have not told me that I should know?" she asked, the routine question you asked anyone in an investigation. That or "Anything else you want to say?"

"I know nothing about my granddaughter's death," she said. "Please believe me."

Callie did without any trouble at all and nodded. "I'm leaving you in here with my deputy at the door. If you need anything, go through him." Then she felt she needed to correct that statement. "But do not try to solve this yourself. Don't call someone in just to ask them questions that are mine to ask. I'm not scolding, ma'am. I'm more like keeping everyone in their own lane so we can get to the bottom of this as efficiently as possible."

She still needed a little more direction, and Mrs. Poe seemed the most aware of everyone and their potential motives. "Pauline doesn't have a dog in this fight, does she?"

Mrs. Poe peered down her patrician nose and said, "But oh, she does."

Callie did an about-face. "Does. . .?"

"Have a dog in the fight."

Callie leaned against the bed. "Such as?"

"She roots for Allan. And I'm known throughout the culinary world and still hold sway there."

"Why is any of that an issue?" The chef held no grudges against any of them. Quite the opposite. She'd be honored to have the Poes' gig on her resume.

Sooner or later Pauline would have to be interviewed again, but more about professional issues. What, in her professional opinion, may have been used against Allan? And what did she suspect happened to Kimi? Why didn't she leave *Maelstrom Manor* when the crap first started hitting the fan?

Mrs. Poe paused. "She knows more about me than I do about her," Grandmother said. "I'll leave it at that. We err on the side of caution, don't you think?"

This sounded more. . . ego-related than crime solving. Callie touched the quilted covers. "I'll be back in a bit. Nap if you can. Tonight will be long and tomorrow even longer."

"Kimberly," Mrs. Poe said, but Callie halted her, not wanting that woman alone in this room, impacting. . . or threatening. . . or interrogating the matron on what was fiscally to happen to the Poes.

Then for a quick second, Callie wondered if Mrs. Poe had mistaken her for the daughter. "Ma'am?"

"I thought I heard Kimberly out there."

"Kimberly's in no shape to console you, ma'am."

Mrs. Poe's mouth flattened. "I meant I could console her," she corrected. "I'm way stronger. She's all pretense."

She halted long enough for Callie to wonder how much the woman wasn't saying.

"It's my fault, you know," Mrs. Poe said, in a déjà vu moment Callie'd had with Allan upstairs. "I should have trained her harder. Been way less forgiving when she fell short. She was the one who felt most entitled. Eddie works hard, but he doesn't have the depth of talent Kimberly has. She's lazy now, and I must assume that was the result of her upbringing."

If the woman was spilling thoughts, Callie would let her. "And Lacey?"

"Mediocre in intelligence, people skills, and motivation. Rests on her family's laurels."

Callie could see all of this, but nothing solved a thing right now. This woman was more exhausted than she cared to admit. "Let's leave all that for later, ma'am," Callie said. "Kimberly is being tended."

The grandmother slid lower into her bed, and Callie smiled, rose, and left the bedroom, closing the door softly behind her. But she dropped that smile in telling Raysor that he was to guard that woman like she was the President.

Callie marched past the Poe calamity, arguments still taking place, Raysor strategically listening while acting like he wasn't, and made her way to the study.

Callie's hand rested on the knob when Lacey trotted to her. "I need to be in there with her," said the sister.

"No, you don't."

"She's scared."

"I'll be there."

Lacey looked stunned. "But she's scared of you!"

"She shouldn't be if she isn't guilty of anything."

"She needs an attorney," Lacey said.

"I'll give her the option," Callie said, hand still on the knob. She waited for yet another excuse by the woman that Callie could slap down. "You're welcome to call your own attorney."

Lacey blinked fast. "Do I need one?"

Callie always found that cliched response funny. "I don't know. Do you?"

Then when Lacey hushed, fearing that anything more said would hurt her, she huffed at Callie, as if that mattered.

"Please return to the group," Callie said, slipping into the study. She directed Annie to leave and assist Raysor, taking Lacey with her, then Callie told Shannon to remain seated.

"You cannot confine me like this," the nurse said. "I've been held prisoner, and I intend to file a complaint."

"Actually, I *can* hold you," Callie said, assuming her place at the desk like before. "We caught you in the middle of a probable crime."

"You have no evidence," Shannon said.

"We'll let forensics and Mrs. Poe's statements decide that."

Stymied, Shannon pondered what to say next, which gave Callie time to set up the audio.

She read the date and time into the recording. "The best you can do right now, Ms. Kirby, is cooperate. Forensics is collecting evidence. Fingerprints will be yours. We'll learn what was in the cup you forced at Mrs. Doris Poe, before she swatted it out of your hand."

"Nothing was in the cup."

"You're sticking with that? If I were a betting person, I'd wager something harmful was in that tea the way this household functions. You don't question second nature habits."

Tension spread over the nurse such that Callie could smell the fear. "Your buddy Lacey was concerned what you might tell me. What could that be?"

Wide-eyed and flushed, Shannon couldn't put words together.

"You know," Callie continued. "You're the one who changed my whole perspective regarding this investigation. I'd about decided the first two attempts at poisoning Allan's food were a family prank as everyone professed. With the third *prank* becoming murder, I'm no longer sure. Chances were that third caper was meant for Allan as well, though that no longer matters in the grand scheme of things."

"You're wrong," Shannon said.

Raising a brow in false surprise, Callie asked, "Which part? The first prank? The second? The third? All three?" She held up an extra finger as if shocked with sudden intuition. "Or the fourth? The one where you tried to kill the head of the entire family."

Shannon hushed, her gaze darting.

Experience gave Callie familiarity with the likes of Shannon. Before the nurse would speak again, she'd run everything through her head once, then twice, and each time she'd worry more about how guilty she sounded. Repeatedly until she was her own worst enemy. That is, unless Callie managed to goad her into reacting before she thought.

"Did Lacey put you up to the tea? You know, so nobody questioned a Poe?"

That drew a rise from the nurse, but then she caught herself.

"Or," and Callie gave a dramatic pause, well-rehearsed from her days in Boston dealing with far worse than Shannon, "did Lacey perform the third *prank*, and tell you to remain silent about it."

Shannon sat still and quiet.

"Or," Callie said, going a note higher in tone, "did she tell you to deal with Grandmother Poe while everyone was occupied? Sort of keeps her hands clean, doesn't it? Saves her place in the will, which would benefit you in the long run as her partner."

"But the attorney said there was no will."

There it was. "He was told to tell y'all that. To see how you and everyone else would react. Mrs. Poe is still a shrewd woman, Ms. Kirby."

Shannon blushed.

Callie waited to see if Shannon would ask the right question.

She thought a little too long, in Callie's opinion, and about the time she figured Shannon had not taken the bait, the nurse asked, "So which is the right will?"

"None with your name in it," Callie replied.

"What about Lacey?"

Callie ignored Shannon's question. "You're making me need to go back and reinvestigate Lacey, asking what she thinks you did that she doesn't want you to tell me about. Lacey's more interested in you than her relatives from the look of things. One family member poisoned, one killed, and one a victim in an attempted assassination, or so we'll see when forensics gets through. Ironic. Guess you ought to be honored she favors you over family."

Shannon thought. "Lacey hired me. She talked Grandmother Poe into hiring me, so she oversaw me."

"Yet Lacey didn't offer to get you an attorney, but I bet she's calling her own as we speak. She wants to get her version of events represented first. Before her family can. Before you can."

Horror seeped under Shannon's skin, eyes wide.

"I guess you're a loyal employee, Shannon, the way you commit crimes to benefit your employer."

With condescension, Callie shifted her chair, backing from the desk. "You stay seated right here. I'll go chat with Lacey. Chances are she'll be way more talkative about events, about details. . . about you. Then I can come back and we can hold a more substantial conversation. How's that sound?" She stood, straightening her shirt, but leaving the recording app running on her phone.

"I never poisoned anyone, I said."

Callie scrutinized the woman, like she was a child seeking for the right truth to tell. "I'll go see how Lacey spins this."

The nurse wilted.

"What happened to your oath, Shannon?"

Shannon's head turned toward the wall in what could be shame.

Leaning hands on the desk, Callie lowered her voice. "You were doing all you could to prove your love and assist in Lacey collecting an inheritance."

"We're a couple," she said, like that made everything right.

Callie whispered, "You keep telling yourself that."

"You weren't here for any of this."

"Maybe that's why I'm asking you questions?"

A tear trickled over Shannon's cheekbone, and not until it reached her jawline did she speak again. "She spiked Allan's water to take advantage of whatever had been done to him earlier. Everyone would think the first person did the third time, too."

"You mean Lacey?" Called asked, for the record.

"Yes, Lacey."

"Are you saying she didn't do the earlier two tamperings?" Callie sensed a sign of breakthrough.

Shannon shook her head, her tears regular now.

"If she didn't, who did?"

A shrug.

"Speak, please."

"I have no idea."

"So, you don't know if Lacey did it or not. How did Kimi die? I mean, exactly. Which poison? How was it administered?"

Shannon deflated, her body sagging from what Callie saw as giving in to the truth. You made or broke a case in such moments.

"Kimi drank from Allan's glass," Shannon said, barely over a mumble. "Nothing was meant to kill him, just scare him away. I told Lacey the correct dosage."

"This wasn't an herb or plant?"

"No."

"Are you going to make me ask?" Callie said, bored by this woman. She tired of the fact that these people had everything handed to them to include lineage and an intact family but abused the hell out of both privileges. "What did you use?"

"Arsenic. Old-fashioned, simple, tasteless, colorless. . . I gave her the dosage for a healthy man." Then she jerked up and corrected herself. "I mean a dosage to make him ill, not kill." But she'd said too much, done too much, and seemed to understand that there was no backing up now. She collapsed forward, forehead on the desk, and cried. "But. . ." She couldn't complete her sentence.

Callie finished for her. "Kimi being sixty pounds lighter made the act fatal."

Shannon nodded from the desktop while still hidden in her crossed arms. Callie mentioned for the recording's sake that the subject nodded yes.

Allan and Pauline had confirmed Lacey handled the place settings, and that Shannon was not there.

Shannon sat up, her makeup a wreck, cheeks blotchy. "It all went wrong. But I didn't do anything. Lacey did."

"Gotcha. You just supplied the weapon."

"Right . . . no, wrong. . . I didn't mean for this to happen."

Callie came around the desk. "Shannon Kirby, stand up. You're under arrest for the murder of Kimi Poe."

The nurse didn't fight back. She gave no denial. She also didn't do as she was told.

"Shannon Kirby," and Callie went to grip the right wrist, the one closest.

But the nurse leaped to her feet, her head catching Callie in the breastbone then up and under her chin. But between the surprise and seeing a few stars, Callie managed to hold onto the wrist, and Shannon wound up on the floor, a knee in her back.

No doubt all could hear the wailing in the dining room. Callie called for Annie. "Officer Greer?" She felt her chin for a cut, some red coming back on her fingers.

"Right here, Chief." She'd crossed the living room at the first sound of trouble. "Whatcha need?"

"Your cuffs for one. Then babysit this one." Callie moved past Annie, patience gone for Shannon, and not much left for Lacey Poe.

She did a stutter step upon reaching the dining room.

Beverly.

Damn, she'd forgotten she'd called her mother.

Chapter 35

Callie

LACEY STOOD NEXT to Callie's mother. She was having a conversation with Beverly like she'd known the woman for years. Odd. Beverly wasn't looking all that comfortable with whatever was being said, though. Maybe Lacey was making sure she wanted Beverly to be with her mother? Maybe Beverly was waiting for her own daughter to clarify for the family.

Raysor remained on guard at Grandmother's shut door, bless him. Eddie stood off with Allan and Pauline. Ogden sat alone up the stairs, to remain alone while remaining alert.

"Where's Kimberly?" Callie asked.

"Upstairs in bed," Eddie said. Callie was good with that.

"Forensics is packing it in," Raysor said. "They'll call you tomorrow. They collected a lot of stuff and said give them a while."

She scanned the gathering, reading the room, and an eeriness crept into her chest. While she'd have a bruise there from Shannon's head butt, this wasn't that. Callie approached her mother, and Lacey mashed tighter against Beverly. Not the first smidgeon of light shined between these two who'd never seen each other before.

Callie didn't recognize that look in her mother's eyes. A look almost of distress. Beverly had never done fear, not in front of her daughter. Even when her husband died, Beverly held it together. Even when Callie almost died on a case, her mother kept it together.

Callie regarded Raysor for a better read. Whatever this was with Beverly, he was clueless. Nobody else in the room showed anything other than an exhausted residual mourning for Kimi.

Lacey, however, made hard eye contact with Callie, and with nobody in her line of vision but Callie, nobody else noticed. Meanwhile Callie attempted to appear unaffected.

"My attorney is on his way," Lacey said.

"Good," Callie said. "Let's go wait in the study with your partner."

"Here is good." She gave a tight grin. "I've enjoyed meeting your mother. She introduced herself to us. Said you thought she might like to keep my mother company. How thoughtful."

Why couldn't Eddie have handled this new guest like he had any other?

Why was everyone oblivious that something was up with this Poe sister?

"Mother," Callie said, regretting her earlier call to draw her here. "I don't need you involved in this investigation. You were to come to my house, not here. What made you show up here?"

She needed Beverly gone for her own safety.

Even the slightest admonition, however, heightened Beverly's arrogance. Nobody told Beverly Cantrell what to do, how to do, or where to be. Everything was her idea, or at least she had to alter yours in some way.

"I'm sorry, dear. I misunderstood. Forgive me."

Her mother was playing along.

Raysor's eyes narrowed at Beverly being so. . . congenial.

Then Beverly began to hum. Neil Diamond. *Girl, You'll Be a Woman Soon.*

She and her mother had so little in common, short of Callie's father, but one world they shared was Neil Diamond tunes. When Beverly lived on Edisto for entire summers at a time, while her husband was busy being mayor of Middleton and Callie was a child, she'd stack Diamond albums three and four deep on the turntable and play them *ad nauseum.* Callie had hated the tunes until they became a part of her, and she'd come to have favorites.

Edisto meant listening to Neil. When the house had changed hands, they'd each ensured they owned duplicate copies of the Diamond library. The song Beverly hummed came from his earlier work, from a 1967 album titled *Just for You.*

Instinctively, Callie played the lyrics in her head. Verse one. The chorus.

Beverly watched her daughter and continued the low hum.

"What are we doing, Chief?" Lacey asked, a small discomfort creeping in at the hesitancy. Despite the six additional people, a sense of a bubble had formed around the three women.

"Waiting," Callie said, having to go back mentally to the end of the first verse and start over. It was all she could do not to hum it for clarity.

Yes. Second verse.

Knife.
Ending things.
Up to you.

Callie fixed on Lacey. "Forensics will confirm everything."

"Confirm what?" But she didn't wait for an answer. "Never mind. I don't have to talk to you. My attorney said so."

"Then listen," Callie said.

But the sister seemed afraid to do that. "Shannon gave Mother the tea, not me."

"Duh," said Ogden from up on the stairs. "We all sort of caught her, genius."

"Shut up, Ogden," Lacey said, tight lipped and remaining stiffly against Beverly.

Thank God he hushed. They didn't need Lacey to lose control. Seemed only Callie and Beverly realized Lacey Poe approached becoming unhinged.

"I didn't hurt Kimi," Lacey said, unconvincing.

"It wasn't Shannon," Callie said, like she knew.

Everyone else in the room seemed to be putting their own pieces together to their own idea of the puzzle.

Lacey had held onto Beverly too tightly and for far too long. Standing open in the dining room hallway was not the place to tackle, grab, or go after her, either.

"Were you after the damn money?" Kimberly asked, suddenly reappearing at the top of the stairs. She'd reappeared, having put her puzzle together more quickly. Between the clarity that comes with death and an organically shared knowledge between sisters, or maybe her being alone to think in her room without the distractions of family, Kimi's mother seemed to be the first to understand.

Kimberly used Ogden's shoulder as support to step around him. Feeling the firmness of her grip, he stiffened to aid her descent. "You stupid *bitch*," she screamed down at her sister.

Lacey did a half step to the side, forcing Beverly to move in kind. "Shut up, Kimberly. It was Shannon's plan." She'd spit her lover's name out like a rancid grape.

Kimberly paused, unable to talk and step at the same time. "You two have functioned as one since you talked Mother into hiring her. If she had a hand in killing Kimi so did you, bitch."

Fists clenched, Kimberly rushed toward her sister, each step unstable until she was freefalling.

Lacey pivoted, a steak knife in her grip.

Callie snatched Beverly firmly by the wrist and yanked her forward, the older woman stumbling past into the living room to her knees.

Raysor's body weight and girth shoved Kimberly backwards onto the stairs while in the same fell swoop wrapped big meaty fingers around Lacey's wrist. The weapon dropped with a clatter onto the hardwood floor, his grip keeping her from falling.

Everyone jumped back, their breaths in audible chorus. Kimberly, however, laid across several steps, sobbing, her son no longer mercurial, instead rubbing his mother's shoulder.

Once Raysor had secured Lacey in cuffs and hauled her out of sight, Callie moved to her mother. Beverly remained seated on the rug, shaken.

"My legs don't work," she whispered to her daughter.

Callie stooped. "Give yourself a moment. You're probably in shock." She reached out to touch her mother before realizing that wasn't something she was used to doing. They had never been touchy feely in Callie's forty plus years.

But Beverly extended her arm. "Help me up."

Callie did, not letting go until her mother was steady. Once Beverly stood firm, Callie returned her attention to the others. Eddie, Ogden, and Pauline tended to Kimberly who'd come undone. Allan remained where he'd been before, seated on a dining chair, stunned, not willing to insert himself into any more drama.

"You might as well spend the night at my house," she said, turning back to her own mother. "Don't need to make that long dark drive back this late."

Beverly straightened her clothes, messed with her hair, then took in the scene. "Where's the Grandmother? Is she invalid? Isn't she why you called me to come?"

"You don't have to do this, Mother. You've been through enough. Go to my place and relax."

But Beverly stood strong. "You asked me to do a job, which I intend to do. You never ask me to help, and I'm not bowing out the one time you do."

Unsure whether she meant her statement as a compliment or a slur, Callie suddenly understood. A mother loved to be needed, which was why Mrs. Poe accommodated her children, even if to a fault. That need was why Sophie brought mystery cookies, to check out who had upset her baby girl. That need was why Beverly interfered so much in Callie's and Jeb's lives. It was why Callie quit drinking and pushed Jeb to pursue college.

Beverly needed this.

"She's in her bedroom," Callie said, caving to the guilt. "Kimi's death this evening hit her hard. I doubt she's sleeping but if she is, please let her. I'm keeping her distant from. . . all of this. That's why my deputy is standing guard."

Beverly's mayoral dignity seeped back in. "Well, I came all this way to help, and I see my assistance especially warranted now. Fill me in on each of the people here so I'm not totally ignorant when I go in there." She studied her daughter as if waiting for an admin assistant to brief her on the day's agenda.

Callie began with the three siblings. . . the brother, the mourning sister, and the murderer. Then the grandchildren. . . the prodigal, the deceased, and the broken. Grandmother needed no introduction. Beverly was familiar, and what she hadn't known, she'd gone home after lunch today and done her research.

After her quick briefing, Beverly patted her daughter on the cheek, a move she hadn't done before, then took her royal self to the bedroom. She lightly rapped on the door, and after a moment, eased in, introduced herself, then peering back at Callie gave a hand motion that all was good.

Yet in looking around *Maelstrom Manor* right now, this family was anything but good. Never would be. Not that they ever had been from all Callie had learned these last few days, but what little had been good was gone.

The night would be long. Deputy Raysor and Officer Annie Greer would escort Lacey and Shannon to Walterboro since Edisto didn't do lockups, having to rely on the county's jail facilities. Callie would interview the rest of these people, tying up loose ends, filling in gaps that Lacey's attorney would attempt to take advantage of.

She ran down Raysor and Lacey in the study, on the opposite side of the room from Annie and Shannon. "Give me your attorney's number so I can tell him to meet you in Walterboro."

Lacey gave the information, but as Callie started to dial from her own phone, Shannon cried out. "That's my attorney, too, right? Tell him about me, too."

Callie held up her phone, stopping short of the last two digits. "Is he your attorney?" she asked.

Shannon looked at Lacey. "He's mine, too, right?"

"Only if you can afford him," came the reply.

Shannon paled. "Honey, that's not right. You know I can't afford that kind of attorney. Tonight was your idea. I just accommodated you."

Which was why Shannon would not share Lacey's attorney.

A prosecutor was going to have a ball with these two. "Is he the family attorney?" Callie asked.

"He handles criminal stuff, but we haven't used him often," Lacey said.

Raising her brow, Callie dialed the last two numbers. "If he claims family conflict of interest, he might not be handling you either, Lacey."

This time Lacey paled.

Chapter 36

Callie

IT WAS ALMOST four in the morning when Callie saw the last Poe out of the study. She could've waited until the next day to query them, but the remaining family seemed as eager to get this done as she did. Nobody saw her to the door. Nobody thanked her. Everyone disbanded to individual rooms upstairs and assumed the police chief would lock up behind herself.

The bottom line was nobody could say who tainted Allan's tea on his first night or the oatmeal cookies the next morning. After speaking to the Poe children and grandchildren, Callie wasn't feeling hard line truth in any of them. She'd interviewed Pauline last, who continued to stand by Allan versus the Poes, and yet Callie got nowhere.

She moved to the kitchen, especially parched after so much questioning, hunting for bottled water, still leery of eating or drinking anything from that refrigerator or pantry. She'd told Pauline and each of the Poes to empty the kitchen, because no telling what was in opened bottles, wrapped in plastic, or frozen that might still be potent in some manner. Who said tonight's dinner, the latest toxic happening, was supposed to be the last one?

Southern Silver Spoon sat on the counter, open and covered in fingerprint dust. Ruined. If that wasn't a metaphor for this family nothing was. She used a spoon to turn pages, winding up in the notorious chapter on toxic plants. There were underlines, circles, and arrows all over the place but in assorted pens and different handwriting styles. Some were faded pencil marks. Various ballpoint pens from fine to full points. Someone used a fine black permanent marker. A community cookbook open to suggestions.

"Callie," came a whisper from the kitchen doorway.

She turned as Beverly entered. "Sorry it's so late, Mother. I had no idea tonight would go how it did. My goal was for you to be a listener and hopefully see the grandmother to sleep. While she spoke to me a bit, I still sense secrets. Her family is in crisis."

"Well, she wasn't ready to go to sleep," Beverly said, moving to her daughter and spying the cookbook, picking up the same spoon Callie had used to turn pages. After a moment she tsked, not saying why.

"It's sad," Callie said, turning to rest her butt against the counter.

Beverly looked up from the pages. "Is this a lot of what you do?"

The lone chuckle bubbled up weary. "No, Mother. God, no." There had been bodies her mother knew nothing about, and Callie would keep those secret, like she hadn't told Jeb every danger she'd experienced in Boston, and there had been many. Here, however, he assumed things were simpler and less perilous. He'd personally witnessed a couple of situations, but she'd convinced him they were anomalies.

The truth was policing had its hazards. When such events occurred, success was often measured in how well she kept the tourists oblivious to how close they'd been to a problem.

"No, this is one for the record book, Mother." She sighed at how tired she was.

Soon the inky blue horizon would show its bruising, then pink up as the sun yawned awake. The palmettos would change from black shadows to greys, the last to gain color as the day arrived.

A long chat with Mrs. Poe could wait until tomorrow, after she was more rested and less pained by loss. Beverly, however, had a town to run, and when she was there, amidst her rushed responsibilities, she spoke in staccato and code, her brain engaged with what she had waiting on her to-do list dictated by her staff. Now, however, her mother was hers. "Exactly what did Mrs. Poe and you talk about?"

"Children," she said. "And grandchildren."

"I hope she did most of the talking."

Beverly gazed at her daughter in sarcastic disbelief. "Try to remember what I do for a living. . . what I've done most of my life."

Callie wasn't sure what that meant.

"People," Beverly explained. "I listen to them, identify the problem, and do my best to assist them through a solution."

Not a bad description for a mayor. Callie wondered why that hadn't been hammered into her head growing up, which might've helped explain all those times she was coerced into attending fundraisers, television appearances, and swearing-in ceremonies. "Go on."

Beverly had always carried a stoic, I'm-in-control air morning, noon, and night. But tonight, that persona was absent. "She blames herself for everything, Callie. She's so shattered."

Damned if her mother wasn't tearing up.

"I'm so happy you had me come sit with her, Callie. She's lost. God help me, but I hope I eased some of that burden."

Beverly appeared quite sad for her. "She was too hard on them, she said. She didn't trust them to walk without her, make decisions without her, or carry on the name well enough. She was afraid to let loose the reins. We spoke a long while about that." Beverly swallowed, and Callie pretended not to see her mother trying to push down feelings.

This was not the mother she was accustomed to. This was true empathy.

Callie almost asked about the wills. Who was in the real will? Personally, Callie would've willed most of the estate to the three siblings and half shares to the grandchildren. Fair and even.

What was the grandmother to do now with one grand dead and one daughter the culprit? Grounds for a new will.

This family had been dismantled in three days. How does an eighty-year-old matron who spent her entire adult life setting up an empire as a legacy cope with it crumbling around her before she died, too old to adjust?

Beverly reached over and wiped a tear off her daughter's cheek. "They'll adapt, dear."

The endearment of *dear* had always rubbed Callie wrong, but tonight it delivered a measure of love so foreign in their relationship.

"We did, if you recall," Beverly added. "Adapt, I mean. I could list the names of who died, who hurt us, who caught us unawares, dear, but no need. Look at me, but better yet look at you. And even more, look at Jeb. We regrouped and accepted our new journey. Each and every time."

Callie fought what to say. This was not the normal Callie and Beverly show.

"Sit," her mother said. "I'll fix you some coffee."

Callie held up both hands, palms out. "Um, not sure you want to eat or drink anything in this house, Mother. We have no idea what additional plans someone may have had, or where they may have hidden the ingredients."

"Oh." Beverly moved from the counter as if it were contaminated.

Opening the refrigerator, Callie found bottled water for herself, and a diet cola for her mother, then escorted her to the back porch, setting the bottles on a table between two chairs that overlooked the Atlantic.

Beverly opened her drink. "Feels rather odd relaxing at someone's place while they're asleep."

"They won't bother us, trust me," Callie said, taking a long swig of the water, suddenly realizing she'd underestimated her thirst over this long damn night. "Now, tell me the whole of your time with Mrs. Poe. I can look at you and see more to the story. No short cuts."

Beverly did a light shake of her bottle. "Any little perk inside that we can add to this?"

Alcohol would only lengthen things and fog her mother's already tired brain. Beverly wasn't used to being up this late at night without some sort of chaser to support the effort. While Callie had climbed aboard the wagon, her mother had no qualms about keeping her habit alive.

"No, ma'am. No booze. Only the story, please."

"She meant to leave her wealth all to the grandchildren, using this birthday party to entice Allan back," Beverly said. "I took a while to figure everybody out, but Callie," and she took a second. "That strong as granite woman cried. She admitted she'd strangled them with control, held them from their own growth. The result was people who couldn't make decisions.

"The grands, however, had shown daring and potential, she said. Even Ogden, who I believe has always been considered the black sheep. She liked his frustration and need to launch himself away from the control. That was a huge plus in her book."

Callie could see that. She'd even asked Ogden about that. That boy needed to be told that in the very near future.

"Oh, dear, about the granddaughter . . . that precious lady cared so deeply about Kimi," Beverly continued. "She'd pinned the family's future on that girl. Good decision on your part, Callie, advising the family to keep her in the dark for now. I'm not sure she could have handled all of that."

"Another day won't matter," Callie said, sighing on the end.

How did a mother compartmentalize that sort of dilemma. A mother never abandons her child, but for that child to kill the brightest grandchild. . . even a strong, younger person would struggle with finding any sort of peace in that. A conflicting pain she'd take to the grave.

Hues of purple tinted the sky. Callie couldn't see the edge of the water, but she could hear. The tide ebbed in forgiving washes, like the universe understood the need for this peace.

Beverly continued. "She was glad to be rid of Shannon. She wished she'd been more business-like regarding her, but the mother in her allowed the incompetent nurse to stick around for Lacey."

Callie hmphed from behind her bottle. "Lacey had decided her only future was to outlive her mother, collect her money, and avoid the real estate and cookbook work that filled the coffers, Mother. Lazy to the core."

"She knew that, Callie. Even when a child hates you, you can't stop loving them. You can only pray they come around." Beverly whispered, "That poor woman."

"It could still happen with Allan," Callie replied, her words not much louder than the breeze coming in from the beach as she tried not to see herself in Beverly's lesson.

The sky lightened more. The moon was gone and only the brightest stars remained visible. They didn't need to stick around *Maelstrom Manor* much longer, but going home meant breaking this bubble. . . a bubble with so much clarity. Clarity about the Poes hinted at more familiar family.

The ocean wind had almost ceased, and warblers tweeted, shaking off sleep. Beverly's next comment rang crystal in the clean air. "I need to tell you something, Callie."

A part of her didn't want to hear the message. Poe or personal, her gut clenched, knowing full well the message would be unpleasant. What else could such an introduction mean?

Callie took another drink and set the bottle on the side table. "Go ahead," she said.

"Mrs. Poe poisoned Allan."

Shit. "Which time?"

"The first two times."

"Why?"

"To see how he'd react."

Son-of-a-bitch.

Chapter 37

Allan

ALLAN HEARD THE Chief leave with her mother around six, but as hard as he tried to go back to sleep, he couldn't. He and Pauline had tried to discuss and decompress after the officers took Lacey and Shannon to jail, but they couldn't think, brains numb. Too much emotion. Too much stress. Too much shock.

Pressure pushed his chest, and he sucked in long deep breaths.

Finally, he went downstairs, hoping to grab time alone before the others woke up. Unsure what to say to any of them, he realized that they had no idea what to say to him either.

Out of habit he wound up in the kitchen. He slid his phone in his pajama pants pocket to open the fridge, not bothering to check for media headlines. No doubt they were there. The Charleston papers, television and radio stations, then probably the state. Maybe national. The Murdaugh murders had put South Carolina on the map in a heartbeat. The Poes were a triple attraction between the lineage to the author, the real estate business, and the cookbook. So many angles for a hungry journalist. Somebody would be inquiring about doing a true crime story, seeking insider approval from the family.

Grandmother's old publisher would be all over this, wanting to issue an updated edition of *Southern Silver Spoon*.

He'd peeked out for a truck or van with logos from any of a dozen stations, but there weren't even cars on Palmetto, much less the press. It wouldn't take long, though. Who did you hire to take care of that sort of thing, because none of his family would have an inkling of an idea.

Yeah, Grandmother's attorneys would be calling, too.

"Hey, kid." Pauline brushed by him, reaching in the fridge, grabbing some kind of protein drink she'd brought with her. She made sure she had to wrench the cap off. "When the stores open, we've got to find something to eat for everyone. I don't trust a morsel of food in this house. I've already thought of tossing my herb case. One never knows."

"Think the coffee's okay?" he asked.

"Use the pods. Refill the reservoir with fresh water. Drink it black."

Before long he had a cup and they stepped outside, the house stifling. Too many ears were due to wake up soon.

A lone walker strolled the beach.

"You okay?" Pauline asked, placing her hand on his back and lightly scratching.

"I feel like I only got to see Kimi for ten minutes," he said from behind his cup propped between both hands, elbows on the chair arms. "God, I cannot believe all that about Aunt Lacey." He inhaled deeply, stemming emotion he'd hoped was gone. "What's Aunt Kimberly going to do?" Then he thought. "And Ogden. Son-of-a-bitch, of all the family members, we had to lose Kimi." He cleared his throat. "What's this going to do to Grandmother?"

"This will knock the stuffing out of her," Pauline said

"Yeah."

And on that note they went silent for a long ten minutes.

"Nobody owned up to coming after me," he said.

"Don't take this wrong, but the tea and cookies sort of feel unimportant right now, don't they?" the chef said.

He studied her. "Was it you?"

"Nope," she said with nary a pause, like she expected the query.

"Prank?" He sniffed. "I hate that word now."

Her eyes narrowed, still focused on the Atlantic. "Probably. Lacey and Shannon never owned up from what we were told. That sort of narrows the field."

"Unless it was Kimi," he said.

"Unless it was Kimi," she repeated.

Setting his cup on the table, he steepled fingers and rested them over his mouth, elbows still on the chair arms. "I don't care who anymore," he finally said.

"I believe that's wise," Pauline said, but her calmness made him look over.

She knew. She knew who did it. He wasn't in the mood to find out, though. The family had been scarred, and he'd bet all he owned on the fact they wouldn't try anything like that again.

"Interested in a job?" the chef asked.

"Interested in hiring?" he asked back.

"Maybe. Interested in moving to Atlanta?"

"I could do that."

"Two weeks from now okay?"

He didn't want to grin too big in front of her, so his steepled fingers in place, he smiled from behind them.

A scream sounded from inside the house.

Pauline's protein drink crashed to the planked porch floor in their rush back inside.

Aunt Kimberly stood in the hallway to Grandmother's bedroom, half bent over, screaming into her hands repeatedly.

Eddie scrambled down the stairs, barefooted and shirtless, Ogden behind him the same.

Pauline grabbed the aunt's upper arms, trying to make her calm down. "Look at me, Kimberly. Breathe."

Kimberly reduced her breathing to pants, but whines still escaped her in panic. "Mother." She pointed to the bedroom.

Eddie hesitated at the doorway, so Allan pushed past him.

With no sign of distress, Grandmother Poe had died in her sleep.

Chapter 38

Callie

CALLIE READJUSTED her utility belt and was about to leave the house when her mother peered out of the guest room door, not about to fully show herself wrinkled and wadded up after too little sleep.

Callie slid into her room. Mark wouldn't mind his own unkempt appearance or hers at this hour, but Beverly would rather be shot than be seen less than a hundred percent put together.

"Why aren't you sleeping?" her mother asked.

Callie spoke plainly. "The grandmother died in her sleep."

Beverly's gasp was followed by a half step back. "What?"

Callie shook her head, knowing there was no other explanation. The pressure of so much loss and disappointment had been too much for the old lady. One day short of her eightieth birthday.

"I need to go over there," Beverly said.

"You really don't," Callie replied. "You were only affiliated with Mrs. Poe, and she's beyond your help, Mother. I, however, need to get over there pronto. I suspect it'll take me half the day to deal with this."

"I really should go," her mother mumbled, but instead of snatching up clothes and making moves to leave, she sat on the edge of the bed.

Callie wasn't sure whether she meant go to the Poes or go home to Middleton. Callie sat beside her. "You are too tired to drive home. Text your staff you'll be back tomorrow."

Beverly scowled at the suggestion but made no move to do otherwise.

Kimi's death hadn't caught up with the morning news, but Mrs. Poe's would turn up the fire. Two Poe deaths in twelve hours with one family member in jail for the murder of the second youngest was national level reporting. Callie would have to assign the day's uniforms to managing the traffic, along with whomever she could bum off the Colleton County Sheriff's Office. She'd manage everything else.

She and Beverly had discussed getting up at nine or ten and grabbing breakfast, hopefully chatting more. Their unspoken breakthrough early this morning at *Maelstrom Manor* felt like an unconsummated promise, and surprisingly, Callie had hoped to continue their conversation.

"Sunshine?" Mark said, from outside their bedroom. From the sound of his steps, he peered outside first, then closed the front door. Callie came out of her mother's room to find him still in his PJ pants, all that Cajun hair disheveled. "Is that your mother's car? Is she here?"

Callie had sent a long text to her beau, to generalize why she'd been out all night, and to let him know not to disturb Beverly, but clearly he hadn't seen it yet. The text wasn't enough to tell the story anyway.

She couldn't help but tousle those long locks. "Mother helped me on the case last night. We got in at dawn. She's in the guest room."

"Why. . .?" He stopped himself short of asking, *Why the hell would you call her on a case?*

Wow, so much water had passed under this bridge since they'd talked, but Callie hadn't the time to spin out details now. She peered back into the guest room. "I've got to get to *Maelstrom Manor*, Mother." Callie kicked herself for not checking in on Mrs. Poe or not having Beverly do so before they left. But she'd be there for the family today. Her mother had handled the news, but she couldn't hide the shadow of sadness, nor the exhaustion. "Crawl back into bed, Mother. We'll chat later."

"You have got to be kidding me," Mark said, when she came back out and prepared to leave. "Did you get any sleep at all?"

"Two hours." Saying it only made her more fatigued.

"Jeb still at the hospital?"

"What?" she asked, robotically collecting her cruiser keys from the bar, not looking forward to this.

"Callie, I asked about Jeb. Where is he?"

"Yes, yes, he's still at the hospital. Sophie gets released this morning. I'll text him, but if you see him, please tell him not to go over to the Poes or call Ogden. Not yet."

She forgot Mark had no idea who Odgen was. She'd had minimal time to update him like she normally would. Too much had happened too fast.

She drove the mile and a half trip in scant minutes, the ambulance not there yet. The area seemed like a snowfall evening on New Year's Eve before the church bells rang in the new. Callie's arrival, however, lured some residents and a couple tourists to their porches in hopes of learning what drew the police yet again. Not the first time, she kicked herself for not checking on the grandmother and dealing with this under the cover of night.

She walked up the steps and found the front door locked. Allan answered her knock.

"Sorry to bring you back so soon," he said, dull and tired. He motioned for her to enter. "Assume you know the coroner is—"

She nodded. "Who found her?"

"Aunt Kimberly," he said low, not wanting to be heard by family.

"Shit," she whispered back, at Kimberly losing daughter and mother within hours of each other.

In the empty dining room, discreetly she asked Allan how everyone else was.

"Numb," he replied. "All I can say is that we are numb."

"Who have you called?" she asked, not having much to do here short of checking in on Grandmother Poe. She didn't doubt the woman died from a broken heart, but there was a process.

"Called 911, and they said they'd call you."

Which they did.

"We notified her primary attorney," he added. "He's jumping on things from his end in Charleston. Some things slow down, some stop, and a few others have to kick into action, he said. Not sure what all that means."

"Was he aware of Kimi's death?" she asked, not sure how many kinds of attorneys this level of affluence kept on retainer.

"Yes. And he was aware we were gathered for Grandmother's birthday, and that she was using the celebration to solidify her thoughts on the new will."

Callie listened. "You talked to him?"

"Nobody else was really up to it." He leaned in. "Dad is a wreck, and my aunt can't put two words together. Ogden is hopeless. Someone had to step up."

Callie started to ask what the existing will said, but whichever will was in existence involved a dead person, and suddenly she didn't care. She could envision reporters asking who might benefit from all this death though. The hungry bastards. She hated journalists.

"I know a lot has happened in a very short time, Allan, but I can't help but ask. . . what the hell are you going to do?" He looked different. His sleeves were rolled up, and the tattoo showed for all to see.

In slow motion he shook his head. "I keep juggling stuff in my mind, but I'm not sure. There are enough Poes left to make something of the family's enterprise." He glanced toward the kitchen. "And Pauline offered me a job in Atlanta."

"Congratulations," she said, at the same time wondering if he was bailing on the whole Poe nightmare. Who could blame him? He inherited or he didn't, whether he was in New Orleans, Charleston, or Atlanta.

"Thank you, but I'm toying with more than that," he said.

Callie didn't ask. She wasn't sure what to ask.

"I stand to inherit a substantial amount of money, Chief."

Okay, now she was dying to ask the question about who got what in the will. "And?"

"The three grandchildren each receive twenty five percent. The adults share the remaining quarter. Kimi's share gets split amongst the grandchildren."

"And Lacey?" That would be roughly eight percent give or take.

"The attorney explained a Slayer Statute that applies if you killed the person you would inherit from, but not a co-heir."

Callie thought through that. "But Lacey killed Kimi which in essence killed your grandmother."

"I know. I told him that. He told me he had to do research on this, and things might go to court. Lacey tried killing me, a cold thought I try not to think hard about, but instead she killed Kimi. In either case, she might have benefited more from the will, or at least that's how it will be pursued by the family attorneys. There are statutes about killing someone to improve one's status in a will, too. Above my pay grade, Chief. No wonder these people are on retainer."

Yep, the press would have a field day with this.

"As for me, if Pauline's willing, I'll buy out her debt in exchange for becoming partner in her restaurant, maybe pull her under the Poe umbrella one day. Not sure yet."

"That would be a lot for Pauline to swallow," Callie said.

He nodded. "We need to get through some of this bedlam first. But a restaurant perpetuates the best of Grandmother, and her cookbook ought to add to the brand. I fully expect another edition to be republished. I'd love to write a forward or new chapter."

Look at this young man. He'd grown exponentially in three days, risen to the task of underpinning the Poe reputation. While death and tragedy would rate a lot of headlines, the attention would also publicize the name and literary brand.

Callie tapped a finger on his exposed tattoo. "Looks good on you."

"I need to add something to represent Grandmother."

Callie thought silver eyes, but not her place. In any manner, Grandmother would be proud.

He managed to grin. "I trust Pauline, Chief, and if how she's stuck around and endured this mess doesn't say enough about her, I don't know what does."

"She won't mind being affiliated with Poes?"

He gave another grin, albeit a sad one. "She's an entrepreneur but still a bit of an opportunist, Chief."

Callie scanned the rooms in view, vacant with nobody around. "Is everyone in with your grandmother?" she asked, taking them back to the real business at hand.

"Most of them," he said. "Pauline's in the kitchen, trying to fix something we can trust to eat. She's still on payroll for the week, so she's doing her thing."

They wandered toward Grandmother's bedroom, and Callie checked in. Nothing was awry. The assorted draft wills remained in a neat stack. No way to tell who'd read them.

Kimberly sat in a seat scooted up next to her mother's body, arms resting on the bed inches away, head bowed. The woman was spent, and Callie couldn't imagine the weight on her. Like Kimberly, Callie had lost a spouse and a parent, both to violence, but not at once. And she'd not lost her child to violence, the worst of the worst of losses.

Eddie stood at the window, trying to be the one in charge but looking uncomfortable in the role.

Facing the wall with eyes shut, Ogden sat in the same upholstered chair that Grandmother had sat in when talking to Callie the day before.

The family number had dropped to half of its former self. A lot of energy and rivalry gone in an instant, and the steam had released from every one of those left. No longer very Poe-ish.

Allan entered behind her and went to Ogden, like he'd decided to take the Poe's misfit toy under his wing.

Callie left them to their grief and walked out. She passed where Allan had thrown up that first night, where Sophie had collapsed a couple yards from that, and where Kimi had fallen in the arms of her family. She decided to hang in the kitchen until the coroner and ambulance arrived.

Damned if she wouldn't sell this house if she were them. The notoriety would sell the place for far more than market value, which bumped two million.

She crossed through the kitchen to find the back door propped open to the beach, the undulation of the ocean a soothing background to everything.

Everyone who lived on Edisto understood the medicinal value of salt water. Day, night, neap tide, ebb tide, full moon or new, residents could hear the differences. When they needed respite from whatever stained their lives, they sought peace in those waters. Sitting on their porches, lying on the sand, dozing on a towel or languishing at Coots, they used the beach to heal. It's what salt water was known for. It's why people dumped their lives on the other side of the McKinley Washington Bridge, back on the mainland. When that past dared to creep over, the power of the ocean pushed back.

Most of the souls living there carried wounds at all levels of recuperation.

"Kudos to you for hanging around," Callie said.

Pauline stood at the counter, pouring a cup of coffee from a one-cup Keurig, offering the first to Callie before fixing her own. "They hired me to do the job for a week, and that week ain't up."

"Heard you asked Allan to come work with you."

"That boy," she answered, shaking her head. "I save his cooking ass and he saves my restaurant. I take on these gigs because things are still tight in Atlanta. He's a Godsend."

Callie leaned against the sink opposite her, staying out of the way. Pauline was attempting to throw some kind of brunch together that could sit out and be picked at by people who didn't have an appetite. . . who wouldn't wonder what the food contained.

"It was Allan's idea to hire you, I take it," Callie said, not asking or telling.

A soft smile grew on the chef. Softly was the only appropriate way to address anything today. "He did. But of course, Mrs. Poe had to approve of me. That in itself was an honor."

"I see that now. Still seems far-fetched considering the state Allan was in." But then Callie now understood why he'd been beckoned back with a will in play.

"Allan suggested me to his father who took the idea to Grandmother. She had to approve the menu, and her touches were there."

Callie crossed her arms, the half empty cup still in hand. "Her idea to alter the tea or yours?"

"Hers. And she did it herself," came the reply without the first hesitation.

"And the oatmeal cookies?"

"Again, hers. Nobody pays attention to old people, she said."

With an easy scoff, Callie said, "Plus, easy to blame the dead person."

Pauline ceased working. She checked the oven where a coffee cake baked. The timer said ten more minutes.

She refilled her own cup that had been off to the side of the stove, then she took up position against the counter across from the chief. "Let's make something clear."

"Please," Callie said, motioning with her own cup.

"I was offered the position. I accepted. But I had to be familiar with *Southern Silver Spoon* and would accept adjustments only from the matron herself. I had no problem with either condition."

"She was trying to keep others out of the kitchen," Callie said.

"No," Pauline came back. "This was her week. Her birthday, her favorite foods, her family finally all together so she could make some hard decisions. That's what she said. *Make some hard decisions.*"

Made sense. "She was measuring her family, hoping she'd made the right choices in the new will. A will they knew nothing about."

"Yes."

"Allan had to be tested since he'd been gone so long."

Pauline nodded. "Yes."

"Yet you never told him," Callie said.

Pauline recrossed her arms in the other direction, buying time to think. Callie let her, because she'd rather hear it properly and clean. Nothing indicated to her that Pauline was in the process of telling her anything but the truth.

"I could not afford to ruin this for him," she finally said. "He was so nervous about coming home. He wanted back into the family, and he had hoped to impress me as well. I saw that motive a mile away, but the Poe thing, the will thing, was something else altogether. All I could do was cooperate with Allan and his grandmother and keep my fingers crossed that all worked out for the best for him."

"Which is why you had charcoal and goodness knows what else in preparation." Callie winked at her. "Sort of makes you an accomplice, Chef."

Pauline remained unfluffed. "Chief," she started, mirroring the usage of title. "I don't know how in the world you would make that case. If you do, you're Sherlock on steroids."

Callie agreed. Everyone would assume Allan's incidents minor in comparison to what happened to Kimi, were either done by Lacey, building up to some sort of climax, or done by the likeable dead cousin.

No one would dare blame the celebrated matriarch who'd died of grief.

No proof. No witnesses. Nobody else to go to jail. Nobody who cared to file charges.

"You're pretty incredible, Miss Pauline." The chef had weathered this toxic spree and all its entitledness with head high, eyes sharp, and on guard for the young man she'd taken under her wing three years ago but failed to protect. "Are you ever telling Allan?"

Pauline gave a wink. "I see nothing but harm coming from him knowing, Chief. Don't you think the boy's been through enough?"

"He has, but don't you think he deserves full closure? The Poes are still his family. And that family's money is cementing your restaurant's future."

"But who knows?" Pauline asked. "He respected his grandmother. Is that what we need to do to her memory? I don't know. Let me think on it."

Callie didn't want to agree or disagree, nor be there if that discussion ever came around. She rinsed her cup and set it in the sink. Someone knocked on the front door. Time to bring this case to a conclusion.

On the way, she checked messages. Beverly had left a voice mail to meet her at four this afternoon. Leave it to her mother not to check if Callie was available, but this time the message held a sense of sincerity. She'd probably been the last person to see Grandmother Poe alive, and Callie bet that conversation was full of Doris Woolf Poe's regrets that Beverly might have related to.

Chapter 39

Callie

CALLIE PULLED up ten minutes early to her mother's home and looked for the car. Probably in the garage. Winding herself up the walk lined with azaleas almost as old as she was, Callie recalled the pruning, weeding, and sprucing she'd been required to do as a child. The mayor and his wife didn't want their daughter acting entitled, and the outside chores gave the town's people a chance to admire the girl's work ethic, Beverly's early days of grooming her daughter to be the subsequent mayor.

Not until high school did Callie put all the pieces together and dig in her heels about assuming the throne. Beverly, however, never considered it an offer, but more of a requisite, leading to their perpetual rub.

Beverly met her at the door with drinks in hand.

Before Callie could remind her mother about her abstinence issue, Beverly handed over one. "It's virgin, dear. Come in. I have treats in the courtyard. Be right out."

Her mother wore the gold lame slippers she'd bought from Belk's department store for as long as Callie could remember. Wearing them meant Beverly was in for the night.

Callie's money was on Grandmother Poe being the topic.

Seated at the wrought iron table, noting the new seat cushions on the old wrought iron chairs, Callie settled and studied the familiar backyard. What had changed. What needed attention (nothing). Allowing memories of being a child to come back, something she didn't readily allow.

"Dear, we need to talk," Beverly said, closing the French doors behind her and joining her daughter at the table. The cookies were from a German bakery in town that was a particular favorite of the mayor.

Beverly's drink wasn't alcoholic. Callie could tell in the way Beverly sipped. This was serious.

"How's the Poe family?" her mother asked.

"As you might think. They are just shy of destroyed, but they'll come back in one form or another." She knew better than to tell her about Allan's and Pauline's business, or the complexity of the will. That was nobody's news but theirs to tell.

Beverly nodded and blew through pursed lips. "She talked with me a lot, Callie."

Callie didn't interrupt.

"She made mistakes being too hard on her children," Beverly said, "that impacted her grandchildren. She held the reins on everyone, yet they all lost direction." She took a second sip to steady herself. Callie may not like much about her mother, but she understood a lot about her.

Staring at her drink, the stem of her glass rotating between fingers, her mother moved on. "When I shared that you were my daughter and Jeb my grandson, she warned me not to become her. I . . ." and Beverly laid hand on her chest. "I can't think of a proper, worthy word to sum her up."

This was not the Beverly that Callie knew. Her adoptive mother was at a loss in expressing herself. That never happened.

When Beverly didn't go on, Callie reached over and dared touch the hand on the glass. "What, Mother?"

"I don't want to lose my grandson," she said.

Callie empathized. "I don't see that happening. He adores you. You might frustrate him, but he thinks the world of you. Hell, Mother, he corrects me all the time to treat you better." She stroked the back of her mother's hand. "He's totally on your side, trust me."

Her mother's tear fell on the back of Callie's hand.

"I've been chasing you away in trying to drive your lives." Beverly released the glass, sniffled, and turned to observe the same yard Callie had just studied. "I cannot afford to lose either of you."

Callie didn't discount the emotion she was being given a rare audience to. "You're not going to lose us, Mother."

"I drove you to relocate to Boston. I lost years of being with Jeb. I lost years with you."

True, but agreeing would be like grinding salt into a wound. A wound that appeared to be gaping and oozing newfound regret. "He's at your beck and call, Mother."

Beverly seemed to appreciate that, but her gaze was bittersweet. "I don't think I want that, Callie. He needs to be his own man and grow strong. Even if I never see him again, he needs to be his own man."

Callie didn't echo that she felt the same. That would be rude. This was her mother spilling thoughts that she'd dwelled on since leaving Grandmother Poe. Her mother taught her etiquette, manners, and what was truly civil in life, and to steal her mother opening her heart would be. . . heartless.

"I cannot lose the two of you," Beverly went on. "And I need to cut you loose as well, if I'm going to keep you." A slight crease formed in her brow. "That sounds rather profound, doesn't it?"

Callie laughed at her mother lifting the tone with humor. God knows Beverly never dove into a misery pit and stayed there.

The words had been difficult for Beverly. But Callie knew if her mother fully intended to put this fresh vision into place, she'd fail a few times before the habit took.

"How about you calling Jeb and telling him yourself?" Callie said.

Beverly gave little choppy nods with a grin that showed how much she relished her daughter's grace.

"Would I be too sappy to put on Neil Diamond?" Beverly asked.

"Not in the least," Callie said. "Let me."

Beverly almost stopped her, the unsaid being her house her rules. Always had been. "Don't do "Sweet Caroline," though, dear. For God's sake, you'd think people could be more original in their taste."

Callie agreed but said nothing. Let her mother call the shots. The woman was still the matriarch of Middleton, South Carolina, and she'd earned her limelight.

Callie called the office and placed herself off duty, telling them she owed her mother some one-on-one time.

Then she called Jeb and asked if he was interested in a family dinner, with only the three of them. And would he bring the pizza.

THE NEXT MORNING back at Edisto, Callie delayed going into the station needing a chance to explain to Mark where she'd been and who and what had been involved. As a retired agent, he hung on her stories, often offering advice. . . always segueing into an old case of his own.

This was what she used to do with her US Marshal husband, before he died years ago. Also with Seabrook, the chief she replaced on Edisto. . . before he died in her arms on Pine Landing Road. But her old boss Stan had been her mainstay for her entire investigative life. Now that he was involved with Donna Baird, he wasn't quite as available. Still, she had an urge to run him down and relay this week's events. He would ask why she hadn't called him to assist. She would tell him she had the world under control. He would enlighten her to his thoughts on the matter, and she'd argue with him about her skills versus his.

The commonality didn't escape her. She thrived around a man who'd been in the field. And she drank too much when one wasn't at hand.

She sniffed. Mark was up from the smell of breakfast. She put the final touches to her uniform, took a quick gander in the mirror, and headed out of her bedroom. Not only would she chat with Mark, but she'd hang around and wait for Jeb to rise and eat as well. She found both men, however, cooking side by side in the kitchen putting finishing touches to a protein breakfast.

The scent of bacon, eggs, and grits consumed her. "Oh, my friggin' gosh that smells amazing," she said sitting at her regular spot at the small kitchen table for four with embroidered seashell placemats, a steaming cup of coffee already in wait.

They soon joined her.

Her goo-goo eggs, as Mark had nick-named them, sat atop buttery grits, and she used the edges of her toast to corral one bite after another on her fork.

For the first few moments, everyone ate in silence. With bellies soon filled, caffeine opened the talk.

"How's Sophie?" Mark asked.

Callie looked to Jeb for that one. She'd heard some about Sophie's hospital shenanigans talking with Jeb at Beverly's last night.

"Home, totally back to normal, I think," her son said. "Thought today I'd let Sprite and her mom do their thing."

"Meaning video games," Callie said, grinning, loving the idea that her son would be around for the day. "Bummer."

"And how are you doing?" Mark asked. Callie's time at Beverly's had gone until midnight, so she came home to him already asleep.

"This one was more. . . emotional than anything else," she said. "The closest I came to harm was the oatmeal cookies that I refused to eat."

"Yeah," Jeb said, with a sudden thought. "Doubt I'll be eating any of Miss Sophie's cookies for a long while."

"Speaking of that," Callie said. "Since when does she even bake cookies? She doesn't eat them, and in all my years with her, I've never seen her bake. She does candy if anything."

Jeb rolled his eyes. "You're helping make my point, Mom."

"Okay, then speaking of Sprite. . ." But she second-guessed herself. The past three days seemed like months ago, when Jeb had left Callie hanging on their front porch, hinting of how Sprite had been through a difficulty but come out fine. With the Poes, Callie hadn't had the head space to ponder what that might be, and Sophie hadn't come to her. Not the norm. Here, however, was safe. These three souls weren't prone to overreacting.

And now the secret was back to driving her nuts.

"What the hell happened to Sprite that y'all kept secret?" she asked, then wished she'd worded that better.

Hands together in front of his mouth, Jeb peered down his nose at his mother. Mark sat back in his chair, coffee at the ready like he held popcorn at the movies.

"I'm telling you up front, this is a test," her son said.

Callie did a little uptick thing with her mouth. "Okay."

"Sprite had a medical scare."

"What?" Then she remembered this was a test of her reactions. "Sorry."

"She thought she was pregnant, but she was too afraid to test. She was afraid what her mother would say, so she did nothing."

Callie hadn't realized she'd been holding her breath. To think Sprite hadn't even gone to Sophie. "And?"

"A month later, she wasn't."

"Did she. . ."

"Lose it? She isn't sure."

How was he so calm?

"Jeb, son, why didn't you come to us?"

With a knowing look, he gave that question a moment so his mother could answer herself.

Callie tried to put herself in Sprite's shoes. Ignorant about pregnancy but fearful of what her family might think of her, she had juggled the options alone, not wanting to share feelings she could barely deal with herself. Her mother would've dominated her business. Callie would've offered advice, following through maybe too much. Beverly, God, no telling what her reaction would've been.

"So now we're good," he said. "We agreed that she had to share this kind of thing with me, but everyone else was optional. . . her choice, our choice."

Callie blew out a long breath. "And all this crap with your grandmother wanting to hire you, tell you where and how to plan your future. . ."

"Only made things worse. Now do you understand why Sprite was so upset on the porch that day? The mothers and grandmother would've pressured her. Miss Sophie would've swamped her with suggestions and emotions, Mom."

It was hard for a mother to hear she wasn't needed in the middle of a crisis.

"Everyone only wants to help," she said. "Everyone loves you."

"Then trust us. We'll call on you when we need to. But sometimes, we have to find our own way, Mom."

She was sad and proud all at once. "Does Sophie know?"

"Sprite's telling her today. Part of why I'm staying here playing games all day."

Reaching over, she patted his arm, then kept rubbing those muscles, running her hand up and down his sleeve. "Thanks for telling me. Did I pass the test?"

"I'd give you a B," he said.

She grinned. "I'll take it."

They chatted for another ten minutes before she had to leave, giving him several hugs before she forced herself to go.

Once in the car, turning east to take the circle around Palmetto first before going into the station, her thoughts gravitated to Allan from an angle she never would've thought much about until now. Until her own son painted the picture.

Parents and grandparents saw their offspring as their property, their project, their responsibility. . . forever. There wasn't an on-off switch. Being a Poe had smothered Allan. Thinking for himself was frowned on, his hopes corrected and redirected until he took off for a life of his own. Even when he'd found himself in a serious dilemma, he couldn't trust his family to assist him. Instead, he knew they'd dominate, make amends to their liking, to the Poe reputation's liking.

Omitting his domineering family made him solve his own problems, and while he felt he might be slinking back home, he did the opposite. He showed his family how a person was an individual first. A family member second. And family should respect the needs of the one, not demand the preferences of the whole.

She couldn't tend to Jeb's needs for his whole life. Neither could Beverly.

Except for one lone vehicle hoping to catch a Poe coming or going, the press was gone from *Maelstrom Manor* and had moved to Charleston.

The trials would be conducted there or in Walterboro, thank goodness. More visitors might cruise through to see the famous beach house, but Edisto would hopefully fade into the past.

Callie almost passed Dawhoo Street without thought, but now that the Poes were secondary to her day, she had a town to return to. Might as well check on Mrs. Chester.

The dumpster remained, nothing spilling over the top, which was good. But parked in the drive was Johnny Scott's Dodge Ram, the bed filled with debris and construction scraps. Possibly the same ones from two days ago.

She pulled in. Last thing she needed today was Johnny Scott pressuring an old lady about using her dumpster, or worse, the old lady using her well-cleaned firearm to draw a bead on a trespasser.

Remembering the front steps were still under construction, Callie rushed to the back and took steps two at a time. The enticing aroma of cinnamon rolls met her before she reached the top.

She rapped the screen door with enough force to be heard anywhere in the house. "Mrs. Chester?" she called, rapping harder, hoping to interrupt anything untoward going on. "It's me, Chief Morgan. Came to check on you."

When nobody showed, she tried the door, the screen's clasp engaged. She knocked harder. "Mrs. Chester?"

Finally, the sneakered feet could be heard, then the owner of them appeared, wearing an apron. "Chief. Surprised to see you over here this morning." She unhooked the door. "Come on in."

"Been baking this morning," she said, leading the way as before toward the kitchen, the combination of butter, cinnamon, and yeast insanely attractive.

Johnny Scott was seated at the kitchen table, a pan of homemade cinnamon rolls resting on a wooden trivet before him. He had both a glass of milk and a cup of coffee at his place, and a half-eaten roll in his hand. "Chief. How are you this morning?" He held up the pastry, almost embarrassingly cheery. "Look at this. I've never eaten anything so decadent in my life."

"Sit," Mrs. Chester said, and Callie couldn't say no. Not until she better understood.

The baker set a small plate before her, sunflowers painted around the edges and used the spatula in the pan to release two rolls and set them before her. "Eat." Then like a Waffle House waitress, Mrs. Chester set a small glass of milk and cup of coffee before her to chase things down. Then she took her seat, pleased at having diners.

Callie took a bite, moaned at the mingling of flavors, even thinking how Pauline and Allan would be impressed, and swallowed. She took a sip of milk. "I don't get it," she said, a wary eye on Johnny.

Johnny threw up hands, as if turning himself in to the cops. "I admit I was going to slip over this morning to dump trash. And she caught me."

Callie peered at Mrs. Chester. "You didn't. . ."

"Nope. Still secure in the bedroom."

"Pardon?" Johnny asked, but Mrs. Chester hand-motioned for him to continue.

"This fine lady," he said and bowed his head to his hostess, "met me mid-trespass. I tried bullshitting about public usage then sought sympathy about my dumpster being gone. He laughed once back at her. "And she called me out. Then she invited me in for cinnamon rolls." He laughed. "Don't that beat all?"

It did. If consulted, Callie would've told her to tell the man to leave then file a report since this was a repeat offense.

Apron still on, Mrs. Chester helped herself to another roll. "I figured if he's moving to Edisto Beach, he needs to know his neighbors. In a good way. He'd be less likely to take advantage of someone he likes. More likely to protect them, honestly. And nothing melts a heart and bridges an impasse like homemade pastries." She waved at both her guests. "Dig in, people. I can't eat all this myself."

Johnny did. "Told her to call me if she needs anything, gets scared, whatever."

"And I told him I'd reward him with whatever's coming off the stove," she replied.

Son of a gun. Not only had a new resident found a friend, but an old woman had nurtured a protector.

Callie could feel badly about being needed less, but people thinking for themselves wasn't necessarily bad. On the contrary, it could be an incredibly good thing.

The End

Acknowledgments

The themes of this book matter to me. Generational love comes with its share of misunderstandings, and though parties mean well, interactions and reactions can be painful and difficult. The elderly hold wisdom they wish to instill into their offspring. The young do not see the importance. The clashes are real, sometimes temporary, but all too many times permanent. I hope that people read the lessons in this story and take them to heart. Family, while heart-swelling and full of love, can also involve heart-breaking and soul-wrenching conflict. Patience, empathy, and respect are important aspects of keeping a family connected. To my friends, who know who they are, who have gone through a lot this past year, this story is for you. I see you.

Love to my family. While they are older and scattered now, a day doesn't pass that I don't think of each one, praying for their happiness.

Special love to my grandsons Jack and Duke who think their grandmother is famous and smart and world-renowned. Kudos to Jack for writing his first piece of suspense fiction. That's my boy.

Love to my grandson Gary, aka Tinymite, who respects my work and has grown into the sweetest young adult, on his way to being a noble nurse.

Thanks to Vanessa, who listens to my troubles and never fails to console me when the world is blowing around me like a whirling dervish. Lift heavy, baby.

Bless you Paulette, accomplished chef and catalyst for this story. Whether in Southern Florida or the coldest Maine, absorbed in her culinary escapades, I always sense I can hear her cackling laugh. She's one of the happiest people I know. Everyone needs happy people in their life.

Finally, blessings to my readers, who never fail to keep me afloat. *When's the next book coming out?* arrives in my texts, messages and emails day in and day out, but I never tire of answering. Who doesn't appreciate that kind of love?

About the Author

C. Hope Clark has a fascination with the mystery genre and is author of the *Carolina Slade Mystery Series* and the *Craven County Mysteries* as well as the *Edisto Island Mysteries*, all set in her home state of South Carolina. In her previous federal life, she performed administrative investigations and married the agent she met on a bribery investigation. She enjoys nothing more than editing her books on the back porch with him, overlooking the lake, with bourbon in hand. She can be found either on the banks of Lake Murray or Edisto Beach with one or two dachshunds in her lap. Hope is also editor of the award-winning FundsforWriters.com.